MW00852472

ALPHA'S REGRET

JESSICA HALL

Dedication

For my mother-in-law, Tracey. She loved hard and fought like a warrior,
just like Everly, until her last breath.
Also, for Nana Valerie, the woman who raised her, and said goodbye while
this book was coming to life. The same woman who inspired my character,
Valarie.

Strong Women are like a ripple effect. When one stands tall, she lifts the next, and that makes waves of change. But united, we don't just make waves — we create tsunamis.

CHAPTER
ONE

Everly

My pounding head spins as I look around at my surroundings, and I instantly regret drinking so much. Panic courses through me when I can't immediately recognize my surroundings. I can tell I'm in a room; the light coming in through the window is blinding as I try to figure out where I am. The last thing I remember is the annual Alpha meet-up, a costume party I attended with my family. My sister and I snuck off to meet with the other future Alphas. My father always insists I need to 'get in good with them', seeing as I am next in line and will have the pack handed over to me at the end of the year when I turn eighteen. Yet, for the life of me, I can't remember how I got into this room.

I groan, rubbing my eyes and hoping I'm seeing shit properly—the alcohol burning in my system is still making me confused. When I try to roll over, though, suddenly, I become aware of the heavy arm draped over my waist. My head whips to the side, and I pray that the heavy arm belongs to my sister and that we have both passed out somewhere. But my worst fears are realized, and I try to contain my scream of horror when I find a naked man lying beside me. He isn't

1

just any man either, but the 'Blood Alpha' himself, Alpha Valen of the Nightshade Pack. This man owns half the city and is from a rival pack.

My father is going to murder me if he finds out!

"Fuck!" I whisper under my breath before looking down to find myself also naked. The slight discomfort between my legs makes me painfully aware that I tossed my virginity out the window and have absolutely no memory of it. So much for that being a magical moment. *He must be a shit lay*, I chuckle to myself. Of all people, it had to be him.

My phone vibrates on the floor beside the bed, causing me to nearly dive off to retrieve it. My sister's face pops up on the screen. I quickly answer it, whispering into the phone, mindful to keep my voice low. "Hello?"

"Where are you? Dad is going to lose it. I told him you're with me, but he's asked me to come home!" she shrieks through the phone. I glance around before looking out the window, trying to figure out my location. Shit. I realize I'm still at the hotel where the Alpha meet was held.

"Still at the Banks Hotel," I whisper, and she pauses, going quiet for a few moments.

"Oh my God, please tell me you didn't fuck Alpha dickwad?" she whispers, knowing Dad will kill me—probably even disown me—if he ever finds out. Alpha Valen's reputation is scandalous and terrifying. I look over at the Greek God lying in bed beside me, completely passed out and unaware of me standing gawking at him. I would love to see the horror on his face when he wakes up, but he just might get in line behind my father and kill me, too. Shit, they may even conspire together to make my death exceptionally horrific.

"No, of course not. I just fell asleep in one of the rooms here, completely alone," I lie, hoping Ava believes me. I won't get her caught up in my minor issue if Dad asks her; she sucks at lying. She doesn't know she can't get in trouble because of me.

"Shut it. If Dad asks, tell him you stayed with Amber and me. I'll have Amber pick you up on the way; be there in five," she says, hanging up.

I quickly look around, scooping my clothes up off the floor and squeezing into the skin-tight little dress. I toss the stupid-ass fairy wings in the trashcan in the bathroom.

Looking in the mirror, I try to fix my makeup—my face is still covered in ridiculous amounts of glitter, and the eye mask that was painted on my face by my sister still conceals half my face. I chuckle to myself, knowing the Alpha will probably wake up just as confused as me and wonder why he is covered in glitter.

I vaguely remember talking to him, finding myself drawn to him for some reason. But now, as I gaze upon his paralyzed form, I can't help but wonder who took advantage of whom.

I give him one last glance, scoop up my heels, and grab my clutch purse before rushing to the hotel door and swinging it open, only to crash straight into Alpha Valen's Beta. I smack into his chest, and he stumbles back, staring at me.

I recognize him from last night's introductions, though thankfully, he seems to have no idea who I am, as I was at the back of the room when he was introduced. I'm grateful for the paint on my face because he might have recognized me as my father's daughter without it, which is the last thing I need.

He smirks at me, clearly finding it funny that I am running from the Alpha's hotel room.

"My Alpha in there?" he asks. I drop my head, hoping he doesn't recognize me, and quickly nod. I step past him, trying not to touch him.

"Are you alright, or do you need a ride home?" he asks, making me stop.

"What, do you give all your Alpha's one-night stands a ride home?" I chuckle at him, and he smiles.

"Only the pretty ones," he says, and I roll my eyes, waving him off before taking off to meet my sister. We need to hurry home before my dad sends out a search party to run through Mountainview City to retrieve his daughters.

Three weeks later

One night.

That was all it took to throw away everything I have ever known. I knew something was wrong when I felt a bit under the weather for more than a few days. Werewolves rarely get sick. Finally, after spending the last week ill, my father—Alpha of Shadow Moon Pack—had dragged me off to see the pack doctor.

Our home, Mountainview City, is entirely populated by were-wolves, comprising four packs. My father's pack is the second-largest pack, which means we're held in fairly high esteem in the area. Plus, the fact that he only has two daughters means that I, as the eldest, am next in line.

Well, I was until the Doctor returned to the exam room after running some tests and turned that dream upside down. The look of disappointment on my father's face makes my heart clench. One night, one man turned out to be the biggest mistake of my life.

"She is pregnant."

I feel my heart sink into my stomach. No, I can't be. I only had sex once, and I don't even remember because I was trashed. How the hell could this be happening? My father casts a stunned look at me from where he sits before returning his gaze to our pack doctor.

"It's wrong; rerun the test. She hasn't found her mate. She can't be pregnant," my father says. I shrink back in my chair. I'm only seventeen, nearly eighteen, and the number one rule all she-wolves have drummed into our heads is to save ourselves for our mates. This is a huge deal, especially to my father. This would bring shame to our family, that I would break the one sacred rule for she-wolves. Sure, the men fool around (a little bias, anyone?) Yet if we do it—especially someone like me in a position of power—it's frowned upon. I would be a disgrace to the family.

"Alpha, I have tested the urine sample twice," Doc Darnel tells him, but my father shakes his head, not believing his words—or not wanting to.

"No, test it again; it is wrong. My daughter is not a rogue whore," he says, finality in his voice.

I cringe at his words: a woman who falls pregnant to someone who is not their mate. It's the worst thing to be labeled besides a traitor, though they're treated the same.

Rogue whores are forbidden on pack lands, only allowed on neutral territory: the main drag of the city and the two streets behind it on either side. Most she-wolves that fall pregnant in other cities are banished like they do with those that betray or commit treason among the packs; forsaken wolves. Without any pack contact, they turn feral, sending them crazed and mad, and are forced to live outside the cities. No one wants to be on their own out there. It isn't safe, and not how anyone wants to live.

Our city is different. We don't banish women from the city. Our treatment is slightly more... humane, I guess you could say. Instead, we just make them rogues, free to go about their lives but without pack help. I used to look down on them—those women I would see trying to make ends meet for their 'poor choices.' Maybe this is my karma; I will soon be one of them.

Running through this scenario in my head, the room starts to feel like it's running out of air. I wonder if I'm going to pass out.

"Yes, Alpha, I will test it again," Doc Darnel says before rushing out of the room and away from my father's deadly glare. My father starts pacing, and my heart rate quickens when he stops, turning to face me.

"He has to be wrong; you are not like that. You wouldn't shame me this way," he says, looking for confirmation. I shrink back in my chair. The Doc coming back in again stops him from saying more.

"The results are the same, Alpha," Doc says before looking at me with pity.

I swallow, staring wide-eyed at the pack doctor, hoping he can save me from my father's wrath, but even I know the elderly, graying man is no match for my father.

Neither am I since I still haven't shifted.

After shifting on our eighteenth birthday, we can find our mates. I have seen friends and family go through it. It is considered sacred. I wonder, terrified, how much being pregnant will delay the process. Bodies can't shift while pregnant; it is a safety mechanism to protect the unborn pup.

My father growls, turning on his heel and glaring at me, his fists clenched by his sides as he fights the urge to shift. Often, werewolves shift when they lose their temper or are preparing for a fight. Despite how hard he's trying, he's still barely holding back, his eyes starting to flicker black and his body trembling in his anger.

My father has always been so proud of my sister and me, always showing us off and telling everyone about what great daughters we are and what a great Alpha I will be when I take over the pack. I look like him—dark hair and bluish-gray eyes, I got those traits from him—and he raised me in his image, preparing me to take over. But right now, with my face mirrored in his wolf's black orbs, he looks on the verge of killing me. I have never seen him so angry in his life, and that is saying something.

"How far along is she?" Father asks. The venom in his words makes my blood run cold.

"We can have an ultrasound done next week to confirm gestation," Doc tells him, and I look at my hands.

"No, do it now so we can take care of it before word gets out. I won't have a rogue whore for a daughter. This is not to get out, do you understand, Doc?"

Doc nods his head nervously.

Vaguely, I notice my mouth is hanging open as I stare, absolutely gobsmacked at what my father just said. It's going against the Moon Goddess to abort a baby!

"Wait!" I say, finally finding my voice. My father looks at me and the Doc moves away from him when he feels my father's aura rush out.

"Wait for what? You aren't keeping this monstrosity. We can sweep it under the rug, no one has to know, and you can still take the Alpha position; we just need to take care of this poor choice, and then things can go back to normal," my father says. He makes it sound so simple like this isn't a sin against the Moon Goddess.

"No. I can't do that, Father. Please, just let me speak with Mom. We can work this out," I plead with him.

"No, you will terminate the pregnancy, then we go home. Doc, get whatever it is you need. I am not leaving this office until this is taken care of," my father says.

I feel tears brimming at his words. Sure, I don't want to be pregnant, but I am not a murderer; aborting a pregnancy is worse than having a child with someone who is not your mate.

"Alpha, I am afraid if your daughter isn't willing, I can't perform such a thing unless there is a medical reason."

"She is willing, isn't that right, Everly?" my father says, trying to force me to agree, but I meet his gaze head-on. My mind is made up; I won't go through with it.

"No!" I tell him, not expecting his following reaction. In all my life, my father has never hit me, never raised a hand to me, and the shock of his action is more painful than the blow itself as his hand connects with the side of my face. I can feel the outline of his fingers etched into my cheek as a burning sensation spreads across it from his palm.

"Then you are no longer my daughter," he says and walks out of the room.

CHAPTER

TWO

Eight months later

Loved ones come and visit the other mothers on the ward, gushing in excitement over their new bundles of joy, eagerly discussing their new additions to the family. The woman across from me is being doted on by her mate. The support he is showing her, the comfort, makes my heart twist painfully, knowing no one is excited to meet my son. No one is coming to check on me or offer support. No one cares for the boy suckling at my breast. Nobody is coming. It is just him and me against the world.

But that is ok. I will make it work.

The labor was excruciating. It was thirty-four hours and forty-five minutes of pure agony and no comfort, not even from the midwives. They were nothing but rude and mean, telling me to quit crying as I begged them to make the pain stop. I had never felt so vulnerable or alone as when I was in labor.

It was hard enough to grow up with the expectations of being the Alpha's daughter, but then I got pregnant, shunned, and stripped of my title. All for one night. That one night turned my life upside down. How could he throw away his flesh and blood, his own daughter, over her falling pregnant?

How could anything so tiny and sweet be called a mistake?

Hearing the nurse come in, I look up. She grabs my chart from the end of the bed, looking it over before eyeing me. Glasses teeter on the end of her upturned nose. No one tries to hide their disgust; everyone looks down on me because I had a child with someone who isn't my mate. That much is evident, that I have no mate because where is he? Not here beside me like the rest of those new mothers on the ward—my mate isn't here gushing over this newborn baby in my arms.

"You really have no idea who the father is?" she asks, clicking her tongue. I know exactly who the father is, but the last thing I need is for him to hunt me down. I already had that run-in. A run-in I would much rather forget when I told him I was carrying his child.

He didn't even remember me.

Doesn't help that he's a rival pack Alpha. It's just easier pretending I don't know. The shame I have brought my family for being pregnant is bad enough; my father would have killed me for the disrespect of foolishly getting into bed with the Blood Alpha.

I watch the nurse flick her red curly hair over her shoulder. "He is cute; shame his mother is a whore," she sneers, and I see the points of her canines pressing beneath her gums as they protrude past her lips.

"Can I get some Tylenol?" I ask, ignoring her comment. I'm feeling a headache coming on. Besides, I've received multiple comments along the same lines since being here—I don't feel the need to defend myself; there is no point. Nothing I say will make them look at me any differently.

"Sorry, can't. It is not on your charts," she says.

"It's Tylenol. It's not like I am asking for morphine," I tell her.

"Doesn't matter. It isn't on your charts, so you will have to go without," she says, dropping the chart on the table beside me. Most women heal directly after giving birth, but I haven't shifted yet, so I have no such healing ability.

"Can I get something to eat at least?" I ask her. I am starving, and breastfeeding is making me ravenous.

"You came into the maternity ward after the dinner rounds, and breakfast is at 7 a.m.," she tells me. I look at the clock and see it is only just after 8 p.m. I nod, knowing this nurse will not help in any way. Crap, every nurse here is horrible because of my situation. Sometimes, I wish I could leave this city, pretend to be human, and just go about my life with my son.

The nurse leaves, stopping at the blue curtain that divides the beds. "Did you even think of the repercussions for the father by having a child with someone who isn't your mate? Did you think of the poor woman who finds her mate in him and one day learns he fathered an illegitimate child to some random she-wolf?"

Little did she know that I thought of that every day since learning I was pregnant, but it was his choice, too. I fight back the tears from her words as I stare down at my amber-eyed boy; those eyes are definitely from his father, from what I can remember at least. Mine are light bluish-gray.

I've just put my son down after he fell asleep in my arms when I see a nurse walk past. She stops and comes over to me when I wave to her. Her uniform is different; she must be the head midwife or someone higher up on the staff list. Long, pencil-straight hair hangs to her shoulders, slightly obscuring her name tag. I try to read the small writing under her name—Rita—but I can't quite make it out. She must be in her mid-twenties because she seems closer to my age. Well, not really. I am barely eighteen, but still, she looks nicer than the previous nurses. She picks up my chart, flicking through it.

"Is there somewhere I can get some water? Or maybe a cup of tea?" I ask, and she glares at me. My stomach drops. Maybe she isn't so lovely after all.

She presses the buzzer behind my head, calling another nurse, yet she still hasn't answered me. My son starts to stir, and I reach over and grab him out of his crib as another nurse comes in, my stomach cramping from the sudden movement.

"Why is she in here?" the head nurse asks, making me look at her.

I just had a baby. Why else? I think to myself.

The new nurse looks over at me. Her hands tremble slightly—this head midwife obviously instills fear in her colleagues.

"Get her to the unmated section. We don't need her disturbing the mothers in this ward," the woman says before turning her nose up at me and walking out. *Turns out, Rita is a bitch, like the rest of them.* I stare, disgusted by this hospital's bedside manner. The girl in the curtained-off room beside me speaks.

"I knew something was up with her, Hun; her mate never visited her. No one has. Now I know why," she says to her mate.

She's right. We are allowed one person with us constantly while in here. The girl next to me, her mate hasn't left her side since I got here. The person across from me had multiple people come in during the night, and her mate also hasn't left.

I try to ignore their mates gushing over them and tending to their every need while I sit here, getting nothing but sneers and judgment.

The bed moves as the nurse begins rolling me out of the room. Because I am sitting upright, I have to grab the bar that runs along the side to stop from falling back. She wheels me through the maternity ward before going down a corridor; I appear to be leaving the maternity unit altogether. The nurse finally stops at a curtained-off area and places the bed against the wall. The woman then turns on her heel and leaves.

"Wait, can I get some water?"

But she has already gone and didn't even acknowledge my question.

"I wouldn't bother. They won't help us," comes a voice before someone jerks the partitioning curtain away to reveal two other girls. One looks to be in her mid-twenties with long, curly dark hair and sparkling green eyes. The other girl is around sixteen, with her dark blonde hair tied into a messy bun on top of her head.

"My name is Macey," the oldest of them says.

"Hi. Everly," I reply.

"Her name is Zoe. Welcome to the shunned mothers club," Macey chuckles before looking down at her baby. She sighs heavily.

"Don't expect them to help; they won't. Seriously, you're best off getting out as soon as you can," Macey tells me.

"But they are supposed to," I tell her, feeling disheartened.

"Yeah, I have been here two days; baby has a few problems. Half the time, they don't answer when I buzz, and forget about them feeding you. I haven't received anything since being here," Macey explains before reaching to the foot of her bed and pulling a bag toward her. She rummages through it before pulling out a granola bar.

"Here. You must be starving. I was, and I came prepared expecting this," Macey explains.

"You had a baby before?" I ask, unable to imagine going through this again.

She shakes her head. "No, this is my first. My mom was a single mother, too. We are rogues like you," she says.

I open the granola bar, my stomach growling at the sight of food.

"Boy or girl?" I ask the younger girl, who seems rather shy.

"Girl. Yours?"

"Boy," I tell her.

"Thanks," I tell Macey before biting into the granola bar.

"Plenty in there, just help yourself. I brought extras in case there were other girls. Which pack are you from? Your aura feels quite strong for a rogue?" she says, staring at me.

"Alpha blood," I tell her. Her eyebrows raise in shock.

"In that case, you don't have to tell me. I understand why you would want to keep that to yourself. Zoe was born rogue—so was I," she says, and I glance at Zoe, who nods.

"If you don't mind me asking, where are you girls living? Are there any refuges or anything for women?"

"I have a place at a refuge. But I know it's full to capacity," Zoe says, a look of sorrow etching her face as if she wishes she could help more.

"Me? I live with my mom and my brother," Macey tells me.

"Where are you staying? No family would help?" Zoe asks.

I shake my head. "No. We will be alright. I will come up with something," I tell them, hoping that will be true, though I have been living in my busted station wagon, which cost me $500 for the last eight months.

It saddens me that we are pushed aside, but the next day, both girls help me, for which I am grateful. Macey continues to share her food, and she was right—not once did anyone come to check on us, no food was brought to us, nothing. Shunned for having a baby, and we suddenly don't matter anymore.

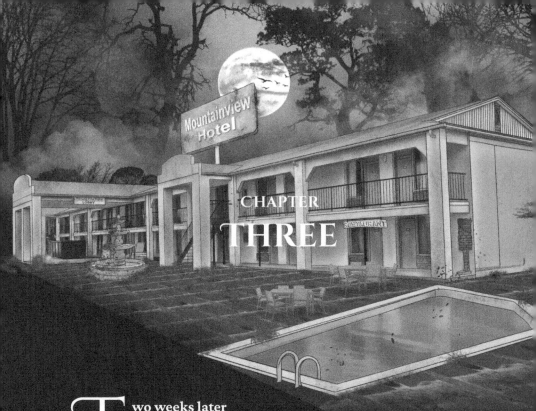

T wo weeks later

Tap, Tap, Tap.

I look up and see a man tapping on my car window, his flashlight shining in before he moves it around, looking in the back. I put my hand up when the light flashes across my face, blinding me. He quickly moves it to the side.

"Ma'am, you can't stay here," the middle-aged man tells me; he must be city security, judging by his uniform. My son—who I decided to name Valarian—stirs, the bright light waking him, and he lets out an irritated cry. The man moves his flashlight away entirely, shining it at the ground, and Valarian stops.

"Look, I've noticed your car here for nearly two weeks; this is a train station." He sighs as I pick up my son out of his fruit box bed and roll down the window a bit so he doesn't keep yelling, thinking I can't hear him.

"You really have no place to go? No family?" he asks.

"No, the council kicked me out of the park," I say matter-of-factly.

He sighs heavily and runs a hand down his face before glancing around the parking lot.

"What about the baby's father?"

I shake my head, knowing that isn't an option. He didn't even believe me about the pregnancy—refused to see me, even when I begged him to let me show him the ultrasound pictures. Every time I tried to call after that, he hung up the moment he heard my voice. After a while, I gave up.

"You know there are people out there that would take him—then you could probably go home."

"I am not abandoning my baby like my parents did me," I tell him, outraged he would even suggest it.

"This is no life for a child. You're young. If you give him up, you could have a normal life. Something to think about: I will give you another week to find somewhere else. After that, you need to move on," he says, and I nod before winding the window up.

I watch him leave before settling my son and putting him back to bed in the fruit box beside me—I have always been paranoid about accidentally rolling on him while asleep. Tugging the blanket up over both of us, I try to get comfortable. Yet, all I can think is. *This is not how I intended to bring my son into this world.* I thought it would be different and that I would have figured out something by now. A single tear runs down my cheek as I think of his words. *"This is no life for a child."* Am I being selfish?

However, the thought of giving him up breaks my heart. He is mine. I loved him and would give my life for my little man. Isn't that enough? I can't deny the bond between us.

W aking up the following day, I groan; it is pouring with rain. It's still early. I rummage through the back for my umbrella before slipping my shoes on. Making sure Valarian is bundled nice and warm, I grab my empty bucket in one hand and pop the umbrella up as I open the hatchback.

Sliding the bucket to the crook of my elbow, I raise the umbrella with the same hand. I then pick up my son in my free arm and make a run for it to the train station bathrooms, paying extra care not to slip on the wet ground. That would be disastrous. Once I get into the large, handicapped stall, I shove the bucket in the sink, filling it with warm water before shimming my pants down to pee. One thing I hate about being homeless is holding my son while going to the bathroom. I can't place him down anywhere, making it hard to use the toilet while making sure not to drop him. When I finish, I slide my pants up with one hand, which is difficult while holding my son, then awkwardly wash my hand before turning the faucet off.

Now the tricky part—holding an umbrella, a newborn, and a now-full bucket of water. Somehow, I manage it and make it back to the car before placing the bucket down and quickly opening the hatchback to my wagon. I crawl in and set my son in his bed before hauling my tiny bucket in. Lathering my washcloth with soap, I give him a wash down before dressing him in a clean diaper and clothes so he's all nice and fresh for the day.

Using the remaining water, I also give myself a wash, longing for a shower. Gosh, I miss showering, something I definitely took for granted. I use the rest stop ones occasionally, but right now, I have no fuel to get there and can't risk spending my limited funds.

When mom and dad kicked me out, I had a small amount of savings. I also worked at the Chinese restaurant on the main street while pregnant to keep saving. The savings didn't last long with buying baby clothes and non-perishable food, though. And now that he's born, I've been spending money on diapers. Not to mention, since my milk dried up from stress and lack of nutrition before I left the hospital, I am forced to stock up on formula and bottled water too. My car looks like a mini supermarket, but I am starting to get low on the formula again. Rummaging through my wallet, I find my last $100. I need to think of something fast. This won't see us through much longer.

Sighing, I lean back on my door, watching the rain. The restaurant won't take me back—I tried that—and my parents obviously aren't an option. His father wouldn't even let me on pack territory when I requested to see him.

I still remember when I got his number to call him that first time; what a nightmare that was. He laughed and said there was no way he would sleep with a seventeen-year-old. To be fair, I was not supposed to be in that part of the club at the hotel. My sister and I wanted to meet the older Alphas, not the young ones that hadn't even reached puberty. So with fake IDs, we snuck in while the meeting was going on in the conference hall. Alpha Valen was just as drunk as I was, so it's no wonder he can't remember me. I barely remember anything. What I do remember is how I felt that night— the pull to him for some reason—and he must have felt it too. I know I didn't imagine it.

Shaking the vague memory away, I grab a granola bar and start eating. My belly is rumbling. Oh, what I would do for a home-cooked meal. I love mom's cooking. She's the best cook!

A tear slips down my cheek and I check my phone, yet I know I will find no missed calls. My father had it disconnected, but I like to look at the photos of when I was still part of the family. I miss my little sister—I wish I could see her, even just once more.

I spend most of the day just trying to figure out what I can do about money. The security guard's words eat at me. *"This is no life for a child."*

I am failing.

I need help and don't know who to ask. When it starts to get dark, the five o'clock train pulls in. I try to light my candle so I can see in the growing darkness, but my lighter has finally run out of fuel. Popping the trunk to get out, I grab my umbrella and glance around, hoping to find someone smoking—someone approachable —to ask to borrow one.

"Excuse me, do you have a..."

The man in his tailored suit walks past, looking down at me. I try over and over again, ignored by everyone that passes. Feeling disheartened, I'm about to hop back in the car when I see a younger man in a neat suit.

I've seen him a few times. He catches the early train and is always home on the five o'clock train. He's always dressed nicely in suits that compliment his brownish-blond hair and green eyes, and his muscular build puts him a good foot taller than me.

The man stares at me warily as I approach, and I stop when I feel his aura—he has Beta blood. He looks familiar for some reason and I finally place him; he is one of the Betas from the Alpha meet. He's Beta to Alpha Valen. I pretend I don't recognize him because he definitely doesn't remember me, and I know he can't feel my aura. I've been rogue for so long now, my aura is almost nonexistent. It doesn't help that I still haven't shifted. I want to, need to, but what do I do with my son?

"Can I borrow a lighter if you have one?" I blurt out quickly before he waves me away; everyone usually assumes I'm asking for money. He stops, staring at me for a second.

"Fine," he says, rustling inside his pocket before handing me a green lighter. I run back to the car and light the candle that sits on a plate in my vehicle. Only, when I turn around, I find him behind me, having followed me the few yards back to my car.

I jump, not expecting him to be so close. "Thank you," I tell him, passing it back. He nods, then begins to leave, walking around the side of my car just as my son cries out.

"Shh, shh, I'm coming," I whisper, pulling the hatchback down until something stops it. I turn to see what it caught on, only for it to be pulled open by the Beta.

"Is that a baby you have in there?" he asks, and my heart thunders in my chest nervously.

Will he call child services on me?

My son cries louder, and I reach for him. The man's eyes dart to him before he sniffs the air. I stare back at him, confused, and tug my son to my chest as if he's threatening to take him away from me.

"It's only temporary; please don't call child services," I tell him, and he cocks his head to the side. His gaze appears to be more thoughtful than scrutinizing.

"Does your car run?" he asks, looking at it before he kicks a tire.

"I have no fuel. I will leave tomorrow, I promise," I tell him, panicking. Maybe he's a council worker? I doubt it because of his expensive suit.

He looks at me, his nose scrunching slightly. "You smell familiar," he mutters.

I swallow, wondering if he remembers me, but he doesn't appear to, and I also don't want him questioning which pack I was from. My father and his Alpha are not on good terms. Yet, maybe if he could get me in to see Alpha Valen, he might help with his son. However, that thought also frightens me—having to face the man who ignored me and refused to even do a DNA test. He declined to come check— stating my claims were lies—but if he just met him, he would see. We can always sense our kin. I stare at the Beta, wondering if he'll leave, but he pushes the hatchback open further before reaching in. I scoot further back, looking for a weapon in case I need it.

"Calm down. I can't leave you here knowing you are sleeping in your car with a baby," he says, grabbing the car seat.

"I will leave; just don't take my son," I tell him. He looks at me like I am mad.

"I'm not." And his eyes mean it. "I want to help." He's being sincere.

"You want to help?" I repeat, slightly disbelieving. I must have heard that wrong.

"Come on, you can stay at the packhouse until I speak to my Alpha," he says, waving me forward. "Grab a change of clothes. We can come back to your car tomorrow," he says.

Terrified, I don't move. It's been so long since anyone has helped me. He sighs before grabbing a bag and stuffing a can of formula, the diaper bag, and some of my clothes inside the bigger bag.

"Come on, wouldn't you rather have a warm house than a cold car?" he asks. I look down at my son, wondering if I should trust him. He grabs the car seat. I climb out, and he hands me my umbrella before shutting my trunk.

"This way," he says, walking to his car. I follow him to his electric blue sports-looking car. I always wondered why he doesn't drive to work. And why would he leave such an expensive car at a train station?

He puts the seat in before scratching his head. "You know how to clip it in?" he asks, and I nod.

"Okay, you put it in, and I will hold your..." His eyes dart to my son.

"Son," I tell him, and he nods, holding out his arms for him. He takes him from me, and I lean in, making sure to keep an eye on him while I clip the seat in before turning around. Retrieving the baby, I clip him in his chair before climbing in beside him. The Beta then passes me the bag before shutting my door.

He turns the heater on when he hops in before glancing at me in the rearview mirror.

"Your son has odd-colored eyes—reminds me of my Alpha's. He is the only person I know with amber eyes besides his father," he says.

I look at the man, and he looks away, looking back at the road. He definitely has his father's eyes, but I keep my mouth shut. Though maybe this would be my chance, he would be able to tell if he saw his own son. We can sense our own family, plus their resemblance is unmistakable.

"Who is your Alpha?" I ask, pretending I don't know.

"Valen, the Blood Alpha," he says, his eyes darting to mine in the mirror again, gauging my reaction to his words. I feel excitement bubble in me, knowing I am correct in who he is.

"He will be fine with you bringing a rogue into the territory?" I ask him.

"He won't be there, and I will speak with him tomorrow. Are you hungry?" he asks, and my belly rumbles loudly at the mention of food. He chuckles at the noise.

"I will take that as a yes," he says, and my face heats. I give my son his binky, his amber eyes peering at me in the darkness of the car.

"What's your name?"

"Everly," I answer him.

"Odd name. What pack were you from, or were you born rogue?"

"No, I was in a pack," I answer. I refuse to tell him which one; it's no secret my family's pack and the Blood-Alpha are constantly at war.

"Your name? I can tell you have Beta blood," I tell him.

"Marcus, and yes, I am Valen's Beta," he says before pulling into a drive-thru. I grab my wallet.

"I don't want your money," he says before ordering for himself. "What do you want?"

I don't say anything, feeling awkward, so he orders two of the same thing.

"Is he asleep?" he asks, and I look at my son. I nod as he pulls up to the next window.

"Climb in the front," he says, which makes me look at my son again, worried.

"I don't bite, climb over," he says while patting the passenger seat. I unclip my seatbelt before climbing over into the front. Placing the seatbelt on quickly, I notice that he doesn't have a mark on his neck; he hasn't found his mate yet. A bite on the neck always means that anyone, man or woman, has been "marked" by their mate.

He opens some cupholders and places the drinks in them before passing me a paper bag.

"You can eat in the car," he says. I thank him and I open his burger box for him, letting him take it out.

Marcus pulls over on the side of the road before flicking the interior light on so we can see before turning in his seat to face me. "Eat. I won't hurt you."

I open the burger box, the smell making my stomach melt. My hands are shaking as I retrieve the burger.

"Are you cold?" he asks, turning the heat up.

I nod my head. It's a lie. I was fine in the car; it's the fact I haven't eaten a hot meal in ages or even just actual food that isn't canned spaghetti or granola bars. I bite into the burger and a sob nearly escapes my lips; I am quick to suppress it so he doesn't hear. I chew slowly, savoring the taste and the warmth. Looking up, I see that he is watching me while eating his burger.

22

I blush, feeling embarrassed that he is staring. He must think I am pathetic. I feel pathetic accepting a stranger's help, and almost crying over a damn burger.

"Thank you," I tell him while taking a sip of the cold Coke. It fizzes in my throat and on my tongue but tastes so good.

"Where is your family?" he asks curiously.

"He is my only family," I tell him, looking at my son.

"They tossed you, didn't they, for being unmated?"

I swallow, looking down.

"My mother was a single mother, not a rogue, though. My dad died and she raised me alone. She struggled, but she had the pack. Must be hard having no one to help at all," he says. I don't say anything. What can I say? I am the disgraced daughter of an Alpha?

We eat in silence, and for the first time in ages, I feel full, yet still, he hands me his fries, telling me to eat them before starting the car again. After twenty minutes of driving, I realize we're getting close to my old pack when he turns onto a road going in the opposite direction.

It takes another twenty minutes of driving through his territory before he pulls up at a large, three-story house. I can hardly see through the darkness of the night, but I can tell it's modern-looking.

"Are you okay? Stepping across didn't make you feel sick?"

I shake my head. It's odd. Usually, rogues feel sick crossing a border, but I don't.

"Huh. Odd," he mutters.

"Are you sure it's okay for me to stay here?" I ask a little nervous about being in pack territory when I am a rogue.

"Yeah, no one is here, and you can stay in my room tonight; I have pack patrol, so I won't be home."

I nod. "The Alpha won't mind?" I ask.

"Na, he won't even know until I see him tomorrow. He's in the city partying tonight; you will have the place to yourself," he says, opening his door. I climb out before walking around the car and grabbing my son. Marcus places my bag over his shoulder and puts his hand on my lower back, showing me to the front door. I watch as he unlocks the door before motioning for me to enter.

S tepping inside, Marcus flicks on the hallway light, and I can finally see better. The entire place is spotless. White marble floors and a massive staircase lead up to the next level. I can't see in the rooms off the side of the foyer; he didn't turn those lights on, but if the foyer is anything to go by, the rest of the house must be breathtaking. It is way over the top; nothing I wouldn't expect of the Blood Alpha. They are the wealthiest pack and have half the city under their claim.

"This way," he says, motioning for me to follow. I trail after him up two flights of stairs before he stops at a black door. He pushes it open to reveal a king-size mahogany bed with a canopy. Matching furniture and a large black rug sit on the floor. Built into the wall is a flat-screen TV, and he turns it on before turning the volume down a bit. To one side, I can also see a door leading to a balcony.

"Obviously, I don't have a crib, but the bed is comfy, and the bathroom is through those doors. It's shared with Alpha Valen's room next door, but I'm sure he won't be by tonight. He'll probably stay at his apartment in the city. Towels are in there, and I will be back to check on you at 6 a.m. I'll take you to see the Alpha then," he says before heading into the walk-in closet and grabbing some clothes for himself.

"The Kitchen is downstairs if you're hungry, and I'll see you later," he tells me before walking out the door. I look around for a moment, then flick the space heater on to warm the room.

"This is nice, Bubba. And tomorrow, you can meet your father," I whisper to him. I can't help but feel a sense of excitement and anticipation. There's no way the Alpha can deny his son once he meets him. He'll know with just one look at him that he is his. He'll be able to sense that. Finally, things were looking up. I'd have help, well, maybe not me, but I know he'll provide for his son.

Walking into the bathroom, I gasp. It's white marble and white tiles with a gold finish. One wall is all mirrors above the basin, and the shower could easily fit three people. But the most exciting part is that the sink is the perfect size to bathe Valarian. He hasn't taken a proper bath since the hospital. I just know he'll love it. I instantly start prepping the sink with warm water, using my elbow to test it before stripping his clothes off and settling him in the water while ensuring I hold his head above the water. He moves his arms and legs, swishing the water and murmuring happily while eating his hands. I chuckle watching him splash.

Once the water gets cool, I get him out. I drain the water and wrap him in a towel before patting him dry and laying him on the bed while I dress him. After his bottle, he falls asleep quickly, almost like he knows he's safe here. I prop pillows around him to ensure he doesn't fall off the bed before walking back to the bathroom, leaving the door open so that I can hear him. After quickly stripping my clothes off, I turn the shower on and step under the warm spray. Marcus didn't mention using the bath products, but I assume it is okay, and use the shower gel and shampoo to give myself the deepest wash I've had in what feels like a year.

Halfway through wrapping the fluffy towel around myself, I suddenly hear voices, drunken stumbling, a woman giggling, and I freeze. Someone is here. I snatch my clothes off the sink basin and am about to run into Marcus's room when the bathroom door opens and a beautiful red-haired woman walks in wearing a skimpy dress. She stops when she notices me. Her extremely tight dress leaves little to the imagination, and she is clearly intoxicated, as a cloud of alcohol wafts in after her.

She looks me up and down before growling at me, her top lip pulling back over her teeth.

"What are you doing in here, rogue?" she barks.

"I... Beta Marcus... He said." My heart thumps wildly in my chest. Stuttering, I attempt to explain when the door is shoved open, and a man storms in. No, not a man, the blood Alpha. He also reeks heavily of whiskey, the smell so strong it burns my nose, yet I can't tear my eyes from his amber ones. He is absolutely gorgeous, even while heavily intoxicated and barely able to stand upright. He's tall, too, and way bulkier than I remember, with dark hair and a five o'clock shadow. But his eyes, those eyes I can't look away from. They glow like the embodiment of autumn.

It feels like someone fried my brain to a crisp, and all I can do is stare, my brain screaming at me, my senses overloaded with his essence.

Mate!

The blood Alpha.

He's. My. Mate.

I know it, feel it, with every fiber of my being, even without having shifted yet. I am of age now, and I feel my heart flutter excitedly. I've found my mate! Taking a step toward him, I reach out to him, but his lips pull back over his teeth to reveal sharp canines. His face, his gorgeous face, is twisted in anger. I gasp, realizing he's too intoxicated to recognize me. Instead, he rushes toward me. His hands grab my throat, and he pushes me against the cold, tiled wall.

"What the fuck is a rogue doing in my house!" he screams before sniffing me. I can't talk; his grip is tight, restricting my airway. He sniffs me again before shaking his head. Then he shoves me back before commanding me.

"Get out of my house now before I have you killed!" he roars, and my stomach sinks somewhere deep inside me. He can't recognize me. I could just as easily be some random rogue whore off the street to him with how drunk he is. However, he keeps sniffing the air, his body telling him something is amiss. It's just that his brain cannot register me at all. My heart sinks.

The woman behind him is clearly enjoying this confrontation; probably hoping he'll kill me; a rogue on pack land. I never should have come here. I never should have gotten my hopes up. Not even my own mate will help me. This was my only chance at showing him that he's a father, and now it just went out the window.

"Wait, but, you're my—" I plead desperately.

"Get out!" he screams, and I flinch, his Command rolling over me. I snatch my clothes from where I dropped them, rushing into Marcus's room and pulling them on. As much as I desperately wish I could continue arguing, his Command leaves me powerless. And the more I fight it, the more it hurts. Alpha wolves, once they reach maturity, can use a certain voice, a Command, that the recipient must obey, by fighting it, the pain grows until they submit to it.

"Come on, baby," the woman purrs, clutching him. Tears brim in my eyes while I snatch my things up, unable to do anything against his Command, unable to explain myself. Wrapping my son in his blanket and tucking him against me, I grab my bag before rushing down the steps.

Pain suddenly tears through me, taking my breath away. Clutching the banister, my stomach cramps, making me cry out and my legs buckle. I grit my teeth, agony tearing my heart apart. They're obviously fucking. I've heard that women know when their mates are unfaithful—can feel it—but I got to meet him with another woman.

I didn't think it would hurt like this; I never envisioned this pain when teachers explained. He hasn't even marked me.

Running down the steps, I rush out the door. It's pouring with rain as a storm rolls across the night sky. And I am miles from my car, yet his Command told me to leave and gives me no choice. Looking around helplessly, I start running, pulling my son under my shirt to shield him from the cold. My legs are moving me with nowhere to go as I desperately try to figure out where to find shelter.

I don't know how long I run for, but I suddenly find myself on the city's main street—the line separating Nightshade Pack from Shadowmoon Pack, my father's pack, my old territory. My old house is only a ten-minute run from here.

Maybe he'll take pity on me; perhaps he might change his mind once he meets his grandson. I can only hope, at least for my son's sake. I swallow, knowing I have no choice, or I'll be in the rain all night with a baby.

Deciding to take my chances, I start running home. I run the entire way before stopping in front of my old home. The lights are all off.

My heart twists as I look up the driveway of the single-story, lavish house. Growing up, I played with the pack kids in this street and rode my bike along the footpath with my sister. My father used to toss the football with us on this very lawn after work when we were little or help us climb the massive tree that sits on the side of the driveway. This was home.

Standing here, I suddenly miss my old life, miss my family; I just hope they miss me too.

Quietly sneaking up the side of the house, I stop at my sister's bedroom window—she's asleep in her bed. I tap on the window and see movement; she flicks her lamp on, squinting around the room before looking at the window. Seeing me waving at her, Ava's mouth opens, and she's immediately on alert as she rushes over. As soon as she throws her window open, I pass her my bag, which she places on the floor before taking Valarian from me, so I can climb through the window.

"Sis!" she cries, hugging me. I inhale her scent, tears flowing down my cheeks, before pulling back to look at her. I am soaked, absolutely drenched, my hair dripping from the rain, but she doesn't seem to notice. She clutches her mouth before a sob escapes her. "I was hoping you would come back." She looks down at my son in awe. "He's beautiful," she chokes out. I gently close the window as she hugs Valarian close, smelling his tiny head.

"Gosh, I've missed you so much. Dad wouldn't let me look for you; he has me on a tight leash," she says, tears streaking down her cheeks. "Grab some dry clothes, take whatever you want," she whispers while pointing at her dresser.

I rummage through her drawers and find some warm clothes, trying to be quiet so I don't wake my parents down the hall. After putting on some of her pajamas, I have to roll the waistband of the pants to hold them up. My sister watches me before she breaks down again.

"You're so skinny," she sobs, sinking onto her bed and looking at my body. She's right—you can see most of my ribs and my hip bones jut out. I've lost so much weight, this is the smallest I have ever been.

"I'm fine, Ava. I'm okay," I try to reassure her, rummaging through my bag to retrieve a diaper. Thankfully, between my shirt and the blanket that was wrapped around him, Valarian was able to stay dry.

She just shakes her head, looking at my son as she rocks him. I sit next to her, and she moves over on the bed to give me space, leaning back against the wall. Together, we watch my son fall asleep in her arms. Laying my head down on her shoulder, I suddenly break down. Ava tries to soothe me, but I can feel her crying silently beside me. Ava was my best friend. It is almost impossible to beat a sister bond, someone who knows your hardships, knows what it's like to grow up with the parents you have, someone who shares every milestone with you and every heartbreak.

How times have changed?

I've missed having someone to talk to. The only interactions I've had were judgmental glares or a few words to show their disgust with me. Nobody asked how I was—nobody cared—and I was stupid enough to believe Beta Marcus would be able to help, stupid enough to think my mate would accept me.

"How is mom?" I ask her, and she shakes her head.

"She's okay; she asked Dad for a divorce when he kicked you out. But you know Mom, she would never leave him," she tells me, and I nod.

It's unheard of for mates to get divorced. The bond stops mates from being separated. It weakens them; two souls, together, or that's how it's supposed to be.

Not for me, I guess. I'm not looking forward to the rest of my life feeling my mate whenever he's with another woman who isn't me. I'm not looking forward to raising our son on my own or being alone.

When Valarian stirs, I get up and grab his formula before realizing I have no bottled water. Ava passes my son to me before grabbing his bottle from my hand.

"How much?" she whispers.

"Four ounces," I tell her, and she nods, opening the door just as my son cries out loudly. I try to muffle the noise and soothe him by giving him his binky, but he spits it out and lets out an ear-piercing scream.

My sister stares at me in panic. Quickly, she tries to close the door, but within seconds it is thrown open and bangs against the wall, causing Valarian to scream even louder.

My father storms in and his eyes instantly find me. A growl escapes him. I cower away, shielding my son. Ava gets between us, trying to shield me from my enraged father, but he shoves her out of the way before stalking toward me.

"Please, Dad, please!" I beg. He grabs my hair, and I scream. So does my son in my arms as I try not to drop him. My reflexes want to pull his hands away; instead, I hold my son for dear life, letting my hair tug painfully from my scalp.

"Mom! Mom!" Ava starts screaming frantically before I hear feet slapping on the tiles in the hall.

"Please, Dad! Mom, help me! Mom, please!" I beg her when she rushes in, her mouth open in shock as my father starts dragging me toward the front door by my hair.

My mother grips his arm, pleading with him. "John, please let her go; she has a baby in her arms."

He shoves her aside before dragging me down the hall to the front of the house.

"Dad, please, it's raining outside," Ava begs. My mother is also desperately trying to stop him. My father doesn't care; he growls at them, ignoring them and my cries. He's just opened the front door when my mother shoves him.

"John! She is our daughter! Please," she begs, tears in her eyes and streaming down her face.

"That whore is not my daughter," he growls, his canines protruding.

"Dad, please, it's freezing outside," Ava begs.

"I said no! I will not have a rogue whore for a daughter!" he screams, his face turning red in his anger.

"Then take him, please. I will stay outside; just don't put him out. Please, Dad, he's your grandson," I choke out. He growls at me, his hand shoving me out the door. He's about to shut the door in my face when I try once more.

"Please just look at him, Dad. He'll get sick. Just one night. Then I will leave," I plead.

My mother reaches for Valarian, but my father pushes her behind him.

"John, at least let me take him! Let me take my Grandson!" my mother cries.

He lets me go, looking down at my son before staring at my mother, who is sobbing, her hands outstretched for him. Those same hands that held mine when I was a little girl, now grasping the air for my son.

"Give him to her, but you stay out. You aren't welcome in my house," he says before walking off. My mother rushes over to grab Valarian before hugging me briefly.

"I will watch him; I'll stay by the window," she says, and I nod.

"Ava has his baby bag," I tell her. My sister clutches my fingers, nodding. Tears roll down her cheeks as her lips quiver.

"It's okay, Ava. I will be fine," I tell my sister behind her before my dad yells at them, making them jump.

"I'm sorry, I have to," my mother says, closing the door. I nod. The curtain in the living room opens, and the lamp flicks on. I see my sister rush off toward the kitchen, and my mother sits on the lounge with him next to the window, so I can see him.

Leaning over, my mother cracks the window so she can speak to me. "He has your nose," she says, smiling sadly at me, and I smile, sitting on the chair out front on the porch. I shiver; my sister's flannel pajamas become soaked as the rain blows toward me where I sit, listening and watching my mother through the window feeding my son his bottle.

At least he is warm and dry, I think to myself. Huddled up on the chair, I tuck my knees to my chest, trying to warm myself and shield myself from the cold and the strong gusts of wind.

It doesn't take long before I start shaking uncontrollably, and my teeth chatter so hard I feel like they'll break. My mother taps on the glass where my head rests—I can see her heartbreak at watching me sit in the cold, stormy weather.

"Shift sweetie. Shift to try to stay warm," she says, placing her palm on the glass.

"I haven't shifted yet," I tell her, and she looks at me sadly.

Shifting is a big thing with werewolves; it is a coming of age. Your wolf is meant to represent your future in the pack. I haven't shifted yet, but when I do, it will not be celebratory like it is for most wolves; it will be purely a necessity. What is there to celebrate? My failures; the fact I am pack-less and homeless; that I am raising a baby on my own because the father refuses to believe he got with a seventeen-year-old; because he can't recognize me as his mate.

CHAPTER

SEVEN

"Shift! Please, Everly. I can't watch you suffer in the rain. Please," my mother begs through the window, sucking in a deep breath.

You can do this, Everly, I whisper to myself. It isn't how I imagined shifting, but I need to put my big girl panties on and do what's required. I tell myself it doesn't matter that nobody will be celebrating for me anyway—not anymore—before stripping my saturated shirt off. I hang it over a railing along the far wall before removing the pajama pants. It's late at night, so I'm pretty sure no one will see me. Even if they did, they wouldn't pay any attention to the Alpha's disgraced daughter.

My mother taps on the window and I look in; my son is drinking his bottle in her arms, gazing up at her, nice and warm. His eyes get heavier and heavier the longer he feeds on his bottle.

"Thank you," I whisper to her. She smiles sadly while nodding her head.

"I'm right here. You don't have to be alone for your first shift," my mother says, and I nod. Others—when they shift for the first time—go running with their family and have a big celebration. Me? I'm shifting to stay warm. I'm transitioning out of necessity while everyone else shifts for celebration. Funny how things work out, isn't it?

I have been able to feel my need to shift for months. However, being pregnant, I couldn't change without causing harm to my unborn baby; once he was born, I didn't have anyone to watch him while I did. This is my only chance.

Swallowing down all emotion, I kneel on the ground, stretch my fingers, and tuck my toes under, so I'm on a sort of tiptoe. My neck cracks first, my face twisting and morphing. Everything stretches and moves, and then I feel the first snap of bone. It is agony. I knew it would hurt—the first shift always hurts, apparently—but I never imagined it like this.

"Don't think of it, just envision your wolf," my mother tries coaching through the glass window.

I dread seeing myself in wolf form. Alphas are supposed to be big, but I've been stripped of my title and my pack; I hadn't shifted on my eighteenth birthday like I should have, and all these things affect a wolf's strength. It's unlikely my wolf will be anything close to what it should have been. I suck in a deep breath, trying to envision what I will look like, and ignore the pain. Will I be a sandy color like my mother or black like my father?

It shouldn't be like this; it wasn't meant to be like this; Dad always promised that he and Mom would be there to help me through it. A scream tears out of me that immediately morphs into a howl as the shift starts.

"Deep breath and shove everything behind it, force the shift, don't wait for it. Force it, Everly," she says.

I throw everything behind it like my mother said, bypassing the agony of shifting. Suddenly, my hands are replaced with paws, my skin is covered in thick fur, and my face becomes more elongated. My canines feel sharp as I run my tongue along them.

I look at my paws and tail, trying to see myself. From the little I can see like this, I appear to be a strange off-white color, almost a blue hue under the moonlight.

Using the glass to get a better look at myself, I see I am pure white, my fur one color, only small, tiny, and thin—so small, I look like an omega as I peer at myself. I look up at my mother in the window holding my son, one hand covering her mouth in dismay. She is clearly shocked at my size, the size of a castaway. I'll be easy pickings for anything that decides to hunt me. And my wolf will only get smaller and weaker the longer I go without my mate.

My father comes over and looks out the window, a stormy expression on his face; he is disappointed. I'm not much bigger than a German Shepherd, which is embarrassingly small. Most rogues would be less insignificant than me. Was this punishment from being stripped bare of everything? This is what's left of me? My father tugs the curtain closed like he can't look at me any longer, like he is disgusted, and I am too.

I didn't know it was possible to feel more shame.

Mortified at how weak I feel, I press my nose against the glass just as a crack of thunder echos in the sky, waking him. When I hear my father walk off, my mother tugs the curtain open a bit before sitting on the couch, so I can see my son. I watch him through the glass, wishing more than anything I could comfort him, but knowing it is best this way. He is safe, warm and, more importantly, dry.

My mother manages to get him to sleep and creates a makeshift bassinet on the couch. Eventually, I fall asleep too, my head resting on the brick ledge under the window.

When the sun starts to come up, I quickly shift back, putting on my drenched clothes while doing my best to carefully ring them out, trying to remove some of the water as I go. Just as I pull the last of the sopping wet clothes on, the front door opens, and my father steps out of the house. I peer up at him from my spot on the ground near the window where I had been crouched. He doesn't even look at me—instead, tosses me some cash rolled up with a rubber band.

"I want you gone before I get home. Don't ever come back, Everly," he says before walking toward his car, not even glancing at me. I reach forward, grab the rolled-up cash, and look after him.

Despite how badly my heart is breaking—he wouldn't even acknowledge me—I still love the man. He's my father, and tossing me away like garbage hurts; it hurts severely, finally making me realize I am nothing but garbage to everyone.

The door opens, and my mother puts her head out to see if he is gone before ushering me into the house.

My sister comes running out with a backpack and some dry clothes. She hands me a towel and I dry myself off before slipping on the jeans, shirt, and hoodie she brought out for me.

"Here, take these," she says, handing me a pair of her Nike shoes. I slip the socks on before placing the shoes on my feet. My mother is still holding my son like she doesn't want to let him go.

"I called a taxi to come to get you," my mother tells me while Ava hands me a bag.

"Some clothes, toiletries, feminine products, girlie stuff. I also put all the cash from my safe in there," my sister says, and I swallow.

"Ava, I can't take that," I tell her.

"You might as well. I can't go to university now anyway. Dad is making me take over the pack next year."

A feeling of guilt overwhelms me—not only did I fuck my life up, but I ruined my sister's too. Now she is being forced to be Alpha. Ava wanted to go to college and study some science thing when I was still set to take over. She is wicked smart, and I ruined her plans by getting pregnant. Ava doesn't look upset, though; just like she's accepted it.

"Take it. My old phone is in there too, and the charger. I will make sure to reload some minutes every month for you, so I can get a hold of you," Ava says, and my mother nods.

"He doesn't have to know. What he doesn't know won't hurt him," my mother tells me.

"So, you will come to see us, visit us?" I ask her, hopeful. Her face drops.

"No, you know I can't, but you can send us photos of... you never did tell us his name," my mother says.

"Valarian," I tell them. They look at me funny, but I thought it went with his father's name. Even though he will probably never meet the man, at the time, I had hoped—now not so much.

"See, you can send a picture of Valarian to us, and we can use video chat; it will be the same," my mother says, only it won't be. It will lack the connection, the physical contact.

Chewing my lip, and I nod, saying nothing. That is as good as it's going to get. I am alone; not even my mother is willing to go against my father for her daughter. I shouldn't have expected her to. It's near impossible for someone to go against their mate.

I never realized how much I missed human touch until I was able to hug my mother and sister, and now no longer feel it—only my son's. I crave contact, any form of interaction, conversation, someone to talk to that can talk back.

"You okay, Everly?" Ava asks, and I nod, seeing the cab waiting out the front. I take my son, my sister's bag she packed for me, and the baby bag.

"I will not see you again," I tell them, letting those words sink in; I'm not welcome back here, and they're too scared to come see me. This will be it. They said they would call, but we all know it will only be texts, if they even manage that much without my father realizing it.

Ava squeezes me tight before letting go and my mother clutches my face, her eyes filled with tears.

"You can do this. You will be alright," she says, her face lined with worry; she knows with how small my wolf is that I will suffer if anyone comes for me. She knows I will not be able to protect myself.

If they knew my mate had also tossed me aside, they would realize I'm basically as good as dead. Without my mate, I will slowly deteriorate until there is nothing left. I won't be able to shift, and I'll practically be human. Once that happens, it's basically the end for me.

"Are you telling yourself or me that?" I ask her.

Her brows furrow; she knows there is nothing out there for me and my son. We are rogue, and nothing good ever happens to rogues; we merely exist among the packs, surviving day to day, praying we don't get picked off by bigger prey because, at the end of the day, no pack would intervene for a rogue, even if they have a child.

I have to hold my son on my lap in the back as the taxi driver takes us to the train station where my car is. We pass a rundown hotel on the way and I think I may have just enough fuel to get my car there. Hopefully, I do. After spending the entire night in the rain, I want a hot shower and something warm in my belly, but most of all, I want the safety of four walls, even if it's only for one night.

I tell myself that one night is all I need, then I can suck it up and figure something out. I hand the taxi driver some cash from the wad my father gave me and watch him go. I have no idea how much my sister snuck into the bag.

Getting my keys from the diaper bag, I unlock my car and climb in, pulling the hatchback down before I realize I no longer have a car seat.

Shit! I think, knowing how long I saved for that car seat. I open the bag and empty my pockets after placing my son in his box bed. My father gave me $525. I snort. *Gee, thanks, Dad,* I think to myself. At least it will buy roughly 16 cans of formula and four boxes of diapers, so it will keep me out of trouble for a while.

Opening the bag my sister packed for me, I find feminine products, hair products, makeup; even some black slacks, a blouse, and some black flats. I'm assuming she placed them here if I manage to get a job interview. I also find her old touchscreen phone and a charger before finding an envelope. Opening it, I pull out a stack of $100 bills. I feel a lump form in my throat; she gave me everything she had.

I know she did. There is nearly eight thousand dollars in the envelope. She gave me all her savings.

I feel a tear slip down my cheek. Turning the envelope over, I see her neat handwriting.

'You can do this. I love you.'

I nod at her words. She's right. I can do this; I can because I have no choice. I will make it work.

After packing up some clothes and refilling the diaper bag, I pack a little bit of food to eat later before changing Valarian. Once he's dressed with a fresh diaper on, I grab my umbrella and toss my bag over my shoulder along with the baby bag, then scoop up my son.

Without a car seat, driving is impossible, so after locking my car, I start walking, deciding to head to the rundown hotel I saw earlier. I wonder how I never noticed it before. Just for one night, I could pretend I'm normal. After that decent shower the other night— before being tossed aside by my mate and son's father—I now long for a tiny piece of normal; some dignity, a chance to feel human, even if it *is* only one night.

The rain has nearly stopped when I reach the two-story rectangular building—Mountainview Hotel. It has peeling paint and the gardens are overgrown; the sign out the front hangs down, and the neon lights flicker as they struggle to remain on; the lines in the parking lot are faded and the hotel numbers on the door are barely visible. At the office, a woman is sitting on a chair out front with a cigarette between her fingers. When I push on the door, the bell sounds and the woman smoking out front speaks.

"I'll be with you in a second; just let me finish this," she says, holding up her cigarette. She stares at me, watching me, her eyes roaming over my appearance before stopping at my son in my arms.

"He's yours?" she asks. I nod, looking down at him and tucking him closer.

"The father?" she asks, and I shake my head.

"Not your mate's?" she asks. I feel tears burn my eyes at her words. I don't know what to say to that.

"He is your mate's, so why are you here?" she asks curiously, pointing to the chair beside her.

She leans over to look at Valarian, taking a closer look at him. She appears to be in her fifties with dark hair cut to her shoulders, her nose pierced, heavy eye makeup, looking comfortable in a tank top and jeans.

"He has strange eyes; reminds me of someone I used to know; amber eyes are usually a family trait. Not many wolves in Mountainview City with eyes like that," she says. "So, the blood Alpha is your mate and his father?" she asks, clearly putting two and two together. I guess Alpha Valen is known for his electric amber eyes. Shocked, I just look at her. She smiles and nods when I say nothing.

"Powerful family, so why aren't you with your mate?"

"He didn't recognize me and kicked me off pack land before I could tell him about his son," I admit.

"And your family?" she asks. I fall silent, and she nods once before speaking, "My parents thought I was a rogue whore too. Funny how things happen."

"So, you have a child?" I ask her, feeling an immediate connection between us.

"Had a child, his father took him."

"So, you are a rogue whore?"

"Such a vile thing to call women; whoever came up with it should be shot. I am many things, but a rogue whore? You and I aren't so different. My name is Valarie, and you are?"

"Everly. This is Valarian," I tell her, and her eyes sparkle.

"It suits; after his father," the woman says.

"How do you know?"

"About his father?" the woman asks, looking at my son. "Only one bloodline I know that has amber eyes. Come on, let's get you a room," Valarie says while getting up. I follow her into the small office.

"I take it you have no ID?" she asks, and I nod.

"I have an old bus pass," I offer, but she shakes her head, waving me off.

"I don't believe you'll give me any trouble. Here, fill this out while I hold Valarian," she says, holding her arms out.

I pass her my son, and she wanders behind the counter, sitting down while I fill out my paperwork, yet I had no address to put down, no credit card that actually works to use as collateral. I put down the number for my sister's old cell phone.

"Are you hungry? I'm cooking a roast, but it's just me and too much for one person. You can join me if you want, say around five; it should be done about then," she says, nodding toward the door behind her. There is a beaded curtain, and the scent of what smells like a lamb roast wafts to my nose. My belly rumbles at the thought of a home-cooked meal.

"How about you get settled in, take a shower, and come through that door when you're done? We can have dinner together. It would be nice to have company. Not many stop over for the night anymore, and you can tell me how you ended up a rogue," she tells me. I dig through my bag to give her cash from the envelope as she hands me my son.

"No, keep it. Be nice just to have company; haven't had anyone stay in months now," Valarie tells me. I look around again. The place is a dump, but it's still nicer than the back of my car.

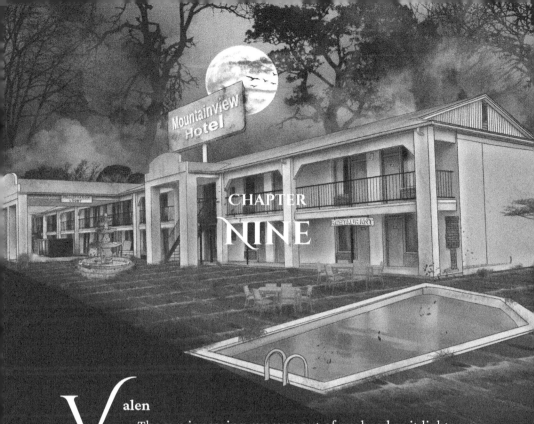

CHAPTER
NINE

Valen

The sun is searing my eyes out of my head as it lights up the back of my eyelids. I am working up the energy to force myself out of bed when Marcus bursts into my room, slamming the door into the wall loudly, the noise rattling my already pounding headache.

"Ah, good. You're up," he says just as I sit up, rubbing my eyes. I wave him off, but he doesn't leave. Instead, he leans on the wall beside my dresser.

"What?" I ask, my head pulsing violently in my skull. I look around my room to find some redhead in my bed and groan, praying I used a rubber. She's tangled in the sheets, and just seeing her there irritates me. Stupid dick, why does it always pick bimbos?

"The rogue girl in my room, where did she go?"

Huh? What the fuck is he talking about? I'm too hungover for his drama this morning. I continue to stare at the woman in my bed, her hair spreading out on the pillow like a web of red. All the while, I ignore my Beta.

"Hey, whatever your name is, get up," I tell her, shoving her shoulder. She groans, rolling over and flashing us her tits. I growl at her, and Marcus snorts.

"Get rid of her," I tell Marcus, getting up to pee. I push the bathroom door open and my senses come alert. I can smell some faint scent in here. It makes my mouth water, but it's barely there. I wonder if the cleaning lady changed her chemicals.

"Valen, the girl in my room, where is she?" Marcus asks, following me to the bathroom.

"What girl?" I mutter, shaking my dick before pulling my pants up. I glance at the trash can and see a used condom. *Thank fuck for that*, I think to myself

"The rogue girl, Everly. I picked her up last night and brought her here," Marcus says, and I pinch the bridge of my nose trying to remember last night.

My head is throbbing—I remember coming home, and the slut in my bed whining about a rogue.

Then it clicks, coming back to me. But I can't remember her face. However, something keeps nagging me about the situation.

"Wait, you brought her here?" I ask, peering over at my Beta leaning on the bathroom door.

"Yes, and she has a name: Everly. Her and her son; I found them sleeping at the train station."

"What?" I ask, horrified, looking at him.

"She had no kid with her," I tell him, and he looks at me, his lips pulling back over his teeth.

"Valen?" he growls. If he were anyone else, I would knock him on his ass for taking that tone with me. He's lucky he's my best friend, or he would be lying unconscious on the floor.

"Grab my keys; I didn't know she had a fucking kid. I never would have kicked her out last night if I had known," I tell him.

"Are you fucking serious? It was pouring rain," Marcus snaps at me.

I suddenly feel terrible as the faint memories come back. I pray I didn't hurt her; I can't totally remember. My memory is hazy, and I am sure I am still pretty intoxicated with the way the ground still keeps moving as I walk.

The woman in the bed stirs, sitting up and rubbing her eyes before running a hand through her hair. I roll my eyes at her while grabbing some shorts and a shirt from my closet.

"Get your shit and get out," I snap at her, scooping up her dress and tossing it at her.

"Baby, what's got into–"

"Don't baby me, get the fuck out of my bed and packhouse," I snap at her. Fuck me, why they gotta be such cling-ons? I make a mental note to avoid redheads. She isn't one of my pack members. Goddess knows where I picked her up from.

"Out, now!" I yell at her, forcing my Alpha aura over her. She jumps up, tugging the dress over her head before grabbing her shoes. On her way out the door, she shoulder-shoves Marcus; I grab my keys off the dresser. I hope I didn't destroy my car again driving home drunk.

"You're not driving; you still look half tanked. Hurry up, maybe she went back to her car," Marcus says. I feel guilty as shit, knowing I kicked the girl out in the rain with a baby. If Marcus brought her here, she must have been in dire straits because Marcus never brings anyone to the packhouse.

"What did you say her name was again?" I ask, wondering why he was so interested in this rogue.

"Everly. She smelled familiar..." he says thoughtfully. "And I can officially say you aren't the only freak with eyes like your father."

"What do you mean?"

"Her son, he had the same eyes as you—freaky as fuck. Could almost pass him off to be your son," he chuckles.

I shove my feet in my shoes, growling at his words. That's the last thing I need: an illegitimate child. It would be another thing for my father to breathe down my neck about.

"What? You never know, you have a new girl on your arm every night. You probably have fifty kids you're unaware of," Marcus laughs.

"How old is she?"

"Dunno, but I could tell she hadn't shifted yet, so must be young," he says with a shrug.

"Well, not mine then; I won't go near jail bait."

"She wasn't that young, probably eighteen. Well, nearly, seeing as she hadn't shifted," he says.

"Did she say what pack she's from?"

"Nope."

"Well, come on, let's see if we can find her. Maybe they might have room at one of the hostels to put her in for a few weeks."

They really need to get rid of that law. We have a few of what the other packs would call rogue whores in our pack—disgusting how the other packs just turn their backs on them.

I sit in the passenger seat of Marcus's car, the motion making my stomach turn as I press my head against the window. I must have nodded off because I wake up to Marcus shaking my shoulder. Looking up, we're pulling into the train station on no-man's land.

"That's her car," Marcus says, pointing to a rundown wagon.

"Well, go on, see if your damsel in distress wants to be saved," I tell him, waving him off. It's pretty overcast today; the storm last night was massive, giant puddles in the parking lot have ducks swimming around in them, making my guilt worse knowing I forced a woman and baby out in this weather. He looks in the windows, and I sigh, tossing the door open and walking over to him.

"She isn't here; I wonder where she went?" he says, looking around before walking off toward the train station. "I will see if the guards are on and if they've seen her,'' he sighs out over his shoulder.

I peer in the windows of the busted-up wagon. The thing looks like a death trap. The car's rear was like a mini grocery department of baby items—tins of formula and diapers—canned food, a quilt, and a pillow. Hardly any personal items, yet I can see a photo album jammed between the passenger and driver's seat.

Marcus comes back, shaking his head. "CCTV shows she left this morning with a bag and her son."

"Might have gone home?" I suggest, and he shrugs. Walking to his car, he opens the back door before pulling out a baby carrier. I help him by placing it beside her car before rummaging around for a pen and paper.

"Leave a note with your number. You think she would contact you?" I ask him, and he nods, finding an old envelope, scrawling his number on it, and putting some money in it to use a payphone if she hasn't got a phone. He places the note inside the baby seat and I look around at the clouds. It looks like the rain is going to come back.

"It will get wet. Give the note and car seat to security to give to her," I tell him, and Marcus nods, walking off toward the train station with the carrier in his arms. Not much we can do when she isn't here, and I need to go crawl back in bed or get my stomach pumped; either would do if it means getting rid of this sick feeling in my guts and this pounding headache.

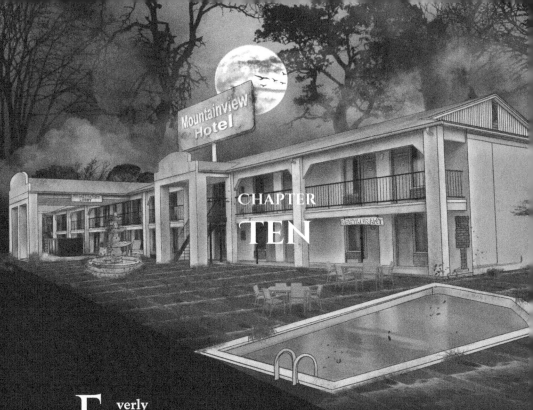

E**verly**

We settle in the room, and I wash Valarian down with a wet cloth—it's a little too cold today for me to give him a bath right now. Once he's settled and napping, I take the longest, hottest shower in ages, trying to wash the memories of last night away.

I found my mate, saw him, and he didn't recognize me. But worse still was knowing he was with another woman. The agony that it caused as I ran home was heartbreaking as well as painful. When Marcus took me there, I hoped that he would recognize our son and we could get the help we needed, that maybe everything could be fixed, especially once I realized he was my mate. It allowed me to hope for the first time in ages, and I caught a glimmer of it only for it to be taken away. Now I'm failing my son once again; that much I do know.

I can't help but feel that way; Valarian will never have a father; I will never again have mine. How I long to go home, where I was the loved and cherished Alpha's daughter. Instead, I am now ashamed and scum, forbidden to speak to my sister in my father's eyes. Not even my mother will fight for her grandchild or me. I know she is hurting, but I could never choose anyone over my son, so how could she choose Dad over me?

My life has fallen apart; I didn't think it could get much worse than all that, but then it ripped out what was left of my heart. I thought my luck was changing when he stepped into the bathroom. Every piece of me was screaming for him. I truly realized how powerful a mate bond is for the first time. Nothing thrilled me more; well, until I saw the look on his face.

The way he yelled at me and ordered me off his territory will stain my memory forever. Then to have my father toss me outside in the rain afterward, forcing me to watch my son being looked after through a damn window, out of reach because I no longer deserve human decency from my own family... it's just too much to process.

I thought I could do this. I thought I was stronger than this. But everyone breaks eventually. Everyone has a breaking point, and I have reached mine. Every damn thing weighing me down suddenly becomes too much and I break. At least no one can see how fucked I really am while I cry in the shower. It washes out the pain I feel until it brings me to my knees.

It is suddenly and startlingly clear how alone I truly am.

Loneliness is deafening and cold—no one to tell you it will be alright, no one to help you pick up the pieces, no conversation. I've lost my sense of self. I'm no one now; just a mom, just another rogue whore for everyone to look down on, even though I am not—he is my mate. But he couldn't even recognize me. I realize how small and insignificant I am to everyone except my baby boy.

Hearing a knock on the door, my head jerks up from where it's pressed to my knees. I get up quickly, shutting the water off and grabbing a towel.

"Everly dear, open the door for me."

"Sorry, just a sec," I call back, checking Valarian before tugging a shirt over the towel to try to appear presentable.

I open the door to find Valarie standing there with a tray in her hands and two plates on it.

"Thought I would come to join you in here. The time must have slipped you by," Valarie says. I quickly take it from her, and she steps inside, walking to the small table.

"Oh, I'm so sorry, I didn't realize how much time passed," I tell her, glancing at the old analog clock on the wall. Was I really in the shower that long?

"It's fine, dear. I could hear you were upset, so I thought I would come and be an ear to listen," she says, and my brows bunch at her words. She points behind me to the bathroom.

"That vent there is directly above my kitchen. It echoes through the pipes. I keep meaning to get someone in to fix it, but no one wants to help a rogue whore," she says with a sad smile. My face heats, and I touch my cheeks.

"I'm sorry. I didn't realize; I hope I didn't disturb you," I tell her. She waves me off.

"You forget I have been where you are. I would have put you in another room, but this is the nicest one left and is functional. The place is falling apart," she says. Valarian starts fussing, and I move to get up but Valarie beats me to it.

"Go get your pajamas on; I'll watch him. Isn't that right, sugar? Yes, I love me some baby cuddles," she says, smiling brightly down at him as she scoops him up into her arms.

"Go on, get dressed, and then we can talk," she says, and I nod, quickly digging through my bag and grabbing some clothes out before rushing to the bathroom. I dress quickly and come back out with my hair wrapped in my towel.

"He is such a sweet boy," Valarie babbles to him. He eventually drifts off, and she places him back in bed.

"So, what made you upset? Why the tears?"

"It's nothing. Everything just got to be too much," I tell her as we unwrap our dinner from the aluminum foil.

We tuck into the food and I tell Valarie everything, bleeding my heart and soul out to her, the pressure lifting off my chest. I didn't realize how talking to someone who listened could feel so relieving.

Valarie told me she also found her mate when she was my age, but since she's an Omega, he didn't want to tell anyone because it would bring shame to his family. These days, it's uncommon for someone to be so prejudiced over ranking. The most heartbreaking part was he never rejected her. Instead, he kept her around, refusing to let her go because he couldn't handle knowing she would belong to someone else.

She said she became just another side piece so he would stay strong; rejecting mates weakens us, yet I think it was disgusting he would force her to endure the agony of being alone.

When she got pregnant, he took her son, said it would be better if he raised him. She said besides pictures, she hasn't seen her son since he was a baby. He doesn't even know she exists because her mate told him she died during the birth. Her story is tragic and gut-wrenching, yet she still loves him despite it.

"Have you thought of moving on?" I ask her, and she shakes her head almost immediately.

"He still comes in every couple of weeks to stay the night," she tells me with a shrug like she never thought about finding anyone else.

"May I ask you something? Something a little personal?" I need to know; I need to know if I will be tortured my entire life.

"You can ask me anything, but then I want to ask you something," she says, and I nod.

"When I found my mate, he was with another woman. The pain... I mean, does it feel like that all the time? Will it feel like that every time he's with someone?"

She swallows, her eyes turning glassy. Valarie sits back in her chair, looking towards the window, and she gulps. "You will learn to endure it. After a while, even welcome it."

"Why would I welcome it?"

"Because it makes you angry. I love my mate, but I also hate him.

53

Sometimes, hating them hurts less than realizing you will never have them. It reminds you to keep on living despite what they do to us. Hold on to that anger because sometimes it is the only thing that will keep you going," she tells me. "I get a prescription, though—powerful painkillers. They help take the edge off, but if he's anything like my mate, it's over before the drugs even set in." She laughs.

"Damn two-stroker; tosses his mate and wonders why he can't fuck right," she laughs to herself, and I snort at her foul language, trying to hold my own giggle. She sighs, and I smile sadly at her.

"So, what's next for you?" she asks.

"Not sure... Probably go back to my car, see if I can get my old job back, though he said no last time I asked."

"How about I hire you? I need help here; not that much can be done to save this dump now." She laughs and I look around the room. "What do you think? Or do you think it's too much work? I could always burn it?" Valarie laughs again, and her eyes sparkle.

I laugh too, thinking that it probably *would* be easier to just burn the place down.

"I've been tempted to, but before me, it was my mother's, so I'm attached to this place," she tells me. "I think it just needs a clean-up, new linens and carpets and some paint. I could go on, but the list would be never-ending.

"So, if you're interested, you can live here for free and I'll provide meals and a wage; say $25 an hour?" she says, and I nearly choke on my spit. I wasn't even making half that an hour at the restaurant when I was working. And that restaurant actually had regular customers.

"Are you serious?" I ask, a little shocked.

"Very. I could use the company and the help. I don't even know where to begin, and honestly, I lost motivation to do it years ago. We can fix this one up first for you and Valarian," she says, looking around.

Tears well in my eyes at her generous offer.

"Don't suppose you got any friends? This might even be a bit much for both of us," she mutters, breaking off a piece of the table, the wood crumbling in her hand. I think of Zoe and Macey from the maternity ward.

"I might know two other girls from the maternity unit; I could try to contact them."

"Rogues?" she asks, and I nod. "Good, tell them I'll give them $25 an hour. I'm good for it. I have more money than I can spend in this lifetime, so it would be great to get some help. It would be nice to see this place up and running again. It used to be the most popular hotel in the city when my mother had it. Also has a function room out the back; weddings used to be held here, but not since it started falling apart."

"So no one comes out when you call?" I ask her. What is wrong with people? Who would turn her away?

"Nope. I arrange workers and they never show up. My mate keeps tabs on my phones; he's paranoid. I know it's his doing," she says with a sigh.

"Well then, I will call the girls and see if they're looking for work. Would it be an issue if they brought their babies to work?"

"Of course, they can; there's even an old play center off the side of the restaurant downstairs. We could fix it up for when they're older and can play, take turns watching them. While they are little, we can just strap the babies to us."

"Macey, I know, has family. Zoe, though, I think is like me; she was a little quiet and a year younger than me."

"Well, it either needs somewhere to stay, there are plenty of rooms. There are units out back, too, but they need a lot of work," she tells me.

"Well, I'll let you rest, and let me know when the girls can start if they are interested. Come down for breakfast in the morning, too. Here," she says, handing me a key. "That will let you into my studio, so you have access to the kitchen if I am not here, which is rare; I have nowhere else to go," she chuckles.

"Thank you, Valarie. You have no idea how much this means to my son and me."

"No need to thank me, Everly. So, I will see you in the morning, and we'll start ordering supplies. There should be a pen and paper in the drawer if the moths haven't eaten them. Write a list of what needs doing that you notice, and we can go over it tomorrow," she says before looking down at Valarian on the bed. She brushes her finger down his little nose, her eyes softening before she clears her throat and nods to me before walking out.

CHAPTER
ELEVEN

I can't believe my luck. I spend all night writing a list for Valarie —everything that I'd already noticed needed doing around the place—but it's a little challenging, considering I don't know what half the place looks like. I also spend a good chunk of time listing ways to advertise the place once it's up and running because she really needs it. I've lived in this city my entire life, and I never realized there was a hotel on this side of town until I drove past in the taxi; and on the main street no less! Valarie won't need this information until the place is ready to open though, which is a long way off. And that's if it even passes the health and safety inspections because this place is literally falling apart at the seams.

After breakfast, I manage to get a hold of Macey and Zoe. Both are eager to find work and are floored with the amount Valarie is willing to pay them, making me realize it wasn't just me that was underpaid and overworked, but rogues in general. Macey's mother said she would watch her baby; Zoe said she would have to bring hers but had a baby carrier and stroller she could use.

Zoe is just sixteen years old—even younger than me—making my heart really go out for her. Her mother was a rogue but died when

Zoe was a child, and she has spent her entire life in and out of child orphanages and refuges. How lonely it would feel to be entirely on your own all your life, though she probably doesn't know any different. She sounds miserable where she is and I spend over an hour on the phone with her. After we hang up, I go down and speak to Valarie, asking if it's alright if Zoe shares the room with me. It has a fold-out bed if Zoe feels weird about sharing the double with me. Valarie seems genuinely excited about someone else coming here and happily agrees.

The following day, I wake up to Valarie calling out to me from downstairs. Sitting up, I see Valarian is still asleep, and my mouth falls open when I realize it's nearly 10 a.m.—we slept in! When sleeping in my car, I was usually up around 6 a.m.

"Everly, wakey, wakey," comes Valarie's voice from the other side of the door as she knocks.

I quickly rush to open the door, embarrassed that I slept so late. Valarie is standing there with a cigarette between her lips, wearing her typical jeans and tank top, an open vest, and steel toe boots. She looks ready to kick ass—hopefully not mine. She really is one tough lady with a heart of gold.

"Finally, you're up. Did you have a good sleep? I didn't want to wake you," she says.

"I am so sorry–" I start, but she waves me off.

"Don't worry about that; I came in with the master key and turned your alarm off. Come, come. I need your help unloading my truck," she says, walking off toward the stairs. I look back into the room. Valarian is sleeping peacefully so I leave the door open before following her down the stairs in my pajamas.

"I've been shopping. Couldn't have Valarian sleeping on that dirty mattress, and now Zoe is coming with her baby. I thought I would grab some things. It turns out, I have a shopping problem. Everything was so cute and reminded me of when I went shopping for my son when I had him," Valarie gushes, her sparkle bright with her excitement. Pointing to the bed of her pickup truck. I blink, shocked. She had indeed been shopping! My hands go to my mouth.

"Valarie..." I am gobsmacked. I don't know what to say; I can't believe she's done all this for two rogue girls she barely knows, one of whom she hasn't even met yet. There are two of everything—everything you could possibly think of! Two cribs, mobiles, crib sheet sets, blankets, and baby toys, some of which both babies are a little too young to play with yet.

"Oh! Check this out; this even has a camera so you can watch them while they sleep," Valarie says, holding up a baby monitor. "Didn't have these when mine was young."

"I don't know what to say; this is seriously the nicest thing anyone has done for me. You've already done more than enough and I only just met you," I croak out, becoming emotional. Big fat tears roll down my face. How could one woman be so kind? She has shown more kindness in the last 24 hours than I received the whole year I have been rogue.

"It takes a village to raise a child; we are going to build our own village," Valarie says before clapping her hands. "Now, let's get this stuff up to the room before the delivery truck comes. We also need to get that bed out; two new ones arrive around twelve. What time will the girls get here?"

"They said ten this morning."

"Well, we better hop to it. Then, I need a coffee and about ten more of these to build up the motivation," she says, holding up her smoke. I chuckle, and we start undoing the straps holding everything in place.

I'm exhausted when I run the last of it up—the room looks more like a baby store than a bedroom now. I shake my head, trying to figure out where the heck Zoe and I are going to put it all. Valarie is taking a break and feeding Valarian a bottle. She's very fond of my son and has commented about four or five times already about his eyes. Her fascination with them confuses me.

Hearing a truck reversing, Valarie hops up, looking out the door and over the balcony.

"Now, please tell me that is your car. Otherwise, I've just stolen someone else's from the train station" she giggles.

"What?" I ask, getting up and walking over to see a tow truck with my car on the back.

"Yes, that's my beast; I would have walked back and gotten it," I tell her, feeling bad she wasted money getting it towed.

"Nonsense! Phil owed me a favor anyway—picked him up once when his truck broke down, said he owed me one—and I simply collected," she says.

The truck door opens, and a big, burly trucker gets out with a beard and balding head.

"Val, where do you want it?" he calls out to her.

"Anywhere, Phil, we have the keys to move it," she calls back to him. Looking at the time, I see it's nearly ten in the morning. I'd told the girls I would meet them out front near the curb so they could find the place easier; they were also unaware there was a hotel here and seemed confused when I mentioned the address.

"Girls should be nearly here," I tell Valarie. She sends me off with a little wave, going back to feeding Valarian and fussing over him. I smile at her. Valarie's whole attitude seems different since yesterday. She appears almost happy—like she's found a new lease on life.

I wait for the girls on the curb until a taxi stops beside me. Zoe gets out and pays for the cab, and I help her grab her stuff from the trunk.

"I never knew this place was here," she says, looking up at the vast hotel. "Kinda creepy—it looks haunted," she adds, and I chuckle. "Anyway, I am so glad to see you again. I've been so excited I barely slept a wink last night." She gives me a big hug.

"So, is this everything?" I ask her, looking down at the stroller and duffle bag.

"Yep, that's everything, our life in a bag. Pathetic, isn't it?"

"Nah. See that piece of scrap metal?" I tell her, pointing at my busted wagon. She nods her head. "That was home sweet home," I tell her, and she laughs. "But seriously, as for baby stuff, don't even worry about it. Valarie went on a shopping spree. The room is packed with 'everything baby'. So much so, we may have to sleep outside to fit it all in the room," I tell her.

"What? Really? How long have you known Valarie?" she asks.

"Met her the day before yesterday. She's lovely. I've never met

61

anyone like her before," I tell Zoe, and she smiles just as a green Daihatsu Charade pulls up next to us, honking its horn a few times.

"Thanks, bro," Macey says, punching her brother in the shoulder and climbing out of it before tapping the roof.

"Hi, girls," her brother calls out, and we both wave to the stranger behind the wheel.

"Fuck off, Blake. Stop hitting on my friends; they aren't interested," Macey scolds her brother. She flips him off and he laughs, driving off down the road.

"Sorry about him. He's a sleaze, so try to stay away from him unless you want another baby," Macey chuckles, shaking her head.

"Noted," I tell her, and she quickly hugs us. She seems eager to get started, but her idea of 'work clothes' is short shorts and a cut-off shirt showing her belly button. At least her hair is pulled into a bun.

"Borrowed the boots from my brother," she says, sticking her foot out to show us. "He's a handyman," she explains when she catches both of us looking at the tool belt around her hips.

"So this is it, huh? Damn, this place is a dump," Macey says as we stand in the parking lot, looking up at the building. The bones are good mostly, but she's right; it's definitely a dump.

"So, you girls interested in helping me clean this dump?" Valarie's voice says from behind us, making us jump.

"Holy crap, you scared me! It... ah... has potential," Macey says nervously.

"For a dump?" Valarie asks, her lips tugging up.

"I didn't mean—" Macey starts to say but Valarie waves her off.

"It's a dump. I may be getting older, girlie, but I ain't blind yet; pretty sure if one of you jumped in that pool over there, you wouldn't come out again—water is probably nuclear. That might actually be that foul smell," she says thoughtfully before shrugging.

"So, you all up for the job? I'll pay on time, and anything this place needs, you let me know and I'll order it in. But there is a catch," she adds. They both nod.

"What's the catch?" Zoe asks.

"We are completely on our own. I have not had one electrician or handyman, not even a plumber out here in over ten years. My mate ruined that shit for me, so if you girls have got any friends who are good with that crap, let me know. If not, we will figure it out ourselves," Valarie tells them.

It's going to be hard trying to source help—an electrician being the main thing because I don't fancy being electrocuted.

"Handyman: my brother—that's where I got the tool belt and tools. Electrician: no idea," Macey shrugs.

"I may be able to help with that," Zoe says, and we all turn to her. She looks sheepish, almost apologetic. "My daughter's father is an electrician. He's a real asshole now that he found his mate and doesn't want her to find out he already has a kid. So I'll threaten to tell her; he either helps when I ask or finds someone that will. Chances are he'll probably find someone else, but I know he'll do it," Zoe says, confidence returning to her face.

"I like you already; you tell him, darlin'," Valarie says.

"So that leaves plumbing which we'll figure out, I guess," I tell everyone, and they all nod.

"So, what do you want to do first?" Macey asks.

"First, we fix the girls' room so it's livable, then we'll start the others, one at a time, and list everything as we go," Valarie says, and we all agree, heading up to the room while Valerie takes the kids to her studio so we can focus on the job at hand.

Everything we're keeping gets piled in the bathroom before tossing all the old furniture over the balcony into the dumpster Valarie had arranged for the renovations. Once that's all out of the way, the cleaning supplies come out. Armed and ready, we start ripping up the carpet.

"Hey, Val," Macey calls over the balcony. Valarie must have answered because she starts talking again. "Have all these rooms got floorboards under the carpet? I was expecting concrete."

"Yeah, why?"

I look down at the exposed floorboards, all in perfect condition—they just need a good clean and polish.

"Because I don't think we should re-carpet. The floorboards are in good condition in this room. If the rest are even half the same, you'll save a fortune by sanding them back and staining them, and if they're like this room, they'll only need a polish" Macey tells her.

"Righty-o, we'll check the others later and see what rooms can be salvaged," Valarie calls back.

We finish stripping the smelly carpet out and toss it in the dumpster. Together, we carry the beds and mattresses up when the truck arrives, and the rest of the day is spent scrubbing the room from floor to ceiling. Valarie brings us drinks and sandwiches at lunchtime—she's so diligent about keeping us fed throughout the day that by the end of it, we are all stuffed and collapse on the couch in her studio.

"So, how many rooms are there?" Macey asks.

I realize I don't know either. I haven't even walked around the building yet, and Valarie said there are units out the back as well as a functions room. I feel nervous; it took us an entire day to clean and fix just one double room!

"Um, good question," she thinks to herself like she can't remember. "Twenty-three rooms, eight units that have four bedrooms in each, as well as the restaurant and function hall. There's a rear garden too. Honestly haven't been out the back in at least three or four years, so Goddess knows what you will find back there; it's a jungle. Then the pool area, laundry room, game room, play center downstairs, and a bar."

"Agh, this is going to kill us," Macey says, pulling some underlay from the carpet out of her hair. She looks at her phone and sighs.

"My brother is here to pick me up; I'll see you both tomorrow. I think early start? That sun was a killer today."

"7 a.m. too early?" Valarie asks, and Macey shakes her head.

"Nope, perfect, see you all tomorrow," Macey says, walking out and giving us a wave.

"Bye," I call after her.

Despite our victory for the day, I can't help feeling overwhelmed. This is an impossible job—so much needs doing—but I just have to remind myself one room at a time. Otherwise, it will be completely overwhelming. No wonder Valarie couldn't do it on her own. It's too much for twenty people, and there are only four of us and two babies. I sigh.

Valarie suddenly reaches for the TV remote on the coffee table, turning the volume up. She always has the nightly news on, but I instantly realize what caught her attention: Alpha Valen is once again on the news.

A video plays out, and my heart lurches into my throat when I recognize the person he appears to be arguing with. It's my father! Both of them are screaming at each other in some club, and my father swings at him. His punch barely misses when Alpha Valen steps out of the way, laughing at him. Suddenly, my father shifts and the recording cuts off; the news anchor says they can't continue playing the video as some viewers may find it distressing. The news then goes on about the old rivalry between my father and the Blood Alpha.

Valarie looks over at me nervously.

"When are they going to get over themselves? Every week one of them is on the news, and quite frankly, I couldn't care less who the Blood Alpha is dating or who shit on whose turf," Zoe says, shaking her head.

"That is not the mental image I wanted in my head," I chuckle.

"Been going for years; maybe one day, they'll both grow up before they lose everything for good," Valarie states, and I nod sadly. Zoe—entirely oblivious to my connection with both Alphas—sighs.

"No wonder the city is doomed with those morons running the place."

"Couldn't have said it better myself," Valarie says, nodding in approval.

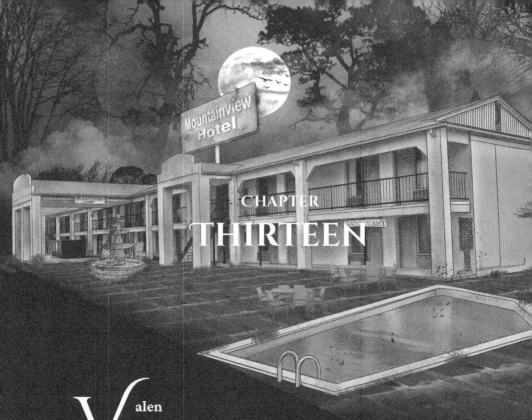

CHAPTER
THIRTEEN

Valen
2 months later

Her hands are clawing at my clothes as we stumble into my room, fingers fiddling with my buttons, lips licking and sucking my neck like a leech. Why does every woman's touch repulse me? I watch as she peels her dress off over her head before I give her a shove, making the backs of her knees hit the bed. She tumbles backward, and I have to fight the urge to laugh as her arms flail about. Yeah, that was sexy—not!

Stripping my pants off, I climb on the bed and tear her panties off. She squeals at the sting of the lace, but I couldn't care less. I need to burn my anger off; Alpha John once again put me in a bad mood tonight. But even as I shove her legs apart and climb between them, I'm already regretting bringing this bimbo home. I want as little of her touching me as possible, yet her hands paw over me. She's mauling every inch of me, wrapping her body around me like a damn octopus and trying to suck on my face like a leech. *Ugh, let's just get this over with.*

I stare down at my dick, cursing it under my breath and willing the bastard to work. This is becoming embarrassing. I was going to be known as the limp dick Alpha. Why the fuck am I having this problem? I have never in all my years ever suffered from erectile dysfunction. Did I break it? What the fuck is going on with me lately? The first time, I thought maybe I was too drunk, but two months have gone by since and I still can't get it up.

"Baby, what's wrong?" the blonde piece I picked up from the club whines at me. I feel like telling her it's her clinging on to me and touching me with her grubby paws that's wrong. Damn whores are always all over me, yet I've had no interest in women lately. They do nothing for me anymore. Fuck, please don't tell me I'm going to be mated to a man. It's got to be too late to suddenly switch sides. I mentally curse my broken cock, but her whining is beginning to aggravate me.

"Will you just shut up? Better yet, get the fuck out!" I snap. I don't know whether I'm annoyed at my broken dick or her whining, nasally voice. I should have known better than to hook up with an Omega—so clingy—but she has nice tits. Too bad, her personality is about as interesting as watching paint dry.

"Did you not hear me? Get the fuck out," I snarl at her. She jumps from my bed, snatching up her clothes and darting out, eyes wide and tear-filled. Fuck her! When my bathroom door opens, I flop back down on my bed and my Beta, Marcus, walks in.

"Man, you need to get laid. You have been nothing but a prick since that redhead was here."

"What redhead?" I ask, tossing the blanket over to cover myself.

"You know, the night you booted that rogue girl out of here," he says, and I try to think back to that night. That was actually the last time I successfully had sex. Every other attempt has been a failure. I prop myself up on my elbow.

"I think that bitch gave me a disease," I tell him.

"Huh? The rogue girl?"

"No, the redhead; that bitch broke my dick," I snap, annoyed. Marcus laughs, shaking his head.

"Well, go get tested or something because if you don't get laid soon, I am seriously thinking of quitting being your Beta," Marcus says, and I scrunch my face up at the idea. No way am I getting anything shoved up my dickhole. Marcus turns, about to leave, when I notice how he's dressed—all done up like he's about to go on a date. I give him the once over. He's an alright-looking man, I suppose. He gets about as much pussy as I do. Relief floods me when my dick stays dead; phew, definitely not gay. It just means that bitch gave me something.

"Where are you going?"

"I have a date because my dick still works so I plan on using it," he announces to me. I growl at him, waving him off. Marcus chuckles and leaves. I watch as he walks out of my room before getting up.

I jump in the shower trying to wash my annoyance away. My thoughts drift off to the Alpha meeting a year ago. It was a costume party; she was dressed in a fairy outfit and covered in glitter. Her mask covered most of her face, but she had blue-gray eyes and plump, pouty lips. I felt drawn to her the moment she walked onto the dance floor, the way her hips moved, and she danced like she didn't have a care in the world.

I was like a moth to a flame, and we were both obliterated. I wish I knew the woman's name or which pack she's from to track her down. I have not been able to forget her for some reason. She always randomly pops up in my head; the way she looked riding my cock and the way her perfect tits bounced above me. I wish she had taken off the mask to picture her better, yet I awoke to find her gone. She disappeared, and I have nothing to go on.

Peeved is an understatement. Usually, I'm the one who does the morning dash before they wake up, but that woman was long gone by the time I woke up, leaving just a faint lingering scent.

I'd awoken to Marcus sitting at the small table drinking coffee and smirking at me.

"Cinderella slipped away this morning, looking rather guilty. It looks like someone finally pulled one over on the big bad Alpha."

Marcus had mocked me and then laughed, thinking it was hilarious. The one woman I actually wanted to know escaped me.

Just the thought of her has my dick stirring to life instantly. I groan, looking down at my hard-on.

"Now you decide to work," I growl, annoyed.

Getting out, I wrap a towel around myself before muttering and heading back to my bedroom. A growl escapes me when I see the Omega sprawled out on my bed. Fucking Marcus! He must have sent her back up here. Looking down, it's still hard. I shrug. I'll just think of my mystery fairy.

"What's your name?" I ask her, and she looks at me like I just proposed to her. Fucking Omegas. I asked for her name, not her hand in marriage.

"Tatum," she tells me while shuffling to the end of my bed too eagerly.

"Well, Tatum, you have two seconds to either start sucking my dick or get the fuck out," I tell her.

She drops to her knees in front of me instantly. Her hands reach for my cock and grip it firmly before wrapping her lips around the tip. I grab her hair before thrusting my dick into her warm, wet mouth. I close my eyes, refusing to look down, knowing the moment I do, it will be over and I'll go limp again. Instead, I thrust into her mouth, thinking of my mystery fairy.

CHAPTER
FOURTEEN

Everly

It always comes out of nowhere. One minute, I'm sleeping—the next, I'm awoken by agonizing pain. I feel my heart pumping in my chest erratically and my stomach cramping terribly. I clutch at it and bite down on my lip to stop from screaming. I don't want to wake Zoe; I know I keep her up at night, and she always hovers worriedly. Usually, it isn't too bad, but tonight it's the worst it's been in two months.

I know he's sleeping with someone. I can tell by the pain ratio. Usually, it's just like an upset tummy, but tonight I feel like my heart is being pulverized, and my stomach twisted in knots. I cry out in pain. I can't help it. I toss and turn until the lights flick on. Zoe isn't going to keep believing it's just period pain. Not after tonight.

"Everly! Everly!" she shrieks, shaking me, but all I can do is cry out and grit my teeth while clutching my stomach. The pain is crippling.

"Should I call an ambulance? I don't know what to do. I'll get Valarie."

"No! I'm fine," I gasp before sweat starts beading on my forehead.

ALPHA'S REGRET

I feel a draft hit me and cold air sweeps into the room. *Please don't last long; please stop.* I beg the Moon Goddess to make it go away.

How am I expected to handle this for the rest of my life? Will it always be this bad? I start sobbing, big fat tears rolling down my cheeks. I hate that Zoe will have to see me this way, hate that he makes me feel this, hate him for what he's made me endure nearly every night on some level—but this is worse because I know he is actually having sex this time, not just fooling around. He's with another woman, and that woman isn't me. Why do I have to be punished for his actions?

Warm hands rub up and down my arms before Valarie's scent wafts to me. The pain grows worse with each second that goes past, making me scream. How did Valarie survive this shit for decades?

"I know sweetie. Just breathe, Everly," Valarie tells me, and I try to focus on her voice to distract myself from the intense pain.

"I think we should call an ambulance. Her pain is worse this time. What if something is seriously wrong with her?" Zoe asks Valarie.

"She'll be fine; it'll be over soon."

"What will be over soon?" Zoe stutters, and I can hear the concern in her voice as I writhe in pain.

"The mate bond; he's with someone and it's causing her pain," Valarie explains to her. I would usually be mad if anyone else spilled my secrets without asking, but I can't be mad at Valarie after everything she's done to help us.

"She met her mate?" Zoe says, her voice soft as a murmur.

"Who do you think Valarian's father is? He's her mate."

"But why is she a rogue whore then? Why would he do that?" Zoe says, and I see her cringe over the word we all hate so much. I blink back tears, nausea bubbling in my stomach.

"She didn't know when she fell pregnant, and I'm afraid her parents would hate her more if they knew who the father is," Valarie explains.

Valarie and I have no secrets; she knows everything now. I trust

71

her more than anyone. She's become like a mother to me. She supported us through everything, and she never turned me away in the two months I've been here. I'm closer to her than I ever was with my own mother.

"Breathe, Everly, deep breaths, and try to sit up for me," Valarie says. I groan, and she helps me up. She hands me my bottle of water off the nightstand, cracking the lid for me before thrusting pills in my hands.

"They'll take the edge off," she tells me, and I rock back and forth. My hands are shaking and I spill water all over me. Zoe grabs the bottle from my hands, and I shove the pills in my mouth, not even questioning what they are. I trust Valarie with my life. Zoe brings the bottle to my lips and I sip it, swallowing the pills down. Tears brim in her eyes as she looks at me sadly.

"Go find a hot water bottle; there should be one under my kitchen sink," Valarie tells Zoe, and she darts out of the room.

"I can't do this. I can't keep living like this," I cry to Valarie.

"I wish I could take it from you, sweetie, I do. I know how hard it is, but you'll get through this, you've gotten through so much by yourself already. Just remember who you are, you're better than him, better than what he makes you feel," Valarie says softly.

"I wouldn't be where I am without you," I tell her.

"The Moon Goddess brought us together for a reason. She won't let history repeat itself; you'll find happiness, Everly. She won't turn her back on you too," Valarie says. I find her words strange but can't make sense of much as another wave of crippling pain washes over me.

Zoe returns with a hot water bottle and places it on my stomach. The pain eases off again and I pray it stays away. *Please be finished, please be done,* I pray, sucking in a deep breath.

The following day, I wake up later than usual; Zoe and Valarie let me sleep in after last night. Sitting up, I spot Zoe sitting on the floor on the rug with Valarian and Casey, her daughter. She has one in the crook of each arm while she feeds them bottles one-handed.

"Tandem feeding," I chuckle, and she nods, looking up at me before smiling sadly.

"Why didn't you tell me? It makes so much sense now," she says.

"I didn't want to talk about it; I don't like talking about his father. He didn't recognize me and tossed me away," I tell her, feeling pain at the very memory. I tried going back to tell him a couple of weeks ago—Valarie told me to try to speak with him again—but I couldn't bring myself to do it. I just kept remembering the look on his face.

The way he'd screamed at me, combined with Valarie's story, scared me even more. What if he tried to take Valarian from me like her mate did to her? I have no title anymore, and my wolf is pathetically weak and so small compared to what I should be. I'm a rogue; hardly Luna material now.

Valarie said the longer she went without her mate, the harder it became to shift until she no longer could. Being rogue also doesn't help, it makes us weaker prey and easy pickings to rob and attack.

I don't know how she's endured this torture for years. One day, I finally saw the man she called her mate. I never caught a glimpse of his face, but last week I saw his BMW pull up and watched him sneak into the office with his own key. Then the next morning, I watched him leave again. I hated what he did to her; I saw her heart break as he left again, and for three days afterward, she could barely get out of bed. She was depressed, and the only thing that worked was me asking her to help with Valarian.

I refuse to become some side piece; I would rather die than live the torment Valarie does. I love her, but I now understand why she couldn't maintain this place. His sporadic popping in and out of her life affected her more profoundly than she was willing to admit. Each time though, I noticed she grew weaker. Each time he left, her mind became fragile for days afterward. She even suffered nose bleeds and tremors. It was almost like watching someone suffer from withdrawals.

"I'll make some coffee. Do you want some?" I ask Zoe. She nods her head and I turn to our small kitchenette. Our little suite is now completely functional—floors are re-stained and polished, the room repainted, curtains removed and blinds put in their place and thanks to Macey's brother, the rickety old pipes have been fixed. In the last two months, we've stripped and fixed all the rooms on the top floor. We're far from done, but each passing day shows progress, and the smile on Valarie's face is worth every ache, sprain, and splinter.

"Valarie said we could take the day off today if you don't feel up to it," Zoe tells me.

"No, I need to work to keep my mind off him," I tell her. She nods her head. I hate seeing the sadness in her eyes when she looks at me. I know she's worried, but it makes me feel even more weak and vulnerable than I already do.

"You have us; we have our village," Zoe says, channeling Valerie. Valarie had told Zoe the same thing she'd told me: we're building our village. The more work we get done, the more I believe she was right. We are building something—a place to call home; a purpose. We just have to remember not to give up. But with the girls and Valarie, I know I've found friends for life.

I've created my own family.

Regardless, I miss my sister terribly, but not once has she called, and Mom changed her number. I am the forgotten child, one who no longer exists in their world, no longer has a place in their lives. I cried for a good hour when that realization hit. Valarie found me on the stairs after I tried for the hundredth time to contact my mother or sister; I just wanted to hear their voices, to know I wasn't forgotten.

"Their loss if they can't see how amazing you are," Valarie says. She sits beside me on the steps, holding my hands.

"You don't need them; they aren't wasting tears on you, so don't waste your tears on them; they don't deserve them," she tells me.

Hearing a knock on the door, I get up and open it. Macey walks in before reaching down and taking Valarian from Zoe. When she straightens, she looks at me, smiling sadly, and I realize Zoe told her. Yet, I feel no anger at my secret being out—I should have told them already.

"So, will you tell us now? I know Valarie knows, but she won't spill, no matter how many times we ask. We won't judge, I swear," Macey says, and I know they won't; it's me who isn't comfortable, me judging myself.

But they're right; I can trust them; they deserve to know. It kind of feels like a relief—freeing—and makes the words leaving my lips easier.

The girls have so many questions, all accumulated over the last two months. I kept my secrets close to my heart. Their biggest was what pack I came from. I knew all their secrets, but I was ashamed of mine for some reason. They had noticed my Alpha aura dwindling; by this time it's almost non-existent. Now they have another secret added to the list. I had refused to tell them the father of my child is my mate. I was ashamed. I thought they would think less of me because my mate didn't want me.

"I am the oldest daughter of Alpha John of the Shadow Pack," I tell them, and they both gasp.

"You're Alpha John's disgraced daughter?" Macey gasps.

"Wait, I thought he only had one daughter. She was due to be the next Alpha?" Zoe says.

"Nope, he's my father, and when he found out I was pregnant, he told me to abort it to cover it up. I said no, obviously, so he shunned me and banished me, stripping me of my title. I was supposed to take over the pack when I turned eighteen."

"Well damn, I feel like I should bare my neck in submission. I knew you had Alpha genes, but I didn't think you were from the second-biggest pack. I thought you transferred into the rogue population from another city," Macey admits. I chuckle at her as she bounces on the edge of the bed, burping Valarian.

"Glad I was sitting down for that news," she mutters, nudging Zoe with her knee.

"Well, remain seated because if you find that scandalous, you are about to have a heart attack at what I tell you next," I tell them.

"Scandalous? You come from one of the most influential families in the city. How would we not be shocked by that, and what could be more shocking?" Zoe says, shaking her head.

I suck in a deep breath. "Valarian's father is Alpha Valen from Nightshade Pack. He is also my mate," I tell them. Their jaws nearly hit the floor. Macey's head turns slowly, her mouth wide open as she stares at Valarian before holding him up in the air.

"You mean to say that I am holding the spawn of Satan himself? That this cute little boy comes from the nutsack of the most vicious Alpha in the city and the notorious playboy of the town?" Macey says, holding Valarian like she expects him to turn into his father and rip her to pieces.

"Yep, and that's it. No other secrets—you know the rest."

"That does explain the eyes. Doesn't his family have some genetic thing with eyes? I think I read that somewhere," Macey says.

"You're worried about his eyes?" Zoe says, looking at Macey before turning back to me.

"Your mate—and the father of your child—is your father's biggest rival. Damn girl, you really don't do things half-assed; you go all in on messing shit up, don't ya?" Zoe laughs. I chuckle as she looks me up and down.

"Yep, the Moon Goddess definitely fucked me over, that's for sure; bad enough he's my mate, but he also had to be my father's biggest enemy."

"Count yourself lucky your father banished you. Could you imagine if the Blood Alpha knew you were Alpha John's daughter and had his son? It would start a war, the city would become a bloodbath, and your father probably would have killed you," Macey says, and I have to agree; maybe things really are working out for the best.

I **0 months later**

Weeks turn into months, and now the hotel is nearly unrecognizable. It was just four rogue women with three babies in tow doing what, I thought, was impossible when we started. At times, it seemed there was no end in sight and all of us wanted to give up. Fix one thing, find another issue; yet we managed it.

Now, here we are, four days before the health and safety inspector comes out to check our progress again. The first time he came out, he gave us a list of issues and snorted in laughter when we told him it was only us fixing it up. He shook his head and said it was impossible and that the place should just be bulldozed.

Nearly a year has passed since then. In that time, we've fixed all the hotel rooms into immaculate suites that match or even surpass the other hotels in the city. Macey and I went 'hotel shopping', as we called it, and sussed out the other nearby accommodations. At each of them, we booked a room for a night to test the services and check out the rooms and decor to develop our own ideas. The function room was one thing most of the other hotels didn't even have, whereas ours is big enough to hold weddings and formal functions.

We've done it up as a winter wonderland inside, elegant yet also sophisticated if needed, depending on the function. Every time I walk into the function room, I marvel at it. It looks like something out of a fairy tale wedding. Twinkling fairy lights hang from the ceiling, coming together in the center of a crystal chandelier—one of the most expensive things Valarie paid for, but the glittering centerpiece of the room.

Besides all the hotel rooms being transformed, the pool area is restored and the property's gardens have been trimmed and well maintained. In the rear gardens, we found four water fountains that still worked, and after a good tidy up, it has a tropical oasis feel.

The restaurant in the main building is fully functional—all appliances have been removed and replaced with better stainless steel and energy-efficient ones. Solar panels have been placed on every building to save money on energy costs when it opens. We also have a children's play area that's fully enclosed and will eventually offer childcare services for employees and guests.

On top of all the renovations, three nights a week, I go to the community college on the street behind us. Valarie paid for my business courses, so on Mondays, Wednesdays, and Fridays, I attend classes.

I only have one month left and I will have finished my studies in accounting, business management, and administration. I just hope I live up to Valarie's expectations. Since meeting Valarie and her taking us in, I'm hopeful for the future and excited for what it will bring.

Our most challenging tasks now are passing the health and safety inspection and finding people to help run the place. We've done all this by ourselves, with a little help from Zoe's child's father and Macey's brother, but we still need more workers to run this place. Four women can't be everywhere and doing everything at once.

All that's left of the big stuff is the front gardens and painting the exterior, which is nearly done, but we've just run out of paint.

Macey's brother is currently trimming the front hedges, and Macey is mowing the lawn with the ride-on mower she borrowed from her neighbor.

"You ready, Everly? I want to get back quickly. Hopefully, we'll have enough daylight to finish that last side," Zoe calls out to me. We're feeling particularly dedicated today.

"Yeah, I'm ready when you are," I call back to her while climbing in Valarie's truck. Zoe climbs in the passenger side and I start the old beast up. Valarie waves from the top balcony with Valarian and Casey in her arms, both smiling and babbling happily as we turn onto the road heading for the hardware store.

"I'm beginning to worry about Valarie," Zoe says, and I hum in agreement. "She's been so ill lately."

"Yeah, me too. I tried to convince her to go see the doctor last week, but she refused, as always," I tell her. Zoe shakes her head and sighs. Last week I walked in on Valarie during one of her coughing fits, only this time it was much different; as she wiped her mouth, her tissue was covered in blood. When I confronted her about it and urged her to seek medical help, she said it had been happening for over a year now and not to worry.

I still worried, and it was all made worse each time her mate stopped in to see her. I've been here nearly a year, but he's like a ghost. I see his car come and go, but I have yet to see the man's face even after this much time. Zoe and I call him 'the faceless Alpha'. That's the only thing we've figured out about him, and that's only by the apparent Alpha vibes he gives off.

"Do you worry that he's slowly killing her? That all this time coming and going is tearing her apart inside?" Zoe asks. I say nothing because I know her mate is the reason she's so sick; I've already noticed it in myself. Going decades without your mate must be pure agony because I feel it with Valen already, and it's been months, not years.

I feel every time he's with a woman, and each time it kills me a little more. Every time I shift, my wolf form is weaker and a little smaller. The longer I remain rogue and without my mate, the worse my wolf side deteriorates. My health has also deteriorated; I'm always sick with the flu or stomach issues, and no matter how much I eat, I can never put on weight. My hair falls out in clumps sometimes, especially when he's been busy fooling around with women. Other times I feel drunk, making me question if he's an alcoholic. So, I can only imagine how badly Valarie suffers after decades of this torture.

The more time goes on, the more I feel him, and it's horrible. It's like the mate bond is pulling me toward him and resisting its taking its toll on me. He has no idea; those times I tried to reach out to him, fear of him taking Valarian stopped me each time. Valarian is mine; I'm raising him, I'm looking after him, and I'll be damned if I let his father take him from me as Valarie's mate did to her.

Pulling into the parking lot of the hardware store, Zoe and I hop out of the car, paint code and cash in hand.

"We need a new paint tray too; I cracked the other one accidentally," Zoe says as we step into the store.

"You grab the paint; I'll grab the tray," I tell her, and we split off down different aisles. Walking down the painting section, I look for the correct paint tray. It needs to be big enough for the roller brushes. Once I find it, I grab a spare just in case. Heading back to the front of the store, I see Zoe waiting in line; she smiles at me, and I step over next to her.

"Four gallons should be enough?" she asks.

"Yes, plenty—and we should have some left over; not much left to do now," I tell her, turning to the front.

My heart skips a beat when a scent wafts to me. I would recognize that scent anywhere. Heart thumping erratically, I swallow as I stare at the man's frame in front of me. He is as tall and intimidating as ever. Emotion chokes me as I observe him. Zoe continues talking away, completely oblivious to me trying to keep myself together.

I watch as he steps up to the counter to be served. He talks casually to the man behind the counter as he pays for his things before turning around and noticing me. He stops dead, looking me up and down.

I gulp, looking up to meet the eyes of my father. We kind of stand there for a second and I wait for him to say something. My mouth is suddenly so dry I can't say a word.

I haven't seen him since the night I found out the blood Alpha is my mate—since the night my own father made me sit out in the rain before kicking me off his territory and telling me to never come back. Despite all that, I miss him, but the look of indifference on his face is enough to say he doesn't miss me.

He snarls, his top lip lifting over his teeth as he looks me over before looking at Zoe, who has finally noticed Alpha John, the second most intimidating man in the city—my father. I open my mouth to try to say something, to ask how mom is, but before I can say anything, he turns and walks out the door.

Not one word. Nothing. The look of disgust on his face is the same as when he found out I was pregnant. I thought it wouldn't hurt me as badly as it did back then. But it does. I blink back tears and gather myself as I step up to the counter with Zoe. She doesn't bother saying anything. What could she say? It would change nothing.

It's one thing when any of us go out and get the inevitable stares for being 'rogue-whores' from everyone else. But my own father— my own flesh and blood—it hurts exponentially more. I just want him to care, maybe ask how his grandson is or how his daughter is. Instead, I get nothing but a look of disgust, like I'm a piece of gum that got stuck to his shoe, and that stings. I'm nobody to him.

Getting into the driver's seat, I look out the windshield and see his car. Refusing to let it get to me, I drive off, not even glancing back. The car is silent on the trip back. Zoe reaches over and squeezes my knee gently, letting me know I am not alone.

Pulling up at the hotel, I finally exhale. I am home. This is home and it's all I need.

All I need is Valarian and our small village family. A family we made, not blood. My father proved there is more to family than just blood. Family is those that are there for you when the rest of the world turns their backs on you. That is family. Unclipping my seatbelt, we got back to work. Suddenly, I feel even more determined to prove I can do this without his help.

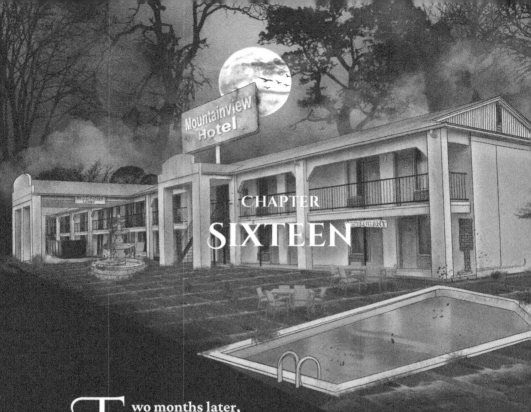

Two months later,

Today is the day, the last inspection to decide whether all our hard work has paid off. Macey, Zoe, and I watch from the balcony as Valarie talks to the health and safety inspector. He had walked around the entire building with his measuring tape and flashlight, clipboard tucked under his arm, and pen behind his ear as he went over every nook and cranny in the place.

We secretly call him 'the birdman'; his nose looks more like a beak and his beady little eyes are too far apart. Macey snorts when a gust of wind has him clutching his toupee. It's chocolate brown and not even close to matching the graying areas on the sides of his head. Down on the front lawn, Valarie watches over his shoulder as he makes notes on his clipboard, giving the place one last scrutinizing look before shaking his head in disbelief.

Finally, he tears off the piece of paper and hands it to Valarie. He walks over to his red sedan and takes off while Valarie stares at the form.

"Come on, we should go see what birdman says needs to be done this time," says Macey. Zoe and I go to retrieve our kids—who are playing happily in their playpen with their blocks—from our room. Scooping up Valarian, I set his feet on the ground and hold his little hands while we carefully walk down the steps to the first floor. He started walking earlier than expected. Last month, he just stood up and took his first steps. He's smart for his age, which is impressive given all the trauma he's been through.

Valarie is still standing in the yard, staring up at the hotel. I can't quite decipher the look on her face, and we approach cautiously.

"He said four rogue women would never accomplish anything on our own without help, ladies," Valarie says, and I sigh, wondering what he's told her needs fixing.

We stop beside her and look back at the huge building; no more peeling paint—the exterior is a beautiful white with blue and light gray trims, the roof painted a deep gray—the hedges are cut to perfection, and flowers hang from the top of the huge porch and along the hand railings. It looks like a brand-new place.

I lost track of the number of times doubts rained down on us, but now, standing out the front looking upon the building a year later, I realize all the blood, sweat, tears, frustration and anger when people refused to help, were all worth it. Four rogue women with no future, no help, and just pure determination gave this run-down hotel a new life.

Every callous, every blister, every cut and graze was all worth it, along with every sleepless night. It all paid off and seeing the look on Valarie's face is priceless. She is a tough woman, with an even tougher exterior, yet not even she can hide her emotion as we stare at what we accomplished.

"So, what's the verdict?" I ask, looking our hard work up and down.

"The verdict, ladies, is we are now open for business," Valarie says casually.

"Well, we will get it done. We can-" Macey starts to say before stopping. I look at Valarie, her lips tugging up at the corners, and

Macey looks around me at her. It takes a few seconds for her words to register.

"Wait, you said..." Macey asks before stopping.

"I said we are open for business; we did it, girls," Valarie says, and we all erupt in squeals of joy, jumping up and down excitedly. Macey howls loudly, and we join her.

It must be a sight from the road to see four women standing near the street howling at the sun and cheering, but we don't care. We did it. We did the impossible. But most of all, we proved to ourselves that we could do anything with a bit of determination, probably stubbornness, and hard work.

We have proven to everyone who said it was impossible that they were wrong and that we are more than just four 'rogue whores' with an unrealistic idea. That unrealistic idea is now very real and standing in front of us, showing us we are capable of so much more than anyone believed of us.

Laughing and walking back to celebrate with the kids, we talk about advertising and hiring. I had an idea about hiring and ran it past Valarie last month.

Four rogue single mothers made this place what it is, so sticking to that, we decided that everyone we hire will be rogue women. A hotel owned and run by rogues, the city's less desirable. Valarie loved the idea, so Macey, Zoe, and I went to every community center and put out word last month that Valarie was hiring.

The next day, the lineup went halfway down the street. It was hard work interviewing everyone, but once we opened, we had fifty staff on rotational shifts. All we have left to find is a head chef. Valarie is an excellent cook and has been teaching me, so for now, that will have to be good enough until we find someone.

We all head into the restaurant and Valarie walks out back to grab a bottle of wine while I gather the glasses. Hearing a cough, I pause, looking out the doors leading to the storerooms.

"Are you okay, Val?" I ask before I hear more coughing.

"Val?" I repeat, walking into the storerooms. I see Valarie

hunched over, having a coughing fit—the worst one I've seen her have—as she gasps for air. The wine glasses slip from my hands, shattering on the tiled floor when I see her collapse.

It's like watching everything in slow motion.

I see her clutch the steel shelf, her hand covered in blood; she turns to look at me, no doubt to tell me not to worry, when she coughs again; blood sprays from her lips and dribbles down her chin as her eyes glaze over; before I know it, she is falling, her skin pasty and covered in a cold sweat. I scream as I see her tumble to the floor and I race toward her, trying to get to her in time, but she crashes to the floor.

"Valarie!" I shriek as I clutch her. Her hand weakly grabs my arm as I pull her head into my lap.

"Call an ambulance!" I scream out. Valarie starts choking, her hand clutching tighter on my arm as I turn her head so she doesn't choke on her own blood while she gasps for breath.

"Hang on, Val, help is coming," I tell her as Zoe races in, grabbing Valarian as he follows Macey and nearly walks over the broken glass. Zoe holds both babies, clutching them as she looks on in horror as Valarie lies gasping for air. Macey is talking frantically on the phone to emergency services while I look down at Valarie in my arms.

"It's okay, you'll be okay," I say as she gasps. Tears stream down my face as I hold her hands—the hands of the woman who has the biggest heart in the world. I admire her strength, a woman bigger than life and who gave me a home. My heart breaks when she squeezes my hands back, trying to comfort me even though she's the one that needs comforting.

"They'll be here in twenty minutes. They're flat out," Macey says, pacing.

Twenty minutes? That's ridiculous! I knew it would be bad because she is rogue—no one cares for rogues, not even the health system—but twenty minutes? Valarie turns her face to look up at me and smiles sadly.

"Where is Valarian?" she gasps, barely audible, and I look over at Zoe.

"He's here," I tell her. Macey grabs him, bringing him over so she can see him, and kneels beside us.

"He looks so much like his father," Valarie tells me. I nod, wiping the tears that are dripping off my chin. Valarian pats her arm, not understanding, and Valarie smiles; I move her hand for her so she can touch his little foot beside her. She closes her eyes, and I see a tear slip down her cheek.

"I am so proud of you girls," Valarie croaks out, and we all nod, all of us crying and blubbering messes as we watch one of the most inspirational women we know suffer.

"Don't speak like that; you will be fine. Help is on the way," I tell her. Valarie coughs as more blood spills from her lips, which now have a sick tinge of blue. Zoe hands me some paper towels and I wipe her mouth with shaky hands.

"Not this time, Evie," she replies. My lips quiver, and my heart breaks at her words because deep down, I know it. I just don't want her to go. I should have pushed harder for her to see the doctor. I bite down on my lip to try to stop it from trembling.

"Listen to me, Evie, I need you to promise," she says, and I shake my head.

"I will listen when you're better. Then you can tell me, then I will promise you anything," I tell her.

"Look after my grandson for me, you promise me that; you promise not to let my son break you like his father did me," she gasps.

"What?" I choke out, trying to hold it together and failing terribly.

"The eyes; he has my son's eyes. You look after him for me. You fight for him, promise you will fight for both," she says before coughing and sputtering. She grabs my hand harder as her body starts heaving violently. My stomach drops. Is she saying what I think she's saying?

"Shh, shh, hold on, Val," I tell her, hugging her and holding her until she suddenly stops, her body expelling what little air was left in her lungs, blood splattering across my shirt and arms.

"I promise," I whisper into her hair, and I kiss her head just as I hear the sirens racing up the street toward us. Zoe races out to get them but I feel Valarie's hand fall limp on my arm, and I know she is gone. Her head rolls in my arms, falling back. Pulling away, I look down at her; her face is slack and the color is gone as she lies limp in my arms.

Paramedics rush in with Zoe, who stops in the doorway, and I look at her and shake my head. The paramedics race to work on her and I get out of their way, taking Valarian from Macey as we watch helplessly while they try to revive her. They work on her for ten minutes. After a while, I hand Valarian back to Macey; she follows Zoe out and to our room to comfort her.

A few minutes later, a man wearing a tailored suit rushes. I know instantly it's her mate. He stops in the doorway and I immediately see the resemblance between him and Valen, his son. That's also when I notice his amber eyes are the same as Valarian's. He stands there, staring down at Valarie as they keep trying to revive her. Eventually, they stop—there is no bringing her back.

He falls to his knees, clutching his dark hair and falling apart. He did this; this is his fault. I know I don't have to tell him because he knows it too. I watch as he breaks, but I feel nothing but numb. Valarie gave me so much and had been my rock for so long. Now she is gone because of the man falling apart in front of me—all because he refused to mark and love her.

Wiping my tears, I look around; the paramedics are on the phone with someone when they bring the stretcher in. I watch as they wheel her out, thinking of what she told me and promising myself I will not let Valen kill me like his father did her. He will not take my son like her mate did to her. I will live for Valarian.

I won't let history repeat itself.

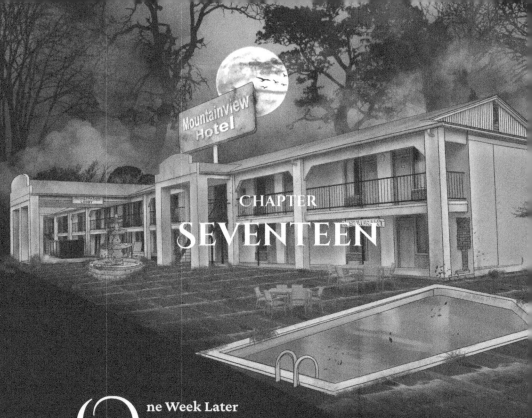

CHAPTER
SEVENTEEN

One Week Later

Alpha Kalen, Valarie's mate, stands across from me as we watch her get lowered into the ground at the rogue cemetery. Zoe and Macey hover beside me; Macey's mother offered to watch our kids at the hotel for us. There aren't many mourners in attendance; just four people and the tow truck driver. Plus her lawyer. I do everything I can to avoid locking eyes with the man responsible for her death.

We all speak, sharing our stories about Valarie—her mate says nothing and remains silent. I wonder what must be going through his head. Does he hate himself as much as I hate him? The fact that he could torture such a wonderful woman, over decades and decades, makes my blood boil. The coroner said she died from organ failure caused by the mate bond; there were no other health issues or explanations.

It pisses me off that he is healthy and alive because he's an Alpha and male, while Valarie is dead because she remained unmarked and female. It feels wrong that women die from neglect of the mate bond. It scares me because my health is already suffering, and if I'm not careful, this could be me. When we got the coroner's report, Macey and Zoe also voiced their concerns, saying I should just mark and mate someone so I don't end the same way. The meeting about her death had been difficult

The coroner was shocked, explaining that he had only seen two cases before because most people keep their mates. He also questioned whether we knew who her mate was to inform them. Kalen, Valarie's mate and Valen's father, said he had no idea as we sat in the office, giving me a pointed look, warning me to not say anything. That meant he saw me when I would catch him coming and going from the hotel, sneaking in like a thief in the night. I couldn't understand why he bothered coming that day if he wasn't even going to acknowledge she was his mate. How did he explain his reason for being there?

I could tell not even the coroner believed whatever bullshit Kalen fed him. I was listed as her next of kin which I was shocked about, but glad to get some answers either way.

Shaking the memory away, I listen to the priest. When the service is finished, Kalen speaks to the lawyer and I watch for a second before turning on my heel and following Macey back to her car.

"Everly? Which one of you girls is Everly?" a deep voice calls out. We all stop, and I look back at the immaculately dressed man. He's an older gentleman, around Kalen's age. Kalen's lips are pressed in a line as he follows after the lawyer, who is practically jogging over to us.

"I am," I tell him. He stops, holding out his hand to me, and I shake it while he catches his breath.

"My name is Joseph. I am Valarie's lawyer. Do you mind if I speak to you for a minute?" he asks, pointing over to a picnic table under the trees by the parking lot.

"Uh, yeah, sure," I tell him, wondering what he wants.

"We'll wait for you at the car, Everly," Macey calls out, and I nod, waving at her. As he sits on the bench seat, Joseph pulls a pair of glasses from the inside pocket of his suit jacket, putting them on before digging through his briefcase. Kalen sits beside him, also curious.

"Why the girl? What does she have to do with anything?" Kalen asks.

"Just wait, please, Alpha Kalen. I will explain. About six months ago, Valarie came to see me, to change her will," Joseph says. My brows pinch together and I look at Kalen, who is glaring at me.

"Ah, here it is, this is her current will. This is for you," he says, handing me an envelope. I notice Valarie's handwriting—the front of the envelope reads *For Everly*. Looking back at Joseph, I nod. Thinking this is all, I begin to get up.

"Thank you," I tell him, about to leave.

"Everly, I am not finished. Valarie was very insistent and went to a lot of trouble to make sure her will could not be contested or changed," Joseph says, looking over at Kalen.

"I'm not understanding," I tell him. Joseph smiles sadly before tugging on his tie and glancing nervously at Alpha Kalen.

"I have known Valarie for thirty years and considered her a good friend, and I am aware of who you are to her, Kalen." Kalen growls, and Joseph puts a finger up, standing up to the man. I sense that Joseph truly cared for Valarie.

"I signed a non-disclosure to not let that information out— Valarie saw to that—but since Everly here is aware of who and what you are to Valarie, I have not broken that, nor do I intend to. But that is why I must warn you, Kalen; Valarie has measures in place that if you fight Everly—if you contest this will I have here—it will be made public information that the Blood Alpha's father let his mate die because of her status."

Contest *what*?

Suddenly it dawns on me. I feel my throat constrict. This asshole was planning on going after Valarie's assets after the way he treated her? I can't believe my ears.

"Status? I fucking loved her," Kalen protests, his eyes narrowing in anger.

"Obviously not enough to look past her being Omega," I snap before I can stop myself. I feel my hands shaking.

"Don't pretend to know me, girl."

"I don't need to know you, nor do I want to, Kalen. Your actions showed me plenty of your character," I tell him, and he growls at me. Ignoring him, I turn my attention back to Joseph.

"What has this got to do with me?" I ask him.

"Well, I need you to sign some documents."

"What sort of documents?" I ask him.

"Valarie left everything to you and your son Valarian. Everything, Everly. The hotel, her bank accounts, her family's money—a considerable amount—everything she owned now belongs to you," Joseph tells me. I swallow, looking up at the tree above me, blinking back tears.

"Valarie was a very wealthy woman, Everly, and everything is now yours," Joseph says, and I sniffle. Kalen growls and punches the table. Joseph jumps when Kalen stands up before storming off toward his car. I stare after him before turning back to face the lawyer.

"Don't worry about him, Everly. This is what Valarie wanted, and I have known Kalen for a long time. He won't risk his reputation to fight this, so what I need from you are some signatures, ID, and bank account details," Joseph says, handing me a pen. I take the pen from him, and he points out where to sign. When I'm done, he gives me the deed to the hotel.

"You just became the new owner of Mountainview Hotel; I look forward to seeing you accomplish great things, Everly. Valarie told me all about you and her grandson," he says, giving me a caring smile.

I open my mouth, glancing around for Kalen, but he's gone already, and Joseph puts a finger to his lips.

"Secret's safe with me, Everly. Valarie was a very depressed woman when I met her; in the last year, I haven't seen her happier. You and Valarian did that," he says, standing up. I shake his hand.

"I will bring some other paperwork over during the week," he says, and I nod, watching him leave before looking down at the deed and the envelope in my hand.

"Thank you," I whisper to her, hoping she can hear me wherever she is. Valarie just ensured Valarian's future, and I could never thank her enough for what she has given us, but I would trade it all in a heartbeat to have her back with us.

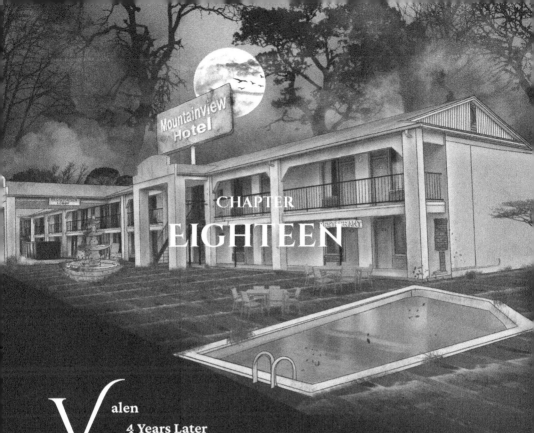

EIGHTEEN

Valen

4 Years Later

I stare blankly at my father as he gives me one of his many lectures. It irritates me to no end that he thinks he can still dictate my life. My secretary comes in, placing a steaming cup of coffee on my desk; my father doesn't even stop talking as he continues droning on, taking another cup of coffee absentmindedly. He sips it before leaning forward and putting it on my desk—the sight instantly irritates me. Two fucking inches away! He knows how much I hate it! I grab his mug and place it on the coaster before sitting back.

"You need to sort your life out, Valen. You are getting too old to be messing around constantly with these whores you play with and getting blind drunk every night. If I had known you would be this irresponsible, I never would have handed the pack over to you."

"My personal life is none of your business; I am a good Alpha."

"You are a fucking drunk!" he bellows at me.

Instantly, I slam the table with my fist. His anger immediately dies down and he continues more calmly.

95

"I am just saying you are twenty-nine years old, just find some bitch and mark her so she can spit out an heir for the pack."

"Not happening; the only person I will be having kids with is my mate," I tell him.

"Twenty-nine years and you still haven't found her. Give up on the idea and just choose a woman. At this rate, you will be my age by the time you have your first child, Valen! This isn't about you. It is about your pack," he says, growling.

I lean back in my chair, grabbing the document off my desk to look at it just as Marcus walks in. Relief floods me at seeing him.

He bows his head to my father. "Alpha Kalen," he says to his former Alpha.

"You're dismissed, Father," I tell him, wanting him gone. He's making my headache worse.

"You can't just dis—"

"I already did," I tell him, cutting him off.

He rises from his chair before grabbing his coffee mug and downing it. He then carefully places it down and storms out. My eyes are on the mug when Marcus moves it back onto the coaster.

"You find out why sales dropped on all our hotels?" I ask him, turning back to the report in my hand.

"I did, and I'm going to check it out myself," Marcus says, making me place the document down.

"Check what out?" I ask him, confused.

"We have competition," Marcus says, dumping some kind of brochure on my desk. I glance at it.

"Mountainview Hotel."

"Since when?" I ask him.

"Look at the star rating."

I glance down and see it has a five-star rating! I read some of the reviews.

"Where is this place? I've never even heard of it."

"That's the thing; it's always been there—under new management apparently. And you won't believe it."

96

"Believe what?" I ask him.

"It's completely run by rogues," he answers, shocking me further.

"I have never noticed this place, and I grew up in the city," I tell him, not believing it's possible. Where did a rogue get enough money to own a hotel?

"It's on the main drag, the first hotel as you drive in from the western borders, backs onto the nature reserve," he says, but I still have no idea what he's talking about.

"Fuck you and your silver spoon; of course you have no idea what I'm talking about. Near the train station. Seeing as you have never used public transportation in your life, you would have missed it."

I press my lips in a line. He's right, though. I usually stick to my own territory and hardly spend any time on the western side of the city; but still, a hotel this size you would think I would notice since it's on the main street.

"Opened three and half years ago. Apparently they are not only cheaper, but they have better services, and I think people are just interested in seeing a hotel run by rogues."

"Great, it's a fucking circus for a tourist attraction. Not that I have anything against rogues, I just have a hard time being fucking outdone by them."

"Well, I will suss it out today."

"Don't bother. I'll go—might book the Alpha meeting there. Alpha John kicked up a stink when he heard we were hosting it and wants it on neutral ground. I have another job for you anyway."

"What's that?" he asks.

"I want you to distract my father," I tell him, and he scrunches up his face.

"Uh, no; last time I had to do that, he gave me a tour of the city I have lived in my entire life," Marcus says. I smirk. "Can't I go with you?" he whines.

"No. I know he's waiting for you to leave so he can give me a lecture on producing an heir, so I need an escape, and this seems perfect," I tell him while holding up the brochure.

"I don't see why I can't come with," he says, getting up. "Oh, and Ashley is downstairs looking for you."

"Ugh, I never should have touched that one; she's like a leech," I groan, and Marcus laughs.

"Yeah, you have to be more careful where you stick your dick," Marcus says.

"Get rid of her for me," I tell him, and he growls.

"Why do I need to get rid of her? I didn't fuck her," he says.

"Fine, just distract my father for me so I can escape," I tell him. He leaves, then mind-links me when the coast is clear, something about asking my father if he's familiar with graphs. My father is always unable to help himself when he wants to show off his knowledge. I know Marcus will give me hell later over it.

Sneaking out, I catch the elevator to the ground floor before walking to the exit, only to see Ashley smile when she spots me. She flicks her blonde hair over her shoulder, pulling down her dress that had ridden up. Don't know why she bothered—I would still see the bottoms of her asscheeks if she turned around.

"Valen, honey!"

"Busy, and don't call me that," I tell her, walking past her. She grabs my hand, and I shake her off, walking out for the valet to notice me. He rushes off to get my car while I stay trapped, standing next to Ashley.

"Want to go out later?" she says, pawing at my shirt. I shove her hands off and she pouts.

"What part of 'I am busy' don't you understand?" I ask her. She says nothing for a few moments, though her face reddens.

"You know, you don't have to be such a prick, Valen."

"*Alpha* Valen, we are not familiar. Just because I stuck my dick in you, don't think it means anything more than that—now get off me," I tell her, putting distance between us.

She starts crying. I roll my eyes; this can't be happening. Seeing people staring, I tell her to shut up, making her cry more. The valet brings my car over and I growl, stomping over and opening the passenger side.

"Get in—I'll drive you home when I'm done," I tell her through clenched teeth, knowing she caught a cab to get here.

She wouldn't shut up the entire time I was driving. Following the GPS, I look for this stupid hotel.

"What are you looking for?" Ashley whines.

I ignore her and then spot it. How have I never noticed it before? The place is huge—and it looks every part a five-star hotel.

This can't be owned by a rogue. The lawns and hedges are well maintained; the exterior has a very coastal, tropical feel—giant palm trees and hanging plants, well-trained vines along the guard rails; a colossal water fountain sits in the center of the parking lot. Getting out, I look at Ashley quickly.

"Stay here, I'll be back in a minute," I tell her. Ashley nods to me and pulls out her phone. I slam my door a little too hard.

Walking around, I inspect the place. The restaurant is packed, every seat is taken, waiters are bustling around inside serving guests. The food smells divine, and I growl in annoyance before opening the restaurant door. I can hear people in the kitchen singing happy birthday when a woman—a beautiful woman—comes out carrying a cake. The staff sings behind her as they follow, and those eating at the tables all stop to sing along as she places it on a table in the corner.

Her scent instantly hits my nostrils and my entire body locks up in shock. All I can do is stare at the woman with her arms wrapped around the birthday girl in the corner—who looks a bit younger than the woman—as they sing to her.

Mate.

My skin starts buzzing, my heart beats faster, and I am consumed by the overwhelming urge to claim her. Suddenly, it feels like there's no one else in the room but us.

My entire body calls me toward the petite woman. Her uniform indicates she's some kind of manager here, and her hair is pulled in a bun on her head, showing off her neck—right where I want to sink my teeth.

Everyone cheers as the younger girl blows out the candles.

"Oh, we need napkins," I hear my mate's melodious voice call out. I feel stuck, entranced by her. My mouth waters as I watch her walk away and back into the kitchen. She's a little skinny—I'll fix that. She also looks tired, but she's the most beautiful thing I have ever seen.

I walk slowly towards another slightly older woman in the corner, who is cutting the cake. Trying not to draw attention to myself, I tap her on the shoulder. She glances at me briefly without meeting my eyes before looking back down in subservience.

"Can I help you, Alpha?" she asks, obviously picking up my aura.

"Yes, that woman that walked into the back to get napkins..."

"Everly, Sir. How can I help you?" she says, straightening up to look at me properly.

Her eyes dart to mine, and she immediately steps back, bumping into the table and the younger girl, who then looks at me. Her eyes go wide, and she clutches the woman's arm. The fear on both their faces is evident. I knew I was feared, but I haven't done anything, only asked a simple question; they're acting like I'm about to go on some killing spree. My reputation is terrible, but I wasn't expecting such fear from two women I've never met before.

"Zoe, go check on Everly," the woman says.

Everly.

Why does her name sound so familiar to me?

CHAPTER
NINETEEN

E verly
    I watch Zoe blow out her candles. Today is her twenty-first birthday and I feel blessed to call her one of my best friends, though she's more like a sister to me—Zoe and Macey fill the places where my family should have been.

I'm happy with how far we've all come. We didn't need anyone; we only needed each other. We got ourselves here.

"Happy twenty-first," I whisper to her, giving her a hug after setting the cake down.

"Oh, we need napkins," I tell her before rushing off back to the kitchen. I go into the storeroom, grab a box of refills and pull a handful out before placing the box back on the shelf. Just as I walk back out, Zoe rushes into the kitchen, her face pale and masked with a look of horror. She smacks straight into me before grabbing my arms.

"What is it? What happened?" I ask, looking around for what scared her. When she doesn't answer, I walk past her to investigate myself—it must be bad for her not to be able to tell me. Zoe fears nothing these days, she's really come out of her shell, so something serious has to have happened for her to be such a nervous wreck.

"You can't go out there," she blurts out, gripping my arms and pulling me away from the door just as I'm about to step through.

"Sir, you can't go back there," I hear Macey call to someone in the restaurant.

"What happened?" I repeat. "Zoe?"

Her eyes go wide as she stares over my shoulder. I grip her arms —whatever she fears must be right behind me. Before I even finish the thought, his scent wafts to me and I straighten up, rigid. Zoe's eyes dart to mine.

My face must mirror the same horror hers does because she grabs my hands, squeezing them tight. I close my eyes, willing myself not to break—he will *not* break me. He already does that nearly every night, and somehow, I've learned to live with it. I won't give him the satisfaction of actually seeing it.

"Your name is Everly, right?" he says, his voice soft and serious.

I fight the urge to shiver hearing his voice. Fucking mate bond. It's bad enough it tortures me; why does it have to affect me this way —every piece of me wanting to throw myself in his arms despite the fact he nearly ruined me. The bond wants that, not me. I am in control. I fought it this long, and I didn't work this hard for every- thing to unravel right now.

"Yes. How may I help you, Alpha Valen?" I ask, turning around. My lungs compress at the sight of him—he's gorgeous, and he fucking knows he is, which just enrages me. Tall, dark, and hand- some. What is it with men? They grow older, manlier, and more handsome while women just fucking age? Damn, my inner mono- logue is out of whack today. 'Fuck' is taking up a good chunk of my vocabulary.

"You know my name and who I am?" he asks.

"I also know what you are too, so how may I help you?" I ask him. I am impressed with how calm I sound, despite screaming internally and wanting to run.

He blows out a breath and runs a hand through his hair before scratching his neck. He looks back out to the restaurant.

"How old are you?" he asks.

"Old enough to know you are my mate, if that's what you are wondering," I tell him. And man, don't I know it? Five years of agony because I know.

He seems taken aback by my tone. I hate him despite the feeling vibrating through the bond that isn't even forged yet. I hate what he put me through, hate how he hung up when I tried to tell him I was pregnant and laughed at me, saying he would never fuck a seventeen-year-old. Well, fucker, you did! And she raised your son herself. Not that I would ever tell him that. Valarian is my world and we don't need this man in our lives.

I step past him and back into the restaurant, managing to avoid his hand as he tries to touch me.

"Can we talk?" he asks. He looks nervous. I get an inkling that he doesn't struggle much with women; he clearly wasn't expecting it from his mate.

"We just did. Nice chat. Macey will escort you out," I tell him, pointing to Macey while I check the dessert displays and grab a knife.

"Look, I know this came as a bit of shock, but I..."

"But you what? Thought I would run off into the sunset with you. Be dying for you to mark me? Uh, no thanks. The door is right behind you. If you just turn around, you shouldn't miss it, but in case you do, there is a green sign above it saying EXIT," I tell him.

"Wow, you are a real piece of fucking work," he snaps, looking hurt.

"Well, unless you are here for a specific reason that isn't about being my mate, then get out."

"Actually, I came here for a reason," he mutters, looking around. We've managed to draw half the restaurant's attention, though we talked rather quietly. I know it must be from his aura. As soon as I dismissed him, he got his hackles up and spilled it out.

"I need to speak to the manager about holding the annual Alpha meeting here," he says before pulling a brochure from his pocket.

"Don't you have your own hotels to do that at?" I ask him.

"I have been asked to hold it on neutral territory."

"Well, we're fully booked," I tell him.

"I didn't even give you the date," he snaps.

"I know, but whatever date it is, the place is fully booked, and if it isn't, I will make sure it is," I tell him, placing the cutting knife and napkins on the table next to Zoe's birthday cake.

"I want to speak to the manager," he says, following me around.

"You're speaking to her," I tell him, clearing a table and walking back out to the kitchen. I scrape the plates before placing them in the sink and turning around, only to almost run into him because he's standing so close. I step back.

"Then I want to speak to the owner."

"You're looking at her," I tell him.

"You own this place?" he scoffs.

"Yeah, is that an issue? Do you feel threatened by my five-star rating compared to your 4.5? Didn't think a rogue woman could outdo you? I bet that's the real reason you're here; you finally realized where all your guests went?"

"Well..." he doesn't finish and instead shuts up.

"It is, isn't it?"

"Yes and no. I wanted to book your function room for the Alpha meeting and also check out the competition. I wasn't expecting to find my mate, though," he says somewhat lamely.

"Well, like I said we are booked out, so if you will excuse me," I tell him, and he growls, stepping into my path.

"Why are you being like this?" he asks.

"Being like what, Alpha Valen?"

"This! I am your mate!"

"I am well aware."

"Then stop. Just let me take you out or something, go somewhere with less of an audience," he says, glancing around at the chefs.

"No, thank you."

"Have you got a boyfriend? Is that it?"

"No! I don't feel the need to fuck everything in sight," I say, my words full of venom.

"Excuse me?" he asks. I roll my eyes, trying to step around him when he blocks me again by placing his arm on the counter.

"I have work to do, please move," I tell him.

"Being an Alpha, I can forcefully mark you to make you submit. Our laws state Alphas can mark their mates if the mate is unwilling."

"Being rogue, I don't give a fuck about status, and if you try that, that just shows your true character and every reason as to why I don't want to be your mate."

"So that's it?" he asks. I shrug, needing him to move. His boxing me in like this is filling my head with his scent, making me want to do things I shouldn't do to him.

"So, you hate me over what the media spills about me? You'll judge me off that? You don't even know me; we just met," he says.

He still hasn't realized who I am. We have met three times now, both times a disaster because he was drunk, and well, I was under-age, so this is on him either way. He should have been able to recognize me the first time.

"I would give you the world, and you wouldn't even give me a chance?"

"No, you would give me Syphilis or some other sexually trans-mitted disease, so I am not interested," I tell him, realizing I'm going to have to touch him to escape. I try to step around him, but he traps me between him and the steel counter, his hands going to either side of my hips.

"Don't pretend the mate bond doesn't affect you the same as it does me, Everly," he says, leaning in. I'm rooted to the spot, completely frozen as he presses his face into my neck. He growls, the sound more like a purr the longer he sniffs before he groans.

"Valen, baby? Valen, where are you?" comes a sugary sweet voice.

Valen freezes and growls at the blonde woman as she rushes in, shock on her face when she spots us.

"Oh, there you are," she says, hurrying over. He glares at her.

"I am not your baby, not your honey, or any other stupid name you think you can call me; get out, Ashley," he snaps so cruelly I actually feel bad for her. She looks between us and her eyes well with tears.

"Get out!" he screams at her.

"But...but..."

"I have work to do, and you should take your girlfriend home," I tell him, using her as an escape. I quickly grip his wrist to move it off the counter, trying not to think about the tingles that rush across my palm, though Valen gasps at my touch.

"She isn't my girlfriend," he says, glaring at her.

"Valen?" Ashley asks, looking hurt.

"You can do better," I tell her as I walk past her and place my hand on her shoulder. She looks at me and smiles sadly. It's odd feeling sorry for the girl he had been screwing.

"That's all you have to say? You aren't angry at her?"

"Why would I be angry at her? Did you expect me to get jealous? Is that the reaction you were hoping for? I haven't got the time or the energy to feel anything for you," I tell him before turning on my heel and walking out.

Macey and Zoe are waiting by the door as I walk out. Macey moves to touch me, but I hold up my hand. She knows instantly not to touch me; she knows I'll break.

"Go, we'll handle this," they tell me.

I rush out the door, heading for one of the apartments out the back that Zoe and I share together. I run through the gardens and up the steps before unlocking the door. The moment I close it, I fall apart.

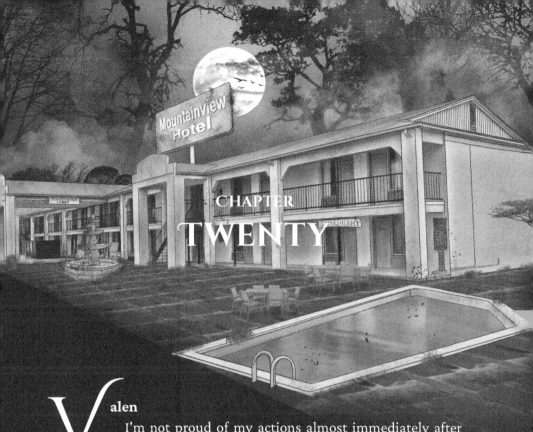

CHAPTER
TWENTY

Valen

    I'm not proud of my actions almost immediately after leaving the hotel and my mate. Ashley won't stop crying and demanding to know who Everly is to me, but I know if I tell her right now, it will be all over the city by the end of the day; the last thing I want is the media hunting Everly down and harassing her. So, I remained quiet the entire drive until I pull up in front of her house. Ashley reaches for me and I pull away.

    I can't stand her touch; it repulses me, and my entire body is pulling me back in the direction of my mate. I know I need to figure something out fast. I don't know how my father survived my mother dying. This is agony, and I've only been away from her for five minutes.

    "Get out!" My voice escapes as more of a growl. Startled by it, Ashley jumps, looking at me nervously, frozen in her seat.

    "Get out," I repeat at her. The Command rolls over her, and her hand reaches for the door handle before hastily getting out.

    "And Ashley?" I start as she climbs out of the car. She stops with her hand still on the open door and looks back in at me.

"Don't come looking for me. Stay the fuck away from me, or you will find yourself living with the rest of the forsaken."

She gasps; I've never banished anyone from the city before. We usually try to avoid forsaking wolves, but she just made finding my mate an entirely new struggle when she couldn't remain in the damned car like I asked. Her puffy, red eyes blink at me in shock at my words before she nods and slams my door shut.

I start the drive home with a sigh, wanting nothing more than to return to the Mountainview Hotel and retrieve my mate. I can't understand why she didn't want me. Wasn't that all she-wolves wanted—to be mated to an Alpha? Yet, she tossed me aside like she felt nothing for me. And she's a damn rogue. She should be jumping for joy!

The chances of an Alpha being bonded to a rogue are rare. It isn't like it's never happened, but most Alphas are bonded to other Alphas. I only know of two other Alphas in the country mated to someone of lower rank. But Everly is the first rogue I've heard of being bonded to an Alpha.

However, I don't care; I just want her. I've always wanted my mate. She could have been a freaking unicorn for all I care. I trusted the Moon Goddess to make the right choice for me, and after seeing her, I can't imagine being with anyone else. My mind is entirely consumed with her, her scent, the tingles that rushed over me when she touched me.

But something is off—right on the tip of my tongue. I have this weird sense of déjà vu, which I know is insane. I definitely would have recognized my mate had I seen her before, but even her name... I swear I've heard that name before. Why can't I place it? Was it in a dream?

One thing I do know is that I have to find a way to win her over. Technically, I could mark her forcefully. It's allowed by our laws, as Alphas can be weakened without their mates. It's considered unacceptable for an Alpha to be debilitated because they were longing for their Luna.

If the Alpha is limited by his mate, the entire pack is put at risk, and I can't allow that. I need her, and she needs me. She will feel the pull; it's inevitable. She's good at pretending I don't affect her, but her heart rate said otherwise, the way her breathing increased at my proximity. But no one can live without their mate, or so I hoped, and she would be mine.

Pulling back into the parking lot of my hotel, I groan when I see my father's car still parked where it was. I was hoping Marcus could get rid of him while I was gone, but what intrigues me is the car parked beside it. A growl escapes me when I see Alpha John's car parked in my reserved parking spot beside my father's. What the fuck is he doing here?

The valet rushes over when I stop the car, toss my door open, and stalk inside, leaving the vehicle running.

The receptionist jumps at the growl that escapes me, echoing off the marble floors and making the windows vibrate.

"Where is he?" I snap at her.

"Conference room one, Alpha, with your father and Beta."

I nod, heading for the stairs instead of the elevator, not willing to wait. I take the stairs on the left and race up to the first floor.

This side of the first floor is mainly office buildings and off-limits to patrons; the other half is sectioned off and all restaurant and bar areas. When I reach the door, I swipe my card to let myself in; the lock clicks before the door swings inward to a corridor. Walking past a few open doors, I can see pack members look out at me nervously. It is no secret that Alpha John and I don't get along.

We are constantly in the media, and a few public incidents recently have the entire city on edge that a war is coming. Honestly, it's inevitable; Alpha John has been overstepping. He wants part of my pack's border and is willing to try to get it by any means necessary, regardless of who he's hurting in the end.

Since the main street and the streets behind it are neutral territories, he can't stake a claim to the land. But that doesn't stop him from driving out those living or owning businesses there. He recently had a few of the smaller pack businesses shut down, burnt out, or even robbed.

Alpha John is a sneaky bastard, never doing his own dirty work—there have even been rumors he's getting help from the higher-ups in the human cities. Unfortunately, without proof—and no one wanting to get involved—there isn't much anyone can do; he has them running scared.

This is really not the time to be having a war in our own city—not when so many people have gone missing recently. We've kept track of how many she-wolves, and even a few forsaken wolves, have gone missing. Talk of hunters coming back has the entire city worried already. The last thing we need right now is for our city to look divided; it would make it easier for the city's human communities to pick us off.

It's no secret that werewolves exist, but that doesn't mean there aren't extremists among the humans who want to eradicate our kind. Our cities have lived in peace now for centuries. However, werewolves and humans have clashed every now and then.

The conference room door bangs against the wall loudly when I shove it open. Marcus is leaning against the wall with his arms folded, looking rather angry about something. My father and John stop whatever they were discussing to look up at me just when I notice another girl in the room. She does not look impressed to be here.

I can tell she's Alpha John's daughter by her scent. He has been struggling with her; she can be quite the troublemaker. I've heard of her a few times, seen her in the papers, and even glimpsed a few inappropriate photos and videos that have surfaced of her drunk and him dragging her out of different establishments.

"Ah, son, just in time," my father says, standing up and motioning for me to sit. I walk over to the table but don't sit down. I don't like whatever the heck is going on here. My father hates Alpha John more than I do—he never did tell me what started their feud—

so I'm a little shocked to see them sitting around chatting like they're friends.

"What the fuck are you doing on my territory?" I ask John.

He sits back in his chair and folds his arms across his chest with a smirk on his face.

"We have a proposition for you." my father says.

"Which I don't fucking agree to," John's daughter says, cutting my father off.

"Ava, you will do as you're told—now sit there and shut up," John snaps, his aura rushing over her; I find it odd that she isn't able to resist. She's definitely old enough to take over her father's pack, so why hasn't he handed it down to her yet? Is it the issue with the media?

"Son, please just take a seat," my father says, and I growl, pulling a chair out and sitting down in it.

"Now, John and I have been in discussions over the last couple of weeks trying to find a way to put an end to this feud. We think we have come up with a solution that will benefit all of us. Tensions are running high in the city, and we need to show those who reside here we are united. But that won't happen if a war is inevitable. So, Ava here is due to take over her father's pack, but with recent issues in the media, it has her pack nervous."

"This is bullshit," Ava curses under her breath and shakes her head. My lips tug up at her defiance, and Alpha John glares at her before he speaks.

"My pack is nervous about my daughter taking over."

"I wouldn't have to take over if you didn't—" she tries to protest, looking at her father with pure hatred.

"Ava, enough! Sit down and shut up. You have caused our family enough disgrace," Alpha John snaps at her. I will give the girl one thing, she has no issues standing up to her father. Instead of backing down, she stands up, placing her hands on the table, and glaring at her father menacingly.

"I am not even supposed to be in the city; I wasn't the one who was supposed to be Alpha. I should have been on the other side of the country in university by now, but you just had to get rid of—"

Alpha John stands up and slaps his daughter before she can say more. Aghast, I jump to my feet, a growl tearing out of me at witnessing him hitting his daughter. It disgusts me that he can smack his own flesh and blood. Sure, she may be a little wayward, but he shouldn't have hit her.

"Sit down. You know not to mention that name," John warns her, his tone threatening, and I wonder who he's talking about. Alpha John always kept his family on his territory. He rarely let his daughter off pack territory unless escorted, but once she turned of age, he couldn't exactly stop her. I know Alpha John's wife is rarely seen, only proving how controlling he is. But if Ava wasn't supposed to be Alpha, who was?

Ava rubs her cheek. Her eyes burn with tears, but she sits back down. Out of the corner of my eye, I see Marcus's jaw clench. My father nods to Alpha John, which pisses me off. How could he condone the man hitting his daughter like that?

"As I was saying, Ava here is supposed to take over the pack. Due to her recent behavior, it is making my pack members nervous, so your father and I have found a way to end this feud and help both packs."

"I don't understand," I tell him, trying to figure out where he's going with this. I can tell my father is suddenly nervous as he loosens his tie, something he always does when he feels uneasy.

"You need a mate to produce an heir. I need someone to help take over the pack; my daughter clearly can't do it on her own and has been troublesome. I need someone that can handle her, keep her in line."

"What? Like you just did by beating her? And what the hell do you get out of this?" I ask, this time turning to my father. None of this makes sense to me; they hate each other. Why would my father suddenly be siding with him?

"Valen!" my father scolds. But it doesn't matter. I'm not about to pretend him hitting her didn't happen or that any of this makes sense. Sure, I'm an asshole, and so is my father, but not once did he ever raise his hand to me, and he sure as hell wouldn't slap a child or a woman.

The outline of her father's hand stings her face like a red glow. I can't help but feel disgusted. Doing that to someone you expect to take over your pack is repulsive. It's obvious that Alpha John needs to retire—he's the oldest Alpha in the city, and clearly his ways of dealing with things are out of date.

Ignoring my father, I turn to John. "I fail to see how your daughter is to help with that issue."

"An arrangement," her father tells me. "We think you should take Ava as your mate. She can provide a strong pup for you, and I can assure my pack they are in safe hands. It would also get rid of the negative media, and the city will look reunited."

"I know you aren't blind to those of our kind that have been going missing of late. We can't be fighting amongst ourselves when we may have an inevitable war coming with the humans," John tells me, but I'm still shocked at what he just asked of me.

I shake my head. No wonder the girl is so angry. I am outraged that my father would even agree to this.

"Just think about it, Valen. This is good for everyone in the city and for both packs. It will end the wars between packs, which benefits both of us."

"No. Now get the fuck out of my hotel; I won't hear any more of this nonsense," I tell them, getting up out of my seat.

"Valen, just think about it. We still have time for you to decide. No need to make hasty decisions. Nothing will be announced until the Alpha meeting in two months. Plenty of time to discuss this some more."

"We don't need to discuss anything. Ava isn't my mate. I will have children with my mate and my mate only. Thank you for the offer, Alpha John, but I am not interested," I tell him, about to walk out the door.

"I will give you some time to think about it, Alpha Valen. The offer still stands, so think carefully. Reputation is everything," Alpha John tells me, his eyes darting to my father, who nods. I couldn't care less about my reputation; I'm comfortable with who I am. Once again, however, I am cut off before I can answer—this time by my father.

"How is the Alpha meeting coming along? Have you picked a location yet?" he asks, effectively stopping me from telling Alpha John to go fuck himself and get off my territory.

"It will be on neutral territory. Now, I think it is time you leave," I snap at both men

"Great," Alpha John says as he gets to his feet. "Well, send us the details, and in the meantime, you can think about what decision you want to make. It would be good to know for certain by the Alpha meeting so we can make an announcement."

"There won't be an announcement. Your daughter is not my mate," I tell him, but he ignores me, instead gripping his daughter's arm and tugging her out of the room. I growl at him.

"Enough. Just think about it, Valen," my father repeats, watching them leave. The moment they do, I turn on him.

"How fucking dare you! You just put me on the spot! You didn't think to fucking ask before making deals with the likes of him? I won't go through with it, and if you try that shit again, I will banish you from the city!" I bellow at him. My father takes a step away from me.

He has always been trying to control every aspect of my life since I took over, but this isn't his choice and is way out of line. I've found my mate. I'm not about to toss her aside for some rivalry.

Alpha John's daughter not being good enough to become her pack's Alpha is not my issue, but this does make things more difficult because now, I have to convince Everly to let me mark her before the Alpha meeting.

I will accept no one but my mate, but I have no doubt that disagreeing will only be the start of my issues with Alpha John and the shadow pack. And I can already tell something is up with my father. He's keeping something from me—there's no other explanation for his behavior. So until I know what it is, I'm going to have to make sure he doesn't find out about Everly.

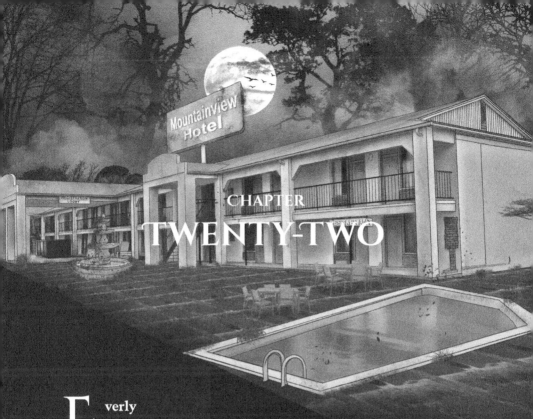

CHAPTER
TWENTY-TWO

E verly

Now that Valen has realized I'm his mate, and after his persistence yesterday, I know it won't be the last time I'll hear from him. He doesn't seem like the type that's used to being knocked back by a woman. But he'll have to get used to it; there's no way I will allow my son to be taken from me. Maybe I've made my point though. Maybe I can go the entire day without dealing with mate dramas.

Stepping out of my office, I groan when I see him again. My heart stops in my chest—he's walking down the corridor toward me. I turn in the opposite direction to escape out the side door and back to the safety of my apartment for a while before I retrieve Valarian from preschool.

"Everly."

"What? Alpha Valen, I'm busy," I call over my shoulder. He jogs after me.

"Too busy to speak with your mate?" he asks.

"Yep, definitely too busy for you," I tell him, continuing toward the door that leads outside and refusing to make eye contact with him.

"Hmm. So you hire liars here? Because that cleaner just told me you should be going on your lunch break right now and that you aren't busy," Valen says before gripping my arm. Sparks rush up my arm, and I jerk away from his touch as I turn to face him. Valen growls at me, and I glare at him.

"Geez, what is your problem? No need to act repulsed by me," he snaps at my reaction.

"I never said you repulsed me, but thanks, I will add repulsion to my list of reasons for hating you," I tell him, though that's a lie; I don't hate him. His arrogance and the fact he can't remember me irritates me, but hate is too strong a word for my mate.

Everything in me is calling me to press against him—to touch him and mark myself with his scent—some primal urge to claim him. But I shove it down, ignoring it. He has my hormones and brain all muddled when he's near, and I want to run from him, disliking the feelings he brings out of me. How can I simultaneously detest and long for someone? It irritates me.

"Why? Why do you hate me? Because of Ashley?" he asks, and I scoff before turning away.

"She means nothing to me," Valen says when I start to walk away from him. He grips my arm again, turning me back to face him. I growl at him and try to shake his hand off, but his grip only tightens.

"Keep your hands off me. You have no right to touch me," I snap at him. His eyes change and turn black, his wolf side pressing forward at the warning in my voice. He clearly doesn't like being challenged by his mate, or is it just my refusal to bow down to him? Or maybe he's butt hurt that I'm not tossing myself at him like the rest of the bimbos he usually has hanging off his arm. I bet that's it! He isn't used to being rejected, and to be dismissed by a rogue must really grind his gears.

His following words prove the latter. "I have every right to touch what is mine, and you are mine, Everly—every inch of you is mine; mine to touch, mine to mark, mine to claim, and I will claim you."

I swallow and try to take a step away when my back hits the wall.

Valen's canines slip from his gums, and he steps closer, pressing me harder against the wall, caging me. His nose moves along my jaw to my neck—the sharp points of his teeth graze my skin. My eyes shut, my breathing becoming unsteady. I hate my own body's reaction to his closeness.

"You don't seem so sure now, Everly. You know who you belong to, and you do belong to me," he says. His breath fans across my neck and I inhale his addictive scent. My own gums tingle with the urge to mark him, claim him as mine, and I try to fight off the instinct that is infused in us.

I feel out of control, my heart rate increases, and my breathing becomes heavy as his scent wraps around me. Valen moves closer— his entire body against mine—and a deep thrum from his chest vibrates against mine as he purrs into me. Yet, my body gives in to his calling, the urge to let him take me overriding common sense. He's using my own instincts against me. Usually, she-wolves are unable to resist the call of their mates. The sound calls me to give in to my mate on some instinctive level, like a sedative that makes my brain suddenly stop working. He nips at my neck, and much as I hate what he's doing, the thought of him marking me also excites me on some level. The experience is bringing forth feelings for him I thought died long ago, reminding me of the urge to nest when pregnant. The hatred is replaced with a longing or compulsion to do what comes naturally but also feels uncontrollable at the same time because it takes free will from us; it's all instinct and urges.

"Do I still repulse you, Everly? Because your body says otherwise," he whispers against my throat before grazing my neck with his teeth again where his mark should be. I shiver when I feel his lips press against my skin before he runs his tongue across my sensitive flesh.

Valen groans obscenely, and his hand skims under the side of my blouse. I gasp at his touch, and my hands feebly clutch the front of his shirt; I don't know if I want to pull him closer or shove him away, my brain and body fighting with each other. But damn, does his body feel good pressed against mine, so warm, and my skin tingles.

I feel the outline of his abs hidden beneath his shirt, his belt buckle digging into my stomach as he presses closer, until every line of him presses against me. A sigh escapes me, and my eyes jolt open at the noise I make. Valen's hand moves higher before he squeezes my breast through my bra and growls softly before nipping at my jaw. I want to shove him off, but at the same time, I don't want him to stop, I want to feel his hands all over me without the clothes in the way.

The sound of someone clearing their throat makes me jolt back into reality, and I jump while Valen growls menacingly. I push him away from me instantly, the fog lifting. As soon as his touch is gone, I miss it. Looking down the corridor, I see Macey and my cheeks heat. She raises an eyebrow at me before tapping her fingers on her wrist. My brows furrow, and I quickly glance at my watch. Shit, I have to get Valarian from the rogue preschool; it'll close soon. I knew I shouldn't have taken such a late lunch! I would typically be waiting at the gate by now; it's nearly 4:30 p.m.

"Zoe?" I ask, and she nods.

"Already gone to get–" she looks at Valen. "She should be back soon," Macey says carefully, letting me know Zoe is grabbing Valarian with Casey. I let out a breath of relief.

"Thank you, Macey. I'll be down soon; I just need to deal with something first."

"Sure, go back to whatever you were both doing. But keep it PG; this is a hotel," she chuckles, and I glare at her before my cheeks flush.

Valen smirks at me, and I turn my glare on him while Macey walks off toward the stairs.

"So, do you still believe you are unaffected by the mate bond?" he asks. I say nothing. How could I when he was practically dry-humping me against the wall, and I was letting him? I shake my head, turning to follow Macey.

"Deny me all you want, Everly; you will give in. You can't resist a mate bond," Valen calls quite confidently. Little does he know, I've been denying my mate bond for years and will continue to.

"I wouldn't be so sure about that. I can be stubborn, and I can guarantee I won't be pining over you," I retort, trying to escape him as he follows me.

"I have other ways to make you give in. Resist the mate bond, but I bet you'll come crawling back if I have this place shut down," he says, and I stop.

"Excuse me?" I snap, spinning around to glare at him. He smiles, and I clench my hands into fists.

"Don't forget who this city belongs to. Fight me all you want, Everly—nothing I like more than a good challenge. But don't say I didn't warn you because I *always* win. You will accept the mate bond and me or..." he looks around, motioning with his hand at my hotel. "I have a lot of influence around here," he says, stepping closer.

"You can't breach me on anything, Valen. Your threats are empty. I know everything is legal; no one can fault this place for anything," I tell him. He shrugs, stepping closer.

"So you won't mind me sending the health and safety inspector around? Nothing to fine you for?" he asks, and I fold my arms across my chest.

"My hotel won't fail anything. Everything is by the book. You won't win, and nothing you do will make me accept this mate bond. Nothing. So go home, Alpha Valen," I tell him before storming away. The nerve of him to threaten me!

"I'll see you tomorrow, Everly," Valen calls out, and I growl at him. I really need to go for a run to burn off some of the anger raging through me. Taking the steps two at a time, I head to my apartment to change, knowing Zoe will be back soon with the kids.

CHAPTER
TWENTY-THREE

I remain in a terrible mood for the rest of the afternoon—I can't concentrate or focus on anything. Two days in a row, I've seen Valen. The bond is buzzing, and it's making it increasingly difficult to function. On top of that, I have his lingering threat and the worry that came with it. He has the power to destroy the hotel we saved, the parting gift Valarie had given to Valarian and me. I feel protective of it; we built this place from its bare bones and gave it back life. I'm not about to stand by and let him take it from us. Yet, I would be powerless against him in a city where rogues mean nothing.

I'd be lying if I said I'm not worried; I am. Macey, Zoe, and I have worked our asses off for years building this place back up. And for him to threaten to destroy it makes my blood boil. The question lingering in the back of my mind remains: would he really destroy this place—harm his own mate's business—all because I refuse to give in to him?

"Uh, Mommy...."

Valarian's worried voice reaches my ears, and I lift my head to look at him. A shriek leaves my lips when I realize I'm burning the grilled cheese. Smoke is billowing from the grill and I rush over, yanking the tray out of the oven, only to forget it's piping hot, and I'm not wearing oven mitts.

My fingers sizzle, and I drop the tray before racing to the sink and quickly turning the faucet on to run my hand under the cold water.

"Casey, don't touch that!" I tell her when she leans down from the kitchen table to pick up the hot tray. She sits back up, and with all the commission, Zoe comes racing in. The smoke alarms suddenly start blaring loudly, and she opens the window above the sink before using a dish towel to waft the smoke out the window.

"Shit, Eve. Are you ok?"

I nod, holding my hand under the cool water—my fingertips are blistered. Zoe uses the dish towel to pick up the tray, placing it on the stove. After discarding the ruined grilled cheese, she uses the broom to smack the fire alarm, jabbing the button and cutting off its deafening noise.

"Let me see," Zoe says, looking around me at my burned hand.

"It's fine; it'll heal," I tell her, and she clicks her tongue.

"You've been distracted all afternoon. What's going on with you today?"

I glance at the small dining table in our cramped, tiny kitchen. Both kids have gone back to their drawings and are no longer paying attention to us.

"He came by again today," I tell her, and Zoe sighs before running her fingers through her hair. I know she worries I'll turn out like Valarie—she and Macey have expressed multiple times they want me to mate with another rogue to ensure I don't die, but other men don't attract me in the slightest. I'd been content on my own; I like my independence and don't need a mate to be whole. However, I can't deny how the bond is affecting me.

"You need to figure something out; last night, you couldn't sleep and were pacing all night, and now you're burning yourself. Go for a run. Val always told you to run it off. Seeing him always weakened her. The more you see him, the more fragile you'll become," Zoe says, chewing her thumbnail and watching me nervously.

Zoe's right; I remember every time that Alpha came to visit Valarie, she would be out of it for days. We would have to force her out of bed. Yet, that couldn't be happening to me. Not yet, surely. Valarie lasted decades before her deterioration got so bad that it killed her. The memory makes me shudder.

"Go, you know you should. When was the last time you even shifted?"

I shrug, knowing she's right. And it had been well and truly over a month.

I hate shifting. It's a constant reminder of what has become of me. Each time, my wolf side becomes smaller and weaker. Yet, if I don't shift, my mental state will start to deteriorate along with my body. When she was still able, Valarie told me that shifting helped ward off the effects of the bond.

Gosh, how I miss that woman. She was one-of-a-kind and one of the best women I've ever had the pleasure of meeting. She would have been a wonderful grandmother had she gotten the chance to live longer. One thing I will never forgive Alpha Kalen for—he killed her. I just have to make sure his son doesn't make history repeat itself.

Valen won't kill me, and he won't get my son; I will make sure of it.

"Go. You can tell me about it later when the kids are in bed," says Zoe. I nod, looking over at them. Valarian's amber eyes stare down at his paper as he works on his picture, concentrating hard, his tongue poking out the corner.

Zoe sets a glass of juice on the table beside him and he stares at it. His lips purse while his brows furrow as he glares at it before moving it onto the coaster. He then does the same with Casey's. Beside him, his pencils are all straight in a row, set perfectly, and even sharpened to the same length. Meanwhile, Casey's is in disarray, and I can see his fingers twitching to straighten them for her.

"Sorry, Valarian, I forgot," Zoe laughs softly before ruffling his thick, dark hair. He looks like his father, a spitting image, and I sometimes notice this particular stare. It's clear there's power in him—he already has a particular atmosphere about him. He's an Alpha in the making, and I'm not sure it will remain hidden. One day, someone will notice he isn't like other rogues. He was born from Alpha parents. Even though I no longer have an aura, he's strong and dominant.

His personality is quite intense for a child. Casey is like any child; though she looks like Zoe, I can see her father in her too. Casey has his lighter blonde hair and brown eyes, though her soft facial features and her nose she gets from her mother.

"Eve, go. The kids are fine," Zoe tells me, and I nod. I feel like I'm failing my son—I hardly have spare time, and I hate spending it away from him when I do. I feel so spread thin, always racing around the hotel and lacking the energy to function by the afternoon, always working, building our village, and his future.

I kiss Valarian on the cheek as I walk around the table to grab my sneakers.

"Can I come?" Valarian asks, and my heart thumps at the thought. He loves watching me shift, not realizing how much weaker I am than a regular werewolf. How was he to know when I am the only one he's seen? But lately, the reserve hasn't been safe.

A few forsaken have come into the city recently—it has been unusual. Though the city's border patrols quickly put them down, it made me nervous about taking my son out there. Since the last encounter was reported, I haven't been out after a group of rogues was attacked.

The packs couldn't care less for rogues, which only makes us more nervous. They've tightened patrols, but not for us; it's no good for anyone in the city if the forsaken get in. Another thing I find odd is the reports of forsaken wolves going missing. Some that stuck close to the city borders and turned feral have suddenly vanished. Those that keep monitoring them haven't seen them.

One thing this city is good at is talking. Rumor spread, yet the missing forsaken wolves are never mentioned in the news. It's like they don't exist. But I know they exist, we've all heard the whispers. Yet, no warning has been given to us rogues to steer clear of the reserve.

Those living in packs were given alternative options for going on runs and extra patrols. None of those options were offered to us. The rogue community is small, so when rogues or forsaken go missing, we know; not that the city cares.

With eleven missing in the last year and numerous forsaken sightings—and three forsaken also vanished—it makes no sense that it's not on the news. It's the first time this many have gone missing. The world is going mad, and it scares me

One of the missing rogues was a cleaner here at the hotel. She has twin girls. Those poor girls. Luckily, their grandmother took them in, and we've still been paying her wage and will continue to do so, despite her missing. We will keep on helping her mother with the twins; we won't forget her.

"Can I come?" Valarian asks.

"Not today, sweetie. Next time, I promise," I tell him, and Valarian pouts.

"None of that; your mother has her reasons," Zoe scolds when he glares at the table and slams his pencil down.

"All she does is work," Valarian mutters and my heart twists painfully at his words.

"I promise next time. It isn't safe right now," I tell him, and he looks at me as I sit on the couch, putting my sneakers on.

"If it isn't safe, why are you going then?"

"Because I have to, I need to shift. You know that, we've talked about this before. Sometimes mommy needs to."

"Fine," he says, straightening his pencils before reaching over and doing the same with Casey's. She frowns at his compulsive behavior. "You promise next time I can go too?"

I sigh and nod my head. "I promise."

"Pinky promise," he asks, holding up his little pinky. I chuckle, getting up and capturing his pinky with mine.

"I pinkie promise," I tell him, kissing his cheek.

"Now, behave for Auntie Zoe, and I will be back soon. We can watch that dinosaur movie tonight if you like after dinner."

"Ooh, and I can make caramel corn," Zoe tells the kids, who nod excitedly.

"Stay away from the fence line," Zoe says, concerned. I look at the clock and nod.

"Two hours max," I say.

"Any longer, I'll send a search party," she replies. I know she would too. Anxiety amongst us rogues is at an all-time high.

Giving one last glance at Valarian, I walk to the front door and hurry down the steps to the path at the bottom. The hotel backs onto the reserve and I head toward the fence line. A large hole had been cut in the mesh fence at some point, which makes it easier for those working here to sneak into the back of the reserve.

The reserve itself is a wetland near the city's border fences. It's also neutral territory, and the only place considered safe for us rogues to shift without causing a disturbance to the packs, which to me makes no sense. Shifting is natural to werewolves, yet we're restricted on where we can go because packs don't want to share any of their safe, protected land with us.

We're considered the undeserving, the nuisances of the city. So we get this one place and one place only, and it just had to be the most dangerous part of the city. The "rogue-approved" territory is on the longest stretch of the border fence line. It's also the weakest, least monitored, and easiest to break through. I plan to steer clear of those fences; we all do, carefully avoiding attention from those on patrol and any possible forsaken wolves that may be lurking and looking for a way into the city.

I have yet to see a forsaken one and I don't want to. The rumors are enough to make me try to avoid them at all costs—cannibalistic, rabid, and crazed. The parts of them that once had humanity are gone, forever stuck in their shifted state, forever the monsters humans once painted us to be.

Slipping amongst the trees, I look around before pulling my clothes off and tucking them into a hollow log before kneeling. I've been finding it difficult to shift the longer I go without my mate. It takes more concentration and feels forced, and unnatural. My body no longer agrees to do as it's told, no longer strong enough to change on demand.

It's a battle made harder each time. I shudder when I feel my bones start breaking—the process is painful, and it shouldn't be. It's like my first shift all over again, and I curse that I ever met Valen as I morph into my wolf, hands becoming paws, two legs traded for four. My vision changes and adapts following the shift. All I want is rest. I'm exhausted already, but I force myself to run.

I run for about an hour before I can barely move. I collapse on the ground next to my clothes before eventually shifting back and changing into them. As I walk slowly back to my apartment, I feel a strange mix of exhaustion, sadness, and anger. The run doesn't seem to have helped as much as I hoped. My feet are dragging as I turn the corner and suddenly smack into a wall. I know this place like the back of my hand and that shouldn't be here. I stumble backward, having bounced off the firm body. Disoriented, I feel a warm hand grip my arm, pulling me back before I land on my ass on the pavement.

A gasp escapes me when sparks rush up my arm and my nostrils are filled with that familiar, intoxicating scent. His breath is warm and heavy in my ear.

"I was looking for you, and the cleaner said your apartment was..." He looks around before looking up at the stairs and pointing to mine and Zoe's apartment.

"This one," Valen says, and I brush away his hand that's holding my arm, my heart thudding in my chest when I hear the kids playing. Valen looks up at the apartment.

"You live with someone?" he asks, cocking his head to the side.

"Yes, Zoe and her kids," I tell him, needing him away from my apartment before Valarian realizes I'm home and rushes out.

"Well, are we going to stand here?" he asks, and I glance at my apartment. "I just want to talk. Please just hear me out."

"We already..." I trail off, stopping suddenly. Valarian pulls the curtain back to stare out, and Zoe quickly closes it, her mouth opening and closing like a fish. She pulls Valarian away just as Valen turns to look up. He waves to Zoe briefly, and she smiles awkwardly.

"Uh, yeah, fine, but my office," I tell him, walking off to the central part of the hotel before he can argue.

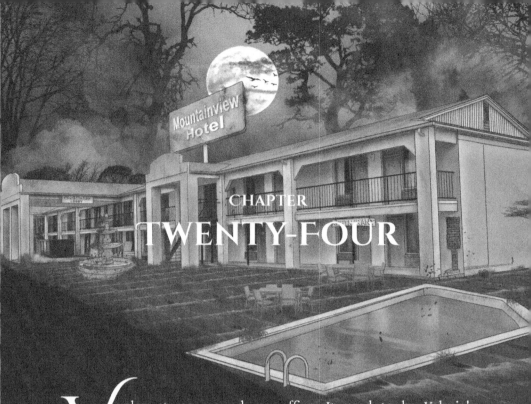

V alen stares around my office. It used to be Valarie's apartment, but we converted it into office space. I found it challenging to come in here before—memories always brought back heartache—so we revamped it, and now the place doesn't haunt me.

Yet, seeing Valen standing here in what used to be her home fills me with sadness. He was her son, and she loved him. Yet here he stands, unaware that this place, the hotel, used to belong to the woman who had given birth to him. What kind of man would he be if she was given a chance to raise him, I wonder?

I watch him for a few seconds, and he stops at the shelving before rearranging it. My brows furrow as I watch him straighten the ornaments, making them line up; it's one thing seeing my son do odd things like that, but a grown man? His movement is robotic and strange as he rearranges the books in alphabetical order on the shelf below. However, OCD isn't a genetic probability, so it has to be a coincidence.

"Why are you here? I wasn't expecting you to stop by," I tell him, remembering his threat to come back tomorrow, yet here he stands.

"I don't need a reason. I own the city, or did you forget?"

I roll my eyes at him. Typical Alpha, thinking the world owes them for being allowed in their presence.

He stops looking around, and I notice the picture of Valarian on my desk. I quickly swipe it off, placing it in the drawer just as he turns to face me. My door opens, and the night secretary walks in.

"Coffee?" Emily asks, her brown eyes sparkling. Though generally shy, she's a cheerful woman and has lasted the longest on the night shift in the foyer. She lives in the rogue commune with her nine-year-old son, working here at night to provide for her child. She actually makes her own coffee from scratch, even growing the beans herself. It tastes terrible. She offered me a cup back when I stopped by her place to offer her the job. Since then, I can't bring myself to drink a single cup—always bring my own.

"No, this won't take–" I try to stammer out politely.

"Yes, please," Valen cuts me off, and I glare at him. Emily lingers for a second, and I nod to her. Valen smiles triumphantly when I give in, yet the joke's on him if he thinks he'll enjoy what she'll prepare for him.

"Now, if only you would give in that easily to the mate bond," he continues, looking at me.

"Not happening. I don't need or want a mate," I tell him and he huffs before pulling out the chair on the other side of my desk. He leans back, folding his arms across his chest, and watches me. I fight back a shiver as my eyes roam over his muscular frame.

"And why is that? What have you got against me? I am your mate, Everly. There is no escaping me, but why would you want to? I am an Alpha. What sort of rogue are you? Most rogues would be begging me to be their mate," he says, and I scoff.

"Not when you keep coming around, no, there isn't any way of escaping you. Do I need to get the authorities involved; tell them I have a stalker?"

"Tell them what you want. As an Alpha, and the most influential one in the city, I have every right to force you to complete the bond, and there is nothing I can't buy my way out of even if there was an issue."

"And here I was thinking I have every right to reject you," I retort. Valen growls, and the door opens. Emily has returned, unaware of the argument she walked in on, utterly oblivious to the tension in the room. She places the coffees on my desk quietly while Valen and I glare at each other, then slips back out. Valen grits his teeth before looking around the room.

"Why? Why would you want to reject your mate?" he asks, sounding like a broken record before getting out of his seat. Looking around again, his jaw clenches tight before turning to glare at the mugs on my desk. I roll my eyes, recognizing that look, and decide to test my theory. It can't be genetic, surely; it's not possible.

"I have my reasons," I tell him before opening the drawer under my desk and pulling out two coasters—Valarian comes down here sometimes and I keep them here for him.

Valen lets out a breath and I hand him one. He quickly places his mug on it and retakes his seat.

"And what reasons are those?" he asks, like he didn't just have a semi-meltdown over a coaster.

"What?" I ask, looking up at him, distracted by his mere presence. I hate the way I feel around him.

"Your reasons—surely you wouldn't judge someone purely by what's in the media?" he repeats, snapping me out of my thoughts.

"Knowing my reasons won't change my decision."

"Nor will it change mine," Valen growls.

"Well, great chat," I tell him, getting to my feet just as I feel his aura rush over me.

"Sit down. You won't dismiss me so easily," he says firmly, and my butt hits the chair hard. Valen bites the inside of his cheek, and I glare at him. "It makes no sense. You should be able to resist me, yet you put up no fight at all," he continues, cocking his head to the side and staring at me.

"I am rogue."

"Yes, but also my mate. You should have some kind of resistance to me," he says, more to himself than me. I add nothing; I have no resistance because my wolf is weak, thanks to the man sitting across from me.

"I have been nice, Everly," he continues with renewed determination.

"You do it and I will hate you forever," I sneer at him, and he pulls back.

"Do what?" he asks.

"You know what. You keep telling me you have every right; you make me and I will make you regret it."

Valen reaches for his coffee, and I stifle a laugh by biting down on my tongue as I stare at the mug in his hand. If he wants to act like an annoying shit, he can drink it then. Maybe I should tell him. But I shove that thought away quickly as I stare back at the Alpha, who seems to think he's the Goddess's gift to women.

"I may have the right to force you, but that doesn't mean I agree with it or will do it. I am not a monster, but I also won't wait around forever. A man of my status doesn't get to wait for a rogue to make up her mind," he says before taking a sip. His cheeks puff out, and he gags, covering his mouth with his hand until he retches again and spits it back into the cup.

"My Goddess, what is that? It tastes ghastly!" he says. I chuckle at the look on his face, and he raises an eyebrow at me. "Do you give that crap to your guests?"

I laugh and glance at my untouched cup. Another fit of giggles leaves me.

"Definitely not—it's reserved for cocky Alphas only," I snort, choking on my laugh. Valen stares at my full mug.

"What?"

"She grows the beans herself."

"Well, she isn't a green thumb; tastes like shit. No amount of sugar would make that taste decent," he huffs before shuddering. I'm in fits of giggles while he continues to stare at me like I'm deranged.

"What's so funny?"

"She fertilizes the plant with her own waste!" I clutch my stomach at the look on his horrified face.

"She does what?" he exclaims in outrage, getting to his feet. "You're lying. You better be damn lying, Everly."

I shake my head and bite my lips to stop myself from laughing.

"Next time I refuse the coffee, trust that I have my reasons. No one loves coffee more than me," I tell him. Valen pales slightly, and I suddenly feel a little bad for letting him drink it.

Eh. He'll get over it.

Everyone's aware never to drink Emily's coffee or anything she brings from home, for that matter. Sweet woman, but she can be strange and believes everything is recyclable.

"Come on then," I tell him, getting to my feet.

"I can't believe you let me drink that," he snaps, following me out of my office to the small kitchenette.

"How was the coffee?" Emily asks on the way past.

"Valen enjoyed it," I tell her, and he growls behind me, though only loud enough for me to hear. Emily beams brightly like she just received the best compliment.

"I grow the beans myself," she says proudly. Valen's hands clench at his sides and he nods stiffly, giving her a smile that looks pained. I nudge him toward the small hall and into the kitchenette. He closes the door behind him.

"If you are going to feed me more shit, I am not interested," he says before spotting the sink and rushing over to it. He rinses his mouth at the faucet before drying his hands on a kitchen towel. Rummaging through the small fridge, I grab out two sodas.

"Not made from anyone's waste, is it?" he snaps at me.

"No," I tell him, cracking mine and taking a sip. Valen does the same, drinking half the can in one go before looking around. I roll my eyes, reaching beside him at his head for a coaster. His hand moves to my hip, and I glare at him, but he smirks back at me.

"Hands off," I spit at him, only for him to pull me closer just as I grab the coasters from the shelf.

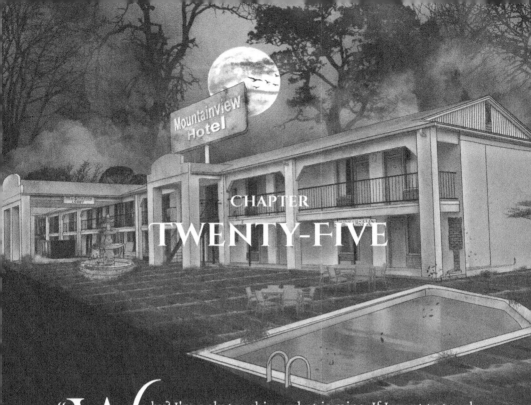

"W hy? I'm only touching what is mine. If I want to touch you, I will, and no one would dare to stop me, Everly. Remember that," he growls before tugging me against his chest. I push off his chest with my hand, trying to escape him.

"Valen, let me go."

"And if I don't want to?"

"I will make you," I growl back at him, though I doubt that. However, a knee to the balls is usually enough to drop any man— even an Alpha.

Valen laughs softly, his hand moving lower before he grabs my ass. I glare at him before thumping his hard chest with my fist that's clutching the coasters. He laughs, plucking them from my fingers. Then his brows furrow and he reluctantly lets me go. I move to the other side, so I'm out of reach. He clicks his tongue, holding up a coaster, and raises an eyebrow at me.

"What?" I ask.

"Nothing. But that is the second time you've done that, like you knew what I was thinking," he says.

Nope, I just know my son, and it seems they share a few odd similarities. I shrug.

"One of the rogue's kid has OCD. I saw you rearrange my shelf."

"Observant, but I don't have OCD—just certain things bother me. Coasters are one of them. Your reluctance to be my mate is another." He mutters something under his breath, too low for me to hear, while shaking his head. I sigh, sipping my soda.

His scent fills the small room, yet I find it oddly calming. However, the quiet is beginning to get awkward as we stand here staring at each other. It makes me question why he came back here tonight. Did the bond pull him back here, or was he here for more sinister reasons?

"You didn't come here because you wanted to talk," I state.

"Not exactly."

I raise an eyebrow at him.

"I was going to mark you." He sighs before wiping a hand down his face when I step away, my lower back hitting the counter. "I won't. I want to, but I won't—not yet, at least. We still have time for you to come around to the decision on your own."

"And if I don't let you?" I ask, horrified at the thought of him marking me against my will.

"You can't just ignore a mate bond. And don't think about rejecting me, Everly, or you will force my hand. I won't have a choice if you do. It will weaken both of us."

"Everyone has a choice, Valen."

"Not everyone—I don't. My father is pushing me to marry and provide an heir."

My stomach twists at his words, thinking of Valarian. "If you can't, what will he do?" I ask cautiously.

"Fuck!" he groans—his eyes darkening—and his aura slips out before he stifles it. "You need to let me mark you. I won't be married off and forced to mate someone who is not my mate."

"You're an Alpha; he can't force you to do anything, and I won't be forced to accept you."

"I have responsibilities to my pack, Everly; my father is going to announce it at the next Alpha meeting."

"Well, I hope you and your future mate are happy together," I tell him, placing my empty soda in the bin.

"How can you say that? What is your issue with me?"

"My issue with you is that you're exactly like every other Alpha; only giving a fuck about titles and pack business; thinking you can go around ordering those beneath you."

"I don't give a damn about titles; you're a rogue. If I cared about titles, I would have rejected you by now—most Alphas would have, given your status. You should be grateful I want you."

"Really? So you admit titles matter then because you just admitted to needing to mark me out of obligation to your pack so you can stay on as Alpha; like I'm some breeding machine made for you to provide an heir, all because your asshole of a father told you to."

Valen growls at me, taking a step closer. "You don't know my father, so don't speak of him that way. He founded this city. Have you no respect? And as for an heir, that is precisely what you were created for; you were fated to me, and therefore belong to me, Everly. You are lucky my father stopped the rogues being tossed from the city and made forsaken. You should be thanking him, not cursing him out."

"And at what cost? Whose lives did he destroy to make sure he got where he is? The only thing Alphas care about is reputation and how much land they own, while the rest of us are cast away and forgotten about. Thank him? He is half the issue with this city he created."

"Oh, for the love of God, I didn't make you a damn rogue. My father isn't responsible for what other packs do. Rogues make the choices that get themselves banished from their packs, I am not responsible for their actions, or yours."

"So you believe every rogue whore decided they wanted to raise their babies alone with no mates or pack support, have their children forced into crappy schools because they can't attend pack ones, work for less than minimum wage while struggling not to be picked off by the forsaken or hunters, forever blamed because they did the one thing all you egotistical men did. They had a child and you all shun them for it. It takes two people to have a baby, Valen, yet only the women are punished for it?"

"So, you're telling me you are a rogue whore? That's how you became a rogue? You weren't born one? I won't raise another person's kid because you wanted to screw around," he says with a growl.

I scoff. This is exactly what I meant; he still shares the same beliefs as his father—the title is all that matters.

"I am not a rogue whore, but it shouldn't matter if I was. This entire place is run by rogue whores, Valen. Not like we tried to keep it a secret," I tell him. Technically, I wasn't lying. I wasn't a rogue whore. My mate fathered my son—I just couldn't let him know about it.

"So this is about your friend you live with, then?"

"What, no," I pinch my brow, letting out a breath. How does he not get it? I click my tongue, annoyed.

"I am offering the chance for you to be part of my pack. You should be happy to have me as your mate; you won't have to be rogue anymore. Isn't that what you want? Don't you want to be in a position of power and not slumming it here with rogue whores?" Valen asks.

I wanted so many things, and not one of them could he give me. I want Valarie back, my family back; I want the rogues to feel safe in their city; I want to be able to walk down the street without being glared at and have people move away from me like I'll steal their mates; I want the pack's views of us to be better.

But most of all, I want the packs held accountable for the anguish they have caused us. We're all the same—only declared different because of who our parents are or because of whom we shared our beds with. Punished for nothing, shamed for making our own choices—-choices that took two people to make.

"I want you to leave is what I want," I tell him, walking out before I slap him.

"You will regret this, Everly; you'll come running back—you'll see. You will beg me to mark you."

I don't acknowledge his words. Instead, I'm angry that he's blinded by what's happening in his own city; the city his father helped build.

The following day, I'm busy organizing a function when a man with a clipboard approaches me with Macey. I recognize him quickly, and he looks around nervously.

"Jim, long time no see. What brings you in here?" I ask, looking at the man who caused us hell while trying to get this place in order. The health and safety inspector taps his notepad.

"We have had a call come in with a few complaints. I am just here to check a few things."

I fold my arms across my chest and raise an eyebrow at him. "This complaint didn't happen to come from Alpha Valen, did it?" I ask, and he clears his throat, clearly uncomfortable with my question. He sighs, looking down at his clipboard.

"I am not at liberty to say," he says when Zoe suddenly comes rushing through the doors, waving both her arms, trying to get my attention.

She slows, spotting the inspector before stopping beside me and leaning close to whisper in my ear.

"There's a tow truck towing your car."

"What!?" I shriek, walking quickly through the gardens and stalking around the front to the car park.

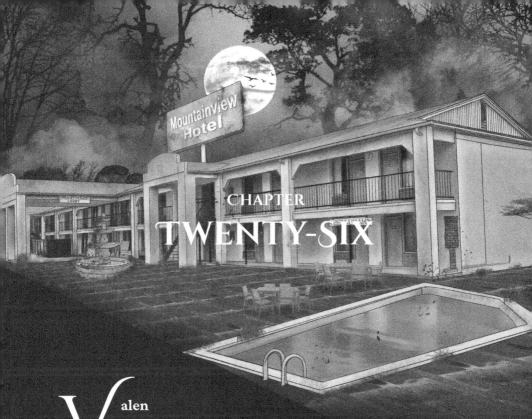

TWENTY-SIX

Valen

If Everly thinks she can just dismiss me and I'll let her, she's wrong. I get what I want, and I want Everly. I refuse to be mated to some girl out of responsibility when I have a perfectly good, but unwilling, mate. My father would choke on his spit if he knew she was rogue, but I don't care. If she is my mate, then I trust the Moon Goddess; she would not give me a faulty one. Everly will be mine—I will make sure of that. Everyone has a breaking point, and I will find hers.

I sit across the road, unable to contain my smile, watching the tow truck pull up to the hotel. I already sent the health and safety inspector in and can see his car in the parking lot from my vantage point.

Her truck was just an added annoyance. The beeping of the reversing truck instantly alerts her staff something is going on. I see Zoe, Everly's little friend, rush out when she notices it backing up to the truck with the Hotel's logo on it. Everly believes she can ignore the mate bond; well, I will make sure she sees me at every turn she makes.

Zoe waves her arms frantically at the driver. One of my men, Dwayne, ignores her as he backs up. The burly-looking man steps out of the cab and stops next to her, looking down at Zoe. I could just make out her telling him to leave, that he was on private property.

"No-can-do, Hun. This car's been ordered impounded for defects," he tells her. I get out and lean on the hood of my car. The tow truck driver spots me and gives me a thumbs up. I nod, giving him the ok to continue, and he starts hooking the old thing up.

It doesn't take long before Zoe returns with a frustrated Everly in tow. Red faced, Everly shoves the man as he starts hoisting her car onto the bed of his truck. Dwayne looks at her, shocked, and I have to admit I am too.

Despite her bold efforts, it's not like she moved him. Dwayne remains precisely where he is; she may as well be a child pushing on a brick wall as she stands frustrated beside him.

She tries to snatch the controller from his hand, but he holds it too high for her to reach and I can't help but find the pure rage on her face funny. Unable to hold it in, I laugh, and her eyes dart towards me.

Gray-blue eyes pin me where I stand before her lips press into a line and her hands ball into fits. She storms over to me in a raging fit, and I fold my arms across my chest just before she stops in front of me.

I find her pint-size rage entertaining; her tiny body is no threat to me. Everly barely comes up to my chin and has to turn her face up to look at me. I smirk back at her, her eyes practically spitting fireballs at me.

Good thing she isn't a witch. She definitely would have cursed me with the look she gave me. She can ignore me all she wants, but Everly can't overlook my influence in this city; eventually, she will be forced to give in.

"What the hell are you doing?" she demands, poking me in the chest with her finger. I snatch her hand, holding it in mine, and she tries to rip it free. Her strength is nothing compared to mine, and something about that bothers me. What if someone grabs her who isn't me? It feels so easy to hurt her, even accidentally. She would never be able to fight them off.

She growls at me, and I realize how non-existent her aura is, like she doesn't have one. Rogues have auras too, weaker and nothing in comparison to a pack wolf, but she has none. Despite her spunk, her growl sounds weak, and if it wasn't for the look of anger on her face, it may have been a purr.

"Let go, and make him stop," she demands.

"Let me mark you, and I will," I tell her, and she snarls at me, her canines slipping from her gums. "Go for it, bite away; I don't care if you want to mark me first. Either way, you will be mine."

"You are fucking infuriating! This won't win you any brownie points," Everly snarls, and I tug her closer before spinning and pressing her against the hood of my car.

Her breathing becomes harder as I press closer to her. God, her body feels good pressed against mine. Her scent makes my mouth water, and I fight the urge to push my face into her neck, losing the battle completely, but instead of shouting, she gasps.

Everly's hand still clutched in mine loosens, and her body goes slack against me when I press closer to her. Her breathing intensifies as I run my nose along the column of her throat to her ear—so warm and enticing. I can hear her heart pounding in her chest as her other hand grips the front of my shirt feebly.

I can tell she is trying to fight off the effects of the bond telling her to give in—telling her to give herself to an Alpha; to me. The vibration of my purr rattles my chest, and before I can stop myself, I run my tongue across her neck. I groan at the taste of her skin on the tip of my tongue. Damn, she tastes even better than she smells, and I have to restrain against my basic instincts to devour her. However, the action seems to snap her back, and she tries to shove me off, fighting against me. I pull back to look at her, only for her palm to connect with my face.

My cheek stings from her slap, and if looks could kill, I would be reduced to dust.

"Get off me, you brute! Stop trying to force me to do what you want."

I rub my cheek with my hand. The contact from her slap made my skin tingle and burn, but I don't move away from her. Instead, I look over my shoulder to see the tow truck leaving with her vehicle on the back.

"Well, seems like you need a lift to the impound yard?"

She growls at me, and I purr back at her before she starts smacking my chest.

"I swear, Valen, you will regret doing that! Tell him to bring it back now! That truck has sentimental value. It was given to me by someone I care about. Now call him—undo it!"

I run my finger down her neck and she shivers under my touch.

My cock twitches in my pants, seeing the effect I have on her. She feels the bond—there is no denying it—no matter how much she hates me.

"Not until you agree to be mine. If you want it back, all it takes is one little mark to sit right here." My finger stops where her shoulder meets her neck, and my gums tingle. I desperately want to mark her as mine, crave for her skin to break under the pressure of my teeth when I give her my mark that will forever lie on her skin, telling the world she is mine.

"Valen, please," she asks, and I look down at her, her face turned, watching the tow truck move down the street, taking away her truck.

"It's just a truck, Everly. If you want it back, you know what you have to do."

Her jaw clenches, and she turns to look back at me. My stomach sinks when I see her eyes teary like she's fighting the urge to cry. It's just a truck, and an old one at that. It isn't even new! Why she would get so emotional over that old thing is beyond me.

"You have no right," she snarls.

"Maybe you forget who I am; I have every right. I own this city, and I say what happens in it, Everly. The sooner you realize that the better it will be for you. I could give you everything you ever wanted."

"Not everything, Valen. You can't give me the last five years of my life back," she says, shoving me away, and I let her.

"If you haven't figured it out yet, Valen, I don't care for your social status or your money; I make my own, I don't need yours, and I certainly don't want it."

"I can make your life miserable, Everly," I say, not backing down.

Everly laughs, which startles me; a threat from the blood Alpha isn't to be taken lightly. She's clearly not stupid, she knows I'm capable of destroying her and those who work for her. I could have her hotel torn to the ground and no one would bat an eyelash, especially over some rogue girl.

"Do your worst, Valen. Don't forget, my reputation as a rogue is minuscule compared to the reputation you have. Who do you think will suffer more when it's tarnished? Certainly not me. They already think I'm the lowest scum to reside in this city. Yet, they still walk through those doors. They still visit my hotel. Miserable? You don't know the meaning of the word—but you will. I will make sure of it."

Turning on her heel, she's about to cross the road when my phone rings. She glances at me as I pull it out to see the towing company name pop up on the screen.

"This would be about your car," I tell her, and she turns back to face me, folding her arms across her chest. I answer it, putting it on speakerphone so she can hear.

"Alpha," Dwayne states. "Am I bringin' it back? Or should I take it t' the yard?"

"That is up to Everly," I tell him, raising an eyebrow. She glares at me. "What will it be, Everly?"

"Go fuck yourself, *Alpha*," she sneers. Dwayne whistles at her tone.

"Wow. So waddya want me to do?"

"Crush it," I tell him, not taking my eyes from her. She takes a step toward me, and her hands clench before she closes her eyes tightly, breathing deeply.

"Alpha?" Dwayne asks.

"I said crush it. Take it to the scrapyard and make sure it isn't salvageable," I tell him. Her eyes snap open and I raise an eyebrow at her. Everly's eyes burn with unshed tears, and she shakes her head. I hang up.

"Could have been avoided," I tell her.

"Yeah, if only I never met you, all of this could have been avoided," she spits at me before turning on her heel and darting across the road. I notice Zoe and Macey waiting out the front for her, and she shakes her head when Macey reaches for her, swatting their hands away before chasing after her. I start driving off, heading home to plan my next move since this one was unsuccessful. I would have to think of another way. She'll give in; it's only a matter of time.

I'm halfway home, yet my thoughts keep going back to her. I need to look into her background, find out more about her. That might help explain why she's so difficult and why she would be so upset about a car. I also want to know what she did to become a rogue, since she isn't a rogue whore. But I don't know her last name. Though, that should be listed on the hotel's registration, shouldn't it?

For some reason, I can't forget the way her lip trembled when I said to crush her car. It makes me feel like an asshole. It makes no sense, though; she has enough money to buy another one; she owns a damn hotel, for goodness' sake. There is no way in hell I would be caught dead in that old piece of junk. She should be thanking me for removing it; now she has reason to buy another. Suddenly, I blanch.

"Fuck!" I say and swerve off to the side of the road. Pulling my phone out of my pocket, I quickly call Dwayne.

"Hello?" he says.

"Where are you?"

"Next door at the scrapyard, doin' what you asked."

"Don't let them crush it."

"What?"

"Please tell me they haven't crushed it yet," I say. "The car. Tell me you haven't crushed the car."

"Oh shit," he says, and I hear banging around in his truck and the sound of a door being slammed before yelling for them to stop. My heart pounds in my chest while I wait for what seems like hours, praying it wasn't destroyed.

I hear more banging before a rush of heavy breathing. Dwayne sounds like he's just run a marathon. He's a big guy and sounds like he's on the verge of a heart attack when he grabs the phone again.

"Eh, that was close. Good thing ya called—another second 'n it would have been crushed into a can."

I let out a breath of relief while he tries to catch his breath, panting heavily into the phone.

"What do you want me to do with it?" he asks after a moment, sounding more normal.

"Put it in my garage out of sight, cover it over. I don't want my father seeing it if he stops over."

"Sure thing," Dwayne answers, and I go to hang up when I hear his voice again. "Hey, boss?"

"Yeah, what is it?"

"She's yer mate, ain't she? I ain't seen ya try this hard t' git a girl in a while; figured she must be special if yer trying to make 'er chase after ya," Dwayne says.

"Keep it between us; I don't need my father knowing for now."

"Yeh, we all know 'e hates rogues. But by the look on her face when she spotted you, she hates Alphas more."

I sigh. It does appear that way.

"Oh, 'n you might wanna have patrols sit around 'er perimeter; forsaken been spotted multiple times the last couple of weeks. That hotel backs onto the reserve—not a safe place right now. Yer dad pulled all the patrols away to focus on the pack's perimeters only."

I growl, feeling anger flush my face. He had no authority to do that. Only Alphas do, and he no longer holds the title.

"Thanks. I will handle it; I'll get Marcus onto it straight away."

CHAPTER
TWENTY-SEVEN

Everly

Tears of frustration streak down my face as I storm away from him. Zoe and Macey stand there waiting, but I'm too upset to speak to anyone; I just want to run into my office and shut the door. Both of them follow me inside, Macey clutching a piece of paper in her hand.

"You ok?" Macey asks and I nod. However, I feel anything but ok. That was Valarie's car. I know it's silly, but it was hers, just like everything of hers I keep down in the storage lockers. I can't bring myself to throw anything away.

"We will get it back," Zoe offers, and I shake my head.

"He had it crushed when I refused to let him mark me."

"Asshole! I'm sorry, Everly," Macey curses and I sniffle. It isn't their fault. Macey clears her throat and I glance at her resting on the edge of my desk as I use a tissue to wipe away my childish tears. Buying another is no issue, but I loved that car because it was hers.

"The Inspector..."

"Crap, I forgot," I tell them, getting up, and Macey waves me away, holding a piece of paper out to me.

I take it from her and read it. A sound of annoyance leaves me when I see what's written on it.

"This is bullshit! They're to the standard; he checked last time!"

Macey nods.

"He said he'll be back in a week to check the guard rails are fixed and the fence around the pool has been replaced."

"Anything else?" I ask, and Zoe chews her lip nervously.

"He said whatever you've done to piss off the Alpha, you need to fix; that he's been asked to find any fault to shut us down unless you give Valen what he wants."

"You didn't tell him..."

"Of course not."

I nod in relief.

"I'll handle this, then I'll come and grab the kids from school with you," I tell Zoe, who nods.

"Also, one of the fridges is down—I've sent for an electrician," Macey adds as they are leaving. At least this day can't get any worse.

I spoke too soon. Turns out, no electrician will come out—not even a handyman. I went through my contact list of rogues with different trades—looking for anyone that has any skills with appliances or electricals—but found none, and Casey's father is away from the city visiting his mate's family.

When it's time to pick up the kids, Zoe meets me out front of the hotel by her car.

"Any luck?"

"No," I groan.

"We'll figure it out. We still have one running, and we could possibly bring one down from one of the suites."

"We'll have to bring two down—one won't be big enough—and

that means two rooms won't be available until I order a new one; *if* I can order a new one. I have a feeling we'll be struggling to get it delivered."

The following day

Apparently, another forsaken was spotted last night. A few people staying at the hotel decided not to risk it and left, knowing the hotel was a good entry into the city.

Regardless, it's Saturday, and we're waiting for the food delivery to arrive for the wedding this afternoon.

Like I thought, I couldn't get a delivery truck with the new fridge in time. We had a week's wait, and it took six of us to haul two of the fridges down from the apartments out back that run parallel to the functions room. Thankfully, the forsaken sightings have scared off a few guests, giving us extra rooms in the hotel itself to make up for being down two of the apartments that had been reserved for the wedding guests.

I glance at my watch; the food delivery should have come into the city an hour ago.

"What's wrong, mommy?" Valarian asks as I pace frantically out in the loading dock for the delivery to arrive.

"Just waiting for a supplies truck sweetie. What are you doing?" I ask, stopping and staring at him. He has his hand propped up on his chin while he stares down at a sheet of paper. He'd asked for some photos earlier and I'd given him my photo album to pick some out. He'd been working on some school project quietly in the delivery shed which is out behind the kitchen. He's so patient. Casey has trouble sitting still for long, yet Valarian has been out here for an hour with no complaints while we wait for the truck that's severely late.

"Do you have any pictures of my dad?" he asks. I immediately freeze, hair standing up on the back of my neck. I get closer to him to see what he's looking at.

"Um, no, I don't think I do," I tell him, brushing his hair back and glancing at what he was working on.

"This for school?" I ask him and he nods. It's a family tree.

"Casey has pictures of her dad—why haven't you got any pictures of mine?" he asks. I chew the inside of my lip.

There were small, cut-out pictures, and Valarie was at the top, the space next to her empty. I've always tried to be as honest as I could; he knows Valarie was his father's mother and his grandmother. Not that he remembers her very well. The space beside her is empty because I can't risk having him mention his grandfather's name at school.

The next line is a picture of me along with a space that's blank. Coming off my picture were some lines where he had glued cut-out pictures of Macey and Zoe.

"You put them in our family tree?" I smile.

"Yes, they are my aunties and Casey and Taylor are my cousins; our little village," Valarian states.

"That's right; our little village, our family," I tell him, feeling like I could cry. He stares at the blank spots on the page.

"You really don't have a photo of him?"

I shake my head, wishing I could give him one. I could possibly get one off the Internet, but the teachers at school would recognize him instantly.

"What about your parents, and my grandpa?" he asks, pointing to the other vacant spots.

Again, he's asking for something I can't give him, and it makes me feel guilty, but they're just too recognizable. I had my name changed before he was born—I use my grandmother's maiden name, Summers. That's the only piece I had left of my family and a life I no longer have. My father removed all traces of me.

"I'll check," I tell him, and he smiles brightly.

"What were they like?"

"My parents?"

He nods. "You never talk about them."

I think of what I can tell him. I knew this day would come and I dreaded these sorts of questions; the information I could give him is limited.

"Well, my mom looked a lot like me; I have her facial features but my dad's eyes and his dark hair. My dad..." I pause for a second. "When I was little, I used to think he was a superhero; he liked to play and would always play with me and my sister after he finished work."

"You have a sister too? A real one?" he asks, and I nod sadly.

"She used to be my best friend."

"What happened to them? Can I meet them?" he asks.

"Maybe one day," I tell him, though whether that day would come is unforeseeable. My phone starts ringing and Valarian turns back to his work. Glancing at the screen, I see it's the delivery truck I was waiting on.

"You're late," I answer.

"Yes, and it's out of my hands. I've been stopped at the city entrance. I tried to explain and had to wait for some Alpha to get here. They've been searching the truck and only just gave my phone back," the man tells me, and I sigh.

"Everything still cold?" I ask.

"Yes, the delivery is fine, but that Alpha I was telling you about wants to speak with you."

"Which one?"

"Alpha Valen, he said his name was. I'm not too familiar with your kind or their politics, but he asked a bit about you, asked if I was a secret lover; he seems quite intense," he says nervously before clearing his throat.

"I'll put him on," the delivery driver tells me.

"Everly, it seems you have found yourself in another predicament," Valen's voice chuckles from the other end.

"Stop messing around, I need that truck. I have a wedding in five hours."

"Well then, seems like you will want to negotiate then?"

"I am not letting you mark me. Valen, this is my life, my job, it's not a time for me to be messing around and playing games," I snap at him, forgetting Valarian is sitting behind me. I glance over my shoulder and meet his questioning gaze before sighing. "What do you want?" I ask, before quickly adding, "Anything but–"

"Let me hold the Alpha meeting at your hotel," he says, cutting me off.

"Definitely not," I tell him, a pit in my stomach.

"That's my offer; what have you got to lose? It brings more business to your hotel and will get you media coverage for it," Valen says and I roll my eyes. That's the last thing I want. However, that was not the issue—it would be risking Valen finding out who my father is. It would also mean confronting my father.

"So, am I sending the truck back where it came from? I need an answer; you have a lot of seafood in this truck, and it would be a shame for it to go to waste. Plus, this is *way* less of a commitment than you agreeing to let me mark you."

I press my lips together. "Fine, what date?" I spit through gritted teeth, though a part of me is relieved we reached an agreement. I'm just afraid it'll go exactly how I'm thinking, and I end up humiliated or my son is denied. But maybe it won't be so bad and it'll go smoothly? This could be a chance for Valarian to meet my sister and mother.

Yeah, right. Talk about wishful thinking.

"Any date in three weeks. You can pick the date, but it has to be three weeks max," Valen tells me.

"And my delivery?" Then another thought suddenly comes to me. "Oh, and the restaurant fridge blew up, so if you want the Alpha meeting held at my hotel, I need a new fridge delivered in the next hour. Think you can manage that?"

"It will be there in twenty minutes, along with a fridge. I am trusting you not to go back on your word, I advise you, don't. I will text you the numbers, and you can send me the cost and details along with the date."

"I am not giving you my number. Just send it to the hotel email address, and I'll message you back with the details."

"You don't have to give it to me, Love; your delivery driver has it written right here on your invoice. Talk soon," he says before hanging up the phone.

I'm such an idiot! I never should have put my cell number on the company's info. Damn it. I have to think fast about what to do about the whole Alpha meeting issue. On the plus side, my truck is on its way—and a fridge. I'll count it as a win for now.

CHAPTER
TWENTY-EIGHT

The wedding goes without a hitch. For the first time in days, I breathe a sigh of relief. Leaving the night manager to handle the end of the wedding, I settle behind my desk, getting ready to finish up for the day. I'm about to log out when my phone vibrates. It's a text from Valen.

'It's Valen: Still waiting for that invoice?'

I plan on ignoring him and dealing with it tomorrow, but his next text has me scrambling for my email.

'Do I need to stop over and deal with it personally?'

'Sending it through now, and the booking confirmation,' I quickly reply, going through the calendar to find a suitable date. I add it to the schedule just as an idea hits me. If it costs too much, he'll surely decline.

I write up the invoice and send it through to his work email he messaged from earlier in the day. I chuckle to myself when my phone starts vibrating on my desk. I stifle my laugh and pick it up.

"Fifty thousand dollars!" Valen exclaims. I pull the phone away, so he doesn't hear me laughing, before composing myself.

"That extra half-star rating costs a lot. You wouldn't know—you only have...what is it? Four stars?" I tell him, having a dig at the fact my hotel's rating is currently half a star higher than his.

"It's outrageous! What are you serving to make it cost that much! Do I at least get my cock sucked for that much?" he asks.

"Oh, you know, the finest finger food: fairy bread—with premium sprinkles—and hot dogs with ketchup; the good stuff reserved specifically for the Blood Alpha. If I'm feeling generous, I may add in a piñata and goody bags. As for the cocksucking, I am sure that Ashley will do a fine job; I would rather skip on any STDs," I tell him. Valen growls.

"I don't have an STD. You think this will turn me away?" he snaps.

"I am hoping so."

"No, chance. Fine, you want to serve all the Alphas in the City kids party food, go for it. Check your bank in the morning; the money will be there. Oh, and Everly?"

"Yes, Alpha," I say, bored and wanting to go to bed.

"I will be seeing you very soon, and if I am paying this much, it will come with a happy ending from you personally." He laughs and hangs up. I wonder what he means...

I hadn't even gotten back to my apartment when my bank notified me that a payment was placed into the hotel's bank account. That was fast! I groan as I open it and see that it was definitely from Valen.

"Damn it," I mutter. I was so sure he would refuse. Not only is he officially holding the Alpha meeting here, but he's also paid in full, and I now have to host four packs. The girls are going to kill me! The last thing rogues want is to be spoken down to by social elites all night. Plus, the catering team will be fuming when they see they won't just be cooking for one Alpha but four, plus a few neighboring cities' Alphas!

Hmm, I could bribe them with a bonus, maybe?

Stepping inside, I find Zoe watching TV, yawning. She looks back at me over the couch.

"Oh no, what happened?"

"We may be hosting the Alpha meeting. Well, we *are* hosting the Alpha meeting."

Zoe sighs. "This is what you didn't want to tell Macey and me when we asked how you got the delivery truck and a fridge in?"

I nod, chewing my lip nervously.

"Charge him double; that will send him packing."

"I charged him fifty thousand."

"WHAT!" Zoe says, looking floored. "That'll definitely send him elsewhere!" She laughs, but I don't.

"No. No, it didn't," I shrug, pressing my lips in a line grimly. "He paid in full."

"That son of a–...lovely lady," Zoe corrects.

"Shit, what do we do about the kids—Valarian and Casey? Both their fathers will be there, and if Micah is here, guaranteed he'll bring his mate," Zoe says, chewing her lip worriedly. Micah is Casey's father, and he still hasn't told his mate he has an illegitimate child, which worries Zoe because his mate, Ana, is struggling with fertility.

"Maybe we can ask Macey's mom? It's not for three weeks. We have time to figure something out."

"It is what it is," Zoe murmurs with a shrug.

"What about your father?" she asks.

"He'll probably just ignore me, I would say. I haven't seen him since the hardware store years ago."

"Maybe he might be over it; want to reconnect?"

"Maybe, but I don't think so. He tossed me away. Valarian asked me about my family today; also asked about Valen," I tell her.

"What did you say? I saw the family tree thing. Casey brought one home too."

"Valarian added you, Macey, and the girls on it," I smile.

"Damn-well better have! I am the best Auntie anyone could ask for," Zoe states, and I chuckle.

"Did they go down easy tonight?"

"Casey had a tummy ache, but Valarian went down easily. He asked when you would be home, and he was digging around in your room earlier, too. He took some pictures from the photo album."

I nod. "Yeah, I told him he could."

Zoe chews her lip nervously. "He overheard you on the phone earlier—asked what being marked meant."

"What did you tell him?" I ask, wishing I could stop time and keep Valarian from growing up and asking the questions he's bound to ask.

"That mates mark each other," Zoe says, shrugging.

"Shit." I pinch the bridge of my nose, thinking of how many new problems I've had since Valen came back into my life. He's been nothing but a series of unending problems. I didn't blame her for answering, though. What else could she say?

Zoe sighs. "Too smart for his own good sometimes, that boy is."

Two Days Later—**Monday**
We were running late for school drop-off this morning, and Zoe and I both forgot it's crazy hair day. Macey reminded us when we walked out this morning and saw the other kids' hair undone and messy, so we detoured to buy some spray-in hair color. Pulling up at the local grocery store, Zoe runs inside before returning with one can of electric blue hair color and one called *glitter bomb*. We pull both kids from her little yellow Volkswagen. Casey giggles excitedly as her hair is instantly changed to blue. Valarian, however, pouts.

"I don't want to look like a smurf," he says.

"Zoe said it was the only color they had left. It's for a good cause; it's to raise money for the children's hospital and for you kids to have fun," I tell him.

"What about the glitter one?" Zoe asks. Valarian crosses his arms, looking at Casey dancing around the parking lot beside the car in her blue hair.

"No, it will make my hair sticky," he says.

"Come on, Val, just a little," I beg him. Gosh, this child is difficult sometimes. Would it kill him to be a kid for once?

"You will be the only kid without your hair done," Zoe tells him, and he side-eyes Casey.

"Please?" I ask.

"Fine, just one line," Valarian gives in, and Zoe draws a glitter line from the front of his head to the back, then shrugs. You can barely see it in his dark hair.

"Better than nothing," she says, and we count it as a win.

Climbing back in the car, we head to the school. The school is run-down and derelict looking, covered in graffiti, and there are only around two hundred students total. It angers me that only two streets away on this side of the main street is Alpha Valen's prestigious pack school, and across the road, three other pack schools— good schools. Yet, children of rogues or 'rogue whores' are apparently undeserving of getting a proper education. The least they could allow would be actual teachers—some of ours are barely educated enough to teach. Valarian is smart too; he may even be smarter than some of the teachers. The kids' teachers are waiting out the front, all done up in colorful clothes and crazy hair like the students.

When we enrolled the kids in school, Macey, Zoe, and I were given a tour; they barely had a library and only one old computer to be shared among the kids. We decided to raise money for the school, so for two weeks, half of all hotel sales and room fees went to the school. It was clear the packs weren't going to help, but in a way, they did without knowing it by attending the fair we held at the hotel. We raised enough to buy new laptops, and the library actually looks like a library, half the shelves packed with different books.

"I just had an idea on what the bonus from the Alpha meeting can be used for," I tell Zoe.

"I still can't believe he paid it." Zoe laughs.

I point to the run-down play equipment. Macey's daughter Taylor fell off last week and broke her arm after falling through the bridge between the two platforms. "Was going to ask those willing to cater for the event if they would take a double bonus for the night and the rest of the amount goes towards the school playground?"

Zoe smiles. "You know they'll say yes. Look how keen they were for the fair we held; everyone has kids that go here. Thank you, Alpha Valen," she murmurs.

"Yes, but it's also a big ask for them to put up with the Alpha-holes," I tell her, and she snickers.

"True, but they'll be happy to do it, you'll see," Zoe says, smiling more brightly. I can tell she's excited; we all get excited when it comes to helping the other rogues and children.

Opening the back door, I let Valarian out and peck him on the cheek—he instantly wipes it off.

"What's wrong with you?" I ask him. He scowls uncharacteristically.

"Who were you talking to on Saturday?" Valarian asks. He's been in a mood all weekend.

"Just the delivery people," I tell him, knowing exactly what he's referring to. He's been probing me all weekend every chance he got about his father.

"You're lying. You said he couldn't mark you; I heard a man's voice. Zoe said mates mark each other. Why did you say that man couldn't mark you? Is he your mate, is it my dad?" he asks. I glance at Zoe, who mouths *sorry* at me.

"No, sweetie, it was a figure of speech," I lie, but his eyes narrow, seeing straight through me—this kid is too observant. "Is this why you've been upset lately?"

"Why isn't my dad your mate?" he asks with a hint of demand in his voice. Glancing around, I notice the teachers busying themselves, pretending not to overhear. All this over some homework. I sigh, wondering if I can find a way around this.

"Billy said you're a 'rogue whore' and that's why my dad isn't around."

"He said that, did he?" I ask with a growl. Billy is a little punk and he and Valarian are always fighting

"Yep, so I punched him in his ugly face. But then I thought about what he said, and now I want to know!" he demands.

"Ok, we can talk about this when you get home," I tell him, and he glares at me.

"The wind will change, and your face will get stuck like that," I tell him, and he huffs, folding his arms across his chest. His face doesn't budge. "Not here, Valarian."

"Fine, but when I get home, I want to know who my dad is and why I can't see him," he says, frowning. "I don't like them calling you and Auntie Zoe names," he adds, and I smile grimly.

"Well, Billy's dad is a rogue because he spat in his Alpha's face," Zoe adds behind me. Valarian makes a face of disgust.

"See? He's just a nasty boy," I tell Valarian.

"You promise you'll tell me?" he asks.

I sigh and look at Zoe and she frowns.

"I will tell you what I can."

"Pinky promise?"

"Pinky promise," I say, grabbing his little pinky, and his mood seems to lift slightly before he turns around.

Now, I have to figure out what I can tell him without giving too much away.

He rushes off toward the front gate with Casey, and I see Taylor there waiting for them.

"Hey Auntie Zoe, Auntie Eva," Taylor calls, waving eagerly with her broken arm in a cast covered in brightly colored drawings and names.

"Hey, sweetie!"

"Can I come over and swim on the weekend?" she calls back.

"Of course. If you like, I'll even ask your mother for a sleepover," I tell her, knowing I'm off this weekend. It's the first weekend I've had off in a year. The girls insisted, and I was actually looking forward to giving Zoe a break. Macey always jokes we'll never need men because we have each other and are practically married with the way we handle the kids between us.

"Yes!" Taylor fist bumps the air excitedly.

Zoe waves goodbye, and I climb back in the passenger seat with a sigh, missing my truck. However, on the short drive home, I pass Alpha Valen going the other way in his Black Mercedes. The windows are blacked out, but it's the only one of those cars I've seen before; it has to be him.

"Pull over and turn around," I tell Zoe. She looks for a safe place to turn around and we head back the way he was driving.

When we find his car, it's parked in front of the public library and he's already out of it.

"Is that Alpha Valen's car?" Zoe asks, and I nod.

"No. No. Whatever you're thinking, no," Zoe says, pulling in beside it. "What *are* you going to do?"

"He ruined Valarie's car, so I'm going to ruin his," I say. Furthermore, I'm still pissed off about the entire school thing. Seeing the giant school two streets away that no rogue child can attend irritates me. The kids always ask what the big building they can see from the main road is.

The pristine, white sandstone school was erected when the first packhouse was, along with the church the kids also aren't allowed to attend. Pack members are allowed to travel freely where they want, as long as they follow the local pack's rules while visiting other territories. A rogue isn't even allowed to look, let alone attend anything that isn't on the main street or in the designated rogue areas.

Getting out, Zoe squeaks.

"Eve!" she hisses when I grab the cans of hairspray and start digging through her trunk. "What are you looking for?"

"Got a screwdriver?" I ask her.

"You scratch that car, he will lose it."

"Not going to ruin its paint. Besides, this crap will wash off with water," I tell her. She rolls her eyes before rummaging around and passing me a tire valve remover.

"Why do you have that?" I ask. She shrugs, looking up at the sky.

"I may have used it on Micah's car a few times," she mutters, and I raise an eyebrow at her.

"And *you* are trying to stop *me*? You're just as bad as I am."

"He owed me child support," Zoe huffs. I chuckle. I intended to stab the tires, but this will work even better.

I set to work, tossing the can of spray glitter to Zoe, who uses it to cover his car while also keeping a lookout.

The air wheezes out of the tires quickly as I race to the front window and write on it with the blue spray dye.

'Alphahole xx' I write instead of 'asshole'.

His tires all flat, I quickly rush back to Zoe's car and we laugh as we drive away. We did no real damage, but it will be annoying. I wonder why he's at the public library?

"You know he will figure it out?" Zoe says.

"Innocent until proven guilty."

"Who else would be game enough to do that to the Blood Alpha?" Zoe snickers. She has a point—no one crosses him.

"Stuff him; he deserves it for making our kids attend shitty schools and for forcing me to hold the Alpha meeting. He'll live and I doubt he'll bat an eyelash at the cost to get it towed and fixed if he's willing to pay fifty thousand dollars for an Alpha meeting," I reply.

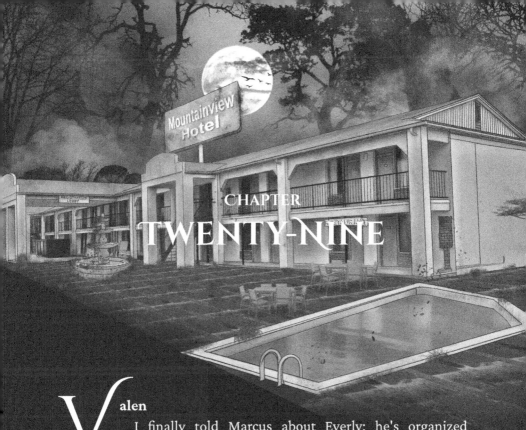

CHAPTER
TWENTY-NINE

Valen

I finally told Marcus about Everly; he's organized patrols to run through the reserve for me to keep an eye on the back end of her hotel. Someone broke the fence and I'm arranging for it to be fixed. Hopefully, sometime today, someone will be able to go out there—otherwise I'll go myself.

Marcus and I just finished at the library. No luck. We found no records of an Everly Summers before five years ago—nobody by the name Everly at all. The only thing we managed to find was the hotel's data and something stating she was in the hospital almost five years ago, yet it doesn't say what for or which part of the hospital. The lady behind the counter told us to try the werewolf council because she can't even access her own files for some reason.

"The name sounds so familiar," Marcus says, shaking his head. "It's right on the tip of my tongue. I just can't, for the life of me, figure out where I've heard it. And don't you think it's a little odd that not even you can access her files?"

"Obviously," I tell him.

"She has to be hiding something. Why are there no records of an

Everly or a Summers? Everly is a unique name. I'm sure I don't know anyone with that name, but somehow it just sounds so familiar," Marcus repeats.

We're about to head to the council chambers to look in the birth records, or any records for that matter—even bank statements. Marcus hits the button on his key fob and the blinkers flash, signaling it's unlocked. Then we both stop dead in our tracks.

"What the hell! What happened to my car!" Marcus shrieks, rushing over to his beloved car. He just bought it a week ago, having liked mine so much. I press my lips in a line, glancing around for any culprits, and spot the library's security cameras that point at the parking lot.

"Alphahole?" Marcus says, and I walk over to the front of his car. "They've mistaken me for you. Which bastard would do this?" he growls angrily.

"They removed your tire valves too," I point out, gesturing to his flattened tires. He starts shaking, fur sprouting along his arms in his anger. He spent all day yesterday polishing and cleaning it, and even made me take my shoes off before I got in it this morning.

"When I catch this fucker..." he seethes.

"Well, you're in luck," I tell him, pointing to the cameras and cutting him off. He smiles, rubbing his hands together.

"Their asses are mine," he growls, stomping toward the library entrance again. Heads will roll when he catches them. Unless...

I suddenly have a sneaking suspicion that Everly's name is all over this. No one else would dare touch anything belonging to me. I smile at her tenacity to try to get revenge. Chuckling to myself, I follow Marcus—I may have to stop the riot he will no doubt cause in his wrath.

The woman at the counter smiles when we return, pushing her glasses up the bridge of her nose.

"You're back, Alpha, Beta. What can I help you with this time?" She smiles pleasantly.

"I need to see your security footage," Marcus all but growls. The woman startles, shrinking in her seat. I grip his shoulder, tugging him away as his aura rushes out; a few people glance at us nervously.

"May we look at the security footage, please, Agatha? Someone has trashed his car out the front."

"Certainly, Alpha, right this way," she says, jumping down from her seat and disappearing behind the counter. I lean over to look at her—her head barely comes to the top of her desk. How in the world does she climb onto that stool? She's so short, she's probably barely taller than a child, and a small one at that.

Marcus glares around at the people, looking for the assailant. I chuckle, shaking my head as I nudge him toward Agatha, who walks out from behind the counter.

"Holy shit, you're short," he says as though he doesn't realize he spoke his thoughts out loud. Agatha glares and I elbow him.

"What? She is! She's the perfect height for–"

"Zip it," I tell him. There's no telling what kind of trouble Marcus would get himself into when he's angry like this.

"Well, she is," he mutters, following her. She leads us to the back of the library and unlocks a door before pushing it open for us. She glares at Marcus, who pretends not to see as he walks in.

"I will be at my desk if you need help; the password is 'Red-moon'," she says before sticking her nose up like it will make her taller and walking away.

"Bet her wolf looks like a chihuahua," Marcus laughs before walking over to the laptop. He types in the password, then begins flicking through the files to find the parking lot video. After pulling up today's date, he starts rewinding. The security footage isn't the best.

He stops it at the point we pulled into the lot. I watch our blurry figures walk into the library and about five minutes later, a little yellow Volkswagen pulls in beside his car.

I instantly recognize not only the car, but the blue uniform Zoe has on and the black one Everly always wears.

"Their faces are too fuzzy. Does it zoom in?" Marcus growls, hitting the button a little too hard.

"No need, I know who they are," I tell him with a laugh.

"Who? Take me to them. I'll smack them into next week."

"Woah, Rocky, settle down. You really want to beat on a girl?"

"How do you know it's a girl? That could be anyone," he says, squinting at the blurry figures on the screen.

"One, because I know the car; two, I recognize the uniforms."

Marcus turns in his seat to look at me.

"It's my mate and her friend she lives with. She saw my car the other day. I bet she thought your car was mine," I chuckle.

"Your bond trashed my car?" he snaps, glaring at the screen.

"Appears so."

"Well, you better say something to her, or I will," he growls.

"Don't worry about it. I'll handle it," I tell him, pulling my phone from my pocket and sending Everly a text.

'Where are you?'

It takes her a few minutes for her to reply.

'Work, where else would I be?'

'Didn't happen to stop by the library today, did you?'

'No, been at work all morning, us rogues have no need for books. We aren't entitled to an education.'

I briefly wonder what the meaning of the last part of her message is. I have no doubt it's to have a dig at me about something out of my control.

'Next time you want to vandalize my Beta's car, check for security cameras. I have a very pissed-off Beta to deal with because of you.'

'Well, tell him I am sorry his Alpha is an Asshole. I thought it was yours. I will double-check next time.'

'There will be a next time?'

'.... Depends'

'You are playing games with the wrong person, Everly, you won't win.'

'$50k in my bank account says otherwise. But get this: you paid $35k too much; the rogue school says thank you for your considerable donation

to their play equipment. Would you like mini sausage rolls and party pies to go with your frankfurts and fairy bread?'

'I would prefer you, served on a silver platter. Think you can organize that?'

'I prefer gold.'

'Gold it is then.'

'Dreaming!!!'

'Only of you. So, would you like to come and apologize for your misjudgment? I accept all kinds of begging, sexual favors, but it could all be forgotten and forgiven for a simple mate mark?'

'Hard pass. Beta Marcus should choose his friends more carefully, and his cars, apparently.'

Beta Marcus? How does she know my Beta's name? I know he's in the public eye a lot, but he's never mentioned by name. And the rogue school? We have rogue schools, sure, but why would she give them so much money?

I need to check out this rogue school her friend's kid goes to. Maybe generosity is the way to get in her good graces. But first, I must get even for my grumpy Beta. I doubt me giving money away to the rogue school would be a good enough punishment for him.

"Why are you smiling like an idiot, Valen? What about my car?" says Marcus—his anger clearly hasn't evaporated.

"Send it for detailing," I tell him, waving him off. Marcus growls as I start dialing Richard's number. He works at the city's police station and is usually on highway patrol.

"Yes, Alpha?"

"Hey, Rich. I have a favor to ask."

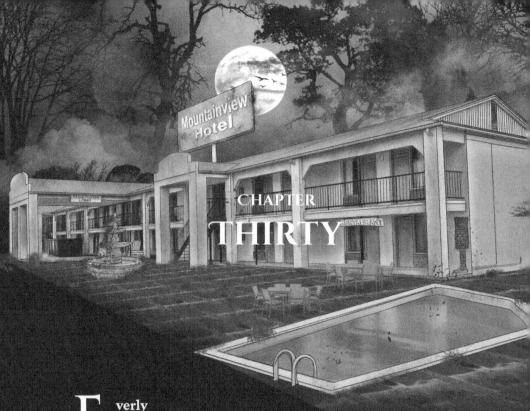

E verly
We're just pulling out of the hotel to go pick the kids up from school. I managed to find an old photo on the internet today of Alpha Valen when he was a teenager—hopefully that will quell Valarian's burning curiosity and the questions he has about his father.

I still have no idea what to tell him about his father being my mate, or if I should even tell him that part; he'll question me more. I'm hoping to find a way around that one. We're almost there when we hear sirens go off behind us just as Zoe pulls onto the school's road. She curses under her breath, and glances in the rearview mirror.

"Shit," I say. "I wonder why they're pulling us over? You're not doing anything wrong." Maybe Zoe was accidentally speeding?

Zoe's brows furrow and she pulls over onto the side of the road. She immediately rummages for her registration papers from the glove box, nearly spilling the contents on the floor as she digs for her insurance and registration documents. A moment later, the officer knocks on the window and she winds it down.

"Afternoon, ladies," he says. Zoe looks at him like a deer in head-lights; I watch her hands tremble nervously. Her sudden fear confuses me.

"Afternoon, officer," I answer when she says nothing and only stares at the man. I give him a brief wave.

"License and registration," he asks, holding his hand out for the documents in Zoe's hand. Zoe fumbles and I raise an eyebrow at her. Why is she so nervous?

"Here, sir," she stammers, passing her documentation to him. He looks it over briefly and hands it back to her.

"I am afraid I have to book you for..." he pauses, walking around the car before kneeling in front of her Volkswagen and looking under it. He gets up, walking around to my side, checking the exterior of the car.

"...bald tires," he states.

I raise an eyebrow before I grit my teeth. Fucking Valen—it had to be him. This cop doesn't even look like he knows why he's pulling us over and it's clear he's looking for any reason to target us.

"They're brand new!" Zoe argues.

The officer shrugs and starts writing her a ticket just as Macey suddenly pulls up behind us.

"Friend of yours?" he asks, and I look over the back seat to see her getting out of her car.

"Is everything alright, officer?" Macey asks, coming over and stopping beside him. He doesn't even glance at her, just continues jotting down on his notepad.

"Yes, your friend here has bald tires."

"Bald tires?" Macey asks, looking at the wheels, clearly none of which are bald.

"Yep, I'm giving her a ticket; she shall have fourteen days to fix the issue or I will pull her car from the road," he explains.

"This is bullshit," Zoe mutters.

"Pardon, ma'am?" the officer asks with a coy smile on his lips.

"Nothing, sir," she grinds out through clenched teeth, looking back out the windshield. Her knuckles turn white as she grips the steering wheel and I see a bead of sweat run down the back of her neck. The officer chuckles before handing her the paper.

"I'll be seeing you later," he states.

"Hopefully not," Macey says and he laughs, wandering back to his car.

"Are you alright? You totally freaked out when he tapped on your window," I tell Zoe. Macey stops next to her window, watching the officer walk back to his car.

"Zoe?" Macey asks when she doesn't answer me. Macey looks at her, concerned.

"That's Micah's father," Zoe admits.

I gasp, swiveling my head to look back at the man as he pulls away and back into the traffic.

"His father is a cop? Does he know about Casey?"

"No, of course not," Zoe says.

"I thought when he pulled me over... I don't know. I thought maybe he found out about Casey and would take her from me," Zoe breathes.

"No one is taking our kids from us," I reassure her, but she grips the steering wheel tighter. I rub her back and she takes some deep breaths.

"Come on, we should get the kids," I tell her, and Macey reaches in, giving her hand a squeeze before going back to her car.

Macey leaves first and we pull out behind her. We're nearly at the school when she, too, gets pulled over by the same officer.

"That prick!" I growl, watching Macey pull over to the curb in front of the school. Other parents are staring at her and the officer when he gets out of his car.

We pull up a few cars down from her. Macey is standing on the sidewalk, arms folded and looking furious.

"What did he get *you* for?" I ask when she catches up with us.

"Apparently, my blinker is broken, and even though I've been using them all day just fine, he reckons me turning them on was a fluke," Macey states, glaring at the officer, who appears to be having far too much fun. The bell sounds and the children rush out. Macey, glancing at the kids, suddenly touches the officer, pulling his attention away from the students pouring from the school.

Zoe quickly rushes over, shielding Casey with her body and keeping her out of sight of the officer. Casey is staring at her mother as Zoe forces her in the car and straps her in quickly, clearly wondering why she's in such a rush. The other kids coming out all eye the officer and murmur that he has a gun. The other Rogue parents also rush off quickly, probably thinking he'll start booking everyone. I shake my head, holding my hand out for Valarian and helping him into the car.

"Want us to take Taylor?" I ask and Macey shakes her head.

"No, go ahead. I need to drop her at mom's anyway," she calls out, making sure to cut off any view of us behind her as she leans on her car. Once we're in and pulling away, I see Macey opening her back door and buckling Taylor into her booster seat.

We drive off and Zoe lets out a breath of relief. It's short-lived; as we're about to pull into the hotel's driveway, we hear sirens blaring and the cop car coming up behind us at high speed.

"For fuck' sake, not again!" Zoe says before her eyes dart to Casey in the back of the car.

"Swear jar," Casey calls out.

"Casey, duck down in your seat for me," Zoe tells her, and her little brows push together. Valarian studies them with his ever-watchful gaze as he glances between the officer and Casey, ducking down in her seat.

Zoe mutters under her breath. I see the officer get out of his car in the rearview mirror. Zoe immediately does the same, to prevent him from spotting Casey. As the officer approaches the car, I see him purposely peer into the trunk and rearview mirror. Just as he basically presses his nose against the window, Casey looks up. He looks next at Zoe, confused but mostly angry.

That's all it takes: one glance and you can sense your family, relatives, or mates—unless incapacitated by drugs or alcohol.

"That's my son's.... kid?" he snarls, pressing his hands against the glass and looking in while Zoe tries to stop him.

"Why do you have her? How... I don't understand. Open this door now!" he bellows.

I get out of the car quickly. Zoe is pulling on the officer's arm as he tries to make his way to Casey's side of the vehicle.

"I will arrest you for kidnapping," he snarls at Zoe.

"Get away from her! You aren't taking her!" Zoe says, trying to shove him away from the car.

"Just try to stop me. Move."

I stand in front of Casey's door and he grips the handle before pushing me out of his way. Casey starts crying when I stumble, catching myself before I fall.

I look in the window to see Casey climbing out of her seat and moving closer to Valarian, who wraps his arms around her.

"Move, lady, I need to double-check something," he snaps at Zoe, who tosses herself in front of the door, blocking him from opening it. Seemingly without thinking, she shoves him and I gasp.

"Get the fuck away from my daughter," she growls in warning, her eyes turning obsidian and her canines and claws slip out.

The officer growls at her, but she doesn't budge. He goes to grab her, but she slashes his arm with her claws. Furious now, he lunges at her, fumbling for his handcuffs. As he tries to snap them on her wrist, his gun falls from his holster.

The officer tosses her against the side of her car, trying to restrain her. Zoe struggles and I try to grab him to make him let her go. I've never seen anything like it before. Zoe is completely wild and crazed as she continues lashing out, her protective instincts kicking in.

A sick feeling grows in the pit of my stomach as I realize I'm watching my worst fear play out before my eyes. Seeing this, I think about how it would feel if someone took Valarian, and the pain hits me in my heart. Just as I'm thinking this, I feel a sharp pain collide with the side of my face. The officer backhands me, tossing me off, and I hit the ground. He looks at me briefly and curses. I feel blood trickle down my lip.

"I didn't mean that. Fuck! He'll fucking kill me," he says while trying to restrain Zoe. Both kids scream as they watch. Through my haze and headache, I hear a car skid to a stop. I turn to see Macey jump out of her car in a fury before she grips the officer's shirt, ripping him off Zoe, and he stumbles back, shocked. Macey gets between them as I scramble to get to my feet.

"There are kids present, officer. Do you really want to scare your granddaughter?" she snaps at him, and he halts his advance toward her.

"So she is?" the officer asks, looking in the back window.

"Please, please," Zoe begs, dropping to her knees and falling apart in her desperation.

"Answer me!" the officer roars at Zoe and takes a step toward her, but Macey growls, taking a step toward him too, her claws slipping out.

"Yes, yes, she's Micah's," Zoe says, looking at him pleadingly. The officer looks between Macey and Zoe before barging past Macey to get to the car.

The officer steps forward and Zoe tries to stop him, but he flings the rear door open and leans in. He reaches for Casey, but she flinches away from him before sniffing the air.

"Come here, sweetheart. Poppy won't hurt you," the officer says, holding out his hands to her. Casey looks at her mother, and Zoe's shoulders sag, her face streaked with tears and running mascara.

"I swear, if you try to take her, I will do everything in my power to stop you—spend every cent we have to fight you for custody if you try to take her from Zoe," I threaten him. The officer looks at me, pulling Casey from the car. I grip his arm. "You take her, I will call my mate—I will call the blood Alpha," I growl low enough for only him to hear. He stops, glancing at me. I didn't want to use his name, but it has the right effect; he instantly pauses.

"You... you won't tell him... I didn't mean to make you..." he glances at my split lip.

"That depends; give her daughter back," I tell him, and Zoe jumps to her feet and reaches for her. However, the officer turns his back on her and sits Casey on the hood of her car.

"Does Micah know about her?" he asks, looking at Zoe.

"Yes, he knows," Zoe tells him and the officer growls but turns back to Casey brushing her hair from her face.

"What's your name, princess?" he asks her.

"Casey," she whispers shyly, wiping her eyes before glancing at her mother. She reaches for Zoe and the officer looks at her.

"He never told us. He and his mate are having trouble conceiving," the officer states.

"That is not my issue, or Casey's. Ana doesn't need to know about her," Zoe tells him.

The man nods, looking at Casey and smiling sadly. "Can I bring my wife, Olena, to meet her?" he asks.

"Are you going to tell Ana that Micah has a daughter?" Zoe asks.

"No, but I will be saying something to my son. Does he help with her?" he asks.

"He pays child support," Zoe says, placing Casey back in the car. She buckles her in, and the officer looks over her shoulder, his eyes going to Valarian for a second.

"He's mine," I tell the officer when I see him looking at Valarian curiously.

"Does Valen know?" he suddenly asks, and I swallow. Valarian looks at me questioningly.

"No, he doesn't."

"He has his eyes, the resemblance is uncanny," the officer remarks, and I look away.

"I will let your wife meet Casey, but only if you don't say anything to Alpha Valen about Valarian; let Everly tell him when she's ready," Zoe says quickly. The officer thinks for a second, looking in at Casey and waving to her.

"You *will* tell him? I know his father has been putting pressure on him to marry and give him an heir, even lined up an arranged marriage with Alpha John's daughter, Ava," the officer shakes his head.

"What?" I ask, trying not to let my tone sound as surprised as I feel. The officer shrugs.

"That's the rumor going around the city. Valen said no, but if he doesn't show he has an heir soon, his father will cause trouble. You're best off telling him before his father finds out about your son. I won't take Casey from her mother, but Kalen *will* take your boy if he finds out about him, especially if he finds out you're a rogue before Valen marks you; reputation is everything to Kalen," the officer states. And don't I know it; Alpha Kalen ruined his own mate, all because she was an Omega.

"He isn't Valen's," I quickly state. It's clear the officer knows I'm Valen's mate, but I can deny Valarian being his son. The officer snorts and laughs while shaking his head.

"The eyes are a dead giveaway—also his little Alpha aura. I can already feel it, so I bet you can too. He is definitely an Alpha in the making; no need to lie to me. Alpha Valen told me you were his mate. But he never mentioned a son. His resemblance and aura will give the boy away to anyone paying close enough attention to him, Everly. I suggest you tell Valen soon—I would hate for you to lose your son," the officer says, closing the rear door. I can see the questions burning through Valarian's gaze as he listens.

"You have a week. After that, I will have no choice but to tell him. I'm sorry. Also, I kind of need to give you a ticket again for something. Valen will ask questions if he doesn't see multiple tickets—he told me to harass you and your friends. Don't worry, I won't lodge them, but I need it for appearance's sake; unless you try to stop me seeing my granddaughter. My wife will be so excited," he gushes, beaming happily at Casey, who waves to him.

"You can see her, but Ana must not know," Zoe says.

"Never liked her much; snobby piece of work that woman is. Can

I bring my wife by over the weekend? You ladies work at the Mountain View Hotel?"

"We own it," I tell him, and his mouth opens in disbelief.

"But you're rogues."

"And that doesn't make us any less capable," I tell him.

"I guess not," the officer says, looking at us all in shock.

While I feel relieved that the officer didn't take Casey, I can't help the sinking feeling in the pit of my stomach. I'm worried that too many people know my secret. I know it's only a matter of time before Valen finds out, with the city being a gossip mill. It's inevitable. No secret stays buried forever, and I can see this is one of those secrets that will eventually come out.

The officer picks up his gun and puts it back in his holster before glancing at me.

"You won't tell your mate about?" he points to my lip.

"It can stay between us, as long as you stick to your word and don't try to take Casey. Everyone knows not to cross the Blood Alpha —I have a feeling he won't take too kindly to anyone that hurts his mate."

He nods, glancing at the car. "I'll see you on the weekend, Zoe," he says, inclining his head to Zoe, who nods before climbing back in her car.

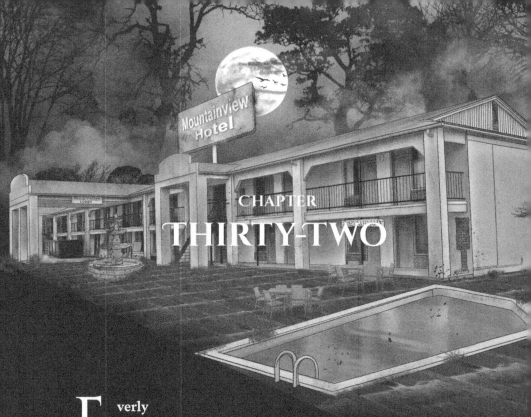

CHAPTER
THIRTY-TWO

Everly

I've been trying to avoid the conversation all night, but Valarian has followed me around the hotel like a bad smell, and as we head to the apartment, I have no choice but to face the pint-sized Alpha. I never thought I would fear my son, but his aura is in full force. All afternoon, people had been glancing at him as he trailed after me while I worked. I could see their curiosity—there's no way I could deny what he is, that he's an Alpha child. Even Zoe has been wary around him, and as soon as we finished for the day, she practically bolted to bathe Casey, leaving me with my fuming son.

Valarian slams the door loudly as he walks in after me. I'm not used to him acting out of anger—he never even threw tantrums as a baby. At least he held his tongue while I finished work. When I'm finally home, I take my shoes off to rest a bit. But there's no hiding from his ever-present gaze. The officer had said too much in front of him.

"You lied to me," Valarian states as I flick on the kettle. I grab two mugs down from the cupboard, intending to make him hot chocolate, but he smacks my hands as I go to set the mugs on the counter. The glass shatters on the ground at my feet. I press my lips together at his acting out. I know he's mad, but there was no need for that.

"Enough!" I snap at him, and he glares at me.

"You lied," he says before growling, which startles me.

"I did not lie; I just didn't tell you the whole truth."

"You said my father wasn't your mate. You said he didn't live in this city," he accuses.

"I never said that; you just assumed he didn't live here, and I simply let you believe you were correct."

"I hate you," Valarian snarls at me, tears burning his eyes. His words twist my stomach painfully and I'm hit with waves of guilt.

"Valarian, you don't understand. It isn't safe for you to know him," I try to explain.

"Why? I hate that everyone says you're a rogue whore; that everyone treats us differently. I see the way people look at you because we aren't part of a pack because you don't have a mate," Valarian says.

"We don't need him, I don't need him, we do fine on our own," I try to tell him while trying to put a comforting hand on his shoulder.

"You may not want him as a mate, but I want my dad. I don't want to be the rogue whore's son, I don't want to be treated the way everyone treats you. I want my dad," Valarian cries.

Pain radiates through my chest at his words—the rogue whore's son. He hates how people see me, see him, and that realization hurts more than anything else he said. It was one thing for an adult to be embarrassed, but for him to be embarrassed for who people think I am...

For the first time in a long time, I'm ashamed of the title bestowed on me. I rub a hand down my face, trying to find a way to explain.

"Well, you can't have him. He—"

"Does he know about me?" Valarian cuts me off, and I look at him. His bottom lip quivers and a tear escapes, rolling down his cheek. I reach for him again, but he steps away from me.

"Does my dad know I exist?" he asks again.

"As I said, Valarian, it isn't safe."

"For you or for me?" he demands. This boy is so much more intelligent than I give him credit for, more observant than I even realized. He's far more advanced than he should be for a child of his age.

"He doesn't, does he? Was everything you said a lie? What about your family?"

I sigh. "My family tossed me away when they found out I was pregnant with you; they threw me away because I was a rogue whore."

"But the officer, he said this Valen was your mate, that I looked like him."

Of all the times Valen could mess with me, why did it have to be when my son was present to witness?

"Alpha Valen is your father. He is also my mate," I admit to him.

"Then why isn't it safe? He has a pack. We could be a real family."

"We are a real family, Valarian; we don't need him to be a real family. We have Zoe and Macey and everyone here," I explain.

"It's not the same," he protests.

"It is. How do you know it would be different?"

"It's not the same!" he screams at me.

"Sometimes family isn't what you expect it to be, Valarian. My family doesn't want me, they don't want you. You have people here that are family to us. They want us."

"And my father? Would he want me if he knew about me? Does he want you?"

I drop my head, and my shoulders sag. "It's not safe."

"Why?" Valarian screams, his face turning red.

"Because he will take you from me!" I yell back at him just as Zoe comes out.

"Everly?" Zoe asks before pointing at the door; five long marks have been gouged deep into the wood. Valarian is looking at me with fear in his eyes for the first time. Startled by his fearful expression, I look down to see my claws have slipped out. Zoe tugs Valarian away from me and he lets her comfort him, something I should be doing, not her.

"Go! Run it off, Everly," Zoe says, and Valarian rushes off to his room.

"Valarian!" I call after him, but Zoe grips both my arms.

"Go, calm down. You can talk to Valarian tomorrow when everyone is more level-headed."

Valen

Officer Richards called just as I was sitting down for dinner. I smile when I see the phone ring, wondering how long it will take before I receive an angry call from Everly, complaining about officers harassing her and her friends.

"Richards," I answer.

"Alpha, I did what you asked, but no more. I can't do it tomorrow."

"And why is that?"

"Well, for one, she threatened me with you for starters, and secondly, I don't want to ruin my chances with Zoe."

"What do you mean 'ruin your chances with Zoe'?"

"I... um... turns out my son has a daughter. Zoe agreed to let me bring Olena to meet her."

"Wait, Micah has a daughter?" I ask, perplexed.

"Yes, Zoe's child is my granddaughter; I met her today when I pulled her over."

I sigh. No doubt, Micah has some explaining to do, and Micah wanna do the right thing by Zoe and her kid.

"That's fine, Richards. You've done enough," I tell him.

"Thank you, Alpha. I can send you the tickets if you like?"

"No, it's fine. I trust you," I tell Officer Richards before hanging up. I barely placed my phone down when it rings in my hand again and I see my father's face pop up on the screen. Marcus is across the table from me, quietly stewing over his car, and I hand him the phone.

He glances at it and grits his teeth before rolling his eyes and answering it.

"Alpha Kalen," he answers in a bored tone. I hear my father ask where I am before Marcus answers.

"He's taking a shit. Ate something and has been running back and forth from the toilet all night." I grit my teeth and glare at him from across the table, and he smiles. "Yep, has a severe case of runny ass, crapped his pants in the elevator too; shit explosion."

My fists clench, and Marcus smirks at me, knowing if I speak, he'll have to put me on the phone.

"I will be sure to tell him. Night, Alpha." Marcus hangs up the phone and I growl at him.

"Was that fucking necessary?" I snap at him.

"Answer your own damn phone then," he retorts. "Oh, and your father recommends Imodium; apparently you can get it from a pharmacy," he taunts.

"What did he want?"

"He wanted to know if you made up your mind about Ava," Marcus shrugs before cutting into his steak.

I'm not marrying that woman; I want nothing to do with Alpha John, and the fact my father meddled still pisses me off. Me rejecting her will undoubtedly cause a war between packs, but I refuse to marry that girl.

"Richards?" he asks. I shrug.

"He said he won't help anymore."

"So that's it? She gets away with wrecking my car?"

"She didn't wreck your car. Besides, I'm planning on heading over there tomorrow; you can come if you want?" I smile and his eyes light up. Marcus has been begging me to take him there all day so he can give her a piece of his mind.

"About time I get to meet this woman that has you swooning and begging at her feet. Plus, I want to meet the woman who trashed my car and thinks she can get away with it," he adds.

I roll my eyes at his dramatics. "Oh, she can get away with it—she's my mate."

"If you expect me not to say something to her, you are sadly mistaken; she crossed the wrong Beta."

"You do realize you are her Beta too, right?"

"Only once you mark her."

"Be nice," I tell him, digging into my dinner. I can't help but feel the excitement bubble up within me, knowing I'll be going to see her tomorrow.

"What do you plan on doing about your father?" Marcus asks me. "Maybe tell him you found your mate," he offers, and I nod.

"Yeah, I don't think I have a choice now," I tell him honestly, and he hums in agreement. It's best we sort this feud out before it becomes an all-out war.

"All I know is I can't wait to meet her. If she has you this worked up, I bet she's a real crazy one in person," he laughs. I glare at him, and he shrugs.

"Well, she must be crazy. Who rejects an Alpha, especially a rogue woman?" he says.

"Any luck on her last name?" I ask.

"Nope, not really. I did find a Summers, however, but it was a maiden name."

"Are you going to leave me in suspense or tell me? Maybe that's how she became rogue? Maybe she divorced someone?"

"Doubtful, plus I doubt there's any relation because I can't see the Alpha shunning a family member."

"There are no Alphas with the last name Summers," I tell him, confused about what he's getting at.

"No, not an Alpha but a Luna; Summers is the maiden name of

Alpha John's wife—Claire Summers," Marcus tells me. I sigh. Another dead end.

However, something bothers me. There was something Ava had said to her father before he cut her off. But I'm sure it was a coincidence. If Alpha John had another child, we would know about her by now. Just look at Ava; she was a huge handful for him. If he had another child, he wouldn't be allowing the wayward one to be his successor, surely.

CHAPTER
THIRTY-THREE

Everly

I came home from my run to find Valarian sitting at the dining room table trying to use my laptop. My mood has lifted now I've gone for a run, but I'm exhausted as I untie my laces and slip my shoes off. The run really zapped my energy, and I had to take the long way around because someone fixed the hole in the fence. Tomorrow, I'll have to send someone to open it up again—or maybe install a gate, which would be ideal because we can lock it off at night. Zoe is watching TV with the volume low, barely audible. She smiles at me and gives me a nod, turning back to the TV and pretending to be watching it, when I know she's just keeping an eye on Valarian.

Valarian looks up at me—his cheek is red from resting it on his hand while he tries to use the laptop. Walking over to him, I run my fingers through his hair before bending down and kissing his forehead.

"What are you trying to do?" I ask him, glancing at the computer screen before standing and pulling out the chair beside him. He lets out a breath before looking at me.

"I wanna know who my dad is—why he left us. But I don't know his last name, and Auntie Zo' said to wait for you," he says. I can tell he's been crying; his eyes are all puffy and red, and he sniffles before plucking a tissue from the tissue box and blowing his nose.

He folds his damp tissue into a perfectly neat square before getting up, placing it in the bin, and washing his hands. I turn the laptop toward me before typing 'Alpha Valen Solace'; images and news articles pop up. Valarian takes his seat next to me and looks at the screen before looking over at me, and I gesture toward the laptop.

"That's your father," I tell him. He turns back to look at the screen.

"We have the same eyes," he says, looking at me. His own amber eyes peer up at me, lashes wet from crying. I nod sadly at him.

"Yes, you have his eyes; it's a genetic trait on the male's side," I tell him, and he glances back at the pictures of his father on the screen.

"When I got pregnant with you, I didn't know your father was my mate; we met at an Alpha meeting, and we were both drinking..."

"So you kissed and I was created?"

I chuckle at his words, and so does Zoe behind me.

"Yep, that pretty much sums it up," I tell him.

"So if you didn't know he was your mate, how did we end up rogue?"

"Because my father kicked me out. Because he thought I was a rogue whore, and I refused to terminate the pregnancy—I chose to keep you," I tell him honestly.

"So, I'm the reason you're a rogue?"

"No, I am. Me being a rogue is not your fault, and I would choose you every time. If I could go back, I would still choose you. You're my life."

He pauses, seeming to think, his face scrunched up in concentration. I cup his cheek, brushing my thumb over his cheek.

"Why were you at an Alpha meeting?"

"Because I used to be an Alpha. I was next in line to take over my father's pack."

He looks even more confused.

"So, did you only just find out my dad was your mate?"

I sigh before rubbing my eyes and shaking my head.

"I've known for a while. When I first found out I was pregnant, I tried to tell your father and he didn't believe me. I saw him again a couple of years later, but your dad was a bit tired and had too much to drink so he didn't recognize me. He was confused, and I think he thought I broke into his house, so he kicked me off his territory," I tell him.

"So, you never had a chance to tell him? How long ago?"

"Nearly four years ago now, when you were just a baby."

"So, you've known all that time... but I heard Auntie Macey say that Grandma Val died from not being with her mate—that not having your mate can kill you."

I bite my lip. "You shouldn't listen to adult conversations, sweetie."

"But is it true? Did she die because her mate didn't want her?"

I nod sadly, looking away. "But it won't happen to me; I have you to live for. I won't die, Valarian. I have too much to live for, you being the biggest," I tell him, and he nods, looking at the screen. He clicks on some photos, making them larger so he can see his father's features better and the pictures are clearer.

"Am I like him?"

"You are so much better than he will ever be."

"So he's a bad man?"

"No, I don't think so. Well, I don't think it's intentional; I think he's just perceived that way, kind of like how I'm perceived to have done something wrong. People believe things about people that may not be true. It's not fair, but it sometimes happens."

"I've seen him on the news fighting, and I saw him in the papers. I thought something was strange about him; I always felt funny when I saw his picture, but I didn't realize he was my dad," Valarian says.

"We recognize our own family. It's built into us to recognize family."

"So, he would know I was his son just by seeing me?"

"Yes, and that's why I can't let you meet him," I tell him.

"Because he'll take me from you?" he asks, and I nod. Valarian seems to think for a second as he stares at the screen, scrutinizing the picture of his father out in front of the hotel he owns.

"I can print his picture off for you if you want?"

He looks over at me and smiles sadly. "That's ok, I think I'll go to bed now," he says, getting up and taking the laptop with him. He kisses my cheek before looking at Zoe on the couch.

"Night, Auntie Zo'."

"Goodnight, sweetie," she replies, and I watch him leave.

"I'm sorry; he asked for the laptop..." she says once he leaves.

"It's fine, Zoe. I should have just told him."

It's the middle of the day, Valarian is at school, and we're in the middle of the lunch rush when the entire restaurant falls silent. Glancing up from the front counter, I groan internally when Alpha Valen walks into the restaurant. A smirk crosses his lips as he approaches me.

Zoe notices him and rolls her eyes before coming over to me. "I'll go check if the meat delivery has arrived; seeing as the Alpha-dick is here, we don't need any more unexpected disturbances or missing truck interferences," she says, glaring at him before walking away.

Valen approaches the counter and I can feel everyone watching us curiously when he leans on the counter, acting like he owns the place.

"Heard you had an eventful day yesterday with Officer Richards?" he chuckles.

"Yes, thanks to you. And you can pay for Zoe and Macey's fines," I snap at him.

"I'm sure if you go down to the office and explain I'm your mate, the fines will be dropped," he says, and I roll my eyes at him.

"Of course, they will be," I spit at him. He laughs.

"You already knew that, though, didn't you? Officer Richards told me something very interesting last night," he says, and my stomach drops. Richards said he wouldn't tell Valen about Valarian—at least not yet.

"Seems I am your mate when it benefits you?"

"Huh?"

"You *didn't* happen to threaten Officer Richards by using my title?" He smiles, and I glare at him before his words register, because I had done that. Heat rushes over my face.

"Lapse in judgment," I tell him.

"Oh, I don't mind. But if you want to use my title, I would rather it be because we share it and not just you throwing it around when you want to get out of trouble."

"I'm sorry. I won't do it again. But I wasn't going to stand by and watch him take Casey from Zoe."

"He wouldn't have; he's a good man."

I roll my eyes at him and turn away, only for him to grip my wrist and turn me back to face him.

"Don't walk away from me, Everly. Are you trying to upset me?"

I don't get a chance to answer before the restaurant door opens again. My stomach feels like it just dropped onto the floor as Beta Marcus walks in. He has his head down and is stuffing a set of keys into his back pocket, but it's definitely him.

"Had to park in the parents-with-strollers parking; no parking–" His words abruptly cut off when he looks up and stares directly at me. Shock crosses his features and his eyes go wide, then he tilts his head to the side. I pray he forgot me, but his following words prove he remembers exactly who I am.

Beta Marcus's face lights up and a smile splits his face as he begins walking over to us.

"I knew I heard that name before! Everly, it's me. You, remember me? Ah, it's been so long. I sometimes wondered what happened to you. I thought you left the city," he says, rushing over and enveloping me in a hug. Alpha Valen seems startled and pulls away, observing us closely.

"You must be mistaken," I try to tell him, trying to get out of his firm grip when he sets me on my feet and holds me at arm's length. I feel my heart thumping into my chest, all feeling gone from my body.

"No, I never forget a face. A name yes, but a face... You really don't remember me? The train station? You asked to borrow a lighter, then I took you to the packhouse."

I say nothing, trying to escape him and Valen, who is observing the scene playing out in front of him with a look of confusion on his face.

"We looked for you but couldn't find you. I even left a note with the security guards. Gosh, I can't believe it's really you," Beta Marcus says.

"Wait, you two know each other?" Valen asks suddenly, and we look at him. I quickly shake my head. My heart is pounding in my chest, and I feel like I'm about to pass out.

"Yes, she's the rogue girl—the one from the train station. Remember we went looking for her?" Marcus briefly explains before turning back to me.

"So, where did you go? Have you been here all this time? You work here? Oh, and your son. What was his name... Valcon... Volcom... Gosh, her son has the freakiest eyes—like yours," he says, gesturing to Valen before continuing excitedly, "The only person I've seen with the same eyes other than your father. So where is he?" he asks, looking around, utterly oblivious to my state of panic.

"Everly isn't a rogue whore; she hasn't got a son," Valen says, and Marcus looks at him, then groans, holding his hands out.

"How do you not remember? I bitched you out for days about tossing her and her kid out!"

"And what train station? I'm lost. What is going on here?" Valen demands, looking between both of us. Marcus sighs.

"Everly, the rogue girl you chucked out of the packhouse, remember? Years ago. We went looking for her at the train station. We left her car seat with the train guards, remember?" Marcus says.

I just want him to shut his mouth. At this point in the conversation, we have the entire restaurant's attention and Valen is staring at me like it's the first time he's met me.

"You were at the packhouse?" Valen asks, shaking his head. He seems confused for a moment before his head suddenly snaps up and a look of anger crosses his features; his top lip pulls over his teeth as he snarls at me, his eyes narrowed.

"Wait, you have a son? You lied to me?"

"I didn't lie."

"You have a fucking son," he growls, and Marcus steps between us.

"Woah, Alpha, what's got into you?"

"She lied," Valen snaps, pointing an accusing finger at me. "My fucking mate said she wasn't a rogue whore; she fucking lied."

"Wait, this is the Everly you were speaking about? This girl right here—she's your mate?" Marcus says while looking back at me. Bravo, idiot, you finally put it together.

"Yes, *she* is my mate."

"Please keep your voices down," I hiss at them when I hear people start murmuring that Alpha Valen has found his mate.

"Is this some joke to you? Do you really have no morals, just like the rest of the rogue whores? You think I can just accept some illegitimate child? Fuck, the press will have a field day with this scandal!"

"I never expected you to accept anything! Now get out!" I spit at him, unable to take his insults. How dare he? He just assumed like the rest of them. He isn't even going to let me explain, just jumped straight onto the rogue whore bandwagon.

"I won't have a rogue whore as a mate," he spits at me.

"Valen?" Marcus snaps at him.

"No, she fucking lied to me."

"I never lied to you. You were just too blind to see the truth; you don't even remember me! Now get out of my restaurant."

"I was drunk. How was I supposed to remember you from the packhouse? I can barely remember that night at all," he snarls.

"You think that's the first time we met? Got no other memories you want to sift through, Valen? I tried to tell you twice before that," I say, anger rising in my chest.

"What are you talking about?"

"I tried to tell you, and you tossed me away not once but twice— threw me out in the fucking rain! You are no better than your father. No better than mine," I snap at him.

"Don't bring my father into this. What is wrong with you? You knew who I was all this fucking time? All this time, you knew I was your mate?"

"Yes, I knew, and if you still can't figure it out, then go. Leave. I won't have you upset my employees with your prejudices."

"Oh, I am leaving. You are exactly like the rest of them—nothing but a whore—and to think I was willing to look past you being a lowly rogue. But I won't put up with you lying to me!" he screams before punching the counter. I jump at his aggression, and a few patrons duck down like they're waiting for him to explode. A few even hide under the tables when he suddenly turns on his heel and walks out, leaving me with Beta Marcus.

"I... I didn't think... Fuck, I'm sorry, Everly. I'll speak to him. I..." Marcus stumbles over his words, looking in the direction of where his Alpha just stalked off and out the door.

"It's fine. Nothing I didn't already expect from a Solace Alpha— clearly, the apple doesn't fall far from the tree," I tell him, turning and walking off to my office. Tears prick my eyes; I can't believe how terribly wrong that all just went.

I feel livid but also hurt. If I were a rogue whore, Valen wouldn't accept me. The funny thing is, even after everything he just learned, Valen never asked who Valarian's father was, and couldn't seem to get it through his head. For years, I had known who he was and lived through the torment of not having my mate. But all he could hear was rogue whore, blind to everything else, blinded by his own perception and judgment.

Escaping to my office, I lock the door and will myself not to break down when my cell phone suddenly starts ringing in my pocket. I half expected it to be Valen calling to yell at me more. It's not. The school's phone number lights up the screen. As I hit 'answer,' I clear my throat and suck in a deep breath.

"Hello?"

"Hi, this is Patricia, Valarian's teacher. Is this Everly Summers?"

"Yes, Patricia, how can I help you?"

"Ms. Summer, I was calling to let you know we've called the police, and an Amber alert has been put out."

My heart beats faster, thumping in my head, when suddenly someone starts banging on the door. I jump up to open it, and Macey rushes in with a frantic look on her face.

"Ms. Summer, your son... he never returned to class after recess. Now, we do have people out searching for him, but if you could come down to the school, and–"

The phone drops from my hand.

CHAPTER
THIRTY-FOUR

Valen

My entire world came crashing down violently around me. Everything I thought I knew about her was wrong—so very fucking wrong. How did I not see it? She's wrong for me. For a few seconds, I thought I had found my mate, but the mate that was supposed to be my other half turned out to be a liar. She lied straight to my face. I thought when I met her, I could look past it if she were a rogue whore, but now, faced with the truth, I realize how utterly idiotic that thought was.

"Valen, what the fuck, bro!" Marcus says as I walk across the parking lot. I ignore him.

"Valen, you can't just leave–"

"She lied to me," I snarl at him, stalking over to his car—I should have brought my own.

"Keys!" I snap at him, and he fishes them out of his jeans pocket and tosses them at me.

"So that's it? You aren't going to let her explain?"

"What's there to explain? She fucked some man and had a kid;

pretty straightforward, Marcus," I growl while unlocking his car. As soon as I'm in the driver's seat, I start the engine.

"You don't know that?"

"I do know that you said she had a kid, and she admitted it."

"That doesn't mean you know the circumstances, Valen; for all you know, she could have been raped. She could have had him run off on her."

"What do you want me to do Marcus? Either way, she has a kid, and he isn't mine, and my father will kill me if I bring a single mother home to be a goddamn Luna. Plus, that's humiliating for me!"

"My mother was a single mother, your father a single father. What the fuck does that have to do with her ability to be Luna?" Marcus snarls at me. I rub my temples, instantly realizing my mistake.

"Fuck, I didn't mean it like that."

"No, you meant she's a rogue whore. I thought you were better than that prejudiced bullshit. So what if she is? She is your mate."

"Just let me think. I have two weeks until the damn Alpha meeting and no mate to present. Just... FUCK!" I scream, flooring it down the main road, the tires screeching on the road as I take off.

"You can be a real jackass, you know that?"

I chuckle. Don't I know it. But either way, it changes nothing. I will be eaten alive by the vulture press if this shit gets out. People already know she's my mate. What happens if they see her son and put the pieces together? That would make for a great headline.

Marcus fiddles with the radio, my mind racing while he continues to ramble about what an idiot I'm being and yadda, yadda. I'm so distracted that I don't see the light turn red up ahead until Marcus's hand slams against my chest, shoving me back in my seat.

"VALEN!" he screams, snapping me out of my head. I hit the brakes, swerving around the corner, my heart leaping out of my throat as I white-knuckle the steering wheel. The car fishtails up the side street before finally coming to a stop.

"Fuck, that was close," Marcus says, clutching his head as he looks out the window. The front tires are on the curb and we narrowly missed those seated outside the café in front of us. People have their phones out, taking pictures, and I know instantly what the headlines will read:

'*Alpha Valen Drunk Driving*' or '*Alpha Valen Putting the Public at Risk with His Stupid Stunts*', or something along those lines. I hang my head.

"Fucking breathe; it isn't the end of the world," Marcus snaps at me.

"It might as well be," I tell him.

"Why? You get a mate and a kid on the same day."

"Only you would think like that," I scoff before chuckling and shaking my head.

"Just drive. We'll already be all over the front page tomorrow, let's just get out of here," Marcus says, slapping my chest. "And you better not have buckled my rim," he adds, and I roll my eyes.

"I'll buy you new ones."

"Nah, don't worry about it—you already did for your mate trashing my car; they come next week."

"What?"

"Don't leave your credit cards lying around. Besides, it's not like you can't afford it. I just took my bonus early," he says.

"Do I even want to know how much?"

"Nope, but thanks, bro."

I laugh, starting his car up, but this time slowly pulling away from the flashing cameras and the murmuring crowd that has built up around us.

I'm flicking through the stations when something catches my attention. "What's this shit?"

"Amber alert. A rogue, male child wearing black khaki shorts and a blue shirt has been reported missing," the radio host states, and I look at Marcus.

"Well, maybe you won't be splashed all over the papers

tomorrow if they don't find that kid," Marcus murmurs, listening to the description. "Amber eyes...?"

I slam on the brakes just as Marcus's eyes go wide. "Everly's kid?" he asks.

"No, it must be a coincidence," I tell him.

"How many kids do you know that have amber eyes?"

"Well, none; you said he had amber eyes, not me."

"Probably right. We should head back. We have that meeting in twenty minutes anyway."

"Yeah," I sigh, having completely forgotten about the meeting.

"You calm yet?" he asks as I clench the steering wheel and nod once.

"Yep, same shit show, I'm just the idiot shoveling the shit; something I'm used to."

"Thatta boy! After the meetings, we can head back to your apartment and get drunk. How does that sound?" Marcus says.

"Nah, I think I'll stay in tonight."

"Great, that means you can be the designated driver and watch me get drunk," Marcus says, and I roll my eyes.

"Or you can sit at my place and I'll watch you get drunk while I figure out how to get out of this arranged marriage," I tell him.

"Sounds good—as long as I'm getting drunk; I need a drink after all your dramas today," Marcus laughs. We're nearly back at my hotel when my phone starts buzzing. I groan when I see my father's face and number pop up on the screen. I quickly answer it, putting it on speaker so I can continue driving.

"Yes, Dad," I say in a bored tone.

"Where are you? You're late!"

"Pulling into the parking lot now," I lie—I'm still ten minutes out.

"Good, good, so what did you want to tell me about the Alpha meeting? I got your message earlier but forgot to reply—some announcement—is this you agreeing to the marriage?" My father asks.

I completely forgot I was going to tell him today about finding my mate. I hesitate for a second, trying to think. Maybe we can keep her son a secret, send him to boarding school for a year or so. Shit, could I even ask that of her?

I could just mark her and be done with it, nothing he could do then. Marcus eyes me, waiting to see what I say.

"Uh, yeah, we can talk about the details tomorrow; I'll be too busy after the meeting this afternoon," I lie, trying to buy more time to think of something.

"So, you *are* agreeing to marrying and marking, Ava?"

"No, dad, but I think I have a solution to our little issue."

"Valen, this *is* the solution. You need a mate, and this is a good idea—it will calm the packs."

"I said we will talk about it later. I'll see you soon," I tell him before hanging up on him.

"Now what?" Marcus asks.

"Now I need to find a way to get Everly to send her kid away for a bit, so my father doesn't find out about him, and convince her to let me mark her."

"Yeah, right. As if that's going to happen," Marcus laughs. I shake my head. I have no options; either the kid disappears for a bit or I forcibly mark her and order him away.

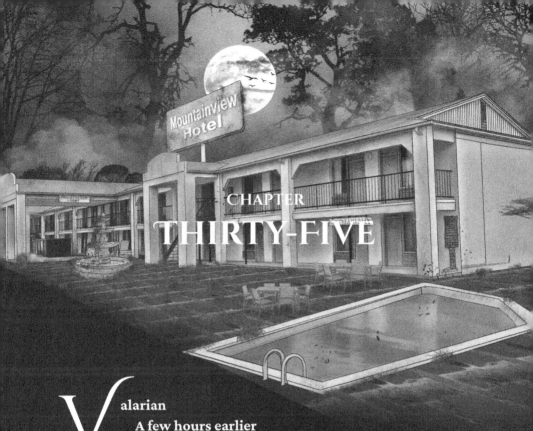

CHAPTER
THIRTY-FIVE

Valarian
A few hours earlier

"Valarian, are you dressed yet?" Mom yells out to me. I grab the piece of paper with my dad's address and a small list I made of his description. Mom said I would recognize him, and the funny feeling I get in my tummy should tell me he's my dad.

"Coming, mom," I call back to her. I unfold the paper again because the corners don't match. Why won't they match? I refold it. Casey walks into the room. I hate how she taps on my door—two taps. It should be three: odd numbers, odd numbers. I try to refold the paper, but her knock irritates me, making me mess the corners up again.

"Valarian, we're gonna be late!" mom calls again.

"Casey, knock," I snap. I don't mean to—Casey is my best friend.

"I forgot. You're so weird, Vally," Casey laughs but knocks on the door again anyway, and I let out a breath. I know the other kids think I'm weird; they all do, but I don't mind when Casey says it; she doesn't say it in a mean way.

"Did you get it?" I whisper to Casey, and she kneels, pulling her bag off her shoulder and pulling out torn pieces of paper.

"I tore them out," she says excitedly before stuffing them back in her bag when we hear footsteps.

"Valarian, come on, come on," Mom says, ushering us out of the bedroom. Casey giggles at our little secret. Today I find my dad. Mom is getting sick. I know she hides it, but I see the puffiness under her eyes, how she's always too tired to play, and lately, she's been falling asleep when she reads to me. She never has time. Time. Time. Never enough time to play with me anymore. Dad will have time for me. I know he'll have time. Or I hope he does; then maybe he can make mom not so tired no more. Maybe then she'll play more. I miss when mom played, but now she gets tired too quickly and needs to rest. She thinks I don't notice, but I notice everything about mom—she's the best mommy.

I follow her out of the house, trying not to think of the torn-out phone book pages—I want the maps. I'm sure how to read the maps, but it can't be that hard. Like a pirate's map, Dad is the golden chest at the end, and I'm gonna find him and surprise Mom. I can't wait to make her smile.

"Valarian, seatbelt," Mom hisses; she's always rushing. I clip my belt in, and Casey does hers. Mom puts the car stick on the D, and the car moves, and we are on our way to school.

We stop at the front of my school. My teacher is waiting out the front. I don't like her, and she always smells funny, like burned grass and cigarette smoke. Plus, she talks too slow. Mom gets out of the car and opens my door before walking me to the gate.

"Auntie Macey is picking you and Casey up. I have roster meetings this afternoon, okay? But I should be home for dinner," Mom tells me with a kiss on the cheek before she rushes back to the car, honking the horn as she leaves. I hate when she does that; the other kids stare.

"Come, come," my teacher calls and tries to take my hand, but I don't let her. Her hands stink bad, like the rest of her, and she always looks like a poodle with her weird puffy hair and big round glasses making her eyes too big for her thin face.

C asey slides the scrunched-up phone book pages to me on the seat at recess. I try to flatten the pages out, looking for the street name that matches the one on the paper, but I can't find it.

"Are you sure these are the right pages?" I ask Casey, and she shrugs.

"How am I supposed to know? You said get the maps, I got the maps."

I huff, trying to think of another way to find my dad. Diego's and Dora's maps weren't this hard to follow, these ones have lots of lines and cross-bits, and none say 'Alpha Valen's home'.

"It's fine. Someone must know where my dad lives," I tell Casey.

"Can I come to find the pirate treasure?"

"I am not finding pirate treasure. I am finding my dad," I tell her, pulling out the spare clothes I smuggled into my school bag. I pull the sweater on over my shirt and the jeans over my shorts. My shorts ride up and give me a wedgie, and I don't like the creases in my jeans. Mom usually gets those out with the iron for me. I don't want creases. They make my pants uneven.

"Don't look, Vally, just don't look, and the lines will go away," Casey tells me, and I nod, stuffing the maps in my bag and putting it over my shoulder.

"You be the lookout," I tell her as we sneak to the front gate. They always leave it open. Casey looks around the corner while eating her anchovy sandwich before giving me a thumbs up. I run out the gate before stuffing my bag in the dead hedges out the front. I glance back at the school. I'm so sneaky! I got out of my school like a ninja!

My feet hurt, and my tummy is rumbling. I've been walking forever, and it's starting to get cold. Mom will be worried. Maybe this wasn't such a good idea after all. I don't know if I'm going the right way. When I get to a man at the traffic lights, I stop. The man is dressed in a suit, like the ones who come to Mom's hotel. He glances down at me when I tug on his suit jacket, then sighs loudly and gives me a mean look.

"What, kid?"

"Do you know where this place is?" I ask, showing him the piece of paper. He huffs and takes it from me, then laughs.

"Alpha Valen's?"

I nod eagerly; he knows where it is. Where my dad is.

"Now, what would a rogue boy want to see him for?"

"I'm not a rogue boy; I am an Alpha like my dad," I tell him.

"Ha, and who is your dad?"

"Alpha Valen Solace."

The man laughs harder. "Is that so?"

"Yep," I tell him.

"Well, my Alpha doesn't have a kid, but I'm sure he'll think this is really funny. Come on then, boy, maybe he'll give you an autograph or let you get a picture with him," the man says, gripping my shirt and tugging me across the road.

"Really, you'll take me to him?"

"Yep, I'm going there anyway. He lives in that big building in the penthouse apartment."

"Do you work for my dad?"

He laughs. "If you say so, kid," he says, and we walk up the hill toward the big building with the bright lights. The door opens as we climb the stairs, and a man that looks like a butler with a funny hat on greets us at the doors.

"Who is that boy, Tatum?" the man in the funny hat asks.

"Some kid who thinks the Alpha is his dad."

"Ha, they all think that. Wonder which rogue whore sent their kid up this time, claiming he fathered it." Both men laugh.

"My mom is not a rogue whore. He is her mate, she told me."

"Whatever you say, kid. They all claim that too, but come on, let's get this over with," he says, leading me inside. The foyer is fancier and much bigger than our hotel's—all white and gold. The elevators are so clean I can see my reflection in them, and something smells yummy, making my belly rumble louder. I forgot to eat lunch, but it must be dinner time now.

"So, what's your name anyway?" the man—Tatum?—asks.

"Valarian, sir," I say as politely as I can.

"Valarian? That's an odd name. Damn, you really could pass as his though; you have the same eyes, now I can see better in the light," the man says, rubbing his chin and staring funny at me.

"And you have a big nose, now that I can see you better—it's bright in here," I respond.

"Ha, funny little shit you are. My Alpha's gonna like you." The man presses buttons on the panel, and we go all the way to the top floor.

"What do you do here?"

"Security work. I kick out the bad guys," he says.

"Do you have a gun?" I ask, my eyes bulging.

"I don't need a gun; I got these," he laughs, showing me his hands as claws slip out of his fingers.

"Cool, like Wolverine! I can't wait to be able to do that," I tell him. He laughs.

"One day, little man, one day you will," he says, and the elevator doors open up to a long corridor. He walks down it before knocking twice on the door. I grind my teeth before not being able to stop myself. I knock on it again.

"Three times, odd numbers, you need to do it with odd numbers, or it's bad luck."

205

He raises his bushy eyebrows at me.

"Whatever you say," he laughs. I hear footsteps on the other side of the door. It jiggles, and excitement bubbles in my tummy; I'm going to bring my dad home to be with us!

The door opens, and I look up to see the man, but I don't get the weird tummy feeling, and he's not my dad. Did Mom lie again?

"Tatum, what brings you here?" the man asks.

"Sorry, Beta, but this boy claims the Alpha is his dad," he says. The man notices me and looks down. He blinks at me.

"I know, freaky, right? Got the same eyes," Tatum says.

"Do you know my dad?" I ask him, but he continues to stare at me. I hear more walking, and I try to see around the man. I sniff the air.

"What is it?" I hear another man's voice ask. The Beta man moves to the side and I see him. The funny feeling in my tummy does big jumps, and I feel my heart racing. The man stops fast, and his mouth opens and closes like a fish blowing bubbles.

"Dad!" I squeal, running to him.

"I found you! I found you! I knew I would find you!" I say, hugging his legs. He's so tall. l feel so happy that I finally found him. Mom will be so happy, too, when I bring him home.

CHAPTER
THIRTY-SIX

Valen

The moment I lay eyes on him, I know he's mine. He suddenly squeals loudly and barrels toward me on his little legs, crashing against me. I imagine the look on my face is of pure horror at first as the pint-sized creature clings to my legs. Tatum and Marcus just stare, gobsmacked—Marcus's is mouth wide open like he's trying to catch flies.

"I found you! I found you! I knew I would find you!" the boy screams, bouncing on the balls of his feet. I pat his back, not knowing what to do with the kid. Yet, touching him only makes this scenario more real. For a moment, I wonder if my drink has been spiked and someone slipped me hard drugs. For a second, I kind of hope they did—until I get a whiff of his scent.

He's a rogue, but his Alpha aura is strong—too strong for just me —indicating both his parents are Alpha born. Only another Alpha would scent the potency of his aura, even as small as he is, but his scent is also familiar.

"So he is yours, then?" Tatum asks, stepping into my apartment. I blink before staring down at the kid, his big amber eyes staring up at me. There's no doubt. He's mine. I nod. Apparently, I have a son? But how? Who wouldn't jump at the chance to have a kid with an Alpha? What woman in the world would hide it? That's assurance for life, having an Alpha's child. What woman doesn't want that?

"Who did you knock up?" Tatum asks. Marcus just rubs his chin, raising a finger in the air like he's about to say something, then closing his mouth before opening and closing it again. It's the first time I've seen him lost for words.

"Everly... she has a..." He doesn't finish.

I pick up the creature that apparently came from my family jewels. I press my nose into his neck, wondering if I smelled right. I nearly drop him when I'm smashed with her mouth-watering scent perfuming out from his pores along with mine.

The boy giggles and tucks his chin as my stubble brushes his neck and face. "Stop, it tickles," he laughs, and I can't help but smile at his adorable cackle before he reaches for my neck with his tiny hands. I place him on my hip, sniffing his head.

"Your mother is Everly Summers?"

He nods. "Yep, and I am Valarian Summers."

Well, that will be changing, I think instantly.

"Mom will be so happy. Now you can be with my Mom. I can take you home to surprise her, and we can be a real family," he says, smiling with all his teeth on display. Somehow, I do not see that happening, but it raises another question: how the hell did I get her pregnant when I hadn't slept with her?

"Valarian?" I murmur, making me wonder if he was named after me—and what a resemblance to my mother's name: Valarie; she died when I was a baby. I like his name, but I'm shocked Everly would name him after me. How did she manage to keep him from me? More importantly, how is he here without her? This can't be real.

"How old are you?" I ask him.

"Five," he answers, holding up his hand, fingers splayed out, and I look at Marcus.

"How?" I ask him, and he shrugs.

"Well, I'm sure you know *how*," Marcus says, and I raise an eyebrow. Of course, I know *how*. But I want to know how it's possible; it makes no sense.

"He's Everly's," I repeat to him, and he nods.

"Get in and close the door," I snap at them both in case someone comes up here looking for me. I definitely don't want anyone overhearing how the mother of my child kept him a secret from me.

"I'm hungry, Dad. I haven't had lunch. It took all day to find you," Valarian says. Marcus walks over to take him, but I tug away, not wanting to put my new son down. Instead, I hug him closer and smell his scent. *God, we smell good together*, I muse.

"I'll make the food then," Marcus says, and I nod to him. I hate Marcus's cooking, but right now, I'm not willing to put Valarian down, as if doing so might somehow make him vanish, and it would all be a dream—one I didn't want but now suddenly can't imagine not having. Please be real; if I wake, and it isn't real, I may just consider that I've lost my mind because who dreams this shit up? And actually desperately want it to be true? I always wanted kids, but never dreamed of actually having them.

"Uncle Marcus will make you something to eat."

Valarian nods and eyes Marcus curiously as he walks away. "He doesn't smell like you."

"I'm an only child, so he's not a real uncle, but he's like my brother."

"Oh, you have a village too? Mom and I have a village: Auntie Zoe and Auntie Macey are Mom's village. Did your dad make you leave too, like Mom's did? He called her names, and we had to build our own family," Valarian states, and I blink, surprised to hear all of this come from him.

"How about you tell me all about your village, and then I think we should call your Mom."

Valarian nods. "So, you aren't coming home with me?" he asks.

"How about we try to bring your mom here?" I tell him while walking into the living room.

"Thirsty? There's chocolate milk?" Marcus calls out to him, and he nods. Marcus continues to the kitchen and I place Valarian on the couch, sitting across from him on the other. Marcus brings him a glass of milk, and he takes it from him, gulping down half the glass before looking around at the coffee table. His brows furrow, but he doesn't set the glass down and I clench my teeth. I know Marcus did it to see my reaction by the smug smile on his face, but I'm shocked by Valarian's following words.

"Where are your coasters? You need coasters," he says, sitting like a statue, as if the thought of placing the cup down would make the world stop.

"Definitely your kid," Marcus says, rolling his eyes before walking off and coming back with a coaster. I watch as Valarian places the coaster on the coffee table when Marcus gives it to him, then makes sure his cup is perfectly centered. The coaster is straight, making me remember Everly finding me coasters when I visited her.

She had said one of the kids of the rogues was a little OCD. Now I wonder if she meant our son. Valarian clasps his hands in his lap, looking around and twiddling his thumbs.

"How did you find me?" I ask him.

"Mom showed me a picture on the internet, and I got maps, but I couldn't find your street. Casey got the wrong maps. And then I found him, and Tatum brought me here."

"I take it you're the missing rogue boy I heard about on the radio?"

"I was on the radio?" he asks excitedly, and I smirk.

Tatum chuckles, watching as he stands by the couch Valarian's on.

"Yes, and I bet your mother is quite worried about you."

"Mom always worries about me."

"I imagine that is what mothers do?" I tell him, and he nods.

"So, tell me more about your village," I ask him.

"What do you want to know?" he says, much happier at the promise of food.

"Do you know which pack your mother came from?"

He shakes his head and chews his lip like he's thinking. "I know Mom had a sister, and they used to be best friends. She doesn't like talking about her real family,"

"So you've never met her parents?"

He shakes his head. "No, they called Mom a rogue whore and kicked her out because Mom had me, but she isn't a rogue whore, right?" he says, his brows furrowing. "Why would they do that to Mom?" he suddenly demands.

I don't know how to answer that, but from what I know, Everly is nearly twenty-three, so that would have made her seventeen or eighteen when she had him. But then Everly's words flood my mind: 'I am not a rogue whore,' she'd said, so that meant she knew who and what I was from the beginning?

"Did your mother say why she didn't tell me you existed?"

He shrugs. "She said she did tell you, but you didn't believe her. Then she said she couldn't."

Marcus also looks at me, and I try to think for a second.

"What do you mean she couldn't? Why couldn't she?"

He scratches his head. "In case you took me from her. Mom thinks I don't listen, but I do. She thinks you would take me away from her, but you won't, right?"

I lean forward and brace my arms on my knees before scrubbing a hand down my face.

"No, I won't take you from her." However, I will if she doesn't tell me how the hell this is possible and also why the hell she kept him from me.

"How old are you?" he asks randomly.

"Me?" I ask; he nods.

"Twenty-nine," I tell him.

"You're old," he snickers.

"You won't think that when you're my age."

He goes to ask something else, but I speak before he can.

"I think we should call your mother, she'll be worried. And I think I should talk to your mommy," I tell him, and he nods.

"So you'll come live with us now?" he asks hopefully, as if it's all so simple.

I pause because I know that isn't going to be a possibility anytime soon. Or maybe it could be...

If only it were that easy. I have no idea—this is the last thing I expected, but I suddenly feel like shit that she's been raising our son on her own, looking after him all this time. All while everyone treated her like a rogue whore.

I pull my phone from my pocket when I realize something else. I met her when she was rogue and kicked her out of my Packhouse. My stomach sinks. I kicked my own son and mate out in the rain when she was homeless and living in her car. The thought sickens me. He was right there all this time, and I did nothing for either of them.

No wonder she hates me.

Marcus places a plate of grilled cheese in Valarian's lap, and he stares at it before looking up at Marcus.

"For real, how is it possible for you to be so much like him when you've never met?" Marcus says, walking off and returning with a butter knife and fork, as well as a place mat.

"There. Happy now?" he asks. I dial Everly's number, listening to it ring. Marcus watches Valarian before speaking again when Valarian still doesn't start eating.

"Yeah, yeah, I'll get you a napkin," he laughs, walking off, and Valarian smiles. I can't help but smile myself. Marcus ruffles his hair when he returns before passing him the napkin.

"Grilled cheese can be eaten with your hands, it's finger food," Marcus tells him, and Valarian scrunches his face up. That's my boy. The phone continues to ring for another few seconds before she finally answers.

"I really haven't got time right now," Everly says, hanging up on me. I shake my head before dialing her number.

"What, Valen?" she growls into the phone.

"Want to explain how I have a boy with amber eyes and a startling resemblance to me sitting across from me?" I ask her, and she falls silent for a second.

"Valarian?" she whispers, fear in her voice.

"That would be him—we need to talk. One of my men will be waiting for you in front of my hotel." I nod to Tatum, and he nods back to me before walking out. "See you soon," I tell her, hanging up before she can say anything. If she wants our son back, she can come to me.

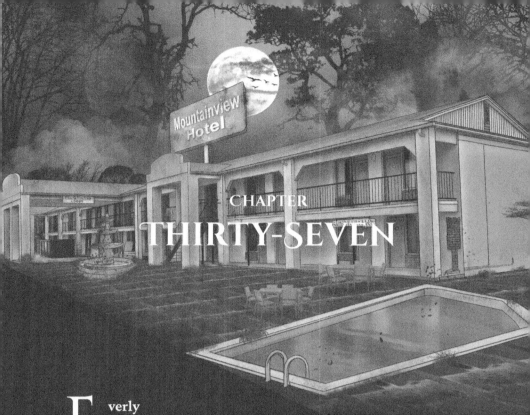

CHAPTER
THIRTY-SEVEN

Everly

My hands tremble as we pull up in front of the hotel. Officer Richards drove me to Alpha Valen's penthouse apartment. The whole ride, I racked my brain trying to figure out how he had Valarian here. Did he spot him at the school and take him? Did Valarian look for him? Or did someone notice the uncanny resemblance between them? I have many questions, but nothing terrifies me more than what happens now that Valen knows he fathered a son.

He'll have to kill me before I ever let him take my son. My nerves are shot, and my eyes burn from spending all afternoon and night bawling like a baby. My mind instantly went to the thought that he was kidnapped, or one of the forsaken had killed him. The relief I felt when I found out he was alive and ok was as crushing as the thought of losing him. There's nothing worse than thinking you lost a child; the what-ifs, the sheer panic, and frantic places your mind takes you are a pure nightmare. My mind had been zooming in and out of the worst-case scenarios. Plus, because he was considered a rogue child, it's not like anyone else really cared that he went missing.

Before having Valarian, it was hard to imagine a life that centered around him. But once he was here, he became my entire world, overshadowing any memory of a life without him.

Once you become a parent, the landscape of fear shifts; it is transformed—weaponized. As a parent, you have someone worth more to you than anything in existence, someone you'd lay your life down for without hesitation, just to ensure they can take another breath.

Without realizing, you take those old fears and wield them like the weapon they became. You're no longer spooked by childhood nightmares like the boogie man; you *become* the boogie man hunter —the shield against those very monsters. But instead of old fears, new horrors flood in the dread of everyday people around you— neighbors, strangers in the park. It's not that you're unafraid; it's that your fear has been redefined because now you're not afraid for yourself. Your fear is for another face, another name—your child's.

Death? It's no longer how you die that scares you. Instead, it's the paralyzing fear of leaving your child alone in a world where no one can love them as deeply as you do.

News headlines about missing children in your area send shivers down your spine. Your mind spirals to the unbearable thought: what if that was my child? Because your child is not just your *responsibility*; they are the axis on which your world turns. They're your reason to rise each day, the beating heart of your existence. To lose one is to lose your very reason for breathing.

The overwhelming dread I felt during those desperate hours of searching surpassed any fear I've ever felt.

So, stepping into the elevator, I finally let myself breathe, knowing Valarian is safe. However, knowing this doesn't lessen my anxiety because now I'm back to fear one: someone taking my child. Except this time, it will be by his own father.

I move from foot to foot as the elevator travels up to the top floor. The hotel is lovely, though I'm shocked to find that Alpha Valen's floor is heavily guarded. Exactly who is he expecting to attack him?

We had to use a key in the elevator to get to this floor. Officer Richards grabs my arm when I step out. He walks me down the middle of the corridor containing one door and five guards. Each one stares at me curiously.

It must be strange for them to see a rogue girl visiting the Alpha. Oh, the scandal that would result in the media if I was spotted here! Officer Richards knocks on the door before suddenly turning on his heel and walking off.

"Psst," I hiss at him, and he stops.

"Where are you going?"

"Work. I was told to drop you off, not hold your hand," he says with a smile. I'm about to retort that he should remain in case this turns into a violent custody disagreement when the door opens and Beta Marcus is suddenly standing in front of me.

"Luna," he says, and I scrunch up my face.

"Yeah, don't call me that. Where is my son?"

He steps aside, motioning for me to come in, and I step past him. The place is all open-plan, and I realize the entire floor is just his apartment. Large windows run the whole length from floor to ceiling, looking out over the city. I bet the view is breathtaking at night.

Hesitantly walking around, I notice another security guard sitting on the couch when I spot Valarian on the sofa beside him—the huge security guard has a game controller in his hand. Valarian glances at me before shrieking in delight.

"Mom!" he squeals, placing the controller he had in his hands down and rushing over to me. But before Valarian reaches me, Alpha Valen scoops him up with one arm before depositing him back on the couch. Valen kisses his head before looking at the security guard, who nods to him in some silent message.

"Stay here. I need to speak to your mother," Valen tells Valarian as I step closer, wanting to see my boy. I try to move toward him. My heart frantically thumps in my chest as I reach the back of the couch, but Valen grips my arm and suddenly starts walking. I stumble as

I'm forced backward before shoving him off, earning me a growl from him.

"Don't fucking touch me," I hiss at him, making sure to keep my voice low so Valarian doesn't overhear as we stand in Valen's over-sized kitchen. Marcus leans on the counter, and my eyes dart to him when Valen steps closer, caging me in with his huge body and pressing me against the counter.

"You want to explain how the fuck we have a son that I had no idea existed until he turned up on my doorstep?"

"Well, for starters, you don't have a doorstep, just a door," I tell, rolling my eyes. If he's going to talk to me like shit, then this conversation is over before it starts. I push on his chest, but he places his hands on either side of my hips, refusing to move.

"I am not in the mood for more of your lies; now answer me," he growls.

"Who the fuck do you think you are? You are not my Alpha. I will not tolerate you talking to me like some child that needs a scolding. Now back up," I tell him, glaring. His aura slips out, and the only thing keeping me upright is his body pressed against mine.

A whimper escapes my lips, having forgotten just how powerful an Alpha aura is when directed at you in anger, and he is angry. No, that isn't a strong enough word. He's livid.

"Don't test me, Everly. You know exactly who I am and what I am capable of. Just remember, if you want to leave here with my son, you better start speaking," he warns. Marcus comes up behind him and grips his arm. My eyes dart to him over Valen's shoulder.

"Valen, calm down," Marcus whispers to him, and he growls but steps back. I breathe deeply when his aura slips off me, allowing me to stand without wanting to collapse in a heap at his feet.

"How?" Alpha Valen says, leaning on the counter. He looks over his shoulder at our son, who is unaware of the tension behind him.

"Gee, I don't know, Valen. Crept into your bed and left without saying a word?"

"What?" he growls, and I scoff. Is he really that stupid? He runs his hand down his face before rubbing his temples.

"Explain. Why would you not tell me?" he growls.

"I did tell you—same as I told you I wasn't a rogue whore."

"I am pretty sure I would remember if I had a son, Everly. Don't bullshit me; it's bad enough you fed that shit to our son," he snarls.

"I did tell you. I also fucking tried to tell you the night you kicked me out of your Packhouse in the fucking rain with our newborn son, I tried to tell you when I was pregnant. Twice. What did you expect me to do? Beg and plead for you to believe me? Because I fucking tried that too, but your secretary kept telling me to fuck off and that she would put a restraining order on me."

"Was I drunk?"

"Which time? Most of our encounters were when you were obliterated. Not my issue that you're an alcoholic. I did my part."

"You are so frustrating. You kept my son from me. My son is rogue because of you," he snaps, pointing an accusing finger at me. I growl at him, and he laughs, tossing his hands in the air.

"Laugh, go on. You think it's funny? You thought it was funny when I told you I was pregnant too, laughed like it was the funniest thing you ever heard."

He stops, staring at me.

"There is no way I would have ignored someone telling me they were pregnant," he says.

"'I would never sleep with a seventeen-year-old, especially a mongrel related to Alpha John'. Well newsflash, asshole, you did!" I spit at him.

"Excuse me?"

"That's what you said, then laughed and hung up on me. I tried to call you back and you said if I ever called with my lies again, you would skin me alive—that you wouldn't be associated with a mutt of Alpha John's," I tell him before looking back at my son on the couch.

"No, wait, repeat that. What did you just say?" he says, looking like his brain is too slow to process information in real-time.

Fuck, does this fool have amnesia to go with his OCD? What a messed-up combination that would be, though, I would like watching him clean the same spot repeatedly. However, I shake that thought away when he steps closer, and I'm forced to take a step back.

"Your last name is Summers," he states.

"It is now—it's my mother's maiden name—my father stripped me of his name the day he stripped me of my title because I got pregnant by you; my father refused to have a rogue whore for a daughter, just like you refused to believe you had fathered the child of mutt," I tell him.

Alpha Valen stares at me. "You are not an Alpha; I would feel it if you were," he says, folding his arms across his chest.

"I've been a rogue for five fucking years—my aura is gone now. You sticking your dick in every bitch you came across for the past four and half years made sure my aura was obliterated. My aura is non-existent because of you," I say through gritted teeth, all the anger from the past five years threatening to spill over.

"What are you talking about?" he snaps.

I snarl. What part wasn't he getting? I shove past Valen before grabbing Marcus by the collar of his shirt and slamming my lips against a startled Beta, who has his hands up in the air. Valen staggers, clutching his stomach, and I release Marcus, who looks like he's about to faint at what I did. Turning to Valen, I point at him.

"Now imagine how bad that would hurt if I fucked him too," I growl at him. Valen's fists clench at his sides, and Marcus puts up his hands, taking a step away from him and me.

"She kissed me," he yaps out when a furious growl tears out of Valen. This time, earning the attention of our son.

"Mom?"

"Everything is fine, honey. Play with your... um... new friend," I tell him, glancing at the behemoth of a man sitting next to my son playing video games; he looks like he should be chasing down the hulk. Valarian stands, looking between us.

"I'll be over in a minute, buddy. Sit down, please," Valen tells him, and he glances between us again before reluctantly sitting back down and returning his attention back to the game.

"Tatum. His name is Tatum," Valen says with a sigh, pointing to the man on the couch beside Valarian.

"Great, are we good now? We all on the same page? If so, I'll grab *my* son and be on my way," I tell him, about to step past him when he blocks me with his arm.

"No, we aren't done yet," Valen says, his lips pulling back over his teeth.

I sigh, folding my arms across my chest. I don't know what else we can possibly have to talk about.

"If you are Alpha John's daughter, how come he's never mentioned you?"

"Did you not listen to a thing I just said? He thought I was a rogue whore—shunned me for it, like all the other packs do. I lost everything because of you."

"But you're not."

"Very observant of you. Now, if you will excuse me, it's a school night, and I need to get my son home."

"He isn't leaving."

"Like hell, he isn't."

"He's my son too. You can't just decide to keep him to yourself."

"And you don't get to wake up one day and suddenly decide to be a mate and father. It doesn't work like that," I retort. He abruptly rises taller, towering over me—then Valarian is suddenly at our side. He tugs on his father's shirt, and he instantly steps back, looking down at the boy.

"I'm tired," Valarian yawns, and Valen looks at me when I bend down to pick him up.

"Have you eaten?" I ask him.

"Marcus made him grilled cheese; he also had some ice cream," Valen answers, and I nod.

"Come, we should get you home for a bath and bed," I tell him, glancing at Valen, who sighs but nods.

"I'll run you home," he says, reaching for his car keys from a bowl on the bench.

"Are you going to come home with us?" Valarian asks his father, and I swallow.

"Not tonight, but I'll pick you up in the morning to take you to school."

I glare at him but keep my mouth shut.

"Really?" Valarian says, brightening up and looking alert.

"Yes, your mother just needs to let me know what time to get you," he asks, raising an eyebrow at me. I suppress a growl, knowing it will only upset Valarian if I say no.

"He gets up at seven."

Valen nods before reaching for him, and I let him take him.

"Come on, we can talk more tomorrow. He should get to bed, he can barely keep his eyes open," Valen says, and I follow him.

CHAPTER
THIRTY-EIGHT

Valen leads us toward the door; I'm relieved he's letting me take our son home. Valarian has his head resting on my shoulder and swiftly falls asleep. However, when Valen opens the door. My footsteps falter, and I freeze when I notice his father talking to one of the guards out front. Valen also stops, and I watch his father laugh at something one of the guards was telling him when he turns. His eyes go to us, standing in the doorway of his son's apartment.

I drop my face into Valarian's shoulder, and Valen steps in front of me, blocking the view I had of his father. Alpha Kalen growls. My heart flutters frantically, and I fight the urge to take a step back.

"Why the fuck do you have a rogue whore in your apartment–" His words cut off as his eyes settle on Valarian in my arms, his head just poking out above Valen's shoulder. He looks at his son and sniffs the air before shoving past Valen. I stumble over my own feet, moving a step away.

Valen's growl resonates off the walls as he tosses his father against the wall, making me jump. A hand grips my shoulder and yanks me backward out of the way. Valen pins his father against the wall, his forearm resting against Kalen's throat.

I look over my shoulder to see who had grabbed me, to find Tatum and Marcus. Marcus jerks me behind him and Tatum grips my arms, holding me steady before Marcus moves to put himself in front of me, acting as a personal shield.

"What is the meaning of this, Valen? That boy..." Kalen growls and looks back over at me. His eyes narrow before shock flits across his face.

"You," he points at me, and Valen growls at his father in a clear warning.

"Everly! And if you ever approach her like that again, Father, we will have issues," Valen warns, his canines slipping from his parted lips, angled toward his father's throat.

"You know her?" Kalen asks, looking back at his son, and Valen sighs.

"Yes," Valen says, letting his father go and fixing the man's jacket. Kalen readjusts his tie before he glances between us. Valarian stirs in my arms and lifts his head before turning to investigate what is going on.

Kalen's eyes widen, and he takes a startled step back as his eyes fall on his grandson when Valarian turns his head to look at him. He looks even more shocked than he had been at seeing the woman to whom his mate left everything she owned.

"Mommy, who is that man?" Valarian whispers to me as he pats the side of my face, trying to get my attention. My eyes remain on the man responsible for killing the woman who made me who I am today.

"He is your grandfather," I tell Valarian while pressing my face to his and inhaling his scent, allowing me to calm some. Kalen blinks and tries to take a step forward, but his shoulder brushes Valen, who has once again moved into his path. Marcus also moves more, blocking Alpha Kalen and taking up a protective stance behind Valen.

"You have a son?" Kalen gasps as he turns his head to look at Valen.

"Yes, and this is Everly; she is my mate."

"What? The rogue whore is your mate?"

"Call her that once more, Father, and see what happens," Valen warns. I'm honestly a little shocked to see him defend my title against his father, and I see Kalen swallow. Kalen waves his hands in the air, and it's clear to me, he's trying to get over his shock.

I shuffle my feet awkwardly and rely on Valen to keep his father in check. Marcus and Valen look over at me, struggling to hold Valarian's weight. Valen's eyes, too, fall on my shaking arms; he moves past Marcus and reaches for his son. I pull back, not wanting Valarian anywhere near Kalen, but Valen growls at me and I reluctantly let him go, allowing Valen to take him—my arms instantly feel empty.

Valen places Valarian on his hip, kissing his temple before reaching for my hand and tugging me toward him.

"Everly, this is Kalen. Dad, this Everly, my mate," Valen introduces us, unaware that no introductions were necessary. Kalen holds out his hand to me, and Valen looks at me expectantly. I hesitantly place my hand in his firm grip. Immediately, Kalen yanks me toward him, inhaling my scent.

Valen growls menacingly behind me, and I see Tatum and Marcus step closer, like they're about to separate us and intervene if necessary. Kalen squeezes my hand painfully, and I grit my teeth. He shocks me by suddenly hugging me, squeezing the air from my lungs, and I feel my back crack.

"Nice to meet you, Everly." But the underlying warning in his tone, I did not miss. Kalen pushes me back, holding me at arm's length, and pulls his face away; his amber eyes meet mine. A chill runs up my spine at the cold look he gives me. Hatred boils in my blood.

"Nice to meet you," I murmur back. The energy rippling off his father cannot be missed, not even by Valen, who looks at his father like he's about to toss him away from me. Kalen pats my arms before he grips my shoulders, and his demeanor swiftly changes.

"We will have to catch up sometime, sort this rogue business out. My son can't have a rogue for a mate; the press would have a field day," he says, his eyes scrutinizing my face when Valen clears his throat beside me.

"We would like to keep things quiet for now, Father, at least until I wrap my head around the fact I have a son and mate," Valen tells him. Kalen pats my shoulder.

"Yes, I think that is for the best, for now," Kalen says before looking at Valarian. His eyes soften as he stares at his grandson, and he pinches his chin between his fingers. Valarian stares up at him curiously, but Kalen's face holds none of the animosity he has towards me.

"He has our eyes, son—looks like you when you were his age," Kalen tells Valen, who nods in agreement.

"What is your name, son?" Kalen asks Valarian.

"Valarian, Papa," he answers, and I fight back the urge to cringe at the endearment Valarian used.

"Good name, a strong one, just like your father's. I look forward to getting to know you better," Kalen tells him, brushing his cheek gently with his thumb.

"Where are you all going?" Kalen asks, turning his gaze to his son.

"I'm taking them home; it's a school night,"

"Your mate and son aren't staying here with you?" Kalen asks before he looks over at me. I look at Valen when he answers, saving me from having to.

"No, I was about to drop them at home."

"Nonsense, there is plenty of room; they should remain here; you will have to mark her, of course. We can't have anyone noticing your mate is a rogue now," Kalen says, and I take a step away from Valen, bumping into Marcus behind me.

"In good time, Father. Now, if you will excuse me, I need to get my son to bed," Valen tells him before he reaches over and grabs my hand. Valen tugs me out of the door after him, and Kalen steps aside at Valen's dismissal. I can feel his eyes on me as I walk with Valen to the elevator. Instinctively, I step closer to him.

I hate that I did, but his father terrifies me more than Valen does. Valen glances down at me for the action, but doesn't say anything as he hits the elevator button. Valarian yawns, mumbling as he tries to get comfortable in his father's arms. Valen tugs me against him and places his arm across my shoulders. For once, I don't shove him away, preferring his closeness and the safety it offers instead of remaining awkwardly at his side under his father's watchful gaze.

"Tatum!" Valen calls, and the monstrous man moves toward us. He stops beside me and looks at his Alpha, inclining his head slightly.

"You are now assigned to Everly and Valarian."

Tatum nods and smiles down at me. "Of course, Alpha," he answers, and I wonder what Valen means when the elevator doors open and Valen tugs me inside. Tatum also steps into the elevator with us, and I let out the breath I'd been holding.

"I'm sorry about my father; he has..." he pauses.

"Strong views about titles?" I offer, and Valen sighs.

"Yes. I'll take care of it."

"No need," I tell him while I reach for Valarian, but Valen pulls away.

"I have him; he's fine. I won't drop him, Everly," Valen says, pressing his nose against Valarian's hair and inhaling his scent.

The drive back to the hotel is silent. I had climbed in the back with Valarian when we got to the car. Valen told me he would get Valarian a booster seat, but I said nothing. I have no idea how long it will be until the novelty of having a child will wear off, so I don't bother to argue that he won't be taking our son anytime soon. Just as the car pulls up out front, I unclip Valarian's seatbelt while Valen parks the car. He gets out quickly before scooping a sleeping Valarian into his arms and tossing his jacket over him to shield him from the rain.

I lead Valen to the apartment I share with Zoe. Tatum follows us, looking around, alert, which bothers me. He surely didn't mean Tatum would be following us, did he? My employees will never get any work done with Tatum hovering around. The man is huge and looks like he belongs in a cave, grinding bones to make his butter, not following a rogue girl and a child around.

"I can take him," I tell Valen, who growls at me and pushes past; he sniffs the air before walking up the hallway, and I follow. Zoe is sitting up in her bed with a book in her lap. She was with me when we got the phone call from Valen about Valarian, so I knew she would have waited up; I'll have to fill her in.

"In the morning," I tell her, and I close her door after she nods to me.

Walking over to Valarian's little room, I see Valen sitting beside him, tugging Valarian's shoes off before he tucks the blankets around him. I watch, safely tucked out of view, as he tends to Valarian, then switches the small lamp off and goes to get up. I move away from the door when Valarian suddenly speaks up, making me pause.

"You aren't leaving me, are you? I need you," Valarian says, and Valen pauses. "Mom needs you too; she won't admit that, though, so don't snitch on me for telling you."

I hear Valen chuckle softly.

"I am leaving, but I'll be back in the morning," he promises.

"Do you pinky promise?" Valarian asks, and I can't help but peek back into the room. Valen stares at his outstretched pinky before gripping it, giving it a shake, and Valarian laughs.

"No, like this," Valarian says, looping his pinky through his father's.

"That means you can't break it. Pinky promises are special," Valarian tells him.

"Ok, I pinky promise I will be back in the morning to take you to school; now get some sleep," Valen tells him, re-tucking the blanket around him. I walk back off to the living room area and see Tatum waiting patiently by the door.

"7 a.m. you said he gets up, right?" Valen asks as he walks up behind me. I nod as he stops beside me.

"You don't have to do the school run, Valen."

"Well, I do now. Apparently, I can't break a pinky promise, Everly, and I want to, I am not asking. He's my son too," Valen says, and I press my lips in a line.

"It's late. I'll let you get to bed. I'll be back tomorrow. Tatum will be outside if you need anything."

"Wait, you aren't expecting him to remain here?"

"Uh, yes. Either he stays, or I do, Everly," he says, his eyes sinking into mine.

"It's the middle of the night. What could possibly happen? We're going to bed. I am capable of looking after my son."

"*Our* son. And you are so capable that our son escaped school and found me? That shows a lot about your parenting skills."

"Don't talk to me about parenting, Valen. Where were you the first five years of his life? I didn't know he would go searching for you; he's never taken off before, so don't you blame me for that."

"Either way, Tatum stays, or I do, so which is it? I won't leave you both unprotected when forsaken are running around at the back of your hotel."

I look over at Tatum. If I had to choose, it would definitely be the giant.

"Fine, but one night only. I won't have him scaring my employees," I say.

"Fine, have it your way. I'll stay tomorrow night then," Valen says before pecking my head and walking toward the door before he stops and turns, looking back at me.

"And you heard my father, Everly; I can't have you running

around rogue. You have a week to get your head around letting me mark you, or I will do it by force if necessary. I won't have my son remain rogue," he tells me, then walks out and closes the door before I have the opportunity to protest.

CHAPTER
THIRTY-NINE

Valen

I can't sleep; all night I toss and turn, knowing they're both over there—so close, yet out of reach. It gives me a little comfort knowing Tatum is there with them, yet everything in my screams I should be the one protecting them, how I have failed. No wonder she hates me. I would hate me too if our roles were reversed.

Now a few past incidents make sense; why I could never hold a relationship to save my life, why I had trouble with my sex life, the sudden bouts of depression seeping into me. Now it makes me wonder if I knew all along on a subconscious level, and it was my body trying to stop me from making the idiotic decisions I some-times did.

She felt it, felt it all, and didn't say anything. When she kissed Marcus, the pain that she caused was brief yet painful all the same. How did she endure years of my infidelity? I may not have known about her, but she certainly knew of me, which makes me groan at how stupid I've been. The countless brothels, the women, and she endured that pain over and over for so many long years.

Five years. For some reason, that number keeps popping up in my head as I try to dredge up any memory that would lead me to her. Why was that number so significant? Besides the obvious, of course. Yet something nags at me, tugging as if it should matter to me. *Five years... five years...* I mutter under my breath. Lurching upright, I feel my breath leave me altogether, and I gasp, nearly choking on my own spit.

The Alpha meeting! The fairy girl! The girl who snuck out on me the following day! Could that have been her? I was pissed off that she left before I even woke. Something tells me it was Everly, yet I never saw her face. Marcus woke me the following day, and she was gone. He said he passed the girl, and I remember it irritated me because I was angry he didn't stop her.

That girl has remained in my thoughts for five years already, and it's one of the things that got me through each night—finding myself often thinking of the girl dressed as a fairy. Yet, I could never explain why she would randomly pop into my thoughts.

Marcus had told me to look for her, but when I checked the registry, I could never find her name, which now makes sense; she was underage. She wasn't supposed to be on that side of the hotel, which was for only adults and....

...and future Alphas.

She shouldn't have been where I was, and I always thought it odd when I went over the registry of attendees. I could never find anyone that even resembled her. No ID had me jumping the way Everly did.

All the weeks I had spent searching the hotel database, and she was in the kid's section! I cringe at that mental thought—don't go there; creepy as hell. Yet, I kind of remember that night, even though I was wasted. I remember how I was drawn to her, and no matter where I turned, I found myself in her vicinity again, drawn to her like a moth to a flame. It had to be her, and it made sense why she would have run. I spent weeks angry that she ran out on me, but it suddenly makes sense because if Alpha John is her father, I can imagine the trouble she would have gotten in if she had been caught with me.

That had been right in the middle of a brutal war. Land was being divided after we bought out half of Silverstone Pack's lands; they fell into hot water with debts, and we settled those debts in exchange for a good-sized chunk of their territory, giving us owner-ship of half the city. A war ensued; too many lives were lost to violence in the streets—constant attacks—though we weren't completely innocent; my pack killed just as many as John's did.

Alpha John was furious. It added fuel to the fire and our feud only became worse, so it makes me curious what changed between my father and John that they're now willing to marry me off to his daughter.

What were the chances I would be mates with one of his daugh-ters? Just not the one they were trying to make me marry. Nothing makes sense; my father hated Alpha John, but now they seem amica-ble, friendly, and it makes me wonder what John has over him. My father is not a man to back down to his rivals—more like stomp on them and kick them to the curb.

My phone buzzes beside where I lie, and I glance at it to see Tatum's number pop up. Quickly opening it, I answer the phone.

"Everything okay?"

"Yes, Everly went for a run. Should I follow her or stay with your son?"

"Um, do you know where she went?"

"I asked, but she said it was none of my business and walked out."

"Just give her space. If she isn't back after an hour though, call me."

"Okay, boss," Tatum says, hanging up.

Going through my phone contacts. I quickly call her, hoping she'll be more talkative on the phone than face to face. We only seem to argue when in each other's presence, but I'm slowly starting to understand why.

"What, Valen?" she answers after the third ring. She sounds tired, her voice strained.

"Tatum said you left the apartment."

"Zoe is there, I didn't leave him by himself. And I figured your friend would watch over him, unless there's a reason I shouldn't be leaving Valarian with him?"

"No, Tatum is fine. He's safe. I was just concerned about where you were going this late at night."

"The reserve. However, I am now headed back home because someone fixed the damn fence again. I had it reopened yesterday afternoon and someone keeps fixing it," Everly curses, and I hear her kick the mesh. I press my lips in a line, knowing it's my fault.

"Uh, that may be my fault. Marcus told me the fence was broken. I sent someone out to fix it."

"Of course it was you," she sighs.

"Well, I'll stay on the phone with you, make sure you get home okay. How was I supposed to know it was intentionally opened?"

"I am capable of getting home, Valen, and it's fine, a lot of us use it as a shortcut. Whatever. I can wait until tomorrow or something," she says, though she sounds like she's almost breathless.

"Please, this doesn't have to be an argument; just don't hang up until I know you're back with Tatum. Do you always go running this late?"

She doesn't hang up on me, so I figure she's giving in.

"No."

"Then why are you running so late?"

Everly doesn't answer straight away, and I glance at the phone to make sure it's still connected.

"Because I need to," she finally says, though it sounds more like a murmur and like there's more meaning to it than that.

"What do you mean?"

"It doesn't matter, Valen. Anyway, I am at my door. Your body-guard is staring at me because I look like a drowned rat from the rain. Can I go now?"

"I just want to make sure you're home safe."

She groans, the noise sounding annoyed.

"Hey, BFG, tell your boss I'm home," I hear her say before I hear Tatum.

I hear in the background, "She's home," and sigh with relief.

"You might as well come in. It's pouring. I can't have you sleep out here; you can stay on the couch," I hear her tell him.

"Uh, just one second," I hear him murmur before I feel the mind-link open up.

"Are you for real right now? Are you seriously asking permission?" I vaguely hear Everly say through the phone. Tatum's voice flits through my head at the same time she snaps at me through the phone.

"Either he can come in, or he leaves. I won't be able to sleep knowing he's outside freezing on my doorstep."

I assume you got what she said?' Tatum asks through the mind-link.

"It's fine," I say to him out loud so Everly can hear too. I cut the mind-link and hear Everly sigh.

"I'll grab you a towel, and if you get beaten in the morning by a petite girl with an angelic face, it's just Zoe; I live with her," Everly warns him. I can only imagine the amused look Tatum would have had at that. I hear him grunt, and I smile, amused that she would warn him she lives with someone. He already knew—he would have noticed the extra scents.

"Okay, can I go now? Tatum is sleeping on the couch, and I'm tired."

"Yes, Everly, goodnight," I tell her, and she hangs up. I sigh. Now to convince her to let me mark her...

I stare up at my ceiling. I can't help but smile, despite the fact she hates me. She still named our son after me. Valarian is my and my father's middle name. All the men in our family have the same middle name; well, except Valarian, obviously, which makes me wonder what it is. Yeah, my dad definitely has a thing for the letter V.

Valen Valarian Solace, what a mouthful that was growing up, yet

I know he also named me in honor of my mother, Valarie, with a mix of his name too.

The Alpha meeting is coming up soon. It won't be long now before I'll have to put everything out in the open. I just hope Everly will let me mark her within the week. I'm not so sure whether I could actually go through with forcibly marking her—not after everything I've already made her endure—and I don't want to give her more reason to hate me.

On the plus side, I now have more excuses to see her since we share a son together. I never gave much thought to being a father. I've always wanted kids because it was expected, but I never really pictured children. However, after meeting Valarian, it's all I want to be now, fuck everything else. I just want my mate and son; want to be a part of his life and hers if she'll have me. Rolling on my side, I set my alarm—I have a pinky promise to keep, and I have no intentions of breaking it.

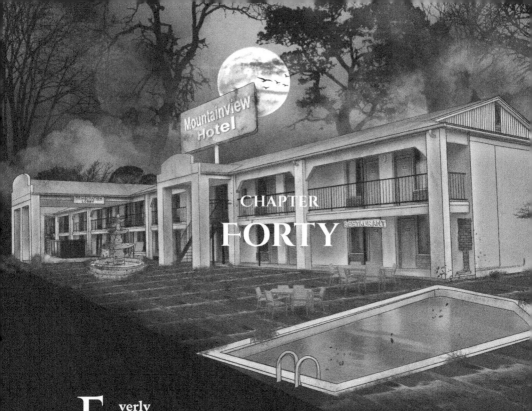

CHAPTER
FORTY

Everly

Yesterday was rough, last night even tougher. I didn't get any sleep; my entire body is aching from tossing and turning. The mate bond grows stronger each time I see him, and the pain of denying it is getting harder to ignore. I roll out of bed to the sound of soft murmurs—that means Zoe is awake. I hear her trying to wake Casey in the room beside mine. Getting to my feet, I quickly open my door to see her in all her bedhead glory. She yawns and smiles at me.

"Morning," she says, turning her attention back to Casey's open door before she does a double take, then steps away from me. Casey starts to step out of her room when Zoe shoves her back inside the door and quickly shuts it. Casey bangs on the door in objection.

"Just a minute, sweetie," Zoe says before gripping my arm.

"What happened? Did that bastard hurt you? I'll fucking kill him," she whispers with venom in her voice.

"Swear Jar," Casey calls through the closed door while I try to figure out what's gotten into her.

"Huh?"

236

Zoe ushers me into the bathroom, turning me to look in the mirror, and I gasp at what I see. There's blood smeared on my face, and the dark rings under my eyes look like I got into a fight. No, lost a fight. I reach for a washcloth and quickly wash my face, but there's no bruising or sign of physical injuries.

"Must be a nosebleed," I tell her, which is something that's becoming more frequent. Whenever I see him, it seems to me that something gets worse—headaches or nosebleeds. I blink at my reflection before leaning in when I notice the discoloration of the whites around my eyes—no longer white but blood red.

"What the fuck?" I whisper.

"You need to figure out something soon, Everly."

"It's fine; I'll go see a doctor," I tell her, though I know it's pointless.

"No, you need to see your mate. Or mark someone."

I stare at her in the mirror. Her eyes are watery and filled with concern as she watches me.

"It's been four and half years, Everly, and you're already deteriorating. What will it be like in another five years? How much worse?"

I shrug. I have no idea, but clearly, that isn't the answer she was after because she stalks off down the hall. The moment I step out of the bathroom, I hear a shriek before her voice reaches my ears.

"The bodyguard, right? Gees, you scared the crap out of me."

Walking into the living room, I find Tatum sitting up.

"You get many break-ins to sleep on your uncomfortable sofa?" he groans, and I hear his back crack. He tosses the blanket aside before making his way to the kitchen and flicking the kettle on.

"Coffee?" he asks, giving Zoe the once over; she's wearing her silky pajamas with kittens on them and rainbow toe-socks.

"Nice socks," Tatum smirks, and she glares at him. He's barking up the wrong tree if he's going to mock her socks; she has an entire collection of those toe-socks, and in the wintertime, she even likes to wear them with her flip-flops. She calls them her 'winter edition' flip-flops. She growls at him, and he purrs back at her, which shuts her up quickly before she purses her lips and narrows her eyes at him.

"Uncle Tatum!" Valarian screams, rushing out. Anyone would think they've known each other all their lives, what with Valarian's excitement. I haven't seen him look so alive in ages. At the same time Tatum scoops him up, there's a knock on the door.

"That would be your father, kiddo," Tatum says, placing him down. Valarian moves to the door and swings it open before bouncing on the balls of his little feet.

"You came back! You came back!!" he squeals eagerly.

"I pinky promised, didn't I?" Valen tells him, picking him up. He steps into the apartment and the place suddenly feels smaller with two bulky men taking up space.

"Coffee, boss?"

Valen nods to Tatum before Tatum turns to me.

"Coff—... What happened to your eyes?" he says, shoving past the table and knocking a chair over.

"Allergies," I state as he grips my face with his huge sausage fingers. Zoe scoffs beside me, and he glances at her before raising an eyebrow at me when I swat his hands away. Valen comes over and grips my face instead, and I jerk away from his tingling touch.

"Allergies?" he questions doubtfully when Valarian suddenly speaks against me.

"Mom gets them all the time—and her nose bleeds. She gets a lot of nosebleeds," Valarian says, and I press my lips in a line. Valen looks at me and his lips part before he nods and looks at Valarian.

"Well, mommy needs to see a doctor. I'll take her," he tells Valarian. I start to object when Zoe adds her two cents' worth.

"Good idea; she sees doctor Mary at the rogue center," Zoe says, folding her arms across her chest, and I notice Tatum's eyes dart to her cleavage.

I glare at her.

"My mate is not going to a rogue center," Valen states before realizing what he said to Zoe, who's also a rogue.

"And why is that?" she says, dropping her hands to her waist and popping her hip. Ohhh, careful, Valen... you may just get into an argument you can't win with her.

"Good enough for rogues, it should be good enough for everybody. Or are you admitting that this city is discriminatory?" she says with a glare.

Valen says nothing, just turns away from her, choosing not to answer. Good thing, too, because Zoe is a firecracker before her morning coffee. Never cross paths with Zoe if she's in a bad mood and hasn't had her morning coffee yet. She may be small, but damn she's got a good right hook. You only have to ask the pool boy to know that—or Macey's brother.

"Okay, how about we get you ready for school, Valarian?" asks Valen while walking off into his room down the small hall. Tatum hands me a coffee, giving me a worried look before handing me an extra cup.

"For the boss."

"Your boss. Not mine," I tell him, stalking off down the hall to find my mate and son. Valarian is pulling his clothes out of the wardrobe while Valen looks around. When I stop beside him, he takes his mug from my hand and sips it.

"Doesn't look like a kid's room," he mumbles to me.

"Valarian doesn't like a mess," I whisper back.

"You know I can hear you, right?" Valarian asks as he lays his clothes on the bed neatly.

Valen chuckles and turns around and Valarian eyes his father's cup before going over to his little desk, pulling out two coasters, and setting them on his bedside table.

Valen exhales just like I've seen his son do many times when he found something relaxing. Apparently, coasters are relaxing. Placing mine on one, I move to his wardrobe, retrieving his shoes from the bottom and placing them beside his perfectly made bed. It's one of the first things he does.

The moment he gets up, he makes his bed. I've even caught him making Casey's or remaking mine. That's one of the reasons I make sure to shut my door every morning. Occasionally, his compulsions become a little much. I'm more of a roll-out-of-bed-every-morning-and-make-the-bed-before-I-climb-back-in-it sort of person.

We help him get ready, and Valen watches everything like he's learning something new. I've applied gel on my son's hair and flattened his collar, but it makes me nervous when Valen suddenly starts unbuttoning the shirt I just buttoned because Valarian is whining about the collar not being completely wrinkle-free. How either of them can spot the tiny crease is beyond me.

"It isn't necessary; I ironed it the other day."

"I can feel it, I can feel it, I know it's there," Valarian cries as Valen undoes the last button.

"I'll do it," Valen tells him, giving him a worried look as Valarian's tone threatens a meltdown.

"Breathe, buddy. It isn't the end of the world; it can be fixed," Valen states, walking out. He stops in the hall and scratches his head before looking back at me.

"Where do you keep your ironing board and iron?" he asks.

"Uh, the laundry room, where else?"

"Well, mine is in my linen closet," he says with a shrug.

"See, I told you and Zoe it belongs in there," Valarian huffs.

"Yes, the dryer puts lint on..."

"...the ironing board," they both finish at the same time, and I fold my arms and raise an eyebrow. Valen chuckles and shakes his head.

"Definitely my kid," he chuckles, walking off to find the laundry room.

The kids are eating breakfast and I'm onto my second cup of coffee when Valen glances up at me briefly while he cuts Valarian's pancakes.

"I'll be by at one to pick you up," he states.

Now what does he want? It's bad enough I've spent my early waking hours with him this morning.

"And why is that? Valarian doesn't finish school until three."

"I'm taking you to see the doctor,"

"No, I'll go myself. You don't need to come to the doctor with me; I'm fine."

"I will pick you up at one."

"Valen!" I spit at him, and he pins me with a glare, his aura slipping out; my grip on my mug tightens.

"I will pick you up at one; it isn't up for discussion."

Valarian glances between us. The tension in the room is so thick you could cut it with a knife.

Tatum clears his throat, and I'm thankful when he changes the subject.

Valen ends up taking Valarian and Casey to school, much to Casey's amusement. She happily kept asking if being Alpha meant he could kill people and get away with it, and if he could banish her teacher for the crime of looking like a poodle.

I shake my head at that, but Valen politely answers all her questions before making the offer to take her to school. Zoe ends up giving in when she gets a call from Casey's father, who she had been trying to avoid since his parents found out about Casey.

Walking through the hotel, I wave at my secretary with a smile as I pass her before escaping into my office. Turning the lock, I move toward my desk, only to freeze. Alpha Kalen is there, sitting behind my desk, one leg crossed over the other in a reclined position.

"Good morning, Everly. I thought it was a good idea that I stop by for a little chat."

I purse my lips, folding my arms across my chest.

"Is that so?" I ask.

CHAPTER
FORTY-ONE

Valen

Casey and Valarian excitedly pull me down the halls of their run-down school. The floor alone is filthy with scuff marks, and I shiver with disgust, fighting the urge to start scrubbing the floor. The classrooms aren't much better; the desks are falling apart as the cheap particleboard chips away and some kids are even sitting on milk crates. I look around to ensure this is a school and not some homeless shelter.

Valarian shows me to his desk—definitely the cleanest one in the room. I watch as he removes a white table cloth from his bag and sets up his desktop. His pencils sit neatly in a row as he places each one out carefully. Casey, however, opens her pencil case and upends it on the table. I see him cringe before he glares at her and starts rearranging her pencils in a straight line.

I don't want to touch a thing in here; this place is a bacterial infection waiting to happen. When the teacher comes in, I have to do a double-take. She indeed has poodle hair, like she chose the style out of a dog magazine; it's short and curly on top, then cascades to her shoulders in a poof of hair; her round glasses are perched on the end of her nose. She taps her ruler on the desk, trying to grab the students' attention. The ruler snaps and she stares at it before tossing it over her shoulder. It lands perfectly in the bin, making me wonder how many rulers she's broken.

"Oh, Alpha Valen. And why are you here?" She looks around nervously at the students, like she thinks I'm somehow a danger to them.

"My son," I tell her, pointing to Valarian, and she giggles. The sound is more like a hyena; damn, she's a strange lady. She waves me over and I glance at Valarian, who rolls his eyes. I gave him a pointed look at his rudeness, but I now understood why he called her a poodle—I have to fight the urge to straighten her poofy hair. As I walk over to her, I get a whiff of something that smells strangely like weed, the kind you smoke. I sniff the air as I stop next to her.

"Are you high?" I whisper to her.

"You would be too if you had to teach this lot. Want some? Got a bit left."

I blink at her. She just offered me drugs! I glance around the classroom, wondering if I imagined it. Surely, she didn't? What sort of school is this?

"Uh, no, but I, my son, and Casey will be leaving now," I tell her, motioning for both kids to come with me. Valarian starts picking his stuff up off his desk when the woman taps my shoulder with her finger, which makes me glance at her.

"I'm sorry, sir, but you are not on either of their contact lists. I cannot allow you to take those children."

"He is my son, and I brought Casey here," I tell her.

"Unless you are on the documentation, I cannot allow you to remove them from class. And as far as I know, Valarian has no father. Everly Summers never mentioned you being his father. He is a rogue, sir, and you cannot just come into a school and claim a child as your own. We have rules and regulations."

Rules. I wonder briefly what their practices are on drugs and teachers offering parents to get high. This woman is getting on my damn nerves; not only is she high as a kite, but she also looks ridiculous *and* is unfit to be teaching grade school-aged children—or anyone for that matter.

"Valarian, Casey, grab your stuff," I tell them.

The entire class watches on as Mrs. Whats-her-name frantically steps in the way as they move to the front of the classroom.

"Sir, I am sorry, but I can't allow you to take them!" she screeches.

Ignoring her, I reach over and grab Valarian's hand, tugging him gently over to me. When her hand falls on my arm, the growl that tears out of me makes her quickly step back away from me.

"Touch me again and you will find yourself out there with the forsaken," I grit out, and she gasps. Casey rushes over to me, stepping beside Valarian and I turn on my heel, leaving the classroom. This is unacceptable, and I can't believe Everly would allow our son to be taught here by a high woman. What is she thinking?

"Where are we going, Dad?" Valarian asks.

"Anywhere but here," I tell him, stalking off down the hall. I slow my steps when I see both kids struggling to keep up with my long strides.

"Aw, and today is show and tell; I brought Mr. Scruffy," Casey whines.

"You show Mr. Scruffy every week, Casey," Valarian tells her.

"I do not," she pouts.

"You do too."

"Na."

"Uh-huh, you do. Every show and tell."

She and Valarian bicker all the way to the car.

"You can do a show and tell at home. Marcus will love to hear about Mr. Scruffy," I tell her, needing them to stop arguing while I think of what to do about this entire schooling situation. When my phone rings, I stop just outside the school's entrance and pull it from my pocket. Everly's name pops up on the screen, so I answer it.

"Why has the school called me to say you have kidnapped Valarian and Casey?"

"I have done no such thing. Technically, I am still on school property," I tell her.

"Valarian's teacher just called me, Valen. Where is my son?"

"Beside me, with Casey. Do you know his teacher is a stoner?" I whisper the last part through gritted teeth. She falls quiet for a second before I hear her sigh.

"Yes, most are. A lot of the teachers there are from the rogue commune. What do you expect?"

"It is unacceptable."

"Well, I haven't got time for this. I'm in a meeting with.... uh... with someone."

"That's fine, I'll watch them. I am not leaving them with her."

"No, Valen, they need to be in school. And I'm supposed to pick up Taylor today."

"And who is this Taylor?" I demand. If she has a boyfriend, he will be very much a dead one.

"Macey's daughter; it's my turn to pick them up today."

I sigh, looking over my shoulder at the school before heading back into the corridor. I stop and look at all the open classrooms before glancing down at Casey and Valarian.

"You know which one is Taylor's class?"

"Valen, you can't just kidnap other people's kids!" Everly screeches through the phone at me.

"I'm not. Get Zoe and Macey to call and give me permission to take them. You have five minutes," I tell her, hanging up.

"Taylor is in our class, Dad," Valarian tells me.

Great. I start off walking back to the classroom to see his incompetent teacher. As I push the door open, the teacher jumps before a smug smile splits her face.

"I see you came to your senses before I had to call the authorities," she says.

"Yes, I have. Which one of you is Taylor?" I ask, and a little girl at the back with an arm cast raises her hand.

"Psst, Taylor, we're going with my dad. We're breaking out of here," Valarian tells her, and her eyes dart to the teacher. Oh, right, stranger danger, I think. Shit, I *would* technically be kidnapping that one...

The teacher's phone suddenly rings. She answers while putting herself between me and the rest of the class—like her tiny, withered frame would stop me.

"Hello, Ms. Summers."

I tap my foot impatiently, listening. Her eyes dart to me before she looks at Taylor and shakes her head.

"Ms. Summers, I can't allow him to take her."

"Oh. Oh right, well put Ms. Aldrene on then." The teacher chats to whoever she was handed over to for a moment, then suddenly holds the phone out to me. I raise an eyebrow at her.

"Ms. Aldrene wants to speak with you."

I take the phone from her grip and place it to my ear. "Hello?"

"Are you seriously kidnapping our kids?"

"Not kidnapping, babysitting. This is not a school," I tell her.

"Well, if you don't like the schooling, Mr. Solace, do something about it. It's the only school here for rogue children. But I swear to God, if you try to take my daughter out of this city, you won't need to fear the forsaken. Alpha or not, I will skin you alive and put you in an ants' nest."

"Are you finished?" I ask her.

"Yes. I trust Everly and Zoe's judgement of you. Now put Taylor on. She won't go with a stranger," Macey tells me.

I walk over to the girl and pass her the phone. She talks to her mother for a second before grabbing her school bag, then nervously hands the phone to her teacher as Casey grabs her hand. We leave the school and I put the kids in the car before jumping in the driver's seat. I look in the mirror at the three kids.

Now, what do I do?

"Where are we going, Mr. Valarian's dad?" Taylor asks, and my eyes dart to her in the rearview mirror. I think for a second—I've never babysat a child in my life.

"What about the movies?"

"We can't go there."

"Why not?" I ask them.

"Because we're rogue; it isn't in the rogue areas," Casey says, playing with her Mr. Scruffy dog that's missing an ear and an eye.

"Well, today you can because you're with me, but first I need to call Uncle Marcus," I tell them, pulling my phone from my pocket and dialing his number. I listen to it ring.

"We have until 12:30. Plenty of time to watch a movie before I have to pick up your mother," I tell Valarian.

"Can we watch the new 'Trolls' movie? I saw an ad last night for it," Casey chirps excitedly.

"Ooh, yes, I want to watch 'Trolls'," Taylor says.

"Trolls suck," Valarian says.

"Majority rules. We'll watch these trolls, whatever that is," I tell him. "Marcus," I say when he answers.

"Yep, what's up?"

"We're going to the movies."

"You're not my type."

"It's not a date, fool."

"Are you saying I'm not dating material?" Marcus says.

"You're babysitting material."

"Ah. Fine, but you're paying for our non-date, and I want a snow cone. What are we going to see?"

"Apparently 'Trolls'."

"Never heard of it. Horror?"

"Uhh." I glance at the kids in the back. "What are the trolls?" I ask them.

"These ugly monster things they love," Valarian answers, folding his arms across his chest and pouting.

"I think it's an action movie. Fitting. Maybe trolls under a bridge or something," I tell him.

"Ugh, fine. And why are we going to the movies?"

"I need help babysitting," I tell him.

"You need help to babysit *your* son?" he asks.

"No, I have acquired two extras for the day."

"Everly has more than one kid?"

"I'll explain when I see you. Just meet me at the cinema," I tell him before hanging up and starting my car.

CHAPTER
FORTY-TWO

Everly

"You look worried," Kalen states. He leans forward before standing up, then motions toward my chair. I walk over to it before taking my seat. Kalen takes the seat on the other side of my desk.

"No. I kind of expected it. You here to what? Threaten me about telling Valen about Valarie?" I ask while pulling my phone from my pocket and sitting it on the desk.

"You think that little of me?"

"Well, you did let your mate die, so what else should I think?"

"I never intended for that to happen. I loved Val, she... I was coming to claim her, and she always hid how bad it was."

"Bullshit," I say, hating him more and more by the minute.

"You think I wouldn't take it back if I could?"

I don't care to hear his excuses, and I know Tatum must be lurking around, so if needed, I only have to call out to him.

"What do you want?" I ask him.

"Let Valen mark you."

I fold my arms across my chest and sit back, I didn't expect that. "No."

"Don't be stupid, Everly. Do you want to turn out like Valarie?"

"And whose fault is that?" I spit at him.

"Fucking stubborn woman. You're just like her. Set in your ways."

"Marking me will solve nothing. Five years I lived with him screwing around. Am I supposed to forget that? Forget him kicking me out in the rain when I tried to tell him?"

Kalen scrubs a hand down his face. "My son won't take anyone besides his mate, and I need some kind of leverage against your father."

"My father is not my issue."

"Don't be so stupid. I am trying to stop a war," he says.

"And you think I'm the answer to it? My father won't care if I marry Valen or mate and mark him. He hates me, and me having a kid with him will only make him hate me more if he finds out."

"You have no idea what's at stake here."

"For you or me?"

"Both."

"Then tell me. I am not a damn mind reader. You need to either be transparent or get out of my office."

"I know you don't trust me, Everly. But I am trying to do the right thing here," he says.

"You're right, I don't, so cut to the chase; what is it you really want?"

"I want my son to be happy. I want my grandson to be a part of his life." He pauses and sighs heavily. "I want to make up for the past. I want to do what's right by Valarie—what she would have wanted."

"How does letting Valen mark me help you with my father?"

"Because when he does, you are going to announce whose daughter you are."

"Excuse me?"

"Valen won't mark Ava now he knows he has a mate."

"I'm not sure that I understand what you're getting at," I tell him just as my phone starts ringing and vibrating on the table. I glance at it and so does Kalen, who motions me to answer it since it's the school.

The moment I answer, Valarian's teacher is screeching at me through the phone. I jerk it away from my ear and placed it on the loudspeaker so I didn't rupture an eardrum. Kalen shakes his head while I try to get her to calm down.

"Ms. Summers! A man has come and stolen your Valarian and little Casey from class! He just walked out with them! He's claiming Valarian is his son!"

I growl, annoyed, while Kalen smiles, muttering under his breath.

"Alpha Valen, ma'am?"

"Yes, do you know that no-good scoundrel?"

I roll my eyes. Alpha Valen isn't the most favored Alpha among rogues. Kalen clears his throat and I sigh, knowing I have to admit there was no kidnapping and Valen is his father.

"Yes, he is Valarian's father. He took him to school for me this morning," I tell her. Kalen nods and folds his arms, obviously happy with my answer. I don't get Kalen; I thought for sure he would be here trying to warn me away from his son, not encourage me to be with him.

I narrow my eyes at him, listening to her tell me I need to fill forms out at the school, that Valen has to hand in his ID, and yadda, yadda—like anyone would actually be able to stop the feared Alpha Valen even if he broke the law; he *is* the law in the city.

"I will speak to him," I assure her before hanging up. I grit my teeth and start searching my contact list for his number before hitting dial and lifting it to my ear. He answers it after a couple of rings, and I snap at him before he has a chance to speak.

"Why has the school called me to say you have kidnapped Valarian and Casey?"

"I have done no such thing. Technically, I am still on school property," he states, and I rub my forehead before pinching the bridge of my nose in frustration.

"Valarian's teacher just called me, Valen. Where is my son?" I ask through gritted teeth. I'm beginning to get a headache.

"Beside me, with Casey. Do you know his teacher is a stoner?" he whispers, and I sigh. It's pretty obvious she is. I don't think a single teacher there is actually sober.

"Yes, most are. A lot of the teachers there are from the rogue commune. What do you expect?"

"It is unacceptable," he snaps at me, and I move the phone to the other ear when suddenly Kalen is holding out a tissue to me. My brows furrow when I feel something dribble on my lips and taste my blood coating them. I take it from him. He watches me, his brows pinching together, then opens his mouth but quickly closes it.

"Well, I haven't got time for this. I'm in a meeting with.... uh... with someone."

"That's fine. I'll watch them. I am not leaving them with her."

Watch them? He won't even know what to do with them. But here I am, stuck in this ridiculous meeting with his father. Though, I don't want to tell him that and have him get it stuck in his head that I'm allowing him to mark me.

"No, Valen, they need to be in school. And I'm supposed to pick up Taylor today."

"And who is this Taylor?" he demands, and I can hear the burning anger in his voice. Kalen chuckles, and I raise an eyebrow at him.

Jealous, Kalen mouths to me.

"Macey's daughter; it's my turn to pick them up today," I sigh, shaking my head, amused that he thought Taylor was a man.

"You know which one is Taylor's class?" I hear him ask one of the kids.

"Valen, you can't just kidnap other people's kids!" I tell him.

"I'm not. Get Zoe and Macey to call and give me permission to take them. You have five minutes." He abruptly hangs up and I curse. Kalen chuckles.

"He thought you were seeing someone. I know my son and he never gets defensive like that," he laughs.

"He has no right to be anything," I tell him before walking to the door and asking the secretary to get Macey and Zoe.

"My son may have a reputation, but he is a good man—far better than me. He would be a good father, Everly."

"What about a good mate? Can you promise me that?"

Kalen sighs heavily. "Look, you want your son safe, right? Protected. Valen is the key to protecting him."

"I have protected him for years, and I don't need Valen's help or your strange help, if that's even what you're doing, or trying to do."

Kalen starts to say something when the door bursts open. Macey and Zoe rush in. Macey, seeing Kalen, glares at him before pointing an accusing finger.

"I swear, Alpha Asshole, if your son has hurt my daughter, you won't be leaving this damn room," she spits at him while Zoe tries to calm her down.

"He's nice."

I raise an eyebrow at Zoe.

"Well, he is to me. And I don't think he would hurt our kids. I spent all damn morning with him and he only wanted to help with his son," Zoe explains.

"My son would never hurt a child. Tell me one article you have read where he has injured a kid. Leave him be; he will just take them out or bring them back if he can't handle them," Kalen offers Macey.

"And you?" Macey asks.

"He was upset that the teacher is a stoner; nothing malicious," I answer. Macey looks between us all and I can hear her heart racing in her chest. She closes her eyes and sucks in a deep breath.

"Sorry. It feels weird. Besides these two, the only ones that I leave Taylor with are my mother and brother."

"Can never be too careful, but my son means well," Kalen says before looking at me. I bite my lip. What is his game?

I dial Valarian's teacher's number.

"Hello, Ms. Summers."

"Yes, it's fine for Valen to take the kids."

"Ms. Summers, I can't allow him to take Casey."

"Macey and Zoe are right here. I'll put Macey on."

"I already called the school on the walk over," Zoe says, and I nod.

"And Zoe already called the front office."

"Oh. Oh right, well, put Ms. Aldrene on then." I hand the phone to Macey, who snatches it up and allows him to remove Taylor from class before demanding to speak to Valen. Kalen raises an eyebrow but remains quiet.

"Hello?"

"Are you seriously kidnapping our kids?" .... "Well, if you don't like the schooling, Mr. Solace, do something about it. It's the only school here for rogue children. But I swear to God, if you try to take my daughter out of this city, you won't need to fear the Forsaken. Alpha or not, I will skin you alive and put you in an ants' nest." .... "Yes, I trust Everly and Zoe's judgment of you. Now put Taylor on. She won't go with a stranger," Macey snaps at him.

She quickly talks to her daughter before thrusting the phone in my direction. Sighing, she runs her fingers through her hair before glancing at Kalen.

"Why is he here?" she suddenly asks, and Zoe turns her head to stare at him too.

"Just here to give Everly my wishes on the marking."

"More like force her hand," Macey mutters. Kalen stands up, and we all take a step back except Macey. I swear she's either stupid sometimes or just fearless.

"We can catch up again later," Kalen says before nodding to the girls and taking his leave.

"What was that about?"

"I have no damn idea, just said to let Valen mark me." I shake my head and laugh. Neither of them do, instead both eyeing the tissue in my hands.

"Maybe you should, Everly. He–"

"No. I–...no," I repeat, remembering every time I had to feel him with other she-wolves; every damn night. How could everyone just expect me to forget?

CHAPTER
FORTY-THREE

Valen

Well, that was not what I expected. What the heck did I just sit through? It was a damn kids' musical with rainbow-colored trolls farting glitter and singing about rainbows. Marcus found the movie far more entertaining than he should have. I wanted to drill my own ears out! And Valarian glared at the screen the entire time, not impressed. But the girls loved it. I was with my boy—definitely not my cup of tea.

"Will you stop sniffing her? You're creeping me out," I snap at Marcus as he places Casey back in the car. She fell asleep towards the end of the movie and he had to carry her out.

"I need to know the soap Everly and Casey's mothers use. The smell makes my mouth water," he says, sniffing her hair again. "Or maybe it's her shampoo? Or detergent even," he muses.

"There's something wrong with you," I tell him, and he growls at me. The sound makes Casey jolt awake as he clips on her seatbelt before climbing into the passenger seat. Marcus starts humming and singing along as Taylor belts out one of the songs from the movie. I raise an eyebrow at him.

"What? It's catchy," he says, bellowing out the song like he was auditioning for the voice. His hands move like he's orchestrating the damn musical. We stop at the traffic lights and I nearly jump out of my skin when he tries to hit some high note, and the girls in the back stick their fingers in their ears. I turn my head to look at him.

"What is wrong with you?"

"Do you think it has a soundtrack?" he asks. I'm about to say no, not wanting to hear a single one of those prancing troll songs again, when Casey leans forward between the seats.

"Yeah, it has one on Spotify! You can download it. Mom downloaded it for me."

Marcus turns, blinking at her before a devious smile splits his face and he hands his phone to her.

"No," I tell him before suddenly Casey is using the voice commands on his phone. Next thing I know, it's fucking blaring through my car speakers! I growl while they all bop along to the lyrics I know would be stuck in my head on repeat for the next few days.

"Right, that's it, I am dropping you off at home," I tell Marcus, unable to take much more of him encouraging the girls to belt out each track. I pull up out front and he pouts.

"Out," I tell him, and he turns, ruffling Valarian's hair. My son growls, trying to fix it. Marcus turns to the girls.

"Got any more movie recommendations?"

"Frozen! Frozen!" they chant.

"It has a singing snowman!" Casey tells him.

"It's a movie date. Also, ask your mother what detergent she uses. I need to get me some of that," he says, and Casey sniffs herself.

"Huh?"

"Your clothes," he says before reaching over and tugging on her braid. He sniffs it.

"Huh?"

"Maybe ask about which shampoo too?"

"Okay, weirdo," Casey says, and he jams his fingers in her under-arm, making her giggle.

"What's that? Huh? What'd you call me?"

"Fine! Fine! You're not weird!" she shrieks as he tickles her.

"That's right. I am awesoooome, and way cooler than Mr. Cranky-pants here," he sings before punching my shoulder. Casey and Taylor giggle before he hops out.

I shake my head, making my way back to the hotel. I now have to take Everly to the doctor. Even if it means throwing her over my shoulder and dragging her ass out kicking and screaming, she's going.

Pulling up at the hotel, I see Zoe waiting out front. I had messaged Everly when I left the cinema to let her know I was on my way over, so I'm a little pissed that she isn't waiting when her appointment is in fifteen minutes.

Getting out of the car, Zoe is already at the door and retrieving her daughter, and she unclips Valarian's belt before I have a chance to even get to him.

"Where's Everly?" I ask.

"In the kitchens helping the chef prepare for the dinner rush. Did they behave?"

"Yes, of course. Uhh, Everly's appointment?"

Zoe bites her lip before pointing toward the restaurant, clearly reading the stern look on my face.

I grunt.

"I don't think she's going. She said she had to wait for an electrician, though Macey said she would handle it. Also, the dinner rush is approaching, and she has to sort out next week's rosters; we have a few off sick at the moment."

I slam the door, which makes Zoe jump. I didn't mean to startle her, but I'm livid. I specifically told her what time, and she insists on working rather than looking after her health.

"You alright with Valarian for a few hours?"

"Of course. He can help me in the children's playgroup."

Valarian sulks. "Why can't I come with you and mom?" he asks, and my heart twinges at his upset face.

"Because daddy is about to drag your mommy to the doctors kicking and screaming," I tell him.

"But she said she would go?" Valarian says. I sigh, and Zoe shrugs before grabbing both of their hands.

"Good luck!" she calls over her shoulder as I stalk toward the restaurant. She's certainly gotten friendlier. I shove the doors open, walking into the kitchen to find Everly rushing around doing Goddess knows what.

"Everly," I call out to her, and she looks up. The entire kitchen also stops and looks over at me.

"Busy. Not now," she says, turning back to her task of helping the chef.

"Nope," I growl, knowing she's planning on ignoring me. I walk over to the steel table she's stationed at before grabbing the knife from her hand. I can see the wide-eyed kitchen hands looking at me, but she's going. It isn't up for discussion.

"What do you think you are doing?" she snaps at me, trying to reach for the knife I pried from her grip. I toss it in the sink.

"You have an appointment."

"Reschedule—I'm busy," she growls, and if looks could kill, she would have turned me to dust. Good thing they don't. I growl back at her, then grab her around the waist as she starts to reach for another knife from the block before tossing her over my shoulder.

"Valen, stop!" she shrieks before punching my back as I start walking out.

"Don't you dare; this is humiliating. I work here! Put me down!"

"Are you going to walk?"

"I told you I'm busy; we're down three people today."

"Wrong answer," I tell her before stalking out into the restaurant. Luckily for her, it isn't full, though I wouldn't have cared if it was.

"I'll walk! I will Goddamn walk."

I ignore her, shoving the door open. I'm honestly enjoying the view of her ass in my face. If only she were sitting on it.

"Valen, stop. I said I would walk."

"Nope, I don't trust you," I tell her. I'm halfway to my car when I feel her teeth sink into my back.

"Agh! You damn cannibal!" I snap at her before biting her ass. I must say, I enjoyed her shriek more than I should as she rubs her plump ass. I swat her hand away, wanting to rub it myself, which earns me a growl as I run my hand over her butt.

"Don't bite unless you want to be bitten back," I tell her as I open my car door.

"I can feel it bruising," she snarls before I deposit her in the passenger seat. I slam the door and point at her through the glass.

"Move, and I will put you over my knee if I have to," I warn her. She looks at me before realizing what I said—the look of horror on her face is comical.

"You wouldn't," she says, her eyes narrowing.

"I would," I tell her before opening her door again.

"Go on, run and find out, Everly," I dare her. She looks like she's seriously considering it. I clip her seatbelt in when she folds her arms across her chest and glares out the windshield.

"Good choice; I spank hard," I tell her, pecking her cheek and side of her mouth.

"You are crossing the line, Valen Solace."

"And you are getting on my last damn nerve. Do I need to make you pinky promise from now on?"

She rolls her eyes and I shut the door before climbing into the driver's seat.

"Wait, where's Valarian?"

"Zoe," I answer, starting the car. "By the way, we're going to the registry tomorrow—I'm changing his last name."

"Like hell you are."

"Hyphenate it then. Either way, he is getting my name," I tell her, pulling out of the parking lot.

She didn't bother arguing after that and remained quiet the rest of the trip.

When I pull up at my Hotel, she looks at me.

"I thought we were going to an appointment?"

"We are. The pack doctor is coming here," I tell her, and she glares at me.

"No," she huffs.

"Suit yourself," I tell her, getting out and walking around to open her door. "Which is it, Everly? I carry you or you walk."

Her canines slip out and her eyes blaze with her fury.

"I will walk," she snaps before getting out and slamming my door. She stalks off toward the entrance, muttering under her breath.

"And you have been getting nosebleeds for how long?" Doctor Pat asks.

"A while," she answers. She kicked up a huge fuss when I refused to leave, and I was curious as to why, so had refused to leave the room. She's only given vague answers whenever he's asked any questions, which is beginning to annoy me.

"Answer his questions," I snap at her, forcing my aura out over her and she shudders before blurting out an answer.

"Four years."

"Does she have any resistance to your aura? She answered the question rather quickly," Doc asks, and I can see the concern in his eyes as he peers down at her.

I shake my head; I barely used my aura. Even Valarian would have been able to fight what I just used, but there was no resistance from Everly—like her own doesn't exist at all.

"Her blood pressure is low; very low. She is also underweight," the doctor says, looking over the top of his clipboard at me. He's been running tests non-stop while his assistant takes notes.

"What about unusual bruising?" he asks, and she shakes her head. I shove my aura out. She growls and jolts in her seat.

"Yes," she spits through gritted teeth before glaring at me.

"Any at the moment?"

I raise an eyebrow at her, about to use my aura, but she blurts out an answer before I have to.

"Yes, my ribs."

"Can I see?"

"I would rather you didn't."

"Everly, remove your shirt, or I will do it for you," I warn her.

"Can't you make him leave? What about confidentiality? Or is that not practiced in this pack?" she spits at the doctor.

"You are his mate. He has every right to be here, being the Alpha. I am sorry, Luna."

"I am not your damn Luna," she says, and I growl at her. Everly rolls her eyes before tugging her shirt off. I was not expecting to see her so purple and blue. Her skin across her ribs looks like she's been beaten. Red and purple blotches cover her ribs and back.

"See? Must be low iron. See? Just my ribs," she says before she starts to pull her shirt on. I snatch it from her, standing up and spinning her to the doctor, who also gasps.

"What are you doing?"

"Your back is worse than your ribs," I snap at her, and she looks under her arms, twisting, trying to see.

"This bruising comes and goes?"

She doesn't answer, as she's too busy inspecting herself.

"What?" she asks, looking up at the doctor.

"Does the bruising remain, or come and go?"

She chews her lip nervously.

"Everly?" I ask. She scowls, and her tongue pokes the side of her cheek as she looks at the ceiling for a second.

"It stays," she murmurs before looking at the doctor, who is actually looking at me. I'm confused.

"What?" I ask, and Everly hastily tugs her top on, covering herself.

"It's infidelity markings; the more people the mate is with, the more it affects the bond," the doctor says.

"I haven't been with anyone since finding her!" I tell him, horrified.

"That may be so, but how many have you been with since Everly knew you were her mate?" He looks at Everly in question.

"I've known he was my mate for just over four years now," she answers, and my stomach drops. I knew that, but to count how many times I had sex in that time?

I swallow, looking at the doctor. "Those are from me?" I ask, and he nods.

"They're called a 'taint' or infidelity marks. Every time you are with someone, it taints the bond. Everly is your bond. Therefore, it taints her. They are apparently quite painful, but if it has been four years, she probably has a good pain threshold of it now; be more like a normal bruise, except it scars the bond."

"But it will go away, right?" I ask, not wanting to be the blame for her remaining permanently disfigured like that.

"Yes, after a while; quicker if you mark her. As long as you remain only with her, of course." He leans forward and pauses, bracing his hands on his knees and sighs.

"Your bond is toxic, and it is essentially poisoning her. Eventually..." He pauses for a moment. "Please don't take this the wrong way, Alpha, but you have been with a lot of women for her body to be deteriorating at such a rate. Most of the time, this is the reaction of a rejected bond, and in the advanced stages."

"What do you mean?"

"She is dying, Alpha. At this rate, it could only be a couple of years, especially if you keep sleeping with other women. You will kill the bond and, in turn, kill her."

Everly gasps.

"But wait, people live like this for decades, not years. I ..." She glances at me. "I've researched it."

"Yes, but you are rogue and also young. I haven't seen this sort of deterioration in a patient before. Given Alpha Valen's reputation with other women, I am afraid you are deteriorating more quickly than most I have seen, which explains your lack of aura; also all your other symptoms."

"So, how do we fix it?" I ask desperately, still feeling sick.

"You mark and mate her. Remain close to build the bond. Bonds are fragile, Alpha. They are supposed to be taken care of, not abused," he says, glancing away. It was like being punched in the gut. So, I did this? I did all of this? I nod, but Everly is shaking her head.

"No. We will find another way," Everly says.

"There is no other way. I am marking you, and that is final."

Doc clears his throat, and I look over at him.

"May I make a suggestion?"

"Yes, please," Everly says and huffs.

"I understand, Everly, you don't want him to mark you. That is, unfortunately, the bond. It hurts; I get it. I get that betrayal is unforgivable, and you have been living with this a long time, clearly."

What the fuck is he doing? Doc looks at me before frowning.

"Maybe if you mark him until you are comfortable accepting the bond, it will help strengthen it and slow down the deterioration, but eventually, he will have to mark you."

"No, I will just mark her and be done with it," I say.

"Alpha, I don't recommend forcefully marking her. You need to understand that you doing that could hurt her more,"

"But you just said..."

He scrubs a hand down his face.

"I know what I said, but your bond has been weakened. Unless Everly wants you to mark her, you could make her worse. You need to remember you being with another woman was basically like rejecting her repeatedly. The bond is damaged. You need to repair it before forcefully marking her. You marking her will not only make her hate you but may shock her system."

"What if she never lets me mark her?"

"We will cross that bridge when we come to it. I would like to reschedule for a month's time," he says, and I nod. Everly also inclines her head slowly—I'm relieved she agreed. Maybe hearing this scared her. It petrifies me. I just found her and may lose her, all because I was an idiot. I make myself feel sick.

I reschedule her appointment and see Doc and his assistant out while Everly waits in the living room. When I return, I find her staring out the window.

"Everly?"

She nods, turning around before walking toward me.

"We should head back," she states, about to move past me when I grab her. "We need to get back." She looks like she's on the verge of tears.

"I know you hate me, but please, just mark me."

"I'll think about it; come on." She moves to step away, but I shove her, pressing her against the wall. She struggles, trying to push me away.

"I know I did this. Let me fix it," I snap at her.

"Valen," she growls, which sounds more like a purr than any threat.

"No. You aren't leaving my apartment until you mark me. Stop being stubborn. I know I fucked up but don't let me be the reason you die. Think of Valarian. Hate me, but fucking me mark me— DON'T KILL YOURSELF BECAUSE OF ME!" I scream at her before shoving my aura over her. I use a little too much and she cowers away from me, making my heart twist painfully in my chest.

I drop IT before resting my head on her shoulder. My breathing is heavy, along with my anger. However, it Isn't aimed at her, but at myself.

"Just take me home."

"You want me to beg? I will fucking beg," I tell her before dropping to my knees. I don't care how stupid it is; I'll do it. Whatever she asks, I will do it.

"Please, if not for yourself, do it for Valarian—don't leave him because of me; don't do that to our son," I plead before it becomes too much.

I couldn't live with the guilt if I killed her. I couldn't. I bury my face in my hands, utterly ashamed of what I've put her through. I did this. I did this to her. I made her hate me. I ruined our bond. I can't remember the last time I cried, but this news is gut-wrenching. I can't take it, knowing I did this. The guilt weighs too heavily, and I know I would never be able to live with myself if she died because of me.

I feel her fingers brush through my hair, making me glance up to see her eyes brimming with tears.

"For Valarian," she whispers, and I nod.

"Please," I tell her, gripping her legs, and she nods before looking away.

CHAPTER
FORTY-FIVE

Everly

I wasn't expecting the answer I received from the doctor; I wasn't even aware the bond could be damaged. Sure, I was used to the pain, but to know he hurt our bond? Nothing about the bond felt weaker to me. I still feel for Valen despite not wanting to—still crave him despite hating everything about him. I just want to go home and snuggle my son, smell his scent, and let him soothe my racing mind.

Yet, the way Valen is looking at me, I can see his fear clearly etched onto his face; can see how much the doctor's words scared him as he presses his face into my neck. Valen finally understands the weight of his actions, and I can tell the burden is heavy for him to carry. His grip on my arms is tight, like he thinks I'm about to drop dead before his eyes. My heart twists painfully in my chest with the way his voice cracks as he speaks.

"You want me to beg? I will fucking beg," Valen tells me before dropping to his knees. He clutches my legs, and if the wall wasn't behind me, I would have toppled over. I can feel his warm breath caress the skin under my blouse where it rode up. I feel the shake of

268

his shoulders—he's falling apart. I know I shouldn't feel bad for him after everything he's done, and maybe it's the bond, but the way he's speaking tells me he knows the pain of losing a mother even if he didn't know her. I wonder what sort of man he would be if she raised him. Would he be the mate I needed him to be, the father he needed to be for our son?

Most of all, I wonder if I can ever forgive him, even if it's only for Valarian.

"Please, if not for yourself, do it for Valarian—don't leave him because of me; don't do that to our son," he chokes out, and before I can stop myself, I run my fingers through his hair, wanting to soothe the agony I can hear bleeding into his voice.

"For Valarian," I whisper, the words not sounding my own as I think of my son—the person in this world that holds all my broken pieces together, the child I carried to term, the child I raised and loved from birth. The one person who loves me back.

"Please," Valen begs, and I glance down at him to see him staring up at me. I tear my gaze away. I promised myself I could do it on my own, and I feel like doing this means I'm giving in, tossing away everything I worked so hard for. But I won't toss my life away; I can't bear the thought of Valarian being in this world alone without me.

"Everly?" Valen whispers, and I look down at the man on his knees, hanging onto me like he can somehow put me back together if he squeezes hard enough. I watch his eyes brim with tears, and my hand moves from his hair to cup his face on instinct. His stubble is rough against my palm, and I brush away a stray tear when he blinks and it spills over.

"I'll do anything, but don't make him grow up without a mom," Valen whispers. His lip quivers as he leans into my hand before kissing my palm—sparks dance across it. I bite my lip and look away from the broken man before me.

"I mark you, that doesn't mean you own me, and you don't force my hand," I say.

"I promise," he says, pulling away. I snort, my own tears spilling when I look back down and he's holding out his pinky.

"I'll even pinky promise."

"You know you can't break one of those? They're sacred," I chuckle. He nods before standing, and I look up at him.

"You won't use your Alpha voice on me? You won't mark me unless I let you?" I ask him, but he shakes his head.

"I won't promise to not mark you; I won't watch you wither away because you're too stubborn; I won't let you get to that point, Everly, so don't ask me to promise you that. Ask for anything else but that."

"But if I mark you, you can just turn around and do the same," I tell him.

"I won't. I won't promise never to do it, but I can promise you not today, though?" he asks, and I sigh. He holds his pinky up and wiggles it, and I roll my eyes.

"I promise to make it up to you; I promise to not use my Alpha voice on you anymore if you promise to mark me before we leave this apartment."

I chew my lip while considering what to do, but he's right; I would be killing myself out of stubbornness if I refuse. And if I refuse, he 'll probably mark me anyway and take his chances.

"Everly?" Valen says, pressing closer so his chest presses against mine. He holds his pinky up and I feel my lips try to tug at the corners over the silly little thing I have with Valarian.

"Okay," I tell him, gripping it with mine. Valen lets out a breath and dips his face toward mine; I press further into the wall I'm caged against. His nose skims across my cheek to my ear. My heart thumps erratically in my chest at what I agreed to.

"Thank you," he whispers next to my ear. His scent overwhelms my senses, and I lean into him, soaking up his scent and inhaling deeply. I feel his hand slip into my hair and a shiver runs up my spine as he turns his head, offering me his neck.

"Please, Everly, just claim me. It can mean whatever you want it to mean. Just do it," he murmurs, and I suck in a deep, shaky breath. I can do this, sure, but at the same time, I hate giving him the wrong idea. Yet my mouth starts watering at his intoxicating scent, overwhelming the part of me that's denying him, and I feel my canines slip from my gums before sinking them into his neck.

Valen grips my hair and presses so close I can feel every hard line of muscle that remains hidden beneath his shirt. My teeth sink in deeply, and warmth blooms in my chest before I feel the tether binding him to me, snap in place. Valen shudders against me, and his emotions slam into me like he just slapped me.

Guilt, overwhelming guilt so strong I nearly choke on it. Yet also immense relief that I marked him. I'm not sure what to think as my teeth pull from his skin and I run my tongue across the mark, sealing it. Valen doesn't let me go. Instead, he leans against me, pressing his weight into me. His face turns toward me, then he leans down and presses his forehead against mine.

"Now you own me," he whispers before glancing at my blood-smeared lips. He moves his hand, cupping my face before brushing his thumb across my bottom lip and wiping his blood off. "Now you have my heart, and it's your choice whether or not you break it. But please don't," he murmurs.

I move my hand to the center of his chest. I can feel his heart thumping beneath it rapidly, like a hummingbird's wings fighting against stormy winds, and he sucks in a deep breath at my touch.

"Don't make me have to," I tell him before looking away. Valen nods, dropping his head on my shoulder and inhaling my scent as he presses his face into the crook of my neck. I have to fight the reaction my body has when his breath sweeps over where his mark should be laid. Every part of me urges me toward him and makes me want to curl up on his lap and let him hug away the five years of pain, let him fill the void that was caused by him. However, I know that's the bond speaking and that his emotions are bleeding into me as if they were my own.

"We should get back to Valarian," I tell him, and he nods before stepping back.

CHAPTER
FORTY-SIX

The drive back is quiet but not awkward; just a comfortable silence. I believe me marking him suddenly made everything more real. Before, it was, in a sense, easy to play off that he's my mate, easier to deny our bond—or our weak one anyway. Now though, people will find out. The entire city will realize Valen has been marked, the paparazzi will go berserk, and now I worry about what that means for Valarian. I can handle the dramas the media will portray, but Valarian is still a child.

I know once it's out, a lot of people will have something to say about it. Also, I can already imagine the rumors: that he knocked up some rogue whore and was forced to take me as his mate. The things I can see them saying about me in papers would sting me, but could damage my son. I'm used to negativity, but no child should have to deal with that.

"I think we should move the date of the Alpha meeting," I whisper.

"You want to push it back?" Valen asks. I shake my head.

"Move it forward. Once the media gets their hands on this story, it will blow up; it should be announced to stop it hurting Valarian."

And my father, I think. I hate the idea of confronting him, yet I know it will be worse if he found out via some news article. I know I shouldn't care what he believes after everything. I'm an adult now, and he no longer controls my life, but for some reason, it nags at me; some part of me believes that he shouldn't find out through a news outlet.

"Anyone says anything about our son, Everly, and they won't have a city to live in," he says, putting his hand on my leg.

"You can't just kick people out of the city; that's not the answer, Valen, and that's not what I am worried about."

"Then what are you worried about?"

"I'm worried about what version of our strange... whatever-it-is..." I sigh, rubbing my temples before looking at him. "They're going to say some horrible shit about you being with a rogue whore. Valarian has only just found out about you—well, about who you are —and I worry that what they say about both of us will have an impact on him."

"Then I tell them the truth—simple."

"It's not that simple. You have a reputation to uphold in this city, Valen; one that holds power."

"I don't care about my reputation, Everly. They can say what they want about me—they do anyway—but if you think I'm going to let you take the fall for all of it, you are mistaken."

"They'll say I'm a gold digger, someone who trapped you. Probably even say Valarian isn't yours."

"That they can't say, you can tell by his aura, plus DNA will shut them up."

"My father is going to lose his mind," I mutter, shaking my head.

"Surprisingly, my father took it pretty well," Valen adds, making me think of Kalen and my meeting with him.

"I saw your father earlier today," I admit, looking back out the window.

"Did he threaten you? If he did, tell me. I'll handle it," Valen says.

"You would really go against your father for a rogue?"

"For you and Valarian, I would go against the entire world if needed," Valen says, and I chew my lip. I can feel he means what he said. Feeling him makes his words hold more meaning, and I don't know what to think about him. He can lie through words, but not through the bond, so to feel that he means exactly what he said kind of throws me off.

"He didn't threaten me. He told me to let you mark me."

He chuckles. "Yeah, he's a good father, strict, but he means well, mostly."

"Is that why he tried to get you to marry my sister?"

"No, idea what he meant by that. He's hated your father for decades. It makes no sense to me," Valen admits, and I can feel his worry through the bond, making me realize he, too, noticed his father's change in attitude.

"Are you worried about your father finding out?" Valen asks as we pull into the hotel parking space. He stops the car.

"Yes and no. I'll be relieved I don't have to keep it a secret anymore, but I'm also scared of everyone's reaction."

"Why didn't you just tell him?"

I raise an eyebrow at him and he laughs.

"Yeah, that was a dumb question," he adds. "Do you think he would have kicked you out if he knew?"

"I've thought of that actually—thought about telling him, especially once I found out you were, in fact, my mate."

"Then why didn't you? Would have saved you being homeless."

"Your father isn't the only one that worries about his reputation, Valen. When he found out I was pregnant, he tried to get the doctor to abort Valarian, sweep it under the rug so no one would know, and I could still take my place as Alpha. Like Valarian was some dirty secret."

Valen growls at my words, and his knuckles turn white as he grips the steering wheel.

"I couldn't do it, so he kicked me out. I believe the reaction would have been the same, if not worse, if he knew you were his father."

"You think he would have pinned you down and made you abort if he knew?"

"No, I believe he would have killed me or come after our son once he was born to use him as a tool against you. I couldn't allow that."

"And now what's changed? Why can you be honest now?"

"Valarian has you. I know you'll keep him safe," I admit. I can tell just by his reaction to having a son. Zoe said it herself too. She knew Valen's intentions were good, unlike some we'd come across over the years.

"Can I ask how you came into the possession of a hotel, being rogue?" Valen asks, looking out at the place I call home—my village. I love this place, not just because of what it has given us but because of where it came from and the history behind it.

"It was given to Valarian and me. We inherited it."

"By your grandparents?"

"No, by the woman who owned it. When you kicked me out of the packhouse, I went home—or tried to anyway. My father was gracious enough to let Valarian in the house after my mother begged him because it was raining. The next morning, dad tossed some money at me and said he never wanted to see me again, that I was causing problems between him and mom, so I went back to my car. I grabbed a few things, walked here, and met a woman," I told him. I look over at the doors where the main front counter is. I can still picture her clearly, like it was yesterday; Valarie sitting out front with a smoke between her lips, rough as guts but with a heart of gold. She was a tough woman. A remarkable woman.

"I thought she was someone staying at the hotel," I chuckle. "She was rogue also. She gave us a fresh start, offered me a job, paid for my schooling—she gave me hope. Then, when she died, she left it all to me."

"Is that how you met Zoe and Macey?"

"No, I met them at the maternity ward. When I was given the job, we needed help to clean it up—the place was a dump. She gave them jobs too, said we would build our own village, that family is what you make it. So once it was running and I found out about inheriting it, that's what I did; I built our village. Our village of rogues."

"I guess I owe her one. She seems like a good woman."

"She was. I can only dream of being half the woman she was. No words can describe how great she was."

"Have you got pictures of what it looked like before? I honestly never knew the place existed," Valen laughs.

"You want to see?" I laugh before opening the door. Come, I'll show you," I tell him.

Valen hops out of the car before locking it and follows me toward the front entrance. The bell sounds as we walk in and the secretary looks up.

"Coffee?"

"No, we're fine, Jenny. Shouldn't you be clocked out?" I ask her, knowing Emily should have been in for the afternoon shift.

"I was finished an hour ago. Emily never showed. I've been trying her cell but no answer."

Hmm. That's very unlike Emily. She never misses a shift.

"She may have come down with that bug that's going around," Jenny suggests. I nod.

"Knock off. I'll handle the front desk until I can find someone to come in."

"Actually, I don't mind. I could use the overtime, if that's alright?"

I turn to face her and she looks down, fiddling with her fingers.

"Your son?" I ask.

She nods her head. Jenny is in her fifties and has a son, who is constantly in trouble, especially with the police. She managed to get him into rehab a few weeks ago, making me wonder what was going on. With everything going on lately, I haven't had a chance to ask how he's doing. He sometimes helped the gardeners and the handy woman here.

"Everything alright?" I ask her.

"Yeah, it's fine," she answers too quickly.

"Jenny?"

"I didn't want to ask because you bailed him out last month already, and I still owe you for that..."

"You don't owe me anything. So what's he done now? You know, we have emergency funds for staff—it's there to be used, to help when someone gets stuck."

Her eyes dart to Valen for a second. I completely forgot he was still behind me. I glance back at him, and he looks at me.

"Nothing. He's doing great actually, but the hospital is making him leave."

"I thought it was a three-month program?"

"It was supposed to be, but he isn't a priority on the waiting list."

"But if he already got in, he should be fine to stay. I'm assuming you're talking about some rehab or medical facility?" Valen answers behind me.

She looks at him for a second before looking at me, then does a double-take of Valen, her eyes zeroing in on the mark on his neck. It's no secret in the hotel that Valen is my mate, yet we rogues stick together, and I suddenly worry what the other women will think. I know they'll be happy I have a mate, but I hope they don't think they can't still come to me.

"You marked him?" she asks.

FORTY-SEVEN

"Yes, but it can't get out at the moment. Now, don't change the subject. What do you need?"

"They're kicking him out unless he's a paying patient. They said they haven't got the beds for a rogue," she answers.

"Bullshit. It's only at half capacity," Valen growls behind me. Jenny looks down.

"It's because he's a rogue, Valen; no one helps rogues. You should have seen us getting this place running. We couldn't even get a handyman in without blackmailing them," I tell him, and he seems appalled at my words. Considering who his father is, at least he doesn't seem to hold the same views of rogues. Well, at least not as strongly.

"How much?" I ask her, knowing how hard she tried to get him in there.

"$11,000," she breathes before rubbing both hands down her face.

"Use the funds. It's what it's for. When he gets out, he can come work at the hotel for a bit," I tell her. That's a big chunk out of the emergency rogue funds, not that anyone will complain—it's what it's for.

"Don't worry about it. I'll handle it," Valen says behind me.

"It's fine, Valen. We have the money here."

"I don't care about the money. They gave him a place there. If he's doing well and not causing trouble, they have no reason to kick him out. That place relies heavily on donations and taxpayer's money. I'm assuming it's the main hospital, since rogues can't use the private ones?"

She nods.

"I'll take care of it. I'll place him in one of the private ones if they kick up a stink, but they won't. My pack funds half of that hospital," Valen tells her with a shrug. "I'll need his information."

She looks around her desk before grabbing a sticky note and writing his name, date of birth, and address on it. She hands it to him, and Valen folds it, placing it in his pocket.

"Are you sure? We have a fund for this sort of stuff," I tell him.

"Positive. But I would like to know more about this fund you have for your employees," he answers.

"Thank you, Alpha," Jenny nods, and I see her shoulders relax like a ton of weight has just been lifted off her shoulders.

"Go home, Jenny. Rest," I tell her, but she shakes her head.

"I'm good until you find someone to take over," she says just as the bell sounds, and I glance over at the door as Tatum walks in.

"Ah, just the man I wanted to see," Valen says, and Tatum raises an eyebrow at him.

"Uh, yeah? Didn't you want me to keep watch again?" Tatum asks him, unsure.

"Nope, change of plans. I'll do it tonight—I have another job for you." He motions toward the desk.

"You want me to move it?" Tatum asks, confused.

"Nope. I want you to man it. Everly is down a staff member."

"What?" Tatum asks before staring at Jenny.

"Yeah... I don't think that's a good idea," I say.

"Are you saying I can't answer some phones and work the front desk?" Tatum asks, like I just insulted his intelligence.

"It's more than answering phones," I tell him.

"Can't be that hard," Tatum says, walking around the desk. Jenny looks up at him wide-eyed before looking at me.

"See? He can handle it," Valen says. Why can I tell this is a bad idea? I pinch the bridge of my nose and shake my head.

"Valen, he's a security guard, not a secretary," I explain.

"See? Killed two birds with one stone. He's now a guard *and* can do whatever Jenny was doing."

"This is a bad idea; I'm sure I can find someone else," I say.

"Nonsense, Jenny will show him. And you can show me these photos," Valen says, nudging me toward my office in the back. I glance at Jenny, and she shrugs before getting up. Tatum takes her seat, and she starts explaining things to him and showing him how to use the different phones.

With a heavy sigh, I give in, though he'll definitely be the most buff secretary we've had manning the counter. He looks out of place behind the desk with its pink stationery.

Unlocking my office door, I step in and move to one of the bookcases, grabbing down the hotel photo album. I sit at my desk, and Valen comes over to stand beside me.

Opening the front page, there's an old black and white photo of Valarie's parents from when they owned it. I pull it out and pass it to him. In the photo, there's a man and a woman holding a baby, which Valarie said was her.

"That doesn't look too bad?" Valen states and I snort before flicking through to the photos Zoe and I took when I first came here. I pass them to him before grabbing another one out. Macey's brother took one of us facing the ruined hotel with our backs to the camera —all four of us standing out the front. Valarie's also in it, cigarette between her fingers as she looks at the rundown place. I hand it to him.

"This the woman?" he asks, and I nod. "And Macey and Zoe. So you all started it together? The place looked like a dump," he states.

"It was," I say.

"So the four of you did all this?" he asks, sounding incredulous.

"Yep, four rogue whores and three babies restored this entire place," I tell him.

"Who took the photo?"

"Macey's brother."

"He didn't help?"

I raise an eyebrow at him. "What are you trying to say?"

"Nothing. Just... four women fixed all of this?"

"We may be women, but we're resourceful. Besides, Macey is more manly than her brother. She fights like a guy, too, so stay on her good side."

He laughs, handing them back. "Noted. She definitely looks like a scrapper."

"Oh, she is. I watched her beat a man with a 20 pound bag of flour once. She hauled it around like it weighed nothing."

"What'd he do?"

"He asked her how much."

"How much for what?"

"How much for a night, Valen. He thought because she's rogue, she's a prostitute; that was when we first opened up. It was a bit of shock when they found the place was run entirely by rogues. We ended up with a few creeps in at first."

"So, how did you handle that?"

"A few of the older ladies started bringing their sons in for the night shifts. Day shifts were easier; Macey would turf anyone that looked at us wrong," I laugh. "Come on, we should check on Valarian and give Zoe a break," I tell him, and he follows me through the hotel to the apartment. I'm stopped a few times by different staff, and by the time we get back to the apartment, it's dark.

Walking in, I see Zoe doing puzzles with the kids. She smiles as she glances over the back of the couch at me before her eyes narrow in on Valen and her lips pull over her teeth. She stands abruptly, pointing an accusing finger at him before remembering the kids are in the room.

I have no idea why she's mad, but I can tell she's livid about something. She steps over the kids and moves toward him. Valen, completely unaware of her anger, says 'hello' to her before she opens the door behind him and shoves him out, slamming it shut behind her. I move to the kitchen window and peered out. Valen has his hands in the air, and I crack the window open a little to eavesdrop.

"You keep your creepy sniffing friend away from my daughter," she snarls. I glance at Casey, wondering what happened. Valarian looks up at me.

"Auntie Zo' is upset because we asked what shampoo and detergent she uses," Valarian explains, which only makes me more confused.

"You tell him to keep his sniffer away from my daughter."

"He just liked the soap you use," Valen tries to explain.

"Casey said he sniffed her repeatedly," Zoe growls at him.

"I'll speak to him, but it was nothing bad. He just said the soap smells nice, jeez."

"It's fucking creepy. You don't go around sniffing people's kids. If that doesn't set off alarm bells in your head, nothing will."

"My Beta is not a creep. He would never harm your daughter, Zoe," Valen says, defending Marcus.

"Keep him away from my daughter," Zoe huffs before going back to the door. She steps in and straightens her clothes, going back to the kids like nothing happened.

Valen returns, looking awkward as hell, but the tension leaves the moment Valarian spots him and jumps up off the floor.

"Dad!" he squeals, rushing over. Valen catches him and picks him up, kissing his cheek and hugging him tightly. "I missed you," Valarian gushes, squeezing tight.

"I missed you too," Valen tells him before setting him on his feet. Zoe watches them, and I notice Casey does, too, before looking up at her mother and snuggling against her. It must be hard seeing Valarian with his father. Casey sees hers, but usually only for five minutes when he stops in randomly before telling her some lie about needing to go to work. Yet, she hasn't seen him since Officer Richards found out.

"Are you staying for dinner?" Valerian asks. "One of the chefs sent up stuffed peppers; you'll like those."

"There's plenty there. She always sends up too much," Zoe says. Having calmed down, her eyes dart to Valen's neck, and she raises an eyebrow at me before smiling. Of course, and she would be happy. I look at her just as Valen speaks.

"I was hoping to stay the night. Tatum is playing secretary in your lobby, and since Marcus is definitely off the table now..." Valen says, looking at me.

"You can stay for dinner, but we don't need a guard," I tell him.

"Please, Mom? He can sleep in my bed; I'll share with him," Valarian whines.

"That's not necessary, Val. We have a couch, but your father has..." I stop, knowing he already admitted to wanting to stay, proving he has nothing better to do.

"One night, and *only* one, Valarian," I tell him before also looking at his father so he knows not to ask for a second night.

"Ah, see? I get to stay for the night," Valen tells him as Valarian tugs on his hand, dragging him towards his puzzle.

CHAPTER
FORTY-EIGHT

It feels strange having Valen under my roof. Awkward. Everything I usually do for Valarian, he suddenly asked his dad to do, like cut up his food. I'm suddenly no longer needed; he asked for his father when it was his bath time. Most of my evening was spent twiddling my thumbs, since I only had to heat dinner up. Yet, Valen never once complained and actually seemed to enjoy his son's constant attention. I dread when he eventually leaves, knowing it will make my bond ache, so I know I'll be taking my pills that are hidden in the cupboard. Hopefully, I can sneak them past Zoe.

Even as I went to put Valarian to bed, he asked if his father could tuck him in. I know it was childish, but nights were the only time I got to spend with him, really, so it bothered me more than it should. I'm so used to juggling things between Zoe and me that it feels unnatural having someone willingly helping us, ruining our usual routine. I suddenly have time on my hands, and I'm not sure how I feel about that.

Once Valarian was tucked in bed, Valen returned to the living room. He scratched the back of his neck before looking at the empty spot beside me on the couch.

I roll my eyes before moving over. He smiles, coming to sit next to me and draping his arm across the back of it.

"Finally, Casey is down for the night," Zoe says, coming out in her pajamas while braiding her hair. I've always been envious of how she can do that. I had tried and ended up only making a knotted mess, yet she does it so effortlessly.

Zoe comes over and sits down on one of the kids' bean bags, the bag almost swallowing her petite frame as she sinks in it.

"I'm so damn tired," she yawns, covering her mouth with her hand. "Ugh, and tomorrow will be worse. We're down three staff in the kitchens, one in the children's' playgroup, two waitresses, and have a full house," Zoe sighs.

"Emily must also have the bug. She never showed up for work tonight," I tell her, getting up off the couch and walking over to the bookcase for my folder.

"I already checked the rosters for tomorrow," Zoe tells me. I sat back down with the folder, going to the events calendar.

"I know. We'll have to manage. I can work the lunch and night rush if you can handle the kids in the morning."

"Sounds like a plan. I'll wake you at eleven. If we're still down the next day, we can swap. Macey already pulled doubles two days in a row," she says, and I nod.

Zoe glances at the planner. "What are you looking for?"

"We need to find a date to move the Alpha meeting forward," I tell her, but the earliest date I can make work would be one week earlier, so instead of three weeks, it would be two.

"The 12th?" I ask him, and he looks over my shoulder, flicking through the pages before scrubbing his hand down his face.

"What's wrong with this coming Friday?" he asks, looking at the empty slot.

"That's six days away, it wouldn't be enough notice. And I am not sure if I can get supplies in early enough," I tell him.

"Get in what you can. The rest I'll organize from one of my hotels and have it sent over. You still want to announce it, right?"

I nod. Best to get it over and done with.

"Then it has to be the sixth. I can go unseen for a few days, but two weeks... Two weeks and the media will come looking for me," he tells me.

"Though, I am a little shocked it's stayed under wraps already. I'm surprised one of your staff hasn't sold the story yet," he says, and Zoe glares at him.

"They aren't staff; they are family. We're all family. We stick together," she says, and Valen sticks his hands up in the air in surrender.

"Settle down; you and Macey are the most aggressive rogues I have ever met, jeez," he says.

"Sorry, I'm just overtired." She rubs her eyes before reaching over and grabbing Casey's sweater off the ground. "Shit, I forgot to wash it," Zoe groans.

I also yawn, my eyes feeling like sandpaper, and I regret taking my pills earlier now that I have to do some planning.

"Grab one of Valarian's for tomorrow," I tell her, and she nods. Her brows pinch together before she suddenly buries her face in it and breathes in.

"What is that? Gosh, it smells good. I want to eat it," she says to no one in particular. Valen raises an eyebrow at her and twirls his finger beside his head, and I chuckle when he mutters, "Cuckoo."

"What? You smell it, then," she snarls, tossing it at his head.

"I wouldn't want to offend you by sniffing your daughter's sweater," he mocks, and she rolls her eyes.

Valen sniffs it before pulling a face. "Ugh, yuck. I can't smell anything but Marcus! Thanks for making me get a whiff of my Beta," he says, shaking his head.

"You can't smell it?" Zoe asks.

"Yeah, I can smell it. It fucking reeks of him," Valen says, rubbing his nose. I take it from him and sniff it.

"Yep, definitely your Beta," I tell him. Zoe rubs a hand down her face.

"I must be more tired than I thought. I thought I could smell vanilla bean and fudge," she pouts for a second. "Now I want vanilla fudge," she mutters unhappily.

"Cravings. Are you sure you're not pregnant?" Valen laughs. Zoe looks at him, appalled.

"Not unless I'm giving birth to a baby bunny vibrator or baby batteries," she spits at him. I chuckle at her, while Valen just blinks, shocked at what she said.

"Go to bed. I'll fill out the order forms," I tell her, laughing. She nods, yawning as she gets to her feet before moving off to her bedroom, muttering about finding some vanilla fudge tomorrow.

"Night, Zoe," Valen chuckles, and she flips him off over her shoulder before disappearing down the hall.

"She is definitely my favorite out of your friends," Valen states.

"What's wrong with Macey?"

"Uh, she threatened to castrate me and put me in an ants' nest. Tell me what is right with that one. Who says that, let alone *thinks* of something like that?"

I laugh before looking over at the table. "Tatum dropped some clothes off for you while you put Valarian to bed. They're on the table," I tell him before reaching over to the coffee and grabbing a pen from the drawer. I sit back, pulling the order forms out to fax off tomorrow. Valen gets up and rummages through the bag Tatum dropped off.

"Can I borrow your shower?"

"You can't borrow it, but you can use it," I tell him. I peek up at him. He has a silly grin on his face, and my lips tug at the corners. "Towels are in the hallway."

"Valarian showed me earlier," he says and walks off down the hall while I turn my attention back to my task.

Valen

Her shower is tiny. Every time I turn or move, I'm knocking crap down off the shower caddy or smashing my elbows on the walls. Getting in, I nearly knocked myself out on the shower head, it's that low! And why is everything pink? Pink shampoo, pink soap, pink shower curtain and floor mats; it's like a pink explosion in here. I didn't pick her as a girly-girl.

I should have used the kids' bathroom, not the joint one between Zoe and Everly's room. Turning back to the task at hand, I grab the pink loofah and sniff it. It smells of Everly, so the fluffy pom-pom pink thing must be Zoe's.

I'm bending down under the shower head, trying to wash the shampoo out when I hear the door open. At first, I think it's Everly until I hear the mention of fudge mumbled. I freeze. That's not Everly.

"Remind me to call Emily tomorrow to check on her," she calls out. Frozen, I wonder what she's doing in there before I hear what sounds like someone peeing. Were they that comfortable peeing in front of each other? Then again, Marcus and I were close, and he had no care about taking a leak in front of me.

"Everly?" she asks. I say nothing before suddenly the shower curtain is ripped back, and we make eye contact.

Her weary gaze goes to my shocked one, and her eyes widen when she screams, scaring the crap out of me. I grasp the shower curtain, trying to shut it while she tries to cover herself where she's sitting on the toilet peeing.

The shower curtain is flimsy. I yank it closed, only for it to rip off, and the motion catches me off guard—I lose my footing on the slippery surface. I somehow end up sprawled out on the floor, my head bent awkwardly in the corner of the shower and my legs spread in a very inappropriate manner, exposing me to a horrified Zoe.

"Shit! Fuck! I thought you– Ugh! I can see your dick and balls! I can see it all! I want to unsee it," Zoe shrieks, covering her eyes. "Everly!"

"Shh, shh, stop! Don't call her in here," I choke out, trying to un-wedge myself. Damn, how embarrassing and awkward. We make eye contact—eye contact!—while both of us are in a very vulnerable state.

"What– Are you alright? Oh my God, you're bleeding! I'll get Everly," she gushes, about to run from the room, but I move, grab-bing her ankle as she goes to dart out.

"I'm fine. Let's just never speak of this moment again," I gasp. My back is killing me, and I reach behind me, pulling out the pink back scrubber that's digging into my rear. I drop it on the floor before looking up at Zoe, who is staring at the ceiling.

"You good, dude? Alive?"

"Just great," I tell her, covering myself with the torn shower curtain.

"Nice chat," she says, quickly closing the door. I stumble out of her death trap shower and over to the mirror. The corner of my ear is bleeding and running down the side of my face. I clean it up before drying and putting on some boxers; we'll add that memory to the 'most awkward situation' file in my head. Man, I can never look that girl in the eye again.

Walking out, I find Everly passed out on the couch. Her mouth is wide open with her head tilted, bent back awkwardly. I sigh, relieved when I realize we didn't wake her.

Scooping her up, she doesn't even stir, making me wonder how much she actually works, since she could sleep through all that noise I just made and Zoe screaming. Walking up the hall, I stop when Valarian calls out as I pass his door.

"Are you sleeping in here, Dad?" he asks, rubbing his eyes.

I peek around his door and give him a nod. "Go back to sleep. I'll be here in the morning when you wake up."

His eyes move to his mother in my arms. "Can I sleep with you and mom?" he asks, suddenly brightening up excitedly and I look down at Everly. I intended to sleep on the couch because Valarian's bed is far too small, but if Valarian is in there, maybe she won't mind?

"Please?" he whispers, but he's already climbing out of bed.

"Okay, but be quiet; we don't want to wake your mother."

"Mom could sleep through a tornado. The only thing that wakes her is her alarm once she's asleep. Auntie Macey let off an air horn, and she didn't even move! I don't know how her alarm wakes her," he says, walking ahead and pushing the door open.

"Really?" I ask him.

"Yep. Probably the medication that Grandma Val gave her. She takes them sometimes when she can't sleep. She took them just before dinner," Valarian says as I place her down on the bed. I thought she took Tylenol, so this was news to me, yet she did give me a funny look when I caught her popping pills like she was caught doing something she shouldn't be doing.

Valarian climbs in the middle, tugging the blankets up.

"Grandma Val works here?" I ask him, climbing in beside him.

"No, she died when I was a baby. She gave us the hotel to build our village," Valarian says, yawning. He places his head on my chest and snuggles closer.

"If you were a baby, how do you know she gave them to your mom?"

"Because I heard Auntie Zoe and Auntie Macey arguing with mom over her taking them, something about them making her infertile. They said Grandma told her to take them only sometimes, if the pain is too bad because they have wolfsbane in them and she shouldn't spend her life numb."

I stared up at the ceiling, feeling guilty. Wolfsbane is poison to werewolves, but it also has medicinal properties in low doses, like pain relief because it kills the nerves and paralyzes you temporarily. Yet, too much can kill you.

"What does infertile mean?" Valarian asks. I don't answer and just ask another question.

"Your mom doesn't take them all the time?" I ask him, and he shakes his head.

"No, Auntie Zoe banned them from the house, but she has a secret stash in the pantry. I saw her grab them out earlier while Zoe wasn't looking. She keeps them in the raisin box. Zoe hates raisins, and so does Casey."

I glance over at Everly, passed out cold. "Get some sleep," I tell Valarian, kissing his head.

"Love you, Dad," Valarian mumbles.

"Love you too," I tell him.

Tomorrow I'll find that stash and confront her, I think to myself as my eyes close.

CHAPTER
FORTY-NINE

Everly

I wake up to pee during the night and realize Valarian is in my bed. No wonder my back is killing me, with Valarian's butt resting in the center of it. However, it's the body beside him that makes me tense.

Shaking my head, I quickly race to the bathroom. I never wake up in the middle of the night and will remain asleep until my alarm wakes me. so I'm a little disoriented as I walk back to the room. Glancing at the alarm clock that resides on the bedside table, I note that it's a little after 3 a.m. Why am I awake? In the pit of my stomach, I know it's the bond—the dull throbbing ache of him being around for so long and the bond trying to pull me nearer, wanting me to seek him out.

I even took some of my pills, hoping the incessant nagging pains would dissipate. I knew they would come on; they always do after seeing him, even if it's only for a few minutes. Plus, I was worried I would sleepwalk and crawl into wherever he was sleeping. The ache... the need to see your mate... is ridiculous.

Bonds are far from a blessing. I would consider the bond to be more of a curse. It was irrational and illogical. Damn, the Moon Goddess really screwed werewolves over with that inbuilt setting in our DNA, as if breaking every bone in our body to shift wasn't bad enough. We didn't even get a say in who our mates were, and we're as good as dead if we don't accept them. Valen is turned, facing Valarian, Valarian's head resting on his arm next to Valen's face.

I carefully pull the blanket up as I climb back into bed, not wanting to disturb them. They both look pretty peaceful.

I eventually drift back off, but not for long before I feel the bed move. I jolt upright, still caught in my dream of forsaken taking Valarian from me. I try to shake the remnants of the dream away to look over at the clock and see I've only been asleep for twenty minutes. What the fuck? More movement makes me look over at Valarian to see he's climbing out of bed.

"What's wrong? Are you okay?" Valen asks as Valarian climbs over him to get out.

"I'm just using the bathroom," Valarian mumbles, half asleep, before walking out of the room. My dream is still fresh; I find myself following him, now paranoid about the forsaken getting in my house and stealing him. He shuts the door and I lean on the wall, yawning. Why can't I sleep? I have to do a double tomorrow. I need to sleep!

I debate whether it might be worth taking another pill, but they also give me terrible heartburn for the first half hour after taking them; the wolfsbane is not a pleasant ingredient in them.

I hear the toilet flush, and Valarian opens the door, rubbing his eyes and yawning before walking off in the opposite direction toward his room.

"Val?" I say. He stops and looks up at me through his half-lidded eyes. He's not coherent at all as he yawns.

"Don't you want to sleep in my room?" I ask him, knowing his father is in there.

"No, you keep kicking me," he mumbles, turning around, walking into his room, and climbing into his bed.

I tuck him in, stuffing the surrounding blankets over him before kissing his head. I don't know what to do with myself now. I check all the windows and locks before rechecking them to ensure I didn't imagine checking them. Anxiety at its finest. I debate what to do. Valen is in my bed, so I don't really want to go back there. I could climb in with Valarian, but he said I woke him from kicking him.

I sigh before heading back out to the hall. I pause as I start to head out to the couch. Every part of my body tells me I'm going in the wrong direction. It's like my body is trying to lead me back to my bed—to where Valen is. I knew the bond would get stronger, now I marked him, but this is ridiculous, making me wonder what will happen tomorrow when he isn't here. Would it get worse with him further away? Would the pain get worse?

My mind and body fight against one another before my body wins, my feet carrying me back to my room while I mentally scold myself for letting them. Valen has moved, now more in the center of the bed where Valarian was.

"I can sleep on the couch if Valarian isn't coming back in. Is that why you were pacing in the hall? Or did you go take more of your pills?" Valen says while yawning.

Pacing? I didn't realize I was pacing. I feel like I'm losing my damn mind. I swallow. I know I should tell him to go sleep on the couch.

"Everly?"

"No, it's fine," I mutter.

"It's fine?" he says, sitting up on one elbow and looking at me. I pull the blanket back, climbing into the bed. My entire body is awake now, every part of me twitchy and antsy. I clench my hands into fists and place them under my ass to stop myself from trying to touch him. What is wrong with me? The pain I'm used to, but the feeling of him so near is making my heart rate increase, my breathing faster, as I soak up his scent that's perfuming the room.

I feel him lay back down, getting comfortable behind me. He sighs loudly.

"Valarian told me what those pills are you're taking."

I say nothing and look at the ceiling. That kid is far too observant for his age; he's like a sponge, absorbing everything he sees and hears.

"Why did you take them? Valarian said for pain, but I'm not sleeping with anyone. Are you addicted to them?"

Did he seriously just ask me that? I haven't got time to scratch my ass half the time, let alone have an addiction on top of my never-ending responsibilities.

"I'm not addicted to them," I answer.

"Are you sure? We can get you help? I'm not judging if you are."

"Valen, I am not addicted to them; I don't take them all the time, only when you... well... you know. And lately, when I see you."

"What do you mean?"

"The bond..." I trail off. I don't want to give him more reason to be around or use it as an excuse.

"Are you going to finish what you were going to say?"

I rub a hand down my face. "When I see you, it's worse than when I don't. The bond recognizes you, tells me to claim you, so you can't be with them."

"But you have claimed me now, Everly,"

"Yes, and now the urge to be near you is even worse, and it hasn't even been 24 hours." My tone comes out harsher than I intended. But thinking the words and saying them are vastly different. Saying them makes anger burn in me at how weak I sound. I'm not weak.

"And that's it? That's the only reason?"

"Yes, Valen. I am not addicted to my pills. You don't—" I break off with a squeak when he moves and grabs me, rolling me as he slides his arm under my head and pulls me closer.

His scent invades my nostrils before I feel him rest his chin on my head. I inhale his scent. The dull ache is instantly stamped down, and I feel my body relax, almost going utterly limp in his arms. I press my nose into the base of his throat. His stubble brushes my forehead, and a rather embarrassing noise leaves my lips that almost resembles a purring moan.

"Better?" he asks, and I freeze, mid-sniff. He chuckles, his chest rumbling, and I go to pull my face from his neck. He growls.

"I asked if it was better; didn't ask you to move, Everly," he whispers, tugging me closer. As soon as he starts purring, I fall asleep within seconds, the sound lulling my waking mind into blissful contentment.

Valen

I get up to the sounds of Zoe getting the kids ready for school. I went to sit up and slide out from under Everly when Valarian comes bounding into the room excitedly. Zoe is hot on his heels as she tries to stop him.

"Valarian, no! Mommy is sleeping," Zoe whisper-yells, but it's too late; the door smacks into the wall with a loud bang. Everly, however, doesn't wake up. I twist out from under her, and Valarian, seeing me moving, races over while Zoe blinks at me.

"You're in bed; I thought you left."

"Very observant, and yes, I'm still here," I tell her as Valarian climbs in my lap before I even have a chance to get up.

"Are you taking me to school?"

I look over at Everly, still passed out, as she moves closer in her sleep, burying her face in the pillow I was using.

"No, Valarian. Your father isn't dressed, and we're running late," Zoe says, coming over and plucking him off my lap. I glance at the clock on the bedside table, and so does Valarian; he would be nearly an hour early.

"We don't need to leave until it says eight three zero, Auntie Zo'," he says, his brows furrowing.

"We'll be late to get breakfast from McDonald's on the way if we don't leave now," she says, hauling him out. Zoe winks at me, and I scrub a hand down my face, trying to wake up.

"Zoe."

She stops at the door and looks over at me.

"Don't forget to call Emily," I tell her, and she glares at me. Her lips press into a line. If a look could kill, Zoe would have murdered me. I chuckle as she leaves, taking Valarian with her.

I hear the kids making demands for their McDonald's breakfast as they leave before lying back down. Everly instantly slides her way back over to me and tosses her leg over my waist before nestling her face back into my neck. Gripping her thigh, I haul her on top of me and hear her sigh, making me laugh softly.

She'll probably kill me, but she isn't complaining right now. I manage to go back to sleep for a while before waking up to wandering hands roaming over my stomach and chest. I blink up at the ceiling to see her still half on top of me. Her head falls back on my arm, and I swallow at the sight of her neck. So tempting. And it would be so easy to mark her while she's out like this. I roll on my side and skim my nose across her neck and shoulder.

Everly has a spicy, floral scent; my mouth waters as I inhale deeply before running my tongue over her neck. Then I freeze. Realization smashes into me just before I give in to instinct, and I quickly rip my face away from her neck, feeling my canines pressing into my lips. I suck in a mind-clearing breath before untangling myself from her. I need to get away from her while she's in this state before I do something that will make her hate me. My stomach twists as I force myself out of the room.

Needing a distraction, I flick the kettle on and start picking up toys and clothes that must be from this morning. Hours have passed when I finally look up, having completely forgotten about the coffee I intended to make. I've managed to clean the entire tiny apartment.

"Shit!" I curse under my breath. Is it weird I cleaned her place? Will she find it insulting? Will Zoe? I pull a chair out from under the table, attempting to make a slight mess, so it doesn't look quite so clean, but all I can smell is bleach—taste it in the back of my mouth. The washing machine makes a noise, singing loudly as the spin cycle finishes, and I walk away to put it in the dryer before stopping, cringing. I need to put the damn chair back straight.

Maybe I *am* slightly compulsive, but I have reason to be. I need the distraction—so I don't walk in there and mark her against her will. I realign the chair, my nervousness making it challenging to stop. Passing Valarian's room, I check it, but his room is already spotless. I place the clothes in the dryer, turning it on before throwing another load on, but it's only half full. I quickly look around, trying to find more clothes, as the washing machine is only half full.

Stopping at Everly's door, I push it open. I need to clean it. I run my fingers over her dresser. When was the last time she dusted? I flick my hand, ridding it of the little bit of grime before scooping up her work clothes and sniffing them to see if they have her scent on them or not. She has so many uniforms scattered around her room. She moves on the bed and I glance at her, but she's still asleep.

Scooping up another handful of clothes that were on my side of the bed, I sniff them just as she clears her throat. I glance at her mid-sniff to find her staring at me. She blinks at me and rubs her eyes, sitting up.

"What are you doing?" she asks.

"Uh, washing?" I tell her, holding up the pieces I just grabbed off the floor that fell under the bed. My eyes dart to what's in my hand. I blink.

"Does that require you to sniff my panties and camisole?" she asks before reaching over and snatching them from my grip. My eyes widen.

"I wasn't! I was seeing if they were clean."

"Well, were they, Mr. Sniffer?"

I clear my throat, standing upright. Well, this got awkward fast.

"I swear, I was not sniffing them in a sordid way. See? I have an armful. I just came in here to see if any needed washing." God, that sounds lame even to my own ears; 'not sniffing her panties in a sordid way'—who says that?

"Did you sniff Zoe's panties too?" she says, pointing to the clothes under my arm.

"What? No! I just grabbed these out of the hamper in the bathroom."

"I'm playing, Valen," she chuckles, tossing her panties and cami to me. I let out a breath.

"But if you're looking for a job, I am seeking a nanny," she laughs.

"Ha, ha, very funny." I pause. "Wait, really?" I could be a nanny, or maybe pappy; nanny sounds a little feminine, but I would if it meant spending more time here.

"No, But hey, you want to clean, one less thing for me to do," she says, swinging her legs over the side of the bed.

"Coffee?" she asks, and I nod, scooping up a dress from the back of her chair. Everly moves to the kitchen while I go to the tiny laundry room and put another load of laundry on.

"Did you organize my pantry?" she asks as I walk back into the living room/kitchen/dining room area. I say nothing, feeling awkward suddenly.

"Where's the coffee?" she asks, rummaging around. I walk over to her, reaching past her, and she jumps when I press against her back.

I grab the coffee jar and sugar and bring them down. "Right here." I found the decorative canisters still in their boxes, along with a whole pile of Tupperware still in the plastic, like they bought them and forgot about them.

"Ah. We've been meaning to use those," she says, turning around.

"Excuse me," she murmurs, squeezing past me. She grabs two mugs and I lean on the counter, watching her.

"I got rid of your pills in the raisin box," I tell her, and her hand stops mid-air.

"You what?"

"You don't need them."

"Valen, you can't just throw things out!"

"Valarian said Zoe banned them from the house, so you can either accept it and call me when you need me or you can tell Zoe they're in the house and I'll give them back," I tell her, folding my arms across my chest. She growls, and I raise an eyebrow at her.

"Is that a purr or a growl? It's a little hard to tell."

She glares at me.

"So, what will it be?"

She turns back to make the coffee.

"Or I could just stay here, or we can alternate between both places. I was going to ask if I could take Valarian for the weekend anyway."

"Valen, you don't even have a room set up for him or anything for a child at your place."

"I'll go get some stuff or send Marcus to. I can look after our son, Everly."

"I'll think about it. Besides, we have the Alpha meeting on Friday. Maybe the weekend after," she says, sliding a coffee over to me.

"Why not this weekend?"

"Valen, we are about to publicly announce we're mates, and that will change things for Valarian. I don't want too much to change too quickly."

"Then stay with him."

"I am not staying at your place. Besides, I have to work."

"Then he'll be fine with me. Or I stay here. Either way, I am seeing my son on the weekend, so choose," I argue.

She ignores me, walking back to her room to get ready for work. I follow, sitting on her bed.

"Uh, what are you doing?"

"Finishing our conversation."

"It can wait, I need to get ready."

"Then get ready. I thought women could multitask, or can't you talk and get dressed at the same time?"

She growls at me, but I refuse to leave, even when she glares at me as I get comfortable on the bed and watch her.

"Valen, out!"

"So, the weekend?"

She snarls as she snatches clothes off the hanger.

E verly
It took ages for me to get rid of Valen. He'd been pestering me all damn day about taking Valarian for the weekend. He finally agreed to leave if he could get Valarian from school and take him somewhere after. I decided to agree, so I could get some fucking work done because once again, we're down more staff. And to make matters worse, no one can get a hold of Emily. Apparently, her son also didn't show up for school.

However, when it was nearly 6 p.m., I began to worry when Zoe hadn't messaged me to say Valarian had been dropped off for dinner as promised. Walking back to my office after the dinner rush starts to slow down, I pull my phone from my pocket, about to call Valen when I smack into someone. Looking up, I find it's Marcus.

"Seriously, I have been looking for you everywhere," he says, shaking his head.

"Uh, okay. Why? But more importantly, do you know where Valen is with my son?"

"At home, I think. He sent me to watch you for the night."

I growl, shoving past him and heading toward my office. Only,

302

when I get there, I can hear banging inside the room and some strange noises. I push my office door open, wondering who's inside before stopping dead in my tracks at the sight before me.

Marcus walks in behind me and bumps into me before freezing beside me. Looking up at Marcus to make sure we're in the same reality, I see his mouth has fallen open in shock before he puts his hand over my eyes. I slap his hand away and try to take a step, about to back out of the room quietly. Then Marcus, of course, makes shit awkward by clearing his throat and drawing attention to the fact we're in the room.

My plan was to back away slowly and pretend I did not just see one of my best friends bent over my desk with her pants around her ankles while Tatum pounds into her. They both jump, and I try to bail, but Marcus is blocking the door with his huge-ass body.

I glance everywhere but at the pair of them, though Marcus has no issues openly staring at them. I elbow him while poor Macey, who looks mortified at being busted, scrambles to put her clothes on.

"You should really put a sock on the door, or maybe just lock it," Marcus taunts. Tatum clears his throat, yanking his pants up.

"We were... um... filing... and..." Tatum glances at Macey.

"And tripped and fell into her vagina. It happens all the time. I, myself, hate when that happens," Marcus finishes for him while shaking his head laughing.

"Fucking filing? Do I look like a damn cabinet, you idiot?" Macey growls.

"If you were, I would definitely stick my files in you," Tatum says as Macey buttons up her blouse; she growls at him.

"Next time, can you pick a room and not my desk?" I ask, still not looking at them. I will definitely be taking some sanitizer to that desk later. Maybe even buy another. I don't think I'll ever look at it again without seeing Macey bent over it.

"I thought you were off at four?" I ask her.

"I did, but Tatum asked for help."

"Wait, why are you still here?"

"I haven't left," Tatum says.

"Jenny didn't show up?"

Tatum shakes his head and shrugs.

"Jenny wasn't on today; Blair was. And she never showed. I tried calling her, and that was when I met..." She glances at Tatum. "...your friend. Did you get a hold of Emily? Zoe tried this morning and couldn't," Macey asks, and I shake my head.

"No, I was about to go over there and check on her."

"Maybe Blair caught the bug too?" Macey says, but this is getting too strange. I've lost two receptionists in two days, and multiple other staff are already sick.

"Okay, call Jenny and see if she can fill in; I'm heading over to the commune," I tell Macey, who picks up the phone.

Shit! Valarian, I think. Pulling my phone out, I quickly dial Valen's phone, which is switched off. I growl and look at Marcus.

"Mind-link your Alpha and ask where my son is."

"If you let him mark you, you could mind-link him yourself," Marcus taunts. I roll my eyes before watching his eyes glaze over. I wait when he sighs.

"He said he's taking Valarian for the night," Marcus tells me, and I press my lips in a line before walking out to the parking lot; I'll pick him up on the way home. When I get out there, I curse, realizing I don't have a car thanks to Valen and turn around to head back home to see if I can borrow Zoe's. Only, when I turn around, I smack into Marcus again.

"What are you doing?" I ask him, seeing that he was following me.

"Uh, coming with you," he says.

"You are not. And you're not staying at my place either. Go home and– Wait, have you got a car?"

"Uh yeah. You think I walked here?"

"Good—you're taking me to the rogue commune," I tell him, looking for his car. I spot the sleek, shiny sports car and start marching over to it.

"Is that where your friend lives?" Marcus asks, chasing me to keep up.

"Yes. She isn't answering her phone, and her son never showed up for school," I tell him as he unlocks his car.

I climb into the passenger seat before sending Zoe a message that I would collect Valarian and that I was going to check on Emily.

Marcus drives me insane the entire drive there; the man could talk the leg off an iron pot. And what is up with his music selection? It sounds like a kids' musical in here!

"What the heck are you listening to?" I ask.

" Trolls' soundtrack, it's catchy. Do you like it?"

"No!" I tell him.

"Casey downloaded it on my Spotify."

"What is up with you sniffing her, by the way. And I would stay the hell away from Zoe. She wants your damn head on a silver platter," I warn him.

"Yeah, Valen told me on the way to the school at lunchtime; said she bitched him out really good. I only wanted to know what laundry detergent she uses. A bit of an overreaction if you ask me," Marcus sighs.

"You wouldn't think that if you had her upbringing—she spent the majority of her childhood in youth homes; she met some damn creeps in her time," I tell him.

"Is that how she had Casey?" he asks, and I shake my head.

"No. And what were you and Valen doing at the school at lunchtime?"

"Getting Valarian to take him to the birth registry."

"Excuse me?"

"Valen got him DNA tested and changed his last name."

"He *what*?" I growl.

"You didn't know?"

"No, I fucking didn't."

Marcus looks away awkwardly, drumming his fingers on the steering wheel.

"I thought you knew Valen had a blood sample taken the night he found out before you got there."

"Why would he need to have his DNA tested? We can tell our own kin."

"Yeah, but the birth registry would need it. They can't tell if Valarian is his or not." Marcus shrugs. "I thought he told you he was taking Valarian from school?"

"Yes, picking him up *after,* not kidnapping him and changing his name! I am going to fucking *kill* him," I growl as we pull into the commune.

As we arrive, the presence of blue and red lights makes us slow down. Officer Richards waves for us to stop as we pull in. We're in a pretty secluded area at the back of the commune, so there isn't any reason for them to be out here. Only Emily and her son live out here because her neighbors kept complaining about the smell of her vegetable garden, so she moved to the other side of the commune away from everyone.

Marcus rolls down his window, and officer Richards comes over and peers in the window.

"Beta, Everly," Officer Richards says.

"What's going on?" I ask him.

"School sent us out to do a welfare check on a woman called Emily and her son. Apparently, neither showed up to the school today; she does the morning reading group."

I nod. Emily always did two days a week at the school, one day for cafeteria duty, the other for reading group.

"So you spoke with her?" I ask.

"You know her?"

"Yeah, she works at my hotel. I was coming to check on her."

Officer Richards runs a hand down his face.

"Her place is a mess, and there are signs of a struggle; forensics are in there now taking blood samples."

Forensics were taking blood samples? I blink, thinking of the last time I saw Emily or her son.

"Blood samples?"

"Yeah, the place is pretty messed up. She put up a fight, but we can't find any sign of her or her son."

"Forsaken?" Marcus asks.

"Unsure. Maybe. But we found a dead one not far into the forest."

"You reported it to Valen?"

"No, we tried—can't reach him. But Alpha John is on his way out; said he would stop by and grab Alpha Kalen. Fucking strange seeing them two talking," Officer Richards says. Marcus nods, and so do I. My brows furrow, wondering why my father is interested in missing rogues.

"I'll let Valen know tomorrow; let us know if you find anything," Marcus says.

I wonder briefly if Kalen would tell my father about Valen and me, but I doubt it. However, I *am* interested in why those two are so buddy-buddy right now. Officer Richards starts to leave before stopping and coming back to the window. He leans in, looking at me, but I'm still stuck on the fact my receptionist and her son are missing.

"Also, Everly, you might want to give Zoe a heads-up."

I look over at him. "What?"

"Amber found out about Casey."

"Fuck. Think she'll cause issues?"

Officer Richards shrugs. "No idea, but she wasn't happy."

I sigh and nod. "I'll let Zoe know."

"I'm sorry, Everly."

"Why are you sorry?"

"They're filing for custody of Casey."

"WHAT?"

"Don't worry, we'll back Zoe up; she's a good girl, and honestly, Amber is just being spiteful."

I curse, shaking my head. Zoe is going to freak out. "Tell your son to back off and get his mate in line; they come after Zoe for Casey, there will be issues."

"I'll speak with him, but you know what the courts are like; he

307

already filed, and Zoe is a rogue."

"That says nothing about her ability to parent," I tell him. Officer Richards nods sadly.

"Which court did he file in?"

"His mate's; Shadow Pack. Alpha John's pack."

Fuck! I was hoping he would have said Valen's pack.

"Wait, she's from Shadow Pack?"

"Uh yes, she's the Beta's daughter."

I blink at him, racking my brain for the name.

"Wait, Amber Zimmer?"

"Yeah, do you know her?"

"Yeah, I went—"

Marcus elbows me, and I realize I was about to admit to going to school with her. She was one of Ava's best friends.

"We should go; I need to get Everly over to Alpha Valen's to pick up Valarian," Marcus tells him.

"Oh yes, Kalen told me it was being announced at the Alpha meeting when I called him. The pack will be stoked that Valen finally found his mate."

"Once they get over the shock of his mate being a rogue?" I mumble.

"Uh, well, yes, but the pack will love you," Officer Richards says. I doubt that, but sigh.

"Well, we should go; keep us updated," Marcus says, winding his window up and turning the car around. "Valen's?"

"Yes. Then I need to go break the news to Zoe," I tell him, and he nods.

"She can fight it," Marcus tells me.

"She's rogue, and the custody case will be heard in my father's pack."

Marcus seems to think for a second. "You think he would interfere?"

"I know he will if he finds out she's my friend."

He nods, and we drive to Valen's in silence.

CHAPTER FIFTY-ONE

Marcus drives me to Valen's hotel, and I can't help but notice the strange looks I receive as I step out of his car. I wait for him before following him inside the grand place; people stare openly. I roll my eyes and fight the urge to tell them off, stabbing the elevator button with my finger a little too viciously in my annoyance.

Marcus raises an eyebrow at me before smirking and shaking his head. Looking around the lobby while we wait, I make eye contact with a few people who stare in shock at seeing a rogue. Anyone would think I had two heads with the way they stare like I'm some mutant. I stare back until they look away.

"Not trying to cause trouble at all," Marcus teases, clicking his tongue.

"I am not the problem—they are," I tell him, and he nods.

"It won't be an issue soon."

"It shouldn't be an issue at all."

Marcus sighs; there's no point in arguing over whose views are right or wrong. The elevator doors open, and I step inside. Marcus pulls a key from his pocket, placing it in the keyhole, and twisting it before pressing the button to the penthouse. I tap my foot impatiently.

"I take it you are not happy with your mate?" Marcus chuckles.

"No, I am *ecstatic*. He changed my son's name without asking, pulled him from school earlier than he said he would, and didn't return him like agreed."

"That was sarcasm, right?"

I huff, annoyed. When the doors open on the top floor, I head straight toward his door, ignoring the startled warriors lining the hall.

Before I can knock on it, the door opens, and Valen takes a step back as I point at him.

"HOW FUCKING DARE YOU! YOU HAD NO RIGHT TO CHANGE HIS NAME OR FUCKING KIDNAP HIM! IS THIS SUPPOSED TO MAKE ME TRUST YOU?" I bellow at him, jabbing him in the chest.

He snatches my hand in his tight grip before jerking me closer and surprising me by pecking my lips before I can stop him.

"Good afternoon to you too, mate," he laughs before letting go and walking off down the hall into the living room. I hear the door close as Marcus walks in behind me. I stalk after Valen angrily.

"That's it? You aren't going to say anything?" I demand.

"Nothing to say; I didn't do anything wrong, Everly. He's my son, and I can look after him for the night."

"I'm talking about changing his name, Valen, and you know it!"

"Coffee?"

"What? No! I am here to collect my son and leave!"

"Firstly, he's asleep, so keep your voice down, and secondly, I need your signature to change his name," he says, pointing to some documents in front of me. "I collected the paperwork for change of name and showed proof of DNA, but I need your signature to change it."

"Shit, my bad, bro. I told her you'd done it," Marcus says, walking in.

"Do you not pay attention?" Valen growls at him.

"Surprised you didn't just pay them off to change it," I snap at him.

"It did cross my mind," he admits. "There's a pen," he says, pointing to it beside the documents.

"I haven't agreed, Valen."

"Well, you can break his heart then and explain why he can't have my name too."

"Too?" I ask, looking down at the paperwork. I read over it to see he's hyphenated Valarian's name—changing it to Summers-Solace. I chew my lip, suddenly embarrassed at my ranting.

"I'm not trying to get rid of you, Everly. I just want it to say he's mine too." He places a mug in front of me before picking up the pen and handing it to me. "So, please sign it."

I take the pen from him, looking at the ridiculously long name.

He talks to Marcus while I read over all the documentation. Before I can change my mind, I cross out Summers and add my ID number and signature. I can't believe I just removed my name from his documents. Well, technically, it isn't my birth name, but still.

Valen takes the documents and glances at them before seeing I scribbled out my last name. His eyebrows raise with confusion.

"So... just Solace?"

"Just take it before I change my mind," I tell him.

"Why? I thought for sure you would argue over your name being removed."

"Because it looks ridiculous, and I don't want him known as 'Alpha Alphabet' with a name that long. Imagine spelling that every time."

He appears to think for a second before humming in agreement.

"Now, my son?" I ask.

"Room to the left of mine," he says, pointing down the hall. He goes back to speaking with Marcus while I wander down the hall to get Valarian. I stop next to the door before looking back at Valen and pointing to it, not wanting to walk into his without permission. He nods, and I twist the handle before entering. It's not at all what I expect to find.

My mouth opens in surprise when I see the galaxy wall decor stickers. For years, I've wanted to decorate his room, but he likes everything plain and simple. I once placed dinosaur pictures on his walls, and Valarian threw the biggest tantrum and said I ruined a perfectly good wall. So, I'm shocked to see his bedroom actually resemble a kid's room and not some showroom that looks like it was never lived in.

The nightlight is a moon, and stars cover the walls from his projection nightlight, sitting on the bedside table.

"Just let him stay one night?" Valen murmurs behind me, making me jump.

"When did you do all this?"

"Today. Valarian helped."

"He let you decorate it?"

"Yes, he even helped me pick; he wanted a room like mine," he chuckles.

"You have stars on the walls?" I laugh.

"No, I've grown out of that now. I also sleep with the light off, too; I am officially a big boy," he chuckles, and I elbow him.

"No, I was telling him about my room when I was a kid while we were at the store. I watched him pick out the most boring stuff for a kid I have ever seen."

"You mean like his room at home?"

"You said it, not me."

I roll my eyes before moving toward his bed. His bedspread also has the galaxy on it. Leaning down, I kiss him, tucking his blanket up higher. With a sigh, I stand up before turning to look at Valen.

"One night, and he has to go to school. If I get a phone call tomorrow saying he isn't at school, it will be the last time, Valen," I warn him. Valen beams like all his Christmases came at once. I shake my head and head out to see if Marcus will run me home when Valen steps into my path.

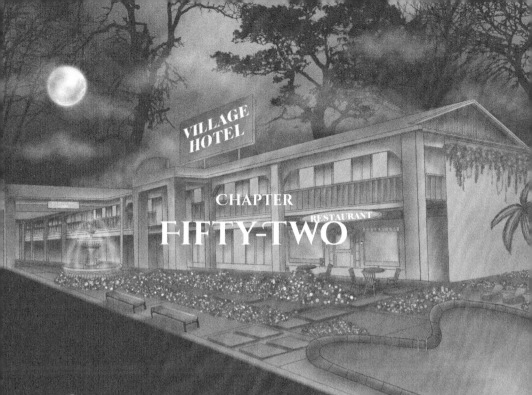

CHAPTER
FIFTY-TWO

I had every intention of coming over here, dragging my son out, and beating this stupid man senseless—though I probably would have needed help to do such a thing—and it all backfired.

"Stay. I'll sleep on the couch," Valen says, gripping my arm.

"You would sleep on your own couch?" I scoff.

"Wouldn't be the first time. Also, pretty sure I've passed out on the floor more times than I can count," he says.

"No. I have to go see Zoe anyway."

"Call her and stay. The hotel will survive without you for one night."

"I don't even have clothes here."

"I own a washing machine and dryer; I also know how to use them."

"Ha, ha, very funny. You're probably a better cleaner than I am with your OCD. But I don't think it's a good idea. I can't," I sigh, rubbing my temples.

Since when did my life become so complicated? I have so much going on. The Alpha meeting is in a few days, my employees are missing, the rest are sick, the drama with Casey's father, and now I have to fight my damn bond every second of the day. I feel like my grasp on control is slowly slipping. All of the stability I've constructed over the years has been thrown out of whack in a matter of days.

"I don't want to confuse Valarian more than he already is," I finally say.

"What do you mean? We're about to announce to the city we're mates, Everly. How would you being here confuse him?" he asks, leading me out of the room and into the hall. He shuts Valarian's door before stopping to look at me.

"Yes, exactly—announcing we're mates, but that's it. I don't want him thinking we're suddenly a family like everyone else. It's different." How does he not get it?

"You are making this different. To me, it's straightforward. I am yours, and you are mine. That's what mates are, Everly. We're supposed to be together, so why do you keep fucking fighting it?"

I don't bother answering. Instead, I go looking for Marcus.

"I sent him home," Valen calls out behind me as if reading my mind.

"You sent him home?"

"Yes, because I hoped you would stay."

"I don't want to stay, Valen. I don't know how I can make it any clearer."

"You know what your issue is? You are so used to being in control that you can't let go. You call me OCD, and yet have you looked at yourself?"

"Excuse me? I am nothing like you. I didn't fucking torture you for years. I sure as hell didn't ask for your Goddamn help; that boy in there? I raised him on my own while you stuck your dick in every bitch in the city and spent the last few years drunk out of your fucking brain. We are nothing alike," I spit at him.

"I have apologized. I can't change it, or believe me, I would. So, stop throwing it in my face every two seconds. I am trying to make this work while all you do is push me away. I know I fucked up, but you could have done more, too; don't put all the blame on me."

"*Done more*? You kicked me off your fucking territory! I tried telling you over the phone, and you laughed at me," I say, the anger building up inside of me again.

"My private life is far from private, Everly. There were plenty of events in the city where you could have come right up to me with him, and I would have recognized him. Fuck, you could have sent me the DNA tests or court-ordered them! You make out I'm a drunk," he pauses for a second, appearing to think before he shrugs.

"Well, I was. But I wasn't drunk every second of every day. I still had obligations to the pack and city. Don't tell me there was nothing else you could have done. And the reason you didn't was because that meant you ran the risk of fucking losing him, so don't put the blame entirely on me! You fucking hate me, I get it, but you also could have found another way. Your hate towards me is why you didn't."

I blink at him when Valarian's voice reaches my ears.

"Mommy?" he murmurs, making Valen spin around to face the hall.

"Why is everyone yelling?"

I go to pick him up when Valen does it before I get the chance.

"Come on, I'll tuck you back in; you have school in the morning," Valen whispers to him, kissing his head.

"Stay or don't. I'm done arguing. My keys are on the counter if you want to leave," Valen says, walking off with a sleepy Valarian in his arms. I can hear him murmuring to him before I turn around and walk into the kitchen to look for his keys. I snatch them up, intending to leave, when I stop, hearing Valarian crying in his room.

Moving down the hall, I stop near his door, listening to Valen try to calm him and wondering if I should intervene.

"I don't want to stay if mommy can't. Does she think I don't want her because I want to stay here? You don't have to make her leave," Valarian sobs. My heart clenches at his words. Does he think I blame him or his father? I'm the one trying to leave. I start to walk in when Valen's voice stops me.

"Your mother is angry with me, not you. She'll come back. Daddy did the wrong thing, that's all."

"But she's leaving and not taking me with her. Why won't she stay?"

"Do you want me to take you home?" Valen asks him.

"But I want her to stay here, too."

I peek in the door to see Valen rubbing his face.

"I'm right here. I'm not going anywhere," I tell him before Valen no doubt tries to retake the blame.

Maybe he's right. Perhaps I could have done more. Or perhaps it's the bond making me think that? Or the fact that Valarian is upset. Although, I did always notice when events were held in the city. We made sure not to organize hotel events on the same weekends. He wasn't wrong about that part; he was involved in many events where I could have approached him. As I move into the room, Valen looks at me before looking at Valarian. "See, she's right here."

"And you'll stay?" Valarian asks. I glance at his father before nodding.

"I'll stay; I just need to call Auntie Zoe. I'll be here when you wake up," I tell him. Quickly, leaning down, I peck his cheek. "Now go to sleep. It's late."

Valarian snuggles underneath his blanket, and I watch as his father gives him a kiss before I walk out of the room.

I walk into the living room and sit on the couch, pinching the bridge of my nose. Valen is still in Valarian's room, and I message Zoe to see if she's still up. I wait for a reply, but I figure she must be asleep when I don't get one. I will tell her tomorrow. It probably wasn't a good idea to tell her over the phone, plus I knew she wouldn't sleep once I told her.

"Are you calling Zoe?" Valen asks, walking out and stopping next to me. He falls on the couch beside me.

"You didn't have to take all the blame," I tell him.

"He'll find out eventually anyway."

"You're right; I could have found other ways to tell you."

"Well, I know now," he says with a sigh before getting up.

"I'll get you some clothes to sleep in unless you are sneaking off; I can distract him until you return in the morning?"

"I told him I would stay. I'll stay on the couch," I tell him. He goes to say something, but I cut him off.

"Your apartment, Valen. I'll sleep on the couch," I tell him, and he presses his lips together, eventually nodding and walking off.

He returns with some clothes and a towel before pointing me in the direction of the bathroom. Everything in his bathroom is ridiculously clean and white. Undressing, I step in and turn the shower dials. Seriously, who has dials?

Water sprays out like a damn tsunami, blasting me in the face, and I place my hands up, shielding my eyes. So much for not wetting my hair.

I turn the other dial only to find water spraying out from the freaking wall, making me shriek when my ass is suddenly pelted with a force that water shouldn't come out at, plus it's freezing cold. I try to shut it off when music starts blaring from somewhere. What the fuck! The bathroom has suddenly turned into a rave! Here I am, being waterboarded while my ass is filled with water.

Is this karma? Did I break a mirror or something? I try covering my ears against the horrid radio blasting from Goddess knows where while trying to shield my eyes and spin the dials in a desperate attempt to shut it off.

"Everly?"

"How do you turn it off!" I scream.

"The blue dial."

"I can't see a blue fucking dial! Your dial is broken!" I shriek at him when another jet of water suddenly comes from the roof—the fucking roof! I shield my head and my ass, forgetting the ears; I'll go deaf, but my ass can't take anymore. I feel like I'm in a car wash, not a damn shower!

Suddenly, the water cuts off, and I hear laughing. Scrubbing my hands down my face, I blink, my eyeballs aching.

"Off," Valen says, pointing to one dial. "On. And that one is pressure," he says, pointing to the third dial, his voice shaking with laughter.

"You couldn't have a normal-functioning shower?" I snap, choking on water.

"Maybe yours are just dated?"

"My ass feels like it just got blasted to the damn moon! Who in their right mind wants an ass-blaster in the shower?"

Valen chuckles, looking down. I suddenly realized that while I was drowning and choking on water, I was also very much naked. A shriek leaves my lips as I shove past him to grab a towel to cover up. Wet tiles and my coordination do not mix well, apparently, and I collide with him, taking both of us out. Valen tries to grab me, but it's not good.

He wheezes as I go tits-and-ass up before landing on the floor on top of him. I can't help but feel like this is some sort of setup, and I'm being punked—surely this can't get any more awkward?

I am so wrong.

I realize I'm looking at his feet, which means I'm on top of him with my ass on his face! How? Just how?

"Your ass really did get blasted," Valen chuckles.

Please, Moon Goddess, strike me down and put me out of my misery! I scramble off; there is no ladylike way I could have avoided him seeing me. Now he's had an internal view! Not even my Gyno got that close and personal with my nether regions.

"Good to know that you wax," Valen adds. His commentary is not necessary. If only he had seen it two weeks ago—it looked like the Amazon Jungle with my winter fur coat. I was foul when I got that call saying I was three years past my last pap smear. Thank Goddess, I was, or he would have been coughing up a hairball.

I snatch the towel off the basin, covering myself and trying to keep some dignity, even though I'm pretty sure most of it went down the drain, along with my speaking ability. I clear my throat.

"Do you want me to fix the shower?"

I nod and hum, looking anywhere but at him. He snickers, trying to contain himself as he turns it on for me. He then takes his shirt off, motioning toward the shower.

"I've already seen you, so no point hiding from me now, Everly," he chuckles before shedding his pants and stepping in.

"Get in the shower, Everly. We're even now; I've seen yours, and you've seen mine. I was just a bit more polite and didn't throw my genitals on your face," Valen snickers, and I growl at him.

I make sure to keep my gaze on his face and not look down, but he raises an eyebrow at me. I roll my eyes, but he's right; nothing much more he can see. So I drop the towel and hop in.

CHAPTER
FIFTY-THREE

Everly

"Can you not stare?" I snap at Valen; his roaming gaze is making me self-conscious. My body is not what he would be used to—my stomach isn't flat, my hips have faint stretch marks, and my boobs no longer sit perky on my chest. My body is ruined from carrying Valarian. He stands there looking like he just stepped out of a sports magazine—all hard chiseled muscle and tan complexion—while my skin is pale in comparison, and I look frumpy.

"Does my staring bother you?"

"Uh, *yeah*. I wouldn't have said it if it didn't," I tell him, turning away from him.

"You've had a baby; that doesn't make you look any less appealing, Everly, so don't shy away from me now," he says, putting his head under the shower spray to rinse the shampoo from his hair.

Easy for him to say; I don't have exes for him to compare himself against, whereas I've seen the girls in the papers that he kept on his arm—even met one of them. As if I wouldn't feel inadequate compared to their perky, fit bodies, while I look like used goods.

I quickly wash before hopping out and wrapping a towel around myself. Valen leisurely moves about as he gets out, not caring that he's standing around naked in front of me. But unlike him, I avert my gaze instead of gawking and keep my eyes strictly above his pecs.

I yank his shirt over my head before undoing the towel, only to realize the pants are gone.

When I try to leave the bathroom, Valen steps into my path. Moving the other way, he does the same thing.

"Trying to escape me?"

"Valen, I'm tired. Please. I don't want to play these stupid games; just move aside," I tell him.

"Always so serious."

"And you're always annoying me. Please move."

"I will, but you have to sleep in the bed with me."

I shake my head; he folds his arms across his chest and looks down at me.

"No."

"Fine, we'll sleep here then," he shrugs, then leans against the door with a devious smile on his lips. I glare at him.

"Fine, but I want the bathtub; you can have the floor," I huff before turning around and walking over to it. Somehow, I don't think his OCD ass will cope with sleeping on the wet floor.

"Are you really that damn stubborn?" Valen asks.

"Yep," I tell him, popping the 'P.'

Valen growls behind me as I climb into the bathtub. I've slept in worse places, but I know he hasn't. He won't last long.

"Everly!"

"Valen!" I retort. His growl bounces off the tiled walls before he suddenly yanks me out of the tub.

"Good thing I'm also stubborn. Would you look at that? We have something in common. And you are sleeping with me," he growls while I struggle to get out of his grip.

"Valen!" I snap. My fists hit his chest as he tries to pull me from the tub. He just laughs as he tosses me over his shoulder. I bang on his back before digging my elbows into it.

"You can be a real jerk."

"Imagine Valarian's little face when he finds you in my bed instead of on the couch," he teases.

"That is guilt-tripping, and you know it. Don't use our son to get what you want."

"What I want is for my mate to sleep in the same bed as me. I never said I would try to *sleep* with you, but your squirming is making it rather difficult."

I dig my elbows in deeper and his back arches as he walks up the hall toward his room. He pushes his bedroom door open with his foot, and I growl at him.

"Do I need to find something to tie you down with, or will you behave?"

"Do that and you will wanna sleep with a towel wrapped around your fucking throat."

"Why would I do that?"

"To stop me slitting it while you sleep," I snap at him.

"Then I'm definitely tying you to the bed."

I stop and growl. "Fine, but I'm the big spoon," I tell him.

"Are you trying to ruin my masculinity?"

"Take it or leave it," I tell him before I'm dumped on the bed. A squeak escapes my lips at the motion, and I snarl again while he chuckles at me.

"Fine, you can be the big spoon," he rumbles as he climbs on the bed, tugging the covers back before climbing underneath them.

"I was happy to just share the bed with you, but if you want to hug me, I'll take it," Valen tells me. I roll my eyes at him but climb underneath his blankets.

Gosh, his bed is comfortable—like a cloud. I'll never ever agree to take the couch again. I realize how uncomfortable my bed actually is, though I'd always thought it was comfortable. I'm pretty sure he just ruined my bed for me now.

"Uh, are you forgetting something? What about spooning me?" Valen laughs.

"I'm too comfortable to move now," I yawn before feeling the bed shift under his weight. Valen pushes my shoulder, wanting me to roll on my side; I'm actually considering biting him for moving me. Although the warmth he offers makes me wiggle back against him.

"I prefer being the big spoon," he says, snuggling against me. He shrieks when I jam my freezing-cold feet between his thighs.

"How can your feet be cold when you just had a shower?" he growls and I snicker.

"If you want to be the big spoon, you also get to be my feet warmer."

His chest vibrates against my back with his growl, but he doesn't move, instead pressing closer. I can't help but succumb to sleep.

The sound of my phone in the living room wakes me. Valen groans behind me, and I blink. The room is still dark, but I can see slivers of light peeking around the sides of the thick blackout curtains.

"Turn it off," Valen snarls, pressing his face into the back of my neck.

I yawn, about to toss the blankets back and climb out to retrieve it, when I realize the tune playing isn't my alarm but my ringtone. The noise cuts off mid-tune.

"Thank God," Valen mumbles. It starts blaring again immediately, and I sit upright. Valarian's voice reaches my ears.

"Hey, Auntie Macey," he says from the living room. I peek over at the bedside table to see Valen's phone on 'charge' and I wiggle out of his grip to snatch it off. I press the power button, and the screen lights up, telling me it's midday. I gasp and lurch upright.

"Valen! Get up! We slept in," I snap at him before hitting his shoulder just as I hear Valarian's footsteps run up the hall toward the bedroom. The door opens further.

"Mom, Auntie Macey said she needs to speak to you about Zoe," Valarian says, holding the phone out. I take it, placing it to my ear.

"Hey, I am sorry I am late. I-"

"Amber and Micah just called Zoe and said they're on their way to get Casey!" she says, and I can hear the alarm in her voice.

"*What*!?" I say, jumping out of bed. I race to Valen's dresser and open drawers, grabbing the first set of pants I lay my hands on and yanking them up my legs.

"I'm not at the hotel. Zoe called me, hysterical. I'm stuck at the morgue—I need you to get to her," Macey sobs.

"I'm on my way," I say breathlessly before pausing. "Wait, why are you at the morgue?" My stomach lurches.

"They think they found Emily; an officer picked me up to identify her."

"Her son?" I ask, fearing the worst.

"I have no idea. Get to Zoe," Macey says before hanging up. My head spins, and Valarian stares up at me worriedly.

"Is Auntie Zoe alright? I didn't want to wake you," Valarian cries as Valen looks around, confused.

"What's going on?" he yawns.

"I need your keys. I have to get back to the hotel," I tell him before turning to Valarian. "Stay with your father, I'll be back." I rush out the door, snatch his keys off the counter, and head for the door just as Valen comes out carrying our crying son.

"Everly, what's going on?"

"Micah's mate found out about Casey; Zoe needs me over at the hotel."

"Is everything alright?"

I look at Valarian, not wanting to say much in front of him, especially since I don't exactly know what's going on. All I know is I let Zoe down. I should have gone home and told her last night about what Officer Richards had said.

"I'll send Marcus to meet you. Go. I'll meet you over there."

I nod and rush toward the front door, hoping I'm not too late.

E**verly**

As I jerk to a stop in the staff parking lot, the scene unfolding before my eyes immediately makes my blood boil. Micah is trying to yank Casey away from Zoe while Casey clutches her mother's clothes, wailing desperately, and staff members are attempting to stop Micah. I open the door, slam it behind me, and dart to them.

"Micah, what the fuck!" I snap at him. Zoe looks up, and I rush over to her side, shoving her behind me and getting between her and Micah.

"Take Casey inside," I tell her when I notice a woman approach, stomping over in a rage. Her blonde hair hangs in loose waves, and her face is made-up, making her look like she's about to step into a photo shoot. She looks every part of the perfect housewife until she opens her mouth.

"Micah, just grab the kid, and let's go!" she snaps.

"Amber, get back in the car," Micah groans, turning to face his mate. I push Zoe toward the hotel doors before looking around for my staff.

"Where is security?"

"The perimeter was breached. They're fixing the fence and are out of radio range," one of them tells me. Fuck! I curse under my breath.

"Like hell, I will. She stole my baby. I should be the only person having your kid, Micah. Now get Casey, and let's leave. She's a rogue whore. Just knock the dumb bitch out. No one will care, and your father will get you off anyway."

Micah scrubs a hand down his face; I can tell he didn't want any of this to happen. But Amber is clearly a nut job and his mate. She'd always been loud and outgoing at school, but I'm shocked to see how cold-hearted she is now. Micah turns to look at me, and I glare at him.

"I'm sorry, Everly. Step aside. I want my daughter."

"Want your daughter? Where the fuck were you for all these years, coming and going as you pleased? Casey barely even knows you!"

"Regardless, she is still mine," he says, trying to shove past me.

"Wait. Everly? Is that you?" Amber says, finally looking in my direction. I glare at her as recognition dawns on her.

"Holy shit, it is you. Everyone wondered what happened to you? Your father said you ran away," she gushes with tears in her eyes. Is this bimbo for real right now? She tries to embrace me, but I step away from her.

"Everly?" Amber says. I can't believe she dares to look hurt in the situation.

"Leave, both of you, or I will be forced to call the police," I tell them. Micah makes a run for the door and jerks Zoe back by the back of her shirt. She smashes against the ground before he grabs Casey, and I move, holding her arm.

"Let her go, Micah," I snarl.

"This has nothing to do with you, Everly, now stand down."

"Like fuck I will. Now LET HER GO!" I yell. He lets go. He appears shocked, and so am I. My aura rushes out harder, and he pales, taking a step back from me. But it wears off quickly, and he snarls at the fact that I commanded him before lunging at me. I shove Casey toward Zoe just as he knocks me down on the ground.

"Fucking command me, whore? Who do you think you are?" he spits, trying to pin me as my head smashes onto the concrete. I see stars for a second, my vision going black, and I hear Zoe scream before hearing a scuffle. My surroundings blur, but he's suddenly gone from on top of me. I hear the sound of flesh on flesh and Amber's blood-curdling scream, making my heart thud, thinking it's Casey or Zoe getting hurt. I turn my head to see Marcus straighten up from pummeling Micah, who is now curled in the fetal position on the ground.

"Zoe? Casey?" I gasp as Amber rushes toward Micah on the ground. Marcus snarls, which makes me look back at him as I get to my feet. My head is pounding, and I can hear sirens in the distance heading our way, but I'm too distracted by the look on Marcus's confused face to notice much else. He turns his head to the side, cautiously looking around me, and I follow his gaze to see Zoe looking white as a sheet of paper, her eyes wide. I rush to her side and grip her arms, shaking her. "Zoe?"

"Zoe?" Marcus repeats behind me. Her eyes are locked on his. I peek over my shoulder at him.

"Casey's mom, right?" Marcus asks her, and Zoe nods. I'm seriously worried she's about to pass out with how clammy her skin is. Is she in shock? Marcus yanks Micah to his feet by the front of his shirt. Amber squeals and rips at Marcus's shirt.

"So, you must be the father?"

Micah nods, terror etching his face, just before Marcus headbutts him with a surprising amount of force. The sound of his nose breaking makes me flinch, and blood spurts out when Marcus's fist connects with his jaw, packing an equal force. Marcus lets him go, and he falls to the ground in a heap just as Zoe faints.

Casey shrieks, and I only just catch her as they both fall forward into me. Tires screech to a stop as cop cars pull up everywhere.

Officer Richards jumps from the first vehicle. Marcus growls, and Officer Richards backs up with his hand on his gun.

"Pull it, and I will end him, Richards. What will be?" Marcus growls at him. His entire body trembles as he fights the urge to shift. I look back at the terrified Officer Richards, who looks at his bleeding son on the ground at Marcus's feet. Amber sobs over him.

"Whatever he did, I'll see it's fixed," Officer Richards murmurs with his hands up.

"Good. Make sure he stays the fuck away from my mate," Marcus snarls before stalking toward me. He grabs Zoe, scooping her up in his arms while I stare, dumbfounded. It makes so much sense now. How did I not see that?

"I spent hours in the laundry aisle trying to find that scent. Not proud to say it, but I even tasted a few, and all I had to do was follow your daughter home, hmm?" Marcus murmurs to an unconscious Zoe.

"Wait, Zoe is your mate?" Officer Richards asks, just as shocked, evidently reading between the lines. Marcus growls at him before holding out his hand to Casey, who looks up at him, his shirt drenched in her father's blood.

"Come on, princess, let's take mommy inside," Marcus says to her consolingly. She looks over at me, and I nod for her to go with him. I'm about to check on Micah when Marcus calls out to me.

"You too, Everly. Leave the bastard. Valen is on his way," Marcus says as he walks toward the hotel doors. I rush ahead of him and open up the door as he stops and looks back at Officer Richards, who is fussing over his son.

"I suggest you get him out of here, Richards. I left him breathing. Valen won't—not for touching his Luna," Marcus tells him. Officer Richards motions some of his men over, who are all staring at me oddly.

"Luna? But she's a rogue!" Amber blurts out.

"Shut it, you over-opinionated mutt," Officer Richards snaps at his daughter-in-law.

My eyebrows raise at his words, and two of the other officers rush over and peel Micah off the ground, who groans in pain.

"You've done it now, boy," Officer Richards snaps at him.

"Uh, Everly," Marcus calls as he nods toward the next door leading into the back of the restaurant. I shut the door and rush over to him. Just as I do, Zoe finally regains consciousness and projectile vomits all over the front of him.

"Well, not the reaction I was hoping for, but still, it's a reaction," Marcus says while Zoe stares wide-eyed at him.

"You're my..."

"Mate," offers Marcus, and she nods like she thought he was a figment of her imagination. I'm beginning to wonder if this whole scenario is a figment of mine too.

"And I just spewed on you," Zoe squeaks. Marcus looks down at the front of his shirt and shrugs.

"At least I can help you shower?" Marcus chuckles. Zoe nods, looking at him like a deer stuck in headlights.

"You can't shower with her. You'll see her privates," Casey says, causing Marcus to jump, having completely forgotten she was there. Great observations; Casey deserves a pat on the back, I think sarcastically.

"Oh, right, we'll shower with our clothes on—can't have that," Marcus agrees with her. Casey nods her head, evidently accepting that answer.

"Want to see where we live? I have all the 'Trolls' movies, and they have a TV show, Valarian doesn't like to watch with me, but you can," Casey says, tugging on his arm and leading him out. I follow them. My head is still throbbing, and once inside, I flop on the couch and call Casey over to me while Marcus goes to help clean Zoe up.

Casey rummages through her movies, putting 'Trolls' on, and I rest my head back on the couch, rubbing my temples.

"Auntie Everly, is my dad going to jail?"

"I'm not sure, sweetie. Are you upset?"

"No, I don't want to go with that lady. They tried to take me from school. Mom drove really fast on the way home, and that crazy woman drove into the side of mom's car in the parking lot."

"She *what?*"

Casey nods, pressing play. "Yep, the school went into lockdown. She said she was my mom, but I already have a mom. The school locked me in a cleaning closet until mom got there, and security dragged them away, but then they chased us."

"No one is taking you from your mother, I promise," I tell her, holding up my finger. I'll sell the damned hotel to pay for the legal bills if need be, but I doubt it will come to that now. Casey nods and grips my pinky.

"Why wasn't Valarian at school?"

"We slept in," I tell her just as the door bursts open and Macey rushes in.

"Oh, thank the Goddess," Macey says, running in and scooping up Casey. She hugs her tight.

"Where is Zoe? Woah, what happened to you?" Macey says, looking at me.

"Huh?"

"You have a huge egg on your head!" Macey shrieks, and I feel my head. Touching the back, I wince. When I pull my hand back, I see blood has stained my fingertips. Great, that's all I need.

CHAPTER
FIFTY-FIVE

E verly
    My head throbs even more as Macey watches me with
    worry. She even prods the bump on my head with her
finger, which only makes it hurt more with her attempt to examine
it.

"It's only bleeding a little; I bet it hurts, though," she says, poking
it again.

I laugh, which causes me to clutch my head in pain. "Uh, yeah,
because you keep poking it," I respond.

"Shit! Sorry," she chuckles and stops.

"Maybe you should shift; it may help heal it a little quicker?"
Macey offers.

That's the last thing I want to do. It always seems like too much
effort to shift these days, and I hate my wolf form. I tire quickly and
don't want to spend the rest of the day like a zombie because I
shifted for a meager bump to the head.

"Maybe later; we still have loads of work today. Oh! The morgue?
Was it Emily?" I ask her. With everything going on, I forgot to ask
her.

"No, it was some homeless woman. She must have stolen some of Emily's clothes. I recognized the tie-dyed shirt, but it wasn't her," Macey tells me, and I let out a breath of relief. Thank heavens. However, it still leaves me wondering what happened to her and what's happening in this city. So many people are missing, and I'm beginning to worry something bigger is going on that we just don't understand yet.

Murders are rare, disappearances rarer in this city, yet multiple have happened in the last few weeks. More problematic is the amount of forsaken trying to get into the city. What are they running from? They mostly stay away. Lately, there have been repeated attempts to breach the city borders. Also, even the forsaken that had been tagged and tracked have gone missing without a trace.

"What are you thinking?" Macey asked, sitting beside me. I shake my head; I have no idea what to think. These days, it seems it's just one thing after another. I look at her, about to answer, when both she and I tense. Both of us look to the hallway, then Macey's head turns to me before she instinctively covers Casey's ears in alarm.

Are they? she mouths, nodding at the hall. My lips press together in a line as I listen to the noises coming from that direction, trying not to laugh. Casey, none the wiser, looks at us.

"How about ice cream? Let's get ice cream," Macey says, scooping up Casey.

"But I want to show Marcus the 'Trolls' movie," Casey complains before jutting out her bottom lip.

The noises become slightly more audible, and Macey hurries to the door.

"Tell Zoe I have Casey," she exclaims, rushing out the door before I can protest.

"Why do I have to tell her?" I groan, getting to my feet before making my way down the hall. I tap on the door and hear things that will haunt my memory forever. Zoe is like mine and Macey's little sister, and there are some things we just don't want the mental image of. This is one of those things, especially when she's making those sorts of noises. I blanch.

Clearing my throat, I knock again. "Uh, Zoe? Macey has Casey while you, um... she just has Casey," I tell her before rushing away and out of my apartment.

Safely outside, I make my way back to the main building and head toward the restaurant. I just step inside when the door leading in from the front bursts open and Valen steps inside looking furious. His eyes scan around the place before they fall on me, and the relief on his face is evident.

"I'm fine," I say with a wave of my hand as he rushes over to me.

A few stragglers have come in for a late lunch and peer over at us. I smack Valen's hand away as he reaches out to me. He starts to say something before he notices we have an audience in here and are prime entertainment.

"What happened?" he asks as he grabs my elbow and leads me out of the restaurant and down the hall toward my office. I spot Casey and Macey in the kitchen with bowls of ice cream. Casey waves as we pass the glass window, and I smile, waving back.

"It's handled, Valen. Marcus handled it; Micah and Amber came and tried to take Casey. I got knocked over, but I'm fine," I tell him as he shoves me through my office door.

"Marcus said you were hurt," he says, examining me while I roll my eyes.

"I am not a child. You don't need you to check me and kiss away any pains," I growl as he pokes and prods me. "Wait, where's Valarian?"

"With my father, I called him over to watch him for me."

I sigh.

"He was a good father, Everly; you don't need to worry about my dad. I trust him with our son," Valen says. Giving Kalen the benefit of the doubt, I let it go. He's never shown any signs he's a threat to our son, and he told me he just wants to be a part of his life.

"And where is Micah now?" Valen asks.

"His father took him away. It's sorted; just leave it be."

"I won't do that. Micah is part of my pack, and he will be punished."

"Punished how, Valen? You can't go killing people over a dispute."

"He hurt you," Valen snarls.

"I'm fine, but you may have to speak to Micah about keeping his mouth shut, and Amber too because they're aware we're mates now. Marcus hammered him pretty good; I don't think he needs another beating."

"Wait, where is Marcus?" Valen asks, only now recognizing he isn't with me. I laugh and cup my mouth, and Valen stares at me.

"What?"

"Zoe and Marcus are mates," I chuckle. His eyebrows almost disappear into his hairline before a thoughtful expression crosses his face. "Huh, now that explains the sniffing," he murmurs. "That makes so much sense. How did I not figure that out?" he says, repeating the exact thoughts I'd had. Both of their weird behavior now made it even more apparent that they were mates, while poor Casey was stuck in the middle of their sniffing.

I chuckle, making my headache worse, and I wince before walking to my desk in search of painkillers. Valen grips my hand when I pull out the packet of Tylenol.

"You said you weren't hurt," he growls.

"I bumped my head, just a headache," I say, snatching my hand out of his grip. Valen stares at me before a growl escapes him, and he starts prodding the bump on the back of my head.

"I'll fucking kill him," he snaps, storming out of the room before I can stop him.

"Wait, Valen! Just leave it be!" I shriek, chasing after him as he makes his way outside to his car.

It beeps as he unlocks the doors before throwing open the driver's side. I race to the other side and slide into the seat. "Valen, stop. Let it go,"

"Get out," Valen growls. Fur is growing along his arms as he struggles to remain in his human form. His eyes flicker with his rage.

"No."

"Everly!"

"No, Valen. Either I come with you, or you don't go."

"Everly!" he snaps, and I raise my eyebrow at him.

"I won't let you hurt him or do something you can't undo. It was a dispute that is over now, and no one needs to die over a bumped head," I tell him. Valen's claws slip from his nailbeds before his fists clench on the steering wheel. He starts to say something else, and I glare at him.

"Micah is Casey's father. He may be a shitty one, but he's still her father. You hurt him and it could upset her, so no, you will not touch him—or whatever it was you intended to do to the idiot," I threaten. Valen seems shocked by my outburst, but I believe retaliating will only worsen things. Zoe doesn't need the added drama when she's about to enter a custody battle against him. This would just add more fuel to the fire.

"You can't expect me to do nothing," he says, looking a bit calmer.

"That's exactly what I expect. The issue is over. Officer Richards looked like he was going to give him hell anyway over the drama he caused. He seemed genuinely embarrassed over his son's actions, and no doubt will deal with him."

"As his Alpha, I can't let it slide when he hurt my mate," Valen snarls.

"And as his Luna, I won't allow you to kill him," I retort, and he seems taken aback by my words.

"Are you trying to pull rank over me?" he scoffs.

"Not trying. I am. If you hurt him, Valen, it will just cause more issues. I don't want the pack hating me before I even join it. Micah and his father are well respected in your pack and this city. I sure as hell don't to want to walk in, disturbing the peace straight away, just because he hurt me before he realized who I was," I tell him.

Valen calms down at my words and folds his arms across his chest, turning slightly to look at me.

"So you're my Luna?" he says, processing everything.

"Shut up and take me to my son," I say. He doesn't start the car; instead, Valen continues to stare at me while I look at the window, trying to ignore his gaze.

"I can't believe you're trying to pull rank over me, and you haven't even let me mark you yet. Now that is bold, young lady," he chuckles.

I fold my arms across my chest and turn my head to look at him. "So what will it be, Alpha?" I ask, and he clicks his tongue, shaking his head.

"Oh, so now we're turning to blackmail?" he chuckles.

"Yep, you want a Luna, I don't want blood on my hands."

"Technically, his blood would be on *my* hands, not yours. I wouldn't want you to break a nail," Valen taunts.

"Broken nails never fazed me, but you make things worse and I may just have to change my mind on this entire Luna business," I say.

"Is that so?"

"Yep," I tell him. He scratches his chin.

"It's not up for discussion," I tell him when he opens his mouth.

"What about a compromise?"

"That would make it up for discussion."

A chuckle escapes, and he shrugs. "How about, I won't hurt him," he growls the last part out, clearly not liking it.

"If?" I stare at him, and he smirks before a cocky smile splits onto his face. "If what?" I repeat, glaring over at him, knowing he'll ask for something that he knows I won't want to agree to.

"If you give me a kiss."

"A kiss?"

"Yep, that's my deal. Take it or leave it," he says.

"What? Right now? Here?" I ask, looking around and praying for an excuse that someone is around. I find nobody.

"One kiss!" I say.

"One kiss," he repeats, looking triumphant. I press my lips in a line and glare at him. He laughs. Mid-laugh, I lean over and peck his lips before sitting back in my seat.

"There. Done," I chuckle, ignoring all the feelings of the bond inside of me.

"Uh, that's not what I meant by a kiss."

"A kiss is a kiss," I tell him.

"That is not what I meant and you know it; I've kissed my father better than that," he growls.

"You kiss your father?"

"That came out wrong. I meant on the cheek, in greeting, not a romantic way!"

I laugh.

"What, you don't kiss people?" he asks.

"Well, I don't kiss my father, that's for sure," I say.

"Stop it; you know what I meant," Valen says, becoming embarrassed at his word vomit. It's strange to feel him through the bond.

"I know what you meant, and I think it's sweet that you give your father a peck on the cheek. Bet that makes him happy that you haven't outgrown your father's love," I tell him. I don't want him to think I think it's weird. It's totally acceptable. It just shocked me that he was that close to his father. Although neither he nor his father appeared too affectionate, Valen was always happy to receive and give our son hugs and affection. It makes me think of my father when I was still his daughter, not his biggest shame.

He, too, was a good father and never turned our affections away until I got pregnant and went from daddy's little girl to daddy's rogue whore daughter. But I'm glad he has a strong relationship with his father. That would never be a bad thing. Though it made the entire Valarie mess more upsetting, knowing how much it would hurt Valen to know his father lied to him all these years.

"So, about this kiss you cheated me out of?" Valen chuckles.

"I did not cheat you. You cheated yourself," I tell Valen as I motion for him to start the car. "I kissed you. It's done; now let's go. I need to get back to do some work."

"Fine, but you still owe me a kiss, and a proper one," Valen taunts while starting the car. "And I *will* make you pay up," he adds as he backs out of the driveway. I chuckle and shake my head at his words.

CHAPTER

FIFTY-SIX

Everly

We drive through the city, but when Valen doesn't turn into his territory, I glance over at him. I'm wondering where we're going when he stops at the police station on the city's main street.

"You're doing this now?" I ask as he unclips his seatbelt.

"Yes, Officer Richards's mind-linked and said his son and Amber are still here. I told him to hold them until I got here," Valen says before getting out of the car. I rush to unclip my seatbelt and jump out, and he starts walking up the steps. My heart races in my chest at the thought of what he'll do.

"You said you wouldn't hurt him," I say in a rush, racing after him and gripping his arm. He keeps walking into the building, and some officers open the door for him as they come out. They tip their hats to him and continue to their patrol cars. I shake my head and look at Valen.

"I said I won't, though I damn well want to. But Amber is part of your father's pack, and Micah is joining it. So if you want her to keep her mouth shut, I need to speak to them and Officer Richards," Valen explains, and I sigh a breath of relief.

Valen doesn't bother speaking to anyone, he just navigates his way around like he owns the place. He probably does; I wouldn't put anything out of his price range. When we come to a locked-off area, Valen taps on the plexiglass window and the officer, who looks half asleep, jolts upright in his seat, nearly falling out of it. He quickly reaches over and hits a button. Valen opens the door and holds it open for me, then grabs my hand, leading me down the long corridor before we arrive at some holding cells.

Officer Richards is leaning against one, though he stands up straighter as Valen enters, baring his neck to his Alpha. I see Amber sitting in a chair behind the hold desk. She glares at me, her eyes narrowed. Valen growls back at her, and she drops her head quickly.

"Alpha, I've spoken to him and he's reassured me it won't happen again," Officer Richards says while shooting a glare at Amber.

"No, it won't. I want them both kept here until after the Alpha meeting," Valen says before turning to Amber. "In cells."

Officer Richards nods to two men. Amber jumps up, shrieking at his words; the noise hurts my ears as they grab her. They drag her, kicking and screaming, toward the cell Micah is in while she throws a full-blown tantrum worse than a toddler. Valen growls and steps toward them before gripping her face.

"You can't command me. You're not my Alpha," she sneers. I can see his rage as his entire body trembles, and the back of his shirt rips as he tries not to shift. Her eyes widen with fear, and I swallow, actually feeling bad for her despite the trouble she caused.

"Be glad I'm not because if I were, I would have stripped you of your title. But your mate is one of my pack and if you don't get your ass in that cell, the only place you'll see him is in the forsaken territory," Valen snarls at her. She gasps, and her eyes flick to Micah in horror.

Valen shoves her face away, and the officers let her go. Officer

Richards opens the cell, and she turns her nose up and walks in as if she wasn't embarrassing herself while acting like a fool or just been humiliated.

Valen turns toward the cell where Micah sits, looking fearful. He's bruised and bloody, but mostly healed from the beating he received from Marcus. Micah cowers when Valen turns his icy glare on him. Valen's shirt is torn, and his skin ripples as he tries to contain himself.

"Consider yourself lucky, Micah, that your Luna is forgiving. You and I both know I am not. The only reason you are still breathing is because of her, so do you have anything to say?" Valen asks him.

Micah turns his head toward me, stutters out an apology, and thanks me for sparing him. I just stare in disbelief.

"Now, if either of you speaks one word of Everly being my mate to anyone, you and your entire families will be considered traitors and made forsaken. Am I clear?"

Amber looks at me but nods her head.

"Take their phones and print off the custody forms."

"Custody forms?" Amber asks, standing up. Micah growls at her.

"Yes, Micah will sign over all parental rights for Casey to Zoe and drop the custody battle. I expect all relevant documentation to be filled out, signed, and filed when I return after the Alpha meeting."

"After the Alpha meeting? I'm supposed to be attending!" she says.

"Tell your father you have food poisoning or something; I don't care. But neither of you will leave this cell until after. If I hear one whisper around town that Everly is my mate, both of you will no longer live in this city," Valen says, before turning to me. Officer Richards clears his throat, and Valen looks at him.

"Um, Alpha, if Micah signs all rights away, does that mean my wife and I can't see her either? It would break my wife's heart, Alpha."

"I never said he couldn't see her, but I want it all legal, so he can't take her from Zoe. If Zoe allows it, I don't see an issue with any of you remaining part of Casey's life, and that goes for Micah too. But if those papers aren't signed and sent off with a copy waiting when I return, I will send your son rogue and he will leave my city; that's if I don't decide to kill him," Valen warns.

"The relevant documents will be here when you return, Alpha. Thank you," Officer Richards says before glaring at his son and Amber.

The other officers bare their necks, and Valen nods before tugging me out of the room and back down the corridor.

"Would you really make them forsaken?" I ask once back in the car.

"Yes. And yes, I would have killed him if you didn't make me promise not to," Valen answers. He tugs off his torn shirt and tosses it in the back before pulling away from the curb.

"Are we going to get Valarian now?"

Valen nods, but by the stern, steel gaze he has out the window and the burning rage I feel through the bond, I know he's fighting with himself not to go back and tear Micah apart.

Just as we're about to turn up the street toward Valen's place, my phone rings. Macey's name pops up on the screen, and I quickly answer it.

CHAPTER
FIFTY-SEVEN

Everly

"I'll be back soon," I say immediately.

"No, it's fine. I got someone to cover you; I figured you were concussed. But Zoe isn't answering and I'm on tonight, and mom has hurt her knee again, so she can't watch both girls. Can you and Valen please, please, come to get Casey for the night?"

"What do you mean Zoe isn't answering? Did you knock on the door?"

Macey clears her throat before speaking in a hushed voice. "I did, but I don't think she could hear me over all the showering sounds coming from the house," she hisses. I snort. Who would have thought?

"They're like damn rabbits. I've been up there twice now, and I swear my ears are bleeding. Anyone would think we're running a brothel with the noises leaving your apartment."

"What's a brothel, Auntie Macey?" I hear Casey asking in the background.

"Uh, a place where people get foot massages," Macey answers awkwardly. Valen chuckles, but turns the car around, hearing her.

"Yep, we're on our way now. Meet us out the front," I tell her.

"Thank the Goddess, but you need to talk to her."

"Why do I have to talk to her? You're the eldest?" I say.

"Because I can't say anything after what you saw the other day, and don't say you didn't tell Zoe; I know you did. And you're the only one not getting laid–... foot massages around here," Macey corrects herself.

"Uh, no, you talk to her."

"I'll rock-paper-scissors you for it."

"Fine. Deal. But don't cry when I win, like I always do."

Valen raises an eyebrow at me and shakes his head. I say goodbye and hang up the phone.

"Are you two seriously going to fight over who's giving Zoe the sex talk?"

"Yes. Unless you want to do it?" I ask hopefully.

"Not a chance. Wait, what do I get for it if I do?" Valen asks, and I fold my arms. I'm not making any more deals with the devil, and I know he'll pick his words wisely, so I won't be able to get out of it if I do. We pull up out front; Macey is waiting with a bag for Casey.

"I threw some of Taylor's spare clothes in it for her, and school was canceled. I just got the notification because of a COVID case."

I sigh and nod. Damn pandemic.

Macey buckles Casey in before stopping at my window and holding her fist out. I roll my eyes, and we quickly play rock, paper, scissors while Valen laughs at us. Macey fist-pumps the air when her scissors cut my paper.

"No!" I cry.

"Sucker, I finally beat you!" she says, doing a victory dance and shaking her ass at me. I shake my head in defeat.

"I expect a total reenactment of the cringiness of that talk about proper behavior in our hotel," Macey says triumphantly.

"Fine, but you get the next awkward talk."

"No way; the last talk still haunts me, when I had to explain to both you girls the importance of pap smears."

"You could have just told us. You didn't have to draw diagrams and demonstrate on our dining room table. I haven't looked at the table the same. And you owe me a desk!" I tell her.

"If I have to give you girls awkward talks, I'll be thorough. Valarie always said get your facts straight, and I did that," Macey says.

"We were mortified," I laugh, remembering.

"Valarie thought it was pretty funny—even helped me do the diagram," Macey laughs. I chuckle.

"Damn, she sounds like a cool old lady," Valen says, and both Macey and I freeze, forgetting entirely about Valen and how casually we spoke of his mother.

"She was. She was a marvelous woman," Macey says with a sad smile. I nod before saying goodbye.

"Love you, Casey," Macey calls. Casey waves.

"Love you too," she retorts, blowing her a kiss. Valen drives out and back onto the highway, and Casey leans forward in her seat.

"Look, Uncle Valen, I brought 'Trolls'. Auntie Macey said I could because it's your favorite," she says, holding up the DVD to show him.

"Uncle Valen?" I ask her.

"Hmm, Auntie Macey said he's your boyfriend and will marry you one day."

"Did she now?" I ask, raising my eyebrow.

"Yep, so that makes him my uncle. But if he's my uncle, how will I marry Valarian? Wouldn't that make him my cousin? But Taylor said she's marrying him and that I have to marry Uncle Fester from the Addams Family, but I told her nuh-uh, I am," Casey says. I snicker, catching Valen's smile as he looks out the window.

"My boy is a lady's man."

I smack his thigh, and he grabs my hand before I can pull it away. Lifting it to his lips, he kisses the back of it, keeping hold of it on his lap when he lowers it again.

"So, can we watch 'Trolls' when we get to your place?" Casey asks hopefully.

"Yes, we can watch it on repeat, if you like," I say.

"Yay! Valarian will be so excited about our sleepover."

"Casey, you live with Valarian. Every night is a sleepover," I chuckle.

"Oh, right. I guess it is," she says, bouncing happily in the back of the car.

The drive is short, and I'm looking forward to lying down. Yawning, I step out of the elevator and follow Valen to his apartment. He unlocks the door, and the first thing I can smell is pancakes. My brows furrow, and I follow Valen in with Casey, who runs ahead.

"Ugh, not 'Trolls'," I hear Valarian whine.

"Oh, where did you come from, little one?" I hear Kalen's voice. Casey points to us down the hall, and Kalen walks over, looking at us.

"I'm Casey, and I came with them."

"Oh, you're back. We're making pancakes," Kalen says, before rushing back to the kitchen as he plates up.

"Pancakes and ice cream for dinner, Dad? Really?" asks Valen disapprovingly.

"You never complained when you were a kid. Want some? I made mountains," he says, pulling a huge tray off the stove. Valen shakes his head with a chuckle.

"Sure, why not? Pancakes for dinner it is, then," Valen laughs.

Kalen is dressed in a suit with a white apron on and a chef hat. He looks like an alien standing in the kitchen.

"And some for Miss Casey," Kalen says, handing her a plate. Both kids race excitedly toward the table with their plates. Just then, Kalen shocks me as I walk to the sink to get a glass of water. He actually hugs me and pecks me on the cheek.

I freeze up, stiff as a statue. "Everly, dear, so happy to see you again," he chirps. I look at Valen, who shrugs and tries to steal a pancake from the tray. His father smacks his hand with the spatula.

"Let me plate it up the way you used to like," he scolds, and I chuckle while Valen seems to pout before stealing one anyway. "You rotten little brat!" Kalen barks at him.

"Has no manners, Everly. Anyone would think a Neanderthal raised him," Kalen says, shaking his head while making a chocolate chip smiley face on Valen's pancakes with two blobs of ice-cream for ears.

CHAPTER
FIFTY-EIGHT

E verly

We ate dinner—or should I say breakfast for dinner, though Kalen seemed reluctant to leave. He was very hands-on, playing with the kids, but we needed to get them showered and dressed for bed, so Kalen said his goodbyes and left, stating he would see us at the Alpha meeting.

"Valarian, time for a shower, buddy; then you have to go to bed," Valen says. Valarian gets up off the lounge, and Casey follows.

"Casey, you'll have to wait until he hops out," I say.

"But Mom showered with Marcus with clothes on. Why can't I shower with Valarian?"

Valarian scrunches up his face, looking disgusted. I just look at Valen, hoping he'll explain, but it's Valarian who answers her.

"Gosh, you can be silly, Casey. People don't shower with clothes on. How would you get clean?" Valarian asks, shaking his head.

"Nah, Marcus did. He told me he was showering with clothes on with Mom."

Probably because he didn't want to tell you he was making

babies with Auntie Zoe," Valarian says matter-of-factly. My jaw drops.

"You can't make babies in a shower. Wait, how *do* you make babies?" Casey asks, and both of them look at us.

Well, that diverted quickly. Valen clears his throat and pulls at the neckline of his shirt, uncomfortable with the direction of the conversation.

"And how does the baby get in there?" she adds.

"Ugh, do I have to tell you everything? The man takes the baby and puts it in a cabbage, and the woman eats the cabbage, and her belly gets fat," Valarian says, exasperated.

Valen raises an eyebrow at his explanation while I do everything I can not to laugh.

"That's not how babies are made; you got that from that cartoon —the one with the cabbage patch dolls," Casey argues.

"Well, how else would mom have a baby?" Valarian retorts.

"Fine—they'll know. Ask your parents," Casey huffs with a pout. I snicker as I bail, leaving that for Valen to find a way out of. As I start to clean the kitchen, both kids look expectantly at Valen, who seems very uncomfortable.

"Umm, they just happen," Valen says.

Really? That was his big explanation to the birds and the bees?

"But how?" Casey asks.

"By showering together," Valen blurts.

Oh boy.

"See? I told you! Marcus was making babies in the shower!"

"You said the man puts the baby in a cabbage, so if he's showering, where does the cabbage come from?" Casey asks, and Valarian pauses to think for a moment.

"I don't know—let's Google it," Valarian says, racing to the table for his father's laptop. However, Valen is quick to get to his feet and snatch the laptop up before he can grab it.

"No, it's bedtime. Shower, now."

"But we want to know," Valarian whines. Valen scrubs a hand down his face before looking over and glaring at me. I smirk.

"Yes, best explain how babies are made, Alpha," I chuckle, and he growls at me while both kids wait for him to answer.

He drops onto the couch with a sigh. "Well, when a man and woman love each other, they do grown-up things which make a baby."

"What grown-up things?" Valarian asks, suddenly very interested in this topic of conversation.

"Like, um, kissing, hugging and adult wrestling," Valen offers, and the kids pull grossed-out faces.

"Wait, is Mom kissing Marcus in the shower with clothes on?" Casey asks, looking shocked.

"Ugh, Casey, I told you people don't shower with their clothes on!" Valarian says.

"Yeah, they do. Or Marcus would see Mom's private parts!" Casey squeals.

"So? People see private parts all the time when they shift. Remember that hippy lady out at the reserve, she took her clothes off before shifting, and we saw her butt and her big hairy front butt."

"Huh, I forgot about that. You're so smart, Valarian," Casey says. "But if Mom and Marcus are kissing in the shower... Oh, oh, oh! I'm going to be a big sister! I always wanted to be a sister," she says, brightening.

"Where are we going to fit a sister? Our house is too small, and no baby is sleeping in my room," huffs Valarian before shaking his head and walking off to the bathroom.

"I'm going to be a sister! I'm going to be a sister!" Casey laughs and dances in the living room.

"I say let Zoe break the news about being a sister. And thanks for the help, by the way," Valen says, coming over and grabbing a kitchen towel to dry the dishes as I wash them.

"By the way, you *are* aware I have a dishwasher?" he asks.

"Yep, I needed an escape. Dishes sounded like a good one," I say.

Once the kids are showered and dressed for bed, I help tidy up their dining room and living room mess.

"Are you staying in our room, or....?" Valen asks hopefully.

"Yes. And you mean your room. I don't live here."

"Yet," he says, and I shake my head at him. "Besides, Zoe will need the extra space since Casey is going to be a big sister."

"I'm sure Marcus has an apartment or someplace?"

"Nope, he prefers to stay at the packhouse."

"Well, if by chance they decide to have kids, I'll move out into one of the other suites at the hotel," I tell him.

"It's not 'if by chance'; more like 'when they have kids.' Marcus has always been vocal about wanting kids. And why would you move into another apartment when you can move in here?"

"Valen."

"What? You said so yourself: the media will go crazy when we announce we're mates. I can imagine the stories already if we don't live together, Everly," Valen says, picking up all the pencils that fell under the table.

"We can work it out," I tell him, watching him set the pencils into their rightful places. That will take all night if he plans on putting them in their selected spot. Shaking my head, I take them from him and jam them in without any order. His jaw clenches. I know he wants to sort them, but Casey will only pull them out again.

"Or you can stop being so damn stubborn and move in here."

"I happen to like being on my own; I don't have to answer to anyone. Besides, I have the hotel, so I need to be there."

"Then I'll move in with you," Valen says.

"What part of 'I like my independence' don't you get?"

"The independence part because we're mates, Everly. Mates live together, not in separate places. Besides, Valarian likes it here, and I want to be with my son."

"I swear, Valen, if you pull shit like Micah, I will lose it."

"Then don't make me. Valarian can't go from house to house just because you're too stubborn about living with me. Either we're mates, or we're not, Everly. So, make up your mind," Valen snaps.

"I'm not saying you can't see him; I'm just saying I don't want to live with you," I say.

"I am sick and tired of your mixed signals! One minute, you're saying you'll be my Luna, and now this," Valen growls before he storms off angrily, and I feel terrible because of the stupid bond.

CHAPTER
FIFTY-NINE

Everly

Valen returns a few seconds later with a towel before marching into the bathroom and shutting the door, muttering under his breath. I hear the shower start and sigh.

He has a point, though. The media would go insane over two mates—especially one holding status in the city—living apart. The scandals it would lead to! I can only imagine the speculation it would cause, and the rift once everyone finds out I am, in fact, Alpha John's daughter.

That's another thing I'm worried about because it *will* come out; secrets always do—they never remain hidden—and I know it will all come out when they dig into my past.

Yet, the thought of having to answer to someone irks me. And if I'm living with Valen, I know I'll have to, plus he could pull rank over me. Yet, the stories that would be in the papers... I can already imagine the headlines:

'PACK RIVALRY KEEPING MATES APART'

'VALEN'S CHEATING WAYS, Trouble With The Notorious Alpha'

Stupid shit. And that would be stacked on top of the ones saying:

353

'EVERLY — THE GOLD DIGGER TRAPPING THE ALPHA'

Fuck! I never thought of the different scenarios, and now they appear endless.

Valen walks out of the bathroom with a towel wrapped around his waist. He ignores me, and I can feel he is upset.

I chew my lip before getting up off the couch, wandering down the hall toward his bedroom, and pushing the door open. Valen is getting ready for bed pulls the sheets back.

"If you're coming in here to tell me you don't want to live with me or to give more bullshit excuses, Everly, I don't want to hear it," he says, climbing in bed and tugging the blankets up. He turns away from me, facing the wall, and I sigh before showering myself and returning to the room.

After rummaging through his closet for a shirt to wear, I climb in bed with him. Through the bond, I can tell he's still festering over our argument and very much awake, though he's keeping his back to me.

"You said earlier you wanted to be my Luna. How do you expect to do that if we live separately?" he says. "The Alpha meeting is in two days. What do you expect me to tell everyone? 'Everly and I are mates, but it's complicated'? This isn't like updating a Facebook status, Everly. I get you don't want me to mark you yet, but at least fucking try."

I remain quiet, pondering my thoughts and his words, when he rolls over to face me.

"What are you afraid I'll do that you keep refusing to try to make this work?" Valen asks.

There are plenty of things I'm afraid of: Valen taking control of everything in my life when I only just got some semblance of the normal back in it; him taking my son; losing the hotel and everyone who relies on that place; I'm worried about the rogue woman losing everything when they have no jobs because I failed them.

But most of all, I'm afraid of ending up back in a shitbox car, living in the train station parking lot with Valarian. I'm scared of losing everything, just like I did before—going back to having nothing and no one. At least with how things are now, he can't control everything. He can't take it from me.

"Anything I say will sound like an excuse," I tell him, and he sighs.

Unless you've lived with the hopelessness of failing at everything and having no one to rely on, you can't understand how terrifying it is to allow someone else to have even the slightest bit of control when you worked so hard to get where you are. Moving in with Valen would be trusting him not to break me again, not to take everything I worked hard for away from me, trusting him not to throw me away like trash like my family did.

"Try to explain. I want to understand, Everly. No bullshit, just tell me," Valen breathes, frustrated.

"I lost everything for our son—everything, Valen. I had no one, only him, until I found that place. No one helped me until Valarie. My father couldn't bear the sight of me. Society displayed me as some vile, home wrecking whore; I lived with that. The other rogue women lived with that. I won't lose it all. I won't go back to that place where I let myself think I would have help, only to find out I wouldn't and that everything could be taken away from me in the blink of an eye," I answer honestly.

I used to use the excuse it was his cheating, the fact he didn't recognize me; but deep down it has nothing to do with that because he's here now, he proved he would stay. It's my own thoughts that ruined everything. I know it's toxic, and my own safety mechanism, but it's the truth. Until you hit rock bottom and claw your way back, no one can tell you not to fear ending up back there again. And that thought terrifies me—I have too much to lose now; I would lose everything, including my son.

"But no one is taking anything from you, Everly."

"You did. I know that it's in the past, I know you want to make up for it, but it fucking haunts me. Do you have any idea how lonely it is when you have a baby relying on you to keep it alive and fed when you have nothing and no one to help? Then, to feel so selfish for forcing that life on a child? Choosing yourself over your own kid because you can't bear the heartbreak of giving them up? You can't bear the thought of letting someone else raise them? I lived with that guilt of thinking I was destroying my son, so I damn near killed myself to earn the right to be his mother—one he deserved. I created a life for us; I won't lose it," I tell him.

"You do deserve him, and none of that will happen again; I'm here now," Valen says.

"Yes, you are, but what happens once you mark me? You make me give up the hotel? Take it from me—from them? Before Valarian, I was oblivious to how this city was run, like any other Alpha. Shunned the rogue whores until I found myself one of them. Zoe, Macey, and I, we built that place. I won't allow you to take it from us —from those that work there. I won't just quit because you want a Luna. And I know you expect that. You expect that because it's what's taught to us. Luna's abide by their Alpha; The Alpha has control. No one should have that kind of power over someone else."

"You think I'll make you give it up?" Valen asks.

"Yes. But I'm also worried about what they'll think when I become one of those that suppressed them in the first place. You marking me doesn't just affect me; it affects them when I become what society wants. What you want," I tell him.

"What do you want, then?"

"What I want is for my son not to be ashamed because he's rogue —I want the stereotypes gone. I want everything I've worked for to mean something, so our son can say that I tried, that I had nothing but made something, something that made a difference. That's why I don't want you marking me. It would be like throwing everything we worked hard for away if you made me give it up—like tossing what I was trying to change away—and all of them will go back to being just another rogue whore. And I will just be another selfish Alpha," I tell him.

"I just want my mate, Everly, that's all."

"You say that now, until everyone starts putting pressure on you to force me to conform to their ways. You think I'll remain quiet in Alpha meetings when they speak garbage about the way they treat rogue whores, or when the packs bring in another law that restricts them more—like the stupid schooling cuts they made last year? It will cause an uproar, one that will reflect poorly on you because you can't keep your Luna in line. You'll pull rank over me, Valen. You'll have control. And when they kick up a stink that I'm speaking against the way they've lived for decades, I know you'll use it against me," I tell him, clutching my head.

Everything is so fucked up, and the stress is beginning to get to me: the stress of the mate bond, the hotel, people going missing, my father, and this stupid Alpha meeting. Tears burn my eyes. I'm so sick and tired of the responsibility, but at the same time, I need to keep going.

"No. You *think* you know, Everly. But I'm not trying to take anything from you. Use your title how you want. Fuck, abolish the laws for all I care; I'll even help you."

I scoff and drop my hands to look over at him. That would go down well, the media would tear shreds off him, and his pack would become a laughingstock. I shake my head. He seems to think it's so easy that I should just accept him because his title could help. But it could also destroy everything.

Valen sighs and sits up on his elbow, looking down at me.

"I mean it, Everly. You want to help the rogues? What better position than one of power? Change the laws, change their views, but do it with me by your side and in your corner. You think you have to solve all their problems yourself; you don't."

"You backing me would start a war, Valen. Wars never solve anything; just get innocent people killed."

"Yes, you're right. But then those wars end up in history books and become everyone's turning point, a reflection of how we messed up and a place to see the error of their ways. You're worried about war? The packs are always at war. Why not go to war for something that will hold value and give a future to someone who otherwise would have none? You have my pack. They will fight for you if you're my Luna. They will fight for the rogues."

My brows crease as I think over his words, yet him saying it and allowing it after he marks me are two different things.

"One thing I've realized since meeting you is that the rogues hold just as much value as anyone else and are capable of more than they realize because not one of your people have ever talked down to me, treated me, or any of those that enter your doors differently. They treat everyone with kindness even though they are shown none. You want to change the laws, change things for the rogues, then let me help you."

"You could go back on your word, though, Valen," I whisper. He could ruin everything because me taking that title gives him everything I own—everything the rogues own.

"I won't. I swear I won't. And I'll prove it." Valen sighs, dropping his head on my shoulder, and groans. He feels defeated, yet I can also tell he understands because his anger is gone.

"How?" I ask.

"Because tomorrow I will open up my pack's schools for the rogue children. And I am shutting down that terrible place you call a school." He lifts his head back up and presses his forehead against mine.

"Besides, when I spoke to Valarian about changing schools, he refused unless Casey and Taylor could come to his new school, so the more, the merrier."

"But what of the rogues that work there? They'll lose their jobs."

"I hear a certain Mountainview Hotel is looking for extra employees... We can help find them jobs. We can work it out," Valen says.

"In a city where rogues can't go past the two streets on either side of the main street unless it's to the reserve, there are no jobs, Valen. No one will hire them."

Valen sighs, appearing to think for a second before pushing his knee between my legs and shoving them apart.

CHAPTER
SIXTY

Everly

I raise an eyebrow at him. He smirks at me without answering as he moves between my legs and rests his arms on my pillow.

"Valen!" I growl, looking away but also not wanting to shove him off because the tingling sensation makes my stomach warm and fuzzy. He chuckles, but presses his weight against me when I don't shove him off.

"Then I will drop my borders for them," Valen says, and my eyes snap to his.

"You would do that?" I ask, and he nods. "Maybe once I do, the other packs may open their borders too."

"Valen, the media will destroy you for that," I tell him, and he shrugs.

"And after the Alpha meeting when I announce my mate is a rogue, it'll give them something else to talk about. I don't care for my reputation, Everly. No matter what, the media will find some way to destroy it, so why not give them something good to talk about? Let them open the debate. Then we can focus on changing their views," he says before leaning down and brushing his nose across my cheek to my ear and down my jaw.

"Valen, it's impossible to think with you doing that," I tell him as his hands bunch up the shirt I'm wearing at my hip.

"Then don't think—just agree. You have no excuses now, Everly."

"I can think of plenty," I breathe out as he nips at my jaw, making me groan and shudder beneath him.

"Are they all to do with the rogues and you thinking I am going to ruin you?" he murmurs before kissing down my neck. I nod, my eyes closing, loving the feel of his lips on my skin. I fight to keep clear my thoughts that are suddenly becoming more hazy.

"Then let me prove it. Tomorrow, I'll drop the borders and open the schools and my pack to the rogues."

"You could just be saying that to get in my pants," I tell him as his hand travels down my hip to my thigh. He laughs softly.

"Well, that would be an added bonus, but you're not wearing any panties, so I don't need to try and get into them."

My eyes fly open at his words. "I thought it would be a bit odd borrowing those when I'm already wearing your shirt," I tell him.

"What's mine is yours," he says while tugging my shirt up higher.

"And what's mine will be yours if you mark me," I tell him, a little bitterly. He pulls his face away from my neck and stares down at me.

"You're worried I'll take everything from you, right?"

I nod and sigh.

"What if I make it, so I can't?" he asks.

"What do you mean?"

"What if I hand my pack over to you?"

"What?"

"I'll stand down—make you Alpha. I'll give you my pack," he says, like it makes perfect sense.

"Valen, I can't ask you to do that! And then what? You become my Luna?"

He seems to think. "Now, that would be a first," he mumbles.

"I'm being serious, Valen," I say.

"So am I, Everly. I mean it; I just want you. Fuck what the other packs think. I'll stand down as Alpha, and... I don't know... just be your mate."

"No, I am not taking your place, and no, I don't want to be an Alpha—Luna maybe—but no, I have the rogues to worry about; I don't want to have to worry about pack issues on top of that. And technically, you would still be Alpha. You can't just stop being an Alpha," I tell him.

He sighs because he knows I'm right, unless I make him rogue or forsaken after giving me his title.

"Yeah, you're right because I have to mark you anyway, so you don't die on me," he says with a huff. "What about a prenup, then?"

"Still holds no legal accountability when you're an Alpha."

"Then I don't know, Everly. What do you want me to do because you don't trust me not to take everything from you."

I chew my lip, trying to think.

"I won't take anything from you. You keep saying I'll toss you away or make you give up helping the rogues; I won't. They're your village, Valarian's village, and his family. So if you don't trust me not to hurt you, trust I won't hurt our son."

"You won't hurt our son," I murmur to myself because I know he wouldn't; I know that for certain. I can feel how much he loves Valarian—loves me. He could hurt me out of spite, but he wouldn't hurt Valarian.

"Of course not. I may be a shitty mate—well, not shitty, but you know what I mean—but I am a good father, Everly. I would never hurt our son."

"Then get a judge to sign everything over to him."

"What?"

"Everything I own is to be signed over to Valarian, with me having total control until he's 18."

"You want a conservatorship?" he asks, shocked.

"Then I have nothing for you to take; it belongs to Valarian."

Valen shakes his head. "No, keep your hotel."

"But?"

"I'll sign everything I own over to you—all deeds, all accounts."

"But you could easily get that back, Valen. You're an Alpha," I tell him.

"But it would still take me months in court," he argues.

"You own the courts," I deadpan.

"Not the human ones, I don't. Everything I own, I will file over to you in the human courts. I can't touch you then and will have to fight for it back the human way," he says, making a face.

"But then I'll look like a gold digger," I tell him and shake my head.

"Then just trust me; for once, trust someone other than yourself. Or give Zoe and Macey part ownership, or something. I can only legally control what you own. I can't control it if it isn't in my name, and Marcus won't ever do that to Zoe," Valen says.

"And you would get a judge to do that? Help me sign it over equally to Macey and Zoe?" I ask, shocked, he would allow me to hand over half the hotel.

"If it means I can have you, then yes. Besides, as you said, they helped build that place; only fair they get half of it. You could probably do it yourself with a lawyer," he says.

"No tricks?" I ask.

"No tricks," he says, smiling down at me.

I nod, actually liking that idea. I can't wait to tell Zoe and Macey.

"Oh, thank God," Valen groans before kissing me.

"Valen!" I mumble against his lips.

"Quiet. You have run out of excuses now," he laughs while his hands claw at my shirt. I suppose I have.

"But you are not marking me until after the Alpha meeting and the documents are signed."

He hums in agreement, pressing himself against me as he nips and sucks at my neck. I moan, trying to keep my head while his lips attack my skin.

"Valen!" I shriek when I feel his shirt tear in his hands, exposing me to him. He pulls away and sighs.

"I said yes. I won't mark you until the paperwork is signed," he whines. "So please let me touch–"

I yank him closer and kiss him. He groans, settling back between my legs. I shiver when he kisses me back, and moan into his mouth when he rolls his hips against me, his erection pressing against the inside of my thigh. I move my hand between us, squeezing his cock through his pants, and he groans, kissing me harder and rocking his hips against me.

"No wrestling. We can't fit Zoe's brother or sister in our house, and I am not sharing a room," comes Valarian's voice suddenly beside the bed. Valen leaps off me and I jump, ripping the blanket up to cover myself.

"What are you doing in here? You're supposed to be in bed," Valen says, clutching his chest like he's about to have a heart attack.

"Casey keeps sleep talking and woke me up," Valarian huffs.

"Come on, I'll tuck you back in," Valen tells him.

"No, I want to sleep in here, so you can't make me share my room," Valarian says, glaring at me. Valen groans, clearly annoyed our son is cock-blocking him.

"But there will be plenty of room if we move in here with your father—two extra rooms," I tell him. Not that I was planning on having unprotected sex anyway, but he doesn't need to know that.

"Really? We're going to live here now?" Valarian asks, his little eyes lighting up, and Valen looks over at me. I nod and he smiles before motioning for Valarian to follow him so he can put him back to bed.

"Fine, but I want a brother, not a sister. I've lived with Casey for so long now. Girls suck, and I'm sick of watching 'Trolls'," Valarian whines.

''Somehow, I don't think it works like that. You don't get to choose," Valen tells him.

"Then just wrestle in a boy way to make a boy," Valarian says simply, like it makes total sense. I chuckle and shake my head.

"I will keep that in mind," Valen tells him while walking him back to his room.

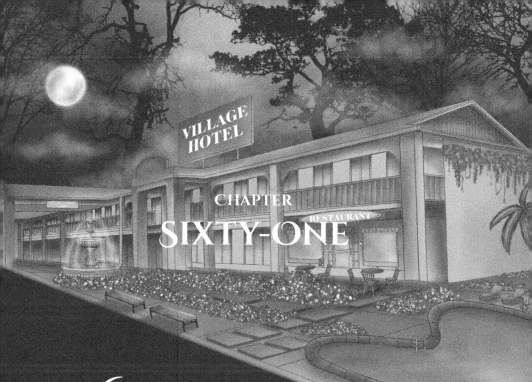

CHAPTER
SIXTY-ONE

Valen

Tucking Valarian in bed takes too long; I'm excited to get back to Everly. Finally! My balls are so blue that I just want her to touch it—even just look at it. I would take anything at this point. I ain't picky. I'll probably blow a load just by the sight of her pretty pink vagina.

Walking to the door, I have a spring in my step until my spawn opens his little mouth.

"Can you read me a book?" Valarian asks. I freeze with my hand on the door mid-escape. Please be a five-page pop-up book with one sentence on each page.

"Sure," I tell him, turning around and stepping over Casey, who is asleep on his trundle. Valarian holds up what must surely be 'The Never-ending Story' with how big it is. It literally is a never-ending fucking story. The thing is at least five hundred pages.

Please be big lettering per page, like one letter a page big letters.

Valarian shuffles over, and I squeeze next to him—having to fold myself like origami to fit on the pint-sized human bed—and open this book which, of course, is to do with space just like his bedroom.

At least it's educational. I groan. Which idiot bought this book? Wait, I did; I was that idiot. I will never encourage nighttime reading again; I get it now!

Valarian looks up at me, blinking and yawning, with his cute little face staring at me expectantly. I start reading and get to some part of the milky-way and glance down, hoping he's asleep, but then I make eye contact with eyes that match mine. He's still awake! Why! Why do you do me like this! I am aware I'm throwing a tantrum, but for the love of God, go to fucking sleep!

Stifling a growl and the urge to toss the book out the window, I continue reading. I know Everly can feel my frustration; possibly feel the weight in my damn balls too. Zoe owes me big for her crotch goblin waking my boy when I could finally get in some sexy time.

Even reading to Valarian, she keeps mumbling about pink unicorns or some crap; I'm damn near tempted to duct tape her mouth shut or put her in the hall. She's lucky she's cute and kind of growing on me. To be honest, she had me at 'Uncle Valen', so I guess I won't disown her yet. I guess I'll let her stay. I continue reading this encyclopedia on space. An hour goes by, and I swear I hear Everly chuckle in the room down the hall. She's enjoying my torment, enjoying my blue balls.

I almost do a happy dance when I notice the fruit of my loins has finally crashed, and carefully sneak off his bed. I step over Casey, only to find her staring up at me, and in her hands is another book.

"Uh, sweetie, my throat is dry," I tell her, and she pouts, fluttering the lashes of her big, hazel eyes. "You can have a sip from my drink bottle, Uncle Valen," she says while beaming and holding it up. That damn word again, but it sounds so endearing. 'Uncle' has a nice ring to it. That's it. Zoe is on my most wanted list. Off with her fucking head.

Casey moves over and rummages on the shelf, pulling out a book that thankfully only has about twenty pages. She holds up her drink bottle to me, and I shake my head. Definitely not drinking from that after she slurped on it.

"For your throat, so you can read," she says, and I hear Everly snicker. She is sorely mistaken if she thinks she's getting out of it or will be by the time I'm done with her.

No amount of willpower could stop the gagging cough as I squirt the tiniest amount of her water in my mouth. The time it takes for me to swallow it and not run for the bathroom and sanitize my mouth is the longest few seconds of my life. It's like forcing myself to swallow a golf ball.

"You can have some more; I don't mind sharing," Casey chirps. Does she not know whose father I am? Does she not see that he gets his strange behaviors from me? Casey insists on me drinking some more of her backwash drink bottle, and I gag. The water tastes slimy. It shouldn't taste slimy. Why is it slimy!

That was definitely spit, and I think... a piece of cookie. I look at the drink bottle and the tiny hole at the top before looking down at Casey. How? I want answers on how she could get a cookie in her drink bottle. It makes no sense, yet I just swallowed it.

Casey, now happy my non-existent thirst is quenched, hands me her book. I'm going to hunt down the author, or director, or whoever invented prancing trolls, and murder them. They deserve death. I understand Valarian's hate for the movie, show, whatever the heck it is.

The girl is obsessed. And I don't mean slightly; I am pretty certain Casey is their number one fan. They should be giving her freebies at this point. She's a walking, talking promotion for them. Even the hair ties in her braided hair have Princess Poppy on them. I settle next to her, reading it to her. I try to skim a few lines to hurry it up.

But she catches me! She is obsessed. I don't know why she needed me to read it. She knows it word for word and could probably recite it backward. After the fifth read-through, she finally passes out, and I make a quick dash for the bathroom and chug down half a bottle of mouthwash before brushing my teeth and finishing the other half of the mouth wash. I needed to cleanse my insides of the bacteria I've just ingested. I shiver at the thought of the germs in that bottle.

I sneak back to my room with a sigh of relief, shut the door, and flick the lock. I mentally debate dragging the dresser in front of it too, but figure surely they can't pick a lock.

Turning around, I look at the bed with a smile, then freeze. Nope, not happening. She's asleep. I did not just ingest a slobbered-on, soggy piece of cookie and drink spit-water and read half the damn library for her to fall asleep before I got back.

Nope, she is paying up.

I briefly wonder if I could get her to pay up for the kiss she owes, maybe kiss my little head instead of my big one. I ponder cursing Zoe and the kids for a few seconds before climbing in the bed like a creeper and stalking my mate. Sneaking between the sheets, I climb between her legs, only for her to knee me in the face.

"Shit. Are you alright?" she mumbles, half asleep. "Valen, it's late," she whines, yawning as I shove her legs apart and grip her ass, dragging her pussy closer for me to feast on. I suck on her thigh, and she jumps as I nip at her skin, working my way to my prize.

CHAPTER
SIXTY-TWO

Everly

It's the feel of warm hands on my skin that pulls me from my sleep. I had tried to stay awake for him, but after the first hour passed, sleep called me, so I drifted off into oblivion. I am still stuck in the remnants of my dream when I feel him grab my legs. Half asleep and startled awake, I act accordingly and bring my knee up, kicking my leg out before recognizing the tingling sensation moving up my thighs.

"Shit. Are you alright?" I gush, hoping I didn't hurt him. Though, why he couldn't just wake me up like a normal person, I don't know. I hear him grunt and curse under his breath before dragging me closer to him.

"Valen, it's late," I yawn, rubbing my eyes when I feel his hands grip my hips and his shoulders force my legs further apart. I have no time to worry about the fact his face is between my thighs before I feel his breath on my skin. A moment later, his tongue and mouth lave the inside of my thigh as he sucks on it, moving his lips ever so slowly to where I suddenly want it.

Sleep is forgotten as arousal teams throughout my body when

his warm breath caresses over my slit. His hot, wet tongue curls between my folds, licking a line to my clit. It's ferocious, swirling and lapping, teasing and tasting as he devours me.

My eyes close as I become lost in the sensation of his mouth on my flesh. My skin prickles with heat, and my entire body becomes hot and flushed. Valen's hands move from my ass to my thighs, and he spreads me wide before dipping his tongue inside me and tasting my desire as it spills out.

His deep, guttural groan vibrates through me as he pushes me closer to the edge. His mouth leaves no part of me untouched as he retraces his path back to my clit and sucks on my throbbing bud that seems to have developed its own pulse.

My pussy clenches as the first simmering ripple of my orgasm washes over me, and I see white—my mind blissfully blank. My back arches as he shoves me completely over the peak, and I'm suddenly free-falling blind through the pleasurable waves of my climax.

My hips roll, and my pussy pulsates against his hot mouth as I ride the tides of my orgasm. His mouth moves to lap at the juices that spill from me. Slowly, I melt against the soft sheets, blissfully relaxed as my body cools down, and I try to catch my breath. I shudder when his tongue flicks over my clit one last time, teasing, tickling, before he crawls up my body and settles his hips between my legs.

His erection rests against my sensitive pussy while he kisses my jaw, nipping at my skin, and I yawn. The little bite he gives me on my shoulder breaks the skin and makes me hiss, and he laughs softly, licking and nibbling my lips as he rolls his hips against me.

"You're not sleeping. I'm not finished with you yet," he growls, and my lips tug at the corners, yet I'm so ready for sleep now.

"Can I do an I.O.U.?" I chuckle tiredly.

"You do owe me a kiss. Don't think I've forgotten," Valen chuckles, nipping at my lips. He rolls his hips against me, making me gasp as he brushes against my clit. I groan, kissing him back when his tongue sweeps across my lips and brushes the tip of my tongue.

My fingers slide through his hair before gripping it and dragging his mouth closer as I tangle my tongue with his. Shivers make him tremble when I trace my fingertips down his side to the waistband of his shorts, pushing them over his hips as I lift my knees and roll my hips against him.

He groans against my lips, helping me get rid of his pants, using his hand to shove them down his legs before kicking them off. He eases his weight back between my legs and moves his pelvis against mine. His thick cock slides between my folds before pressing against my entrance, and I squirm and glare at him, moving up a little before he can shove inside me.

"Forgetting something? I am not having a baby right now," I say.

"No. Nine months sounds about right, though."

I raise an eyebrow at him, and he drops his head against my shoulder and groans.

"Fine," he sighs before sitting up and leaning over to his bedside table. The lamp flicks on, and he rummages through the drawer, removing a foil package. He tears it with his teeth and settles between my legs, rolling the condom on before huffing in annoyance.

"Happy?" Valen murmurs against my lips as he kisses me, and I nod, kissing him back and wrapping my legs around his waist. Suddenly, I twist, forcing him onto his back. As he sits up, he growls at me while I rest my weight against his hips. Hand moving up my thigh to my hips, his thumb brushes over the faint marks that line them from carrying our son. Those golden eyes follow his hands that move up my side, across my ribs to the side of my breast.

He brushes his thumb over my hard, peaked nipple before leaning up to take it in his mouth while his arms wrap securely around my waist. He lifts his weight, dragging us higher up the bed, so he can lean against the headboard. His mouth never leaves my skin as he licks and flicks my nipple, teasing it between his teeth. I moan softly as the bond flares with desire, and I roll my hips against him. Moving my hand between our bodies, I wrap my fingers around his large, thick length and position him.

As I sink down on him, my walls clenching at the feel of his cock filling me. Valen leans his head against the headboard and sighs, while I get used to the feeling of having something inside me after so long. Leaning forward, I kiss him, gently rocking and raising my hips slowly as I find some sort of rhythm. He kisses me back eagerly, his tongue delving between my lips, dominating mine, while his hand slides up my neck into my hair. He grabs a handful, pulling my head back, so his lips can travel down my jaw and neck. My hand falls behind me onto his thigh as I move against him, and he sucks and licks my breasts before clutching me back to him and kissing me deeply.

His hands grip my hips, my skin pinching between his fingers as he moves me faster and sets a new speed. I grab his shoulders as he builds up friction, my pussy clenching around his thick cock soaked in my juices. Faster. Faster. I chase the feeling building inside my stomach. After my breathing turns harsh, I push his hands away, chasing after the sensation, only to slow down again when he grabs my hips once more. His worry slivers through the bond, like he thinks he'll hurt me.

"You won't hurt me, I've had a baby, remember," I murmur against his lips as I kiss him. His worry seems to slip away as he kisses me back.

"Then grip the headboard," he mumbles between kissing me. Reaching up, I grab the headboard above his shoulders while he grips my hips, lifting them before slamming me down on him and making me gasp. His cock bumps painfully against my cervix, but it's a good pain as my walls squeeze around him.

Euphoria slips through me as he continues to roll and lift my hips. Our bodies move in sync and I feel my stomach begin to tighten, feel the heat wash back over my skin, making goosebumps rise all over. His grip tightens, his nails digging in, and I feel his legs tense beneath me just as I come undone.

My pussy clenches, milking him as my orgasm ripples through me. He groans as he finds his release. His grip gradually loosens, and I roll my hips, riding out the remnants of my pleasure before crashing hard into his chest.

Valen's breathing is harsh as we both try to catch our breath. His lips press to my shoulder before he turns his face toward mine, which lies heavily on his shoulder, caressing my lips with his before brushing his nose against mine.

"I love you," he whispers, and I smile, bumping his nose back with mine before pecking his lips.

"What's there not to love? I'm pretty great," I chuckle.

"Is that right?" he teases. Wrapping his arms around my waist, he flips me onto my back.

"Should I be hurt you didn't say it back?" he laughs softly, nipping at my jaw to my lips.

"No."

"Then say it," he whispers, licking the seam of my lips. "Tell me you love me; save my ego."

I chuckle at his words before gripping his face in my hands and pushing him back, so I can see his face.

He's breathtaking when vulnerable. He's beautiful all the time, but the uncertainty of those three words I can see truly worries him.

"I love you, Valen Solace; I have since I found out you were mine," I tell him.

"The whole time?" he laughs, and I chuckle.

"Yep, all that time. I just loved to hate you then."

"And now?"

"I just love you," I whisper, wrapping my arms around his neck and tugging his lips back to mine.

CHAPTER
SIXTY-THREE

E verly

The morning of the Alpha meeting is a rat race trying to get the kids dressed and ready for the day. As I quickly pull a shirt over Valarian's head, he instantly whines as the collar crinkles.

"Valarian, I haven't got time, not today," I tell him. Of all the days he wants to have a meltdown, it has to be the day of the Alpha meeting. It will be held at 3 p.m. I'm already a nervous wreck. The shirt looks acceptable, but Valarian goes into a full-on meltdown, tugging at it and crying. Valen comes over from making his and Casey's cereal and grabs the hem, lifting it off him.

"Calm down. The hotel is fine, Everly. You're stressing for no reason," Valen calls over his shoulder while wandering off to get Valarian a new shirt. He returns with a buttoned one and carefully does the buttons up for his son, making sure not to wrinkle his shirt, before seating Valarian at the table.

My brain feels fried with the list of things I have to check and arrange once back at the hotel, though Valen assured me he would help. How, I'm not sure since Zoe and I will be helping set up and I need him to watch both kids.

"I have to duck down to the council really quick, then I'll head to the hotel to help you," Valen says.

"Well, you need to take the kids with you. Zoe and Marcus are already setting up, and I need to check the restaurant and mark off the catering supplies," I tell him.

"No, my father is watching them for us, and I already asked Zoe, who's fine with him taking Casey too. You just have to meet him downstairs in the wine garden. There's a kids' play area," Valen says, coming over and pecking my lips.

"Wait, what time?" I call after him.

"Just head down after they finish eating. Dad's taking them to the movies and lunch and will meet us at the hotel," Valen calls over his shoulder before walking out the door. I sigh, looking over at the kids, who are happily eating their Froot Loops. Thank the Goddess Kalen is taking them; I don't think I can handle their sugar rush today.

The wine gardens are lovely, though the stares I receive from everybody are beginning to annoy me. I can't wait until the secret's out, just so people will fuck off with their glares.

Casey and Valarian are climbing on the climbing frames and swinging on the poles when I get a text message from Kalen saying he's running a little late. I'm surprised he has my phone number; Valen must have given it to him.

"Ugh, Casey, don't eat that," I tell her, racing over before she actually eats the snail she's lifting to her mouth.

"But why? That lady is," Casey says, pointing to the woman at the table who's eating Escargot. Valarian pulls a face at the woman as she eats one that was on the bed of lettuce on her plate.

"Still, don't eat it. Snail slime is poisonous," I tell her, wiping her hands free of the handful of snails she's collected from the garden.

"Then why is she eating them?"

Ugh, come on Kalen; then you can answer these questions, I internally groan.

"Because they're a delicacy, and they're cooked, not fresh from the garden," I tell her.

"Gross! Why would anyone eat a slug?" Valarian asks, plucking a snail from the garden where I just made Casey drop them. It comes out of its shell and he drops it, pulling a face. I chuckle at him just as a voice from another table reaches my ears.

"Seems Alpha Valen needs to up his standard, especially for the price we pay; letting rogues in here, such a shame," a middle-aged woman says, turning her gaze to me. Valarian growls at her, shocking me, and seems about to say something. I grip his shoulder gently, and he looks up at me; I shake my head.

"Mind your place, boy. Rogue whores and their mutts shouldn't be allowed in the presence of the elite," she sneers, and I glare at her, biting my tongue. I am not about to cause a scene.

"I will have to put in a complaint. It looks like the Alpha is letting all kinds of riffraff in here."

"It appears so, ma'am, because he let you through his doors," I tell her, sick of her whining voice. Her piggish face seems appalled that I would even talk back to her, let alone call *her* the riffraff.

"How dare you? Do you have any idea who I am?"

"No, and I don't care to. I have standards, and you don't meet them," I tell her. She huffs, tossing her napkin on the floor before stomping off just as Kalen steps into the children's play area.

"Sorry, I am late; I got caught in traffic." He turns to look where I'm staring after the woman. "Everything alright?"

"Fine. I need to go."

Kalen nods, and I turn to the kids. Casey is stuffing her pockets full of snails once again. I click my tongue and give them both a peck on the cheek, telling them to behave, before leaving Kalen to deal with it.

"I will find you later, dear," Kalen says, pecking my cheek and hugging me, much to the disgust of those around us. Somehow, I don't think I'll get used to his sudden affections toward me. I roll my eyes before leaving and looking for Tatum, who's supposed to take me back to the hotel. Only when I walk out the front doors do I stop and stare in disbelief.

Valarie's truck.

I blink and take a step back, staring again. Tatum climbs out of the driver's seat and shuts the door. My hands go to my eyes, and I rub them, holding back the tears. I thought he crushed it.

"Is it...?" I couldn't believe my eyes.

Tatum smiles before tossing me the keys—her old keychains are still attached, along with the pendants of four steel cut-out girls and three babies. And three keychain pictures of Valarian, Casey, and Taylor were also still attached. Just seeing them, I can hear them jingle like they used to on her hip when she walked. I kiss the keys, trying not to become emotional over an old truck.

"He didn't destroy it?" I choke.

"Nope, kept it in the garage. I filled it up for you, but she needs a good clean—pretty dusty down there," Tatum says, and I nod.

"Valen said you were stressed this morning. He was going to give it back tonight, but he just called and asked me to give it to you now to help cheer you up," Tatum laughs. It definitely did that. I hug him quickly.

"Thank you!" I tell him before jumping into my truck and reaching over to unlock the glove box.

Relief floods me when I see the letters from Valarie inside. I pull them out, making sure they're all there, including the one for Valen, which is still sealed. I swallow before placing it back.

It had arrived a few weeks after her passing, along with the others for when the babies grew older. It was one of the reasons I was so devastated about the car—I thought they would never find out what was in those letters. The other three go straight into my handbag; I'll put them in the safe back at the hotel. Why I didn't in the first place is beyond me. Her storage locker key—where all her belongings are—is still there too, and I toss that in my bag along with the envelopes.

Starting my baby up, she roars to life.

I smile before pulling out, heading home.

CHAPTER
SIXTY-FOUR

K alen

Something must have happened with that woman I saw leaving. I muse over it as I watch Everly leave. She seems upset. Turning back to Valarian and little Casey, it seems like both are in a mood.

"Papa, can you get us a drink?" Valarian asks, and I smile. He looks so much like Valen when he was Valarian's age; his big amber eyes looking back at me remind me of his father, though Valen has grown out of his dimples.

"Of course. What would you like?" I ask.

"Banana milkshake!" Casey squeals, and I smile before looking at Valarian, though I have a funny feeling I know what he'll ask for, especially if he is, indeed, like his father.

"Vanilla, please."

I nod, happy I am right, before looking around for the servers. Not seeing any, I look at the bar, which only has a small line.

"Okay, wait here; I will be right back. I am just going over there," I point out the bar, which is only a couple of feet away, before stepping through the playground's safety gate.

379

I am excited for the day I planned out to distract the kids. It kind of reminds me of when I used to take Valen out. Every Sunday was our day. Every Sunday was an adventure when he was a small boy, always hunting for unknown places to take him.

I place the kids' milkshake orders and add on some subs to take with us too, before turning to look back at them. I wave to them, then freeze.

They are gone.

Two minutes, if that! I had turned around for only a few moments, and they just disappeared. Racing back to the playground, I search the tunnels, climb into the cubbyholes at the top, and check the slides. They are gone. My stomach drops, my heart racing like a drum at the thought of losing them.

"Hey! The kids, the kids who were in here, did you see where they went?" I ask, grabbing a security guard's arm. He looks behind me at the playground and shrugs.

"I didn't see any kids, Alpha Kalen."

"I want all hotel security looking for a boy and girl. The girl is in a pink dress with, um, um, what is the name?" I try to think of the name of that show she likes, the one Valen complained about. "'Trolls'! It's a pink 'Trolls' dress; the boy is in a light blue, button-up shirt and navy slacks."

The guard starts rattling off their descriptions across his radio before turning to me.

"Their names?"

"Casey and Valarian," I tell him, scanning the wine gardens for any trace of them. How could I lose them, and why would they leave?

"And whose kids are they?"

"My grandkids! Just fucking find them!" I snap, darting off and yanking my phone from my pocket. My hands shake as I punch in the numbers. I have to dial my son's number again, missing a couple of numbers the first time in my haste as I run through the lobby, looking for any sign of them. I manage to dial the correct numbers a few seconds later, still walking as fast as I can and scanning the place while I wait for my son to answer.

"What's up?"

My stomach sinks at the thought of what I'm about to tell him. I feel sick, like I am about to throw up. He and Everly will never trust me again. My heart thuds painfully against my ribs, so hard I am certain I am at serious risk of a heart attack. Do these kids not realize I am old? I can't get a fright like this.

"I lost them. I lost the kids."

"What do you mean, you lost them?" Valen snaps, his voice slightly hysterical.

"They were right there, then I went to get them a milkshake, and when I turned around again, they were gone," I panic, racing through the restaurants and bars, looking for them.

"They couldn't have gone far; I'm on my way," Valen replies.

"Okay. I will call Everly," I tell him, dreading that call.

"No, let's see if we can find them first. They couldn't have left the hotel," Valen says, hanging up.

I have every member of available staff looking for them, the entirety of our security personnel searching, and even a few police have shown up to help me search the damn place when a call comes over the radio.

"Found them. They were in the kitchens, hiding," a chef calls over the radio. The immense relief I feel as I make my way to their location cannot be explained. Pulling my phone out, I call my son back to let him know, and he tells me he is nearly here—no doubt to scold the kids for hiding on me. Walking into the kitchens, I find both kids sitting on milk crates, the chef standing over them with his arms folded, not looking impressed.

"I caught them tampering with the mayor's wife's food," the chef tells me, and I put my hand on my hips.

"Well, haven't you two been up to mischief," I ask them.

"She was mean to my mom," Valarian huffs, and I tilt my head.

"Who was?"

"That lady with the curly hair and pig's nose," Valarian says before getting up and walking to the double doors. He points out a table and my brows raise. Alpha Nixon's wife—a nasty woman.

"What did she do?" I ask him.

"Said we weren't welcome in here, called us riffraff," Valarian says, and I growl.

"You should not have run off like that. You should have told me. Your father is distraught and on his way here," I tell him, and he drops his head. The chef watches as I turn to look at him.

"You didn't serve her the spoiled food?"

"No, caught them just in time, sir."

I nod. "Very well, I will take it to her and make these two apologize," I tell him. He nods, handing me a tray that has escargot and a bowl of soup on it. I give the children a scolding look before noticing a snail in Casey's hand and chuckle. "Were you going to put live ones in her food?" I laugh, shaking my head.

"She's the one who wants to eat slugs," Valarian pouts before glaring out the doors at the woman. I glance around and notice the chef is busy cooking at the back, and no one else is paying attention.

"I saw nothing," I whisper to the kids, placing the tray down and turning my back on it.

"Huh?"

"I saw nothing," I repeat to Valarian, nodding toward the snails in Casey's hands. She pulls more from her pocket. How many did this kid stow away? Valarian giggles and a waitress notices. I nod silently to her. She glances at the table number on the tray, looks out the door, then presses her lips in a line as she snickers.

"I saw nothing either," she says, sending me a wink.

Grabbing the tray, I see the snails have been replaced, and one is even swimming around in her soup.

"Allow me," the server says, and I glance at her name tag. "Thank you, Stacey," I tell her, handing it to her. She nods, smiling at the two mischief-makers behind me who are giggling, before taking the tray out and setting it in front of Alpha Nixon's wife.

She nods and thanks Stacey, while we watch from the kitchens when Valen busts through the doors. Relief is clear on his face, and the kids duck behind me, peering up at him from under my arms.

Valen lets out a breath. "You two have some explaining to do," he scolds before being cut off by the shrill screams coming from the restaurants. I try not to laugh as I watch the woman spit her food out and jump back from the table. Valen turns, looking out at the commotion, while the woman is shrieking and waving waiters over.

The kids are laughing behind me, and I erupt and join them; my son looks at me before folding his arms across his chest.

"What did you do to the mayor's wife?"

"I saw nothing," I tell him, and he looks at the children.

"Papa said we could," Valarian snitches, and I look away. Well, I thought it was quite funny.

"I stand by what I said; I saw nothing."

Valen sighs.

"I hope she chokes," Casey says, pursing her lips and squinting her little eyes at the woman.

"And why is that?" Valen asks her.

"She was mean to Mom," Valarian pouts with teary eyes.

"Seems the woman doesn't like rogues in your hotel, son," I tell him.

"Well, we can't have that, can we?" Valen says, holding his hand out to my grandson. "Let's introduce you both, then, shall we?"

If only I had the balls all those years ago to have Valarie on my arm and by my side, I think guiltily. I won't allow my son to make my mistakes.

"But Dad, she's the mayor's wife!" the child protests.

"And this city is owned by me and Pop. We elected her husband as mayor, and I can easily remove his status," Valen tells him.

"Good, then I want to be the mayor," Valarian says, and I chuckle.

"Aim higher, my boy. No name holds more power than Solace in this City," I tell him, and he looks up at me with a sparkle in his eyes. Oh, he will be a terrific Alpha one day.

CHAPTER
SIXTY-FIVE

Everly

Somehow, we managed to lose one of the cheese platters for one of the tables and the three snack platters! I'd called Valen, who said he would sort it out and bring some from his restaurant. Now that that mini heart attack is sorted, I slide my handbag over my shoulder and finally walk to my office. I just finished stuffing the letters and keys in the safe before my office door opens and Kalen walks in.

He flops into a chair, apparently exhausted, although dressed to impress in his suit. He looks every part the Alpha he should, while I look like a staff member. Not that I own pretty, formal dresses or would even wear them. I prefer organizing the events, not being a part of them.

"Where's Valarian?" I ask him.

"Just dropped him and Casey with Zoe. Valen is taking the platters you needed to the kitchen," he says, looking rather frazzled.

"Is everything okay?" I ask, wondering why he's hunted me down, though people *have* arrived early. However, the function

384

doesn't officially start for another hour. Grabbing the box with the name labels in them for the tables, I tuck it under my arm.

"Oh, we're moving again," Kalen chuckles, reaching for the box under my arm. He takes it from me, following me out of my office.

"Is there a reason you came searching for me?" I ask him. Kalen clears his throat, and I can tell he's nervous about something. After he tells me the long, harrowing story about losing the kids and about the snails, I chuckle.

"You're not upset?" Kalen asks, and I shake my head.

"Nope. I lost Valarian for an hour when he was two. He wandered out of the apartment. I found him in the daycare, the scariest hour of my life. I was frantic. These things happen," I tell him, walking back toward the restaurant just as I spot my father at the end of the corridor. He's wearing a tailored, gray suit, talking to someone with his back to us.

"I also need to speak to you about Valen," Kalen says before stopping and looking at me when he realizes I stopped. He follows my gaze to where my father is talking to someone, then looks at me before glancing at the door beside me. A second later, I find myself stuffed into a storage room where we keep linens.

"Kalen?" I hear my father call out, but luckily, I'm already obscured inside the darkroom. Kalen looks at me and stuffs the box in my arms, shutting the door, but not completely.

"Alpha John, lovely to see you again," Kalen says. I hear my father growl at him.

"What the fuck is this shit I heard from Alpha Nixon's wife saying your son was marrying another?" my father snarls angrily.

"Our deal still stands, Alpha John."

"Not if your son doesn't marry my fucking daughter. We had a deal," my father snarls, and I cover my mouth with my hand, trying to muffle any noises, Unfortunately, I somehow manage to bump a shelf and knock something off it. I quickly dart behind the door.

"What was that?" my father asks, and the door is suddenly shoved open.

"I must have bumped something; I was looking for a bathroom and wandered into a linen closet," Kalen says, his back coming into view as he opens the door, blocking me from my father as he peers in.

"Fucking reeks of rogue in here! Why, of all places, your son would hold it here is beyond me. Did you know this place is apparently owned by a rogue whore? Alpha Nixon's wife told me," my father says. The door shuts again, but once again, Kalen leaves it slightly ajar, and I look between the gap.

"Fucking ironic that the place he holds this meeting is at his own mother's hotel. Though how it ended up out of your hands, I don't know. Must have pissed your dear old mate off for her to give it to some random whore."

Kalen growls at him. "Mind your tone, John. Valarie may be dead, but I won't listen to you talk shit about her."

My father scoffs. "Coming from a man who tossed her aside, I will say what I like," my father breathes.

"Your son better announce my daughter as his future mate, Kalen, or I will tell Valen about Valarie. We had a fucking deal."

"I assure you, my son will take your daughter as his mate," Kalen reassures him, and my father growls.

"He fucking better, Kalen, or your little secret is out," my father says, stalking off down the hall. I hear Kalen sigh and wait a few minutes before I hear his voice.

"Coast is clear, Everly. You don't need to hide," Kalen says, and I pull open the door. He turns to me with a grim smile on his face.

"That's what my father has over you? Why, you were so quick to accept me?" I ask him.

"That is not the only reason, Everly. I made mistakes, ones I refuse to allow my son to repeat. As much as I loved Valarie, I was too worried about my reputation. When I lost her, I realized what I had done. I punished not only her, but I also punished myself," Kalen admits.

"So if Valen doesn't marry Ava, my father will tell him about Valarie?"

Kalen shakes his head. "The deal was Valen has to marry his daughter. He never stated which one."

I cluck my tongue. I can't believe this is happening right now. Nevertheless, I don't understand why Kalen is talking to my father after years of rivalry.

"Why does he want my sister to marry Valen? It makes no sense."

"Honestly, dear, I have no idea; I have tried to figure it out myself. When he confronted me about Valarie, I panicked and agreed. Valarie, I already lost. I couldn't bear the thought of losing my son too," Kalen says. I nod; just the thought of Valarie brings tears to my eyes.

"Anything else to this deal you made?" I ask, wanting to know what I'm up against.

"Yes, Valen has to mark and mate her within the week of the Alpha meeting," Kalen tells me, and I curse under my breath.

"Wait, when you say mate, do you mean to force the heat?" I ask him, and Kalen nods, looking away guiltily.

"He wants to make sure his daughter is with child. He was planning on injecting Ava with the hormones to ensure she got pregnant."

"I do not plan on having another baby anytime soon, so no forced heat. I will let him mark me, though."

"Thank you, Everly."

I shake my head and hold my finger up, telling him to wait.

"I can't carry this secret, Kalen. I can't. You must know how heavy it is yourself. I look at him, and all I see is her," I say. My lip quivers as I think of Valarie, who she was to me, who she could have been to Valen.

"I will let him mark me, but you will tell your son. I have a week to let him mark me, you have a week to tell him; I will not go into this with lies that can unravel us. You want me to be with your son? Then tell him—don't make me have to," I tell him before walking off.

CHAPTER
SIXTY-SIX

E verly

Making my way to the restaurant, I hand the name cards to one of the waitresses, who quickly races around placing them out following the seating arrangements. Valen emerges from the kitchen with a garment bag slung over his shoulder and smiles when he sees me. He's dressed in a black suit, looking hand-some like always. Valarian is also dressed in a suit and is playing with Casey and some other children that have arrived early. Valen comes up behind me and nestles his face into my neck, which earns curious stares when his hand goes to my hip to tug me back against him.

"You're not wearing that," he growls, looking down at my uniform.

"And I am not wearing *that*, if it's a dress," I tell him as he drapes the bag over my arm.

"Ah. Well, good thing it's not. I know you don't wear dresses because I have yet to see you in one. Although you *will* have to wear a dress eventually."

"And why is that, Alpha Valen?" I ask.

388

"Because usually only the groom wears a suit to a wedding, so for one day, you will have to suck it up and wear a dress."

"I like how you assume I will marry you. What if I want to keep my name?"

"We can hyphenate it," he chuckles, kissing my jaw while I pull a face at the thought.

"Fine, Solace it is," I laugh.

"Good choice because I wasn't changing mine to Valen Summers," he says, and I swat his arm with my hand.

"Go get changed," he says, giving me a nudge toward the rear doors that lead to the back, where my apartment is. I sigh, taking the garment bag and heading for my apartment. I quickly change into the white pantsuit he brought before running the brush through my hair and tying it up. Looking in the mirror, I purse my lips. Something is missing. Walking into Zoe's room, I rummage through her make-up bag and borrow some of her cosmetics.

I do a rush job of my make-up, knowing people will already be arriving, and I still have to place a few things out on the tables and check the seating arrangements again. The last thing we need is for rival Alphas and outside Alphas being seated together. Looking in the mirror one last time, I can't help but feel like an imposter.

I suck in a sharp breath and take a moment to pause, trying to find the courage to go out there and face not only my father, but all those Alphas who are here for the announcement.

After today, everything will change. I will no longer be Everly, the rogue, but Luna Everly, and that thought scares me as much as it excites me. How I had changed over the years. Going from scared teenager to terrified but determined mother, having nothing to becoming a hotel owner, and now, changing once more, to Luna. Our village is growing larger, and that responsibility hangs heavily over me. Valarie's voice comes to mind; her saying whenever the health and safety people would mock our attempts to get this place running.

Micah is the worst. Zoe blackmailed him into helping fix the wiring in the place. He walks around and checks the place out, then bursts out laughing in our faces. He finds it hilarious.

"I'm not wasting my time; you'll never get this place up and running," *he mocks with a shake of his head. Valarie refuses to hear it. She steps* *forward, and I see the fear in his eyes—hers hold none. The woman is* *fearless.*

Micah takes a frightened step back at the look she gives him. He dares *not challenge her. There's something with the way she carries herself; she* *doesn't fear pack wolves. No, Valarie is her own pack, and she let us be a* *part of it; she protects us, and this is home. True Alphas preserve their* *home and those that live in it; she's our Alpha. Micah visibly gulps when* *she gets up close and sneers as she looks him up and down. Micah chal-* *lenged her, and she loves a challenge. She says only two words as she* *snatches the tool from his hand. Two words that will always stick with me.*

"Watch me."

Without another word, she turns on her heel and walks to the power *box, shuts off the power off, and undoes the screws holding the cover over* *the exposed wires.*

I shake my head at the memory and smile to myself. It kind of became our mantra—fueled by everyone trying to knock us back. The day before we got the official notice and were told we could open our doors, we sat in the restaurant admiring our handy work. The place looked fantastic.

We were sipping our beers, covered in paint and Goddess knows what else. Valarie was leaning against the counter, watching us. She always watched us. She always let us know how proud she was of what we had accomplished.

"We actually did it," she says, and we nod. All of us are exhausted, yet *our spirits are high.*

"You'll never do it. That's what I'll tell you girls from now on," she *laughs.*

"Watch us," we say collectively with a laugh.

"That's my girls. And they will *watch, and you will show them what* *us rogues are made of,"* she says proudly. It has become our mantra.

I've fallen behind in my night classes, trying to juggle kids, work, and school, and I just feel so defeated. Valarie wanders over to me, cigarette between her lips, where I sit, sulking, looking at my failed test. My bag's between my feet; I foolishly opened the letter right before I was supposed to leave for class. I sigh and rest my head against the brick wall, feeling like I've let her down.

"What are you looking at?" she asks.

"My stupid test; I failed," I grumble.

"Let me look," she says, snatching the paper from my hands. She peers at it and sighs.

"Might as well throw in the towel; you'll never do it." She clicks her tongue, and I squint my eyes at her. One corner of her lips tugs upward very slightly. "Should probably quit this place too; barely made a dent; place looks like crap," she says, motioning around to all the work we slaved our asses off doing all day.

She drags back on her smoke and raises an eyebrow at me. I purse my lips, and she smiles. She crumples up the paper and tosses it into the bin, and I snatch my bag up off the ground.

"Watch me," I say, using those words I heard her say many times over. The challenge is on. She smirks.

"Oh, I am," she laughs. Two little words, but they always put a fire in my belly.

So, with that, I head to the restaurant. Valarie handed this place to Valarian and me; this is my home, and now I'm not only fighting to keep it running, but I'm also fighting for the rogues—our village built from nothing—so there is nothing my father can say or do that can touch me.

We beat the odds; we built an empire. And I won't let one Alpha intimidate me. If Valarie taught me anything, it was to know my worth, and the only one who gets to determine that worth is me, not my father, not my mate, not those who try to suppress me. I no longer have to prove anything to anyone because I proved it to myself, and there is no feeling more empowering than knowing your own worth.

Reaching the rear doors to the hotel proper, I'm instantly bombarded by a flurry of organized chaos as those brought in to help cater scramble with last-minute alterations and tasks. Making my way to the doors to the restaurant, I walk in halfway through the opening speeches, clipboard in hand. I look over the guest lists before walking to the back to check if the chefs need help in the kitchen. The place is already packed, and Kalen is addressing those that attended. I've been to plenty of these growing up, and I know Valen plans to make the announcement at the end of the night.

A few hours in, everyone is mingling peacefully, the Alphas wandering amongst each other to form small groups and chat. Looking over at Valen's table, he nods to the chair beside him, but I shake my head. I still haven't seen my father, and I'm waiting for it. Kalen, I know, wants to keep things civil as long as possible, so I keep my distance, biding my time.

But when a commotion happens toward the back of the room, I recognize my father's voice instantly.

"You fucking idiot! You spilled it all over me!" he yells, standing up. I tilt my head to the side to see Valen stand and look in his direction, along with a bunch of other Alphas. My server fumbles, trying to clean up the mess. Zoe is already quickly approaching, trying to help, with Marcus lingering in the background. Difficult patrons are something we deal with regularly. This is nothing and an easy fix for her.

"Do you have any idea how expensive this suit is?" my father growls at one of our waitresses, Sarah, who looks terrified. Zoe places her hand on Sarah's shoulder.

"May I know what the issue is, Alpha?" she says, a polite determination in her voice.

"Yes, this idiot spilled wine on my shirt!" he grunts, red-faced and flustered.

"Accidents happen, Alpha. I am sure we can organize dry-cleaning or possibly a fresh shirt," Zoe answers quickly while tidying up the table. My father sneers, and Zoe nods for Sarah to go—she rushes off, coming toward me.

"You ok?" I ask her, touching her arm as she escapes the scene, looking rather shaken.

"Fucking prick, he bumped my arm as I was pouring," she says. I nod to the kitchen, and she sighs with relief while I lean against the frame. I chuckle when I see Macey a few tables away, watching Zoe. She looks to be on standby, ready to crack the Alpha with a bottle if need be. She knows who he is, so does Zoe, and not once does she stutter. She's speaking professionally and is doing her job while my father rants about lowly rogues. We've heard it all, and it no longer fazes us. There isn't a name he could come up with that we haven't heard at least once or twice before.

"As I said, sir. We can have it dry-cleaned or replaced for you," Zoe repeats sweetly.

"I want her fired; I want to speak to the manager," he demands.

"You are speaking with one, Alpha," Zoe tells him before waving Macey over.

I'll give my father one thing: he knows how to cause a scene, as everyone is watching with eager eyes. Marcus looks like he's about to drag Zoe away from the threat. Oblivious, at the back, the kids are playing and stuffing their tiny faces with snacks.

"This is Macey, another manager here," Zoe says, introducing them. Macey starts with polite words, ever the professional. Well, that is, until he starts ranting at her and making a fool of himself. I notice Ava shrink in her seat, clearly embarrassed by our father's behavior. Those at the other tables whisper amongst themselves. The woman from Valen's hotel is also seated at my father's table, agreeing and nodding to everything he says.

"Sir, if you don't calm down, I am going to have to escort you from the premises," Macey tells him. And she would, if needed—she has a bat behind the counter, and she isn't afraid to use it. She's already done it many times. Though this is slightly different from the everyday usuals, we deal with—this is a room full of Alphas—that won't stop her.

"Escort me? Who the hell do you think you are? I want to speak to the owner," my father demands. Zoe looks over at me, and I nod to her. She turns back to my father.

"She's on her way, Alpha," I hear Zoe say as I swallow and make my way through the tables. Valen looks like he's about to come with me, but I motion with my hand to stay where he is. I don't need him behind me. I can fight my own battles, and this is *my* hotel, *my* workers, and he's *my* father.

My father sits down while he waits, arms folded across his chest. Macey and Zoe step away, and I take their place.

"Is there a problem, Alpha?" I ask. My father looks me up and down before his eyes dart to those seated at his table, mouth opening and closing like a fish. My mother just stares unblinkingly at me, while my father stumbles for words. Ava, however, snickers before covering her mouth, trying to stifle her laughter.

"Uh, yes. I want to speak to the owner," my father finally says with a wave to dismiss me, clearly over his shock at seeing me. Even while I'm standing here in a room full of Alphas, he'll still try to deny knowing me. That's fine. They're about to find out.

"You're looking at her," I tell him, motioning to myself. If seeing me hadn't shocked him, then finding out I'm the owner definitely does.

"But you're a rogue whore," he sneers.

"No, I am rogue. That word will not be tolerated in my hotel, Alpha. Or should I say, father?" I ask, smiling down at him.

CHAPTER
SIXTY-SEVEN

Everly

The collective gasp that escapes the table is audible throughout the room, and I can see everyone looking in our direction while my father sputters for words. However, Ava simply howls with laughter. So much so that the mayor's wife looks at her as though she's lost it. It's difficult to keep my composure because my sister has the funniest laugh. Ava has one of those laughs that make you laugh because the sound is ridiculous. My mother elbows her and shuts her up effectively with a glare, while my father growls at me. His canines slip from between his parted lips as he glares up at me.

The mayor's wife looks at my father questioningly. "You have another daughter?" she asks, clearly shocked by this news.

Alpha Nixon, who is about my father's age, with thick blonde hair combed to one side, looks outraged as he stares at us all. My father tries to explain before turning his anger on me and his hands slap the table, but I just stare unflinchingly. This is *my* home, and if he wants to deny my existence, fine, but he won't be doing it under my roof. My mother grips his forearm and glares at Alpha Nixon's wife like she's about to take her on. But a growl from my father puts her head down as he glares daggers at me.

"You are not my daughter; you haven't been since the day you became a rogue whor–" His words stop at the same moment I feel tingles rush across my neck as a warm hand caresses the side of it, then moves to my shoulder. Valen's scent wafts to me before I feel his lips graze my jawline, and he buries his face in the curve of my shoulder. My father's anger dissolves, replaced with clear and utter shock. Valen tugs me to his side when his hand moves down my arm to my waist, pulling me closer to him. The room turns silent, so silent you could hear a pin drop.

"I don't think I have introduced my mate," Valen says calmly, though his aura is deadly, and Alpha Nixon's wife drops her head, her cheeks heating. I notice how uncomfortable all the Alphas in the room become, the tension high as Valen—the most prominent figure in the city and strongest, most feared Alpha—addresses my father.

My father huffs and shakes his head before he blows up. Alpha Nixon glares at my father, and my father looks at Ava, who shrinks back in her seat, although the smile never leaves her lips; this is prime entertainment for her.

"I know exactly who this rogue whore is, and she is not your mate," he adds, shooting me a glare.

"See, that is where you are wrong, Alpha John. Everly is no rogue whore. She is my mate and Luna of the Nightshade Pack," Valen says.

"You are mistaken; this girl is a rogue whore. I don't know what she's told you, Alpha Valen, but she has a son. She's tricked you," my father dares to say. Murmurs break out throughout the room.

"You mean Valarian?" Alpha Valen asks before turning to look at the back of the room where all the children are playing. I glance over to see Valarian watching us, and Valen waves him over. Valarian smiles and rushes to his father. Valen bends down and picks him up with one arm.

"Who is that, Daddy?" Valarian whispers, looking at my parents curiously.

"That is your grandfather, grandmother, and your Auntie Ava," Valen whispers to him and kisses his cheek. The whispers in the background grow louder as everyone watches the Blood Alpha, the most notorious Alpha in the city, doting on his son. My father sputters, lost for words, and Valen grips my waist tighter as he turns to look at my father.

"I'd like to introduce you to my son, Valarian Solace. The resemblance is uncanny, don't you think?" Valen smirks, daring my father to deny what he's saying.

Valarian could not be mistaken for anyone else's son; Valen's bloodline are the only ones in the city with a genetic mutation that causes them all to have amber eyes. No other wolf I've come across has that trait, and more than that, they have the same scent, and Valarian's aura can already be felt, showing he's born from not one Alpha, but two Alpha wolves. Anyone looking close enough could tell they are father and son. If anyone has their doubts, no one speaks up. They know better than to piss off my mate.

"The eyes," Alpha Nixon murmurs, looking at Valarian and Valen, then tosses his napkin on the table before turning his questioning to my father. I see a few other Alphas stand and look over at my son and Valen, also recognizing the obvious traits most look past when seeing my son.

Cameras start flashing around us everywhere, and I know this will be splashed all over the morning paper and in news headlines tomorrow.

"Did you know?" Alpha Nixon asks, looking at my parents. My mother has her head down, not liking the change in direction and the accusation behind Alpha Nixon's words.

"How could he? Alpha John had her existence wiped from every database in the city the moment she refused to abort my grandson," comes Kalen's voice as he moves up behind us.

"We had a deal," my father growls.

"And the deal still stands; you said Valen is to marry your

daughter or are you going to continue to deny that Everly, here, is?" Kalen asks, and my father growls before glaring at me.

My father stands, and the veins in his neck bulge and throb with growing anger as he clearly fights the urge to shift. His claws scratch down the table and slice through the thin cloth. His entire body is trembling with rage, and Valen passes Valarian to me before shoving me behind him.

"If you have an issue, John, about who my mate is, I suggest we take it outside," Valen warns him, his tone deadly calm, yet the warning clear. My father knows he is no match for Valen; maybe in his younger years, but not now.

One thing about auras is they're a warning for whomever you're messing with, and Valen's aura outweighs everyone here, proving he's the real king of this city. No one in this room is daring enough to go up against him. He didn't get the title of Blood Alpha by not shedding blood and destroying those who challenge him. My father sneers before looking at my mother, who has remained silent.

"We are leaving," he growls at her. He suddenly stands, grabbing her arm and yanking her up to stand by his side as he does. Everyone at the surrounding tables jumps away. "Ava, now!" my father booms.

She smirks as she stands before speaking loud enough that the entire room hears the words that leave her lips.

"I'll catch you later, sis," she chuckles, pecking my cheek as she moves past me before cupping Valarian's cheek with her hand.

"Gosh, how you've grown, young man. And damn, do you look like your father," she laughs, winking at me. My father growls and snarls, baring his teeth at her, and she smiles before strolling after my father. No doubt she'll pay for that when she gets home, but I can see the defiance and determination to call my father out publicly.

"Well, that was an interesting change of events," I hear an Alpha say from another table. I glance over at the man, and he undoes his tie, tossing it on the table.

"Indeed it is," Alpha Nixon, the city mayor, says as he purses his lips. I turn and stare after my father as he shoves through the exit doors, the media outside snapping photos, and we all hear his furious growl ring out through the night, making them jump away and scatter in fright.

"Back to the celebrations, everybody. I need a drink," Kalen says, breaking the strange tension that has returned.

I pass Valarian back to Valen, and my mate looks at me.

"What's wrong?" he asks, and I shake my head.

"I'll be back," I tell him, darting off and out the doors after my family that just left. The camera lights hurt my eyes as I try to look for the car. Spotting it, I rush over to them before my mother can get in.

"Mom?" I call, and she looks at me before looking back at the car. Seeming to make her decision, she moves toward me. My father gets out of the car again, yelling at her to get back in, but I clutch her hands. His fury is loud enough to keep the media away; no one dares come close enough to hear us.

My mother hugs me as my father growls and screams at her. "I have to go," she whispers with tears in her eyes. She glances at my furious father, who's about to stalk over to her, no doubt to drag her back to the car.

"I'll call you. Now I know where you are, he can't keep me away. I have to go before your father comes over."

"Wait, just let me–" I beg.

She shakes her head and squeezes my fingers. "I have to go. I need to calm your father down. You have no idea what you've just done," she says, confusing me before rushing off and past my father, who was stalking toward her. He stops, looking me up and down and sneering, about to say something before looking over my shoulder. I turn to see what he's looking at, only to see Valen coming up behind me. My father growls before turning on his heel and returning to his car.

Valen wraps his arms around my waist, pulling me against him and away from the car as my father reverses out of his parking spot, then tears out of the place, speeding off down the road. I sigh; what a long night. Valen kisses my cheek before pressing his nose into my neck.

"Are you okay?" he whispers, and I nod, wondering what my mother meant by her words.

"I will be," I tell him before letting him lead me back to the restaurant.

CHAPTER
SIXTY-EIGHT

Everly

Toward the end of the night, everyone had calmed down, and the cleanup began. Despite the exhaustion and aching feet from standing on them all night, after the incident with my father, the night actually turned out well. In addition to introducing me to many people who were actually nice, Valen made an official announcement to the media at the end of the meeting. Now that everything is about to come to an end for the night, I'm eager to crawl into bed. I notice Kalen lingering a little longer when Valen comes over with Valarian asleep in his arms.

"I have people on the way to help with cleaning up; they'll be here soon. Come home; we need to get him to bed," Valen says, leaning down to peck my lips when I look up at him and smooth down Valarian's hair just as Kalen walks over to us.

"Actually, can I speak with you for a minute?" Kalen asks, and my eyes go wide. He isn't seriously going to tell him now, is he?

"Uh, sure." Valen motions toward a nearby table, but Kalen shakes his head and reaches for Valarian. Valen watches him, staring oddly at his father, while my heart beats frantically in my chest. Kalen hands Valarian to me, and I grab him. Valen's brows wrinkle, and I can feel his confusion through the bond.

"We can stay here for the night," I tell Valen, and he nods.

"Fine, I'll be up in a minute; just let me go lock my car back up," he tells his father before walking off.

"I didn't mean right now," I hiss at Kalen when Valen is far enough away.

"I need to get it over with; it's time, Everly. Besides, if I don't do it now, I worry I won't be able to bring myself to do it," he sighs.

I chew my lip, slightly worried about what will happen. Looking toward the car park where Valen went to lock his car, I sigh before nodding.

"I'll get Zoe to watch him for me and I will be back in a minute," I tell him, before quickly escaping back to the apartment. Zoe is setting Casey down to bed when I walk in. Marcus is there, resting on the couch with his head back.

"Fun night," Marcus chuckles while shaking his head.

"It's about to get worse too," I say, and he sits up, but I shake my head instead, quickly taking Valarian to bed and stripping his shoes and jacket off before tucking him in. He'll pitch a fit in the morning about sleeping in his clothes, but right now, I have bigger issues to deal with, like the explosion I'm expecting when the news of Valarie comes out.

"Zoe, can you watch him for me for a few minutes?" I ask her while walking back out to the living room. She's in the process of removing her shoes and looks over at me.

"Of course; is everything alright?" she asks and no sooner than she says it, Marcus jerks upright as we hear a thunderous growl that's clearly an Alpha's roar of rage. My heart skips a beat as I run for the door. Marcus, though, is faster, beating me down the steps as he takes off.

The door flings against the wall with a bang and I cringe at the sound, hoping it didn't wake the kids as I race across the gardens to the restaurant.

Horrified staff stare out the window at the parking lot, and Marcus shoves through them and out the doors. I gasp when I see Valen pummeling his father. Kalen is on the ground while Valen rains blow after blow into his face. Blood sprays everywhere, and I push past my stunned workers and through the glass doors just as Marcus grabs him, yanking him away from his face. Only for Valen to slam his hands into Marcus's chest, launching him backward into the side of a car. His body creates an outline in the metal, and Marcus shakes himself out, looking dazed.

"Valen, stop!" I call out while racing over to him. He snarls and punches his father again. I grab his arm desperately. Kalen isn't even trying to fight back and has his arms up, letting his son pummel him bloody. Valen roars when I grab his arm and yank it back, making me fall backward. My ass smacks the ground, and I grunt at the impact. The hard ground causes my tailbone to ache.

"VALEN, STOP!" I scream, getting to my feet and grabbing him again. My grip on both his arms, however, is ineffective. Having never seen him so angry before, I'm afraid he'll kill his father. Despite my minimal weight compared to his muscled frame, I shove at him; I'm pretty sure that I injured myself in the process. I topple on top of him, and he sits up, but I scramble back and move in front of Kalen as Valen launches himself at him.

Anticipating the impact, I close my eyes, but the crash never comes—instead, a ferocious growl screams from him and my eyes open. The gasp that leaves me stutters as I find myself suddenly nose to nose with his wolf form towering over me, his paw in the air with claws extended, looking for a kill. They abruptly retract as he places the paw on my shoulder. I can feel Kalen shaking behind me as Valen snarls, snapping his teeth at his father's legs. I grab his furry head and pull on his ears to draw his attention away from his father.

"Stop," I say in a barely audible whisper. Valen's eyes still sparkle with tears, and he strikes my hands down with a massive paw. Kalen sits up, blood streaming down his face. Valen paces in his wolf form, trying to find a way past me to reach his father. However, I know he won't attack me to get to him.

CHAPTER
SIXTY-NINE

Everly

"I'm sorry, son," Kalen chokes out, groaning. Turning my head, I look at him. Kalen's face is so swollen he's barely recognizable. He coughs before placing his fingers in his mouth and removing a tooth. Valen's answer is a growl as I rush to help Kalen stand. The sound of cracking bones reaches my ears as I hear Valen shift back behind me. Keeping a grip on Kalen, who is unsteady on his feet, we move toward his car. I fish his keys out of his pocket and unlocked his car for him.

"I'm alright, dear. Go check on my son," he hisses, falling heavily in his seat. With a nod, I turn to find Valen has walked back to his car.

"Valen?" I call, and he turns to look at me as I walk over to him. The look he gives me makes me stop.

"You knew. You knew and said nothing," he says. I bite the inside of my lip and nod. Hurt shines in his eyes as Valen looks at the hotel.

"She gave you this place, didn't she?" he asks.

My lips quiver as he turns his gaze back to me.

"She recognized your son," I tell him, and he sucks in a deep breath.

"You should have told me," he says, and I can feel his heartbreaking, the sadness for a loss he didn't actually lose all those years, the sinking feeling that I betrayed him.

"Valen, wait. Just let me–"

He gets in his car and slams it in reverse, smacking into the brick flower bed in front of the main office before tearing out of the parking lot. The engine of his car roars as he floors it down the street.

"I take it that's what you meant when you said it would get a lot worse?" Marcus says as I rub my arms against the cool breeze. He stops beside me with a groan while rubbing his lower back, and Kalen pulls out of his own parking space before lowering his window.

"He'll forgive you. It's me he's furious at," Kalen says with a sigh. I nod as I watch him leave, feeling like a piece of me is leaving too.

Three days later

The only time I've heard from Valen is via text message. Three days have passed, and he's still angry at me; I know he spent most of those days drunk. I can feel a growing unease sitting in my stomach through the bond. Standing in front of the school, Valarian and I wait for him to come to get him, yet the feeling through the bond tells me he's passed out, sleeping. In no way am I letting my son go with him if he's drunk. I hope it's just my guilt for not telling him sooner.

"What time is it?" Valarian asks me, looking both ways down the street for his father's car. Retrieving my phone from my pocket, I glance at the time and sigh. He's almost an hour late.

"He'll come. He promised on the phone," Valarian says while nodding his head and walking back to the bench seat in front of the school. I wander over to him and sit next to him.

"Maybe he's in traffic?" Valarian says, fidgeting with his fingers.

"How about we call him when we get home? Perhaps he's busy," I offer.

"But he promised he would be here," Valarian says while looking at me teary-eyed. He's been asking for his father since the morning after the Alpha meeting—asking where he was and when he could see his father, and I kept making up excuses.

"Did you have a fight?" he asks, and I turn to look at him. "You did. You upset him and made him leave us, didn't you?" he says, looking angry.

"No, he's upset about his mother," I tell him.

"But Grandma died years ago."

"And people stay sad for a long time," I try to explain.

"Well, you can take me to him," Valarian says, hopping up and walking toward the car. I try to call Valen on the short walk back to my truck, but he doesn't pick up.

"I don't think he's home. We can try to call him when we get back home."

"No! He promised me. I want to see him. I want my dad!" Valarian screams at me. Startled at his outburst, I stare at him before pulling myself together and kneeling beside him, wiping the tears that streak down his cheeks.

"Valarian, I don't think you should see him right now. Your father needs time," I tell him, but he shakes his head.

"What if he needs me? Please, Mom! Please," Valarian begs, and I drop my head and pinch the bridge of my nose. I sigh before looking back at his big, amber eyes filled with tears.

"Fine, but we just knock, and if he doesn't answer, we go home," I tell him. He nods, bouncing on his heels in excitement, then races toward my car, climbing in the back and buckling himself in. Jumping into the driver's seat, we head to Valen's hotel.

The regret I feel upon stepping out of that elevator is instant. No guards stand in the corridor, and the smell of liquor has Valarian pinching his nose. Grabbing his arm, I try to steer him back into the elevator, but he takes off, racing down the hall. I chase after him when he pushes inside the wide-open door.

"Dad! Dad!" Valarian screams excitedly before he falls silent.

Rushing through the door, I can see Valarian standing in the hall, where it opens up to the living room. He looks over his shoulder at me before looking back into the mess. Glass crunches under his shoes as he walks off searching for his father.

"Valarian, wait," I call, trying to catch up to him, only to stop when I walk in and see it for myself. Broken glass lies everywhere, the couches have been upturned, the china is broken, blood is spattered on the walls, and the place looks like it's been burgled. I follow the sounds coming from Valarian to find him standing in the doorway to the bathroom.

"Dad?" Valarian murmurs, and I grip his shoulder. Valen is passed out on the tiled floor.

"What's wrong with him?" Valarian asks, looking around at the mess. I can tell that now he's found his father, he's on the verge of a meltdown as he takes in all the mess and the state of him.

"How about I call Papa, and you stay with him for the night while I look after daddy, okay?" I ask him as he stands there, trembling and looking terrified. His eyes tear up, and he glances over at his father on the floor.

His entire body is now shaking, and he nods his head before stepping into the bathroom and leaning down to shake his father's shoulder.

"Dad?" I hear him murmur, and his father groans but doesn't wake. Valarian leans down and kisses his cheek. Pulling my phone from my pocket, I call Kalen, who immediately agrees to come get Valarian.

Once he picks up my son, I walk back into the house before slowly beginning to clean the place. I'm furious that he let it get this way, knowing full well what his son is like. The place is absolutely trashed and stinks like a brewery. After sweeping up the glass and mopping the floor, I walk back into the bathroom. Now that the hall is clear of glass, I drag him to his room. It takes me 20 minutes to lift him onto the bed. He groans and mumbles but doesn't wake up, and by the time I'm done, I am absolutely livid.

I drive all the way back to my hotel, fuming, and snatch the letter and the keys from his mother's storage out of the safe before driving back. Valen has no excuse for breaking his son's heart as he did. Fair enough, he was pissed at me, but Valarian didn't deserve to see him like that. I also blame myself for bringing our son here.

An hour later, I've found all the liquor bottles in the place and have started tipping them down the drain when a hungover Valen stumbles out of the room, bumping into the TV unit and clutching his head in his hands. Ignoring him, I continue pouring the bottles down the sink when he rubs his eyes.

"Everly?" he questions, seeming confused before his eyes widen. "What day is it?"

"Monday. You were supposed to pick Valarian up," I say, trying to keep the anger out of my tone. He mutters, then groans and clutches his hair, banging on the side of his head with his fists.

"Why are you here?" he asks, staggering to the kitchen counter before falling onto a stool. He drops his head onto his arms.

"Did you not hear me? You were supposed to pick him up, but instead, we come here and find you passed out on the floor in the bathroom. All because Valarian begged me to bring him to you."

"Wait, Valarian was here?" he asks, whipping his head up from his arms.

"Yes, you promised him. Then he walks into this place looking like a shithole with you drunk."

"He saw me?" Valen asks, and the feeling through the bond is one of sheer guilt and panic. He looks around the room frantically, as if hoping to spot Valarian. "Where is he?" he asks, getting up and rushing to his son's room.

"He's not here. Your father has him," I say, and he freezes, snarling and turning on his heel, then stalking toward me.

"You let that man take him?" he growls angrily.

"Yes, because he asked for you and you were unavailable. I understand you're upset, but don't punish your son for it, Valen," I say, walking over to my handbag. I rummage for the letter Valarie sent to me for him after her death. Her handwriting is on the front. I swallow the lump that forms in my throat, and tears prick my eyes from just thinking of her before I turn around.

CHAPTER
SEVENTY

Everly

"She always watched; you just didn't know. She watched you your entire life. Don't let her down by having to watch you destroy yourself," I tell him before thrusting the letter at him.

He takes it, reading his name on the front. "What's this?"

"From Valarie; it arrived in the mail a couple of weeks after her funeral along with a few others," I say, watching him turn it over between his fingers. After shaking my head, I grab my bag from the counter and head for the door.

"She's dead, Everly. He kept her from me, and now she's dead," he says, and I stop. Tears burn my eyes as I turn to face him.

"She is only dead if you believe she is. That hotel is her legacy—hers. All those women and the rogues? She helped build that. I hated your father for so long for what he did to her; I may never forgive him for that, but if he hadn't, none of that would exist. All those people, she gave them their lives back—that hotel gave them their lives back. She isn't dead, Valen. Everything I am, Zoe is, Macey, your son, is her. Gone, yes, but she is not dead because no one will forget what

411

she's given to us," I say. Valen shakes his head before falling back onto the stool. He clutches his head in his hands once more, and his shoulders shake as he breaks down.

"He lied. All those years, he lied to me," Valen cries, and I chew my lip to stop it from quivering before walking over to him. I run my fingers through his hair and gently take the letter from him. He looks at me, and I place it in my handbag.

"What are you doing?"

"Come with me?" I say. He shakes his head. "I want to show you something," I tell him, pulling on his hand. "But first, you need to get dressed; you stink," I tell him, groaning as I pull him to his feet, and he chuckles. He sniffles and tries to kiss me, but I pull away.

"Did you make out with an ashtray?" I ask, scrunching up my face in disgust.

"That bad?" he asks, and I nod, pushing him toward the bathroom. I turn the shower on as he pulls off his clothes. After retrieving a towel and fresh clothes for him, I sit next to the sink basin to wait.

I message Kalen to check on Valarian, and he says that Valarian is already down for the night, asleep; the poor guy must have had a long day.

When Valen gets out, he changes, finally smelling and looking like the man I love.

"So, where are we going?" he asks as I retrieve my bag and keys.

"You'll see," I tell him, leading him down to my car—his mother's old car.

"This was hers, wasn't it?" he asks, stepping aside and staring at it. Biting the inside of my lip, I nod before chuckling.

"She taught Zoe how to drive in this thing. That's why it has a dent in the back," I chuckle, pointing it out. He looks on the back tailgate at the pole mark where she reversed into a sign.

"I almost crushed it," he whispers in horror.

"But you didn't. Good thing too. All the letters were in the glove compartment," I tell him before climbing in. Valen hops in beside me as I start her up. He stares vacantly out the window for most of the drive.

"What was she like?" he asks as we pull up to my hotel.

"I'll show you," I tell him, climbing out of the car. Valen's brows furrow, but he reluctantly gets out. Grabbing his hand, I walk him around to the storage sheds at the far back of the property closest to the reserve.

Digging through my bag, I retrieve the keys, unlock the padlock, and kick the slide lock.

"It wasn't until after she passed, and I was going through her things, that I realized why your father was so afraid to have her by his side. This. This is who your mother was," I tell him, lifting the roller door. The shutter groans as it rolls and bangs open. Leaning in, I flick on the lights. The fluorescent bulbs blink before buzzing and staying on, lighting up the huge shed. Valen gasps and steps inside, and I follow behind him.

The room is not only filled with all her belongings, but her past. "Your mother came from a wealthy family. This hotel was the first one built in Mountainview City. The city was built around it. Valarie's father refused to join any packs as they formed around the city."

"All this is hers?" he asks, looking around the place in awe. I nod. Valarie had plenty of secrets—most I keep close to me, ones I never knew in my time with her but that she trusted me with after her death.

"After her parents passed, they left her this place. Your father discovered her, and they had you, but because of all this, and the uproar she caused in her younger years, your father worried about it damaging his reputation," I tell him, glancing at all the banners, posters, and huge blown-up pictures of all the rallies she attended that hang from the walls.

"She wasn't a rogue whore like everyone thought. I believe she was like me. It wasn't until she died that I understood what she meant when she said that me and her were the same. She was mislabeled, like me. She allowed everyone to see her that way, but she wasn't. Your mother was an activist—an activist for the rogues—and all this and the hotel were hers; her legacy and what she fought for," I explain, grabbing a picture off the wall.

I hand the blown-up newspaper clipping to him. Valarie is pictured front and center, leading the protest with her banner held high. I pass him another; it's of her standing on the roof of a cop car to rally her troops.

"She stopped when she got pregnant with you. Everyone eventually forgot. Then I met her, and she met her grandson, and she started fighting all over again. Only this time, instead of fighting in the streets, she gave the rogues a home, and she asked me to continue it," I tell him, looking around at the memories that were once hers.

Moving to the back, I grabbed an old scrapbook. It's aged and heavy, filled with every news clipping of her son, and at the back are photos of every event he attended that she snuck into. Grabbing another down, that one reveals even more pictures of him growing up. I hand it to him, and he looks down at them before moving to clear off a box. I stand off to the side and watch him look through it.

"She always watched, Valen. She was there; you just didn't know it."

Valen nods, turning the pages. I hand him back his letter before giving him the key.

"I'll let you look. Just lock up when you're done," I tell him before pressing my lips to his shoulder.

"You kept it all these years?" he asks, and I look over at him. My lips quiver, and I clear my throat. This place always reminds me of her.

"Yes, because she wasn't just your mother, Valen. For a while, she was also mine."

Valen nods, turning back to the scrapbook. I smile sadly before turning and walking back to my apartment, wiping my tears as I went.

CHAPTER
SEVENTY-ONE

E verly

I'm not sure how late it is when Valen comes in, but I feel him slip into bed beside me before snuggling into my back. When I wake up later, though, he's gone; his side of the bed is cold. I wonder what time he got up and left. I do, however, notice Valarie's letter has been opened because it's sitting on the bedside table. Picking it up, I place it back in its envelope before tucking it away in the top drawer where it won't get ruined.

Racing around, I quickly get dressed for work. Marcus took Casey to school for Zoey, and she's also running around getting changed, hopping on one foot as she slips her shoe on because both of us are already late.

Kalen had already taken Valarian to school. He'd sent me a picture of him and Valarian at the school gate, so the only thing I have to do today is pick him up when he finishes.

In the meantime, I have a never-ending list of work at the hotel, having fallen behind recently with all the added drama. There's the cleanup from the event to be finished, as well as taking care of the multiple rooms that need cleaning after the place was packed last

415

night. I already feel exhausted just thinking about it all. With a groan, I drag myself down to the restaurant, knowing that's the first major task: taking inventory to order new stock in. However, Zoe comes rushing in halfway through, scaring the living daylights out of me when she squeals loudly.

"Evie, come quick! You have to see this!" she gushes excitedly, waving me to follow her. I hold up my notepad, but she's practically bouncing on her heels with excitement. Placing my notepad down with a sigh, I follow her into the staff lunchroom. It's packed and full of staff members crowded around the small TV in here when they should be working.

"Wha– Jesus, Zoey, I have things to do," I whine at her when she reaches over and grabs my hand, yanking me to the front as she pushes past everyone. My feet halt when I see the TV screen.

Looking for the remote, I notice Sarah has it and I take it from her, turning the volume up. A reporter is standing out in front of the rogue grade school, and huge buses are lined up along the road. The news reporter is positioned between them, but what's most shocking is Valen standing in the background talking to men in construction uniforms.

My brows furrow, wondering what he's doing at the school when the new anchorwoman starts speaking.

"Recently, I received some news that Alpha Valen has made a significant turn for the better, or so he claims. It is not just that he accepted a rogue as a mate; he has opened all of his borders to the rogues, permitting them to pass through or even move into his territory. Alpha Valen stated that other Alphas should accept change and follow suit by opening their borders.

"As you can see behind me," she gestures behind her. "He has also gone a step further and has accepted all students from this rundown school, welcoming them into the pack schools on his territory. His bizarre behavior is believed to be a result of learning the son of his rogue mate, who he also claims is his own child, attends this school," the woman says. She then prattles on about some other crap he was supposedly up to and how I managed to fool the Alpha with outlandish claims that Valarian is his. Turning, I look at all my staff as Zoe shakes my arm.

"Did you know?" she asks. I shake my head. I had no idea whatsoever; he left this morning without telling me where he was going.

"I know he said he would open up the borders, but..." I stop, trying to wrap my head around the news, it seems too good to be true.

"That's not all; he's turning the old school into a homeless shelter. Marcus called me this morning. Valen also put a statement out this morning for any rogues looking for work, telling them they can apply to all his personally owned businesses, as well as welcoming them to apply for any positions available on his pack land," Zoe exclaims.

"We also had workers out at the commune this morning," Sarah says behind her, making me turn to look at her.

"Construction workers?" I ask.

"Yes, they were ripping the fences down that border his pack and said they were building a road into the place," Sarah says excitedly.

I blink, unsure what to say; turning back to the TV, it's footage of kids lining up to get on the buses to go to their new school.

"About time things changed around here. If only the other packs would adopt this change as well," Sarah murmurs, and I look at Zoe, chewing my lip.

"Maybe we can make them?" I tell her, and her brows furrow.

"I'm no longer a rogue; I'm a Luna of the city now. I can petition the council, and remove the laws."

"Girl, do you have any idea how hard that is? I investigated that shit years ago. You need to have at least five council member signatures on that, and as far as I can tell, you'll only get two: yours and Valen's. The other three packs won't agree, and no way your father will sign after the drama from last night," Sarah tells me, and I sigh.

"Alpha Nixon and his wife definitely won't sign," I murmur to myself. So that only leaves one other Alpha and Luna, so I would still be a signature short, and that's if they even agreed.

"Not to mention, you need them to approve it before you can even bring it before the council members. You can put it forth, but that doesn't mean they'll agree to hear it, let alone call in a meeting over it," Macey says, getting up from her spot on the small sofa.

"We'll find a way. I have to petition for it first anyway, which will take a couple of days."

"No, first you need to let Valen mark you. You aren't Luna until he does," Macey tells me with a smirk on her face.

"Right, that too, I guess," I admit. I can't help but feel nervous, though I know I don't need to be; old anxieties are hard to let go of. Yet, looking back at the TV, there is no one else I would rather be tied to than my mate.

CHAPTER
SEVENTY-TWO

Valen
Three hours earlier

My thoughts are all over the place as soon as I wake up. Everly is still asleep beside me, but I don't want to wake her. Rolling over, I spot the letter from my mother. The storage shed was a real eye-opener for me about the struggles she faced. My father, growing up, had never once said a bad word about her, only that she was Omega and he loved her.

He never mentioned she refused to conform to our way of life; he never told me she was one of the original rogues from whom this land was taken.

I rummage through the storage locker for hours. This entire city belonged to her family. In search of a better future for their daughter, my grandparents sold pieces of it off, selling it to the different packs that now reside here under the pretense that it would create a better future for my mother.

Only, it did the opposite, and they were thrust into the middle of a turf war—the very turf they owned, land that was once theirs, only to be turned into what it is today. Two generations of fighters. My grandparents wanted the city to remain free—free for anyone to live without the sanctions the packs brought forth. Instead, the city turned into a prison, one ruled by the packs that bought the land out with the promising to maintain my grandparents' way of life.

Instead, it stripped them from it. Looking at Everly, it's a similar circumstance. She was stripped bare of everything she thought she would have, only to end up placed within the sanctions of the packs that surrounded us. A future set to repeat because of greed and blindness to what they're forcing those less fortunate to endure.

My own son had been forced to watch his mother fight and claw her way to the top. My mother was remarkable in her fight to bring freedom back, and looking at Everly, I now understand why she fought the bond the way she did. Everly has all the makings of an excellent Luna. However, my father messed up, believing my mother would harm his reputation and break the pack alliances. He was wrong; she would have brought about change, and she would have been unstoppable, like Everly will be with me by her side.

Now, I understand what all the fuss is about—all the trepidation and fight. Everly isn't just fighting for the rogues, for my mother, or for herself; she's fighting for the future, for our son. Picking up my mother's letter, I open it and pull it from the envelope, finally finding the courage to read it.

For my son,

If you are reading this, it means my time has come and gone. I know you must have some questions, pent-up anger towards your father. Just know I forgave him. Over the years, I watched you grow from the shadows, and he did a pretty good job. You turned out alright. Turned into the Alpha you were intended to be.

For years, I longed to hold you, though the only way I could was in my *heart, but know, I did try. I fought for you. Even if it was from the sidelines, I always watched, and I held on to the hope I would meet you in person again one day. Now, obviously, it won't be in this lifetime. Don't feel bad for me, though, don't feel sad. I get to leave you my most incredible gift of all.*

Your Luna and your son. I may not have had the chance to raise you, but I've watched her grow, watched her fight—and she will fight—and watched her become a mother to your son, my grandson. Go easy on her; she has a lot of anger towards not just you but the system in which we all live.

She'll fight when the time comes, and I just hope it's by your side and not against you because, I'm sorry, son, she will win. Tell that girl she can't, and she will prove you wrong. You could try to tear everything from her, but it won't work. You don't want to go to war with her. War burns bridges while that woman builds them, just like my hotel.

I had lost all hope until she wandered onto my doorstep. I recognized Valarian the moment I laid eyes on him, of course. He reminded me so much of you, and it was like I was given a second chance at the one thing I missed with you. She gave me drive and reason to keep fighting. When I met Everly and our sweet boy Valarian, I was on borrowed time, waiting for my life to end. For years, this place resembled how my life felt—broken and hopeless. Yet, after finding them, I opened myself up a little bit for the first time in a very long time, invited them in, and gave them a place to stay.

For that, I not only gained a grandson but a daughter too. They gave me life, gave me back my home and my fight. So, in turn, I gave her every-thing. Everything I own. I would say your father won't be too pleased with that knowledge, but he'll understand why in time.

Now, I know you're probably furious that your father lied to you all these years, but just know it was a different time, and I came with a lot of past and baggage. He saw me as a challenge. He wasn't totally to blame, though. I was a wild one. Yet, he loved me still, and I couldn't let go of the anger or my home.

When he took you from me, that was the worst and most harrowing day of my life. For a while, he would bring you to see me, so I was a part of some of your earliest memories until you started questioning. But my hatred for what he did overrode my reasoning. Don't blame him entirely, though; we both made choices we shouldn't have.

It's as much my fault as it was his. You were deprived of a mother, I lost a son, but he lost his mate, his Luna because his reputation was on the line. That was his loss and mine. I've realized over the years that anger and hatred grow, and it slowly destroys us. So let it go. It does no good to dwell in the past. Instead, look forward to the future and what it can be if you allow it. Hatred and anger do nothing but rot your insides, Valen, so let it go.

He was your father and still is. I know he'll regret my passing, regret his mistakes. But that's where history can change. Our past actions are a lesson for the future, so take those lessons from us; don't blame, don't hate, rejoice that you found Everly and Valarian.

Don't let this be your biggest regret. Don't rule by emotion, rule with a level head, and make sure it's with your family by your side. I'm proud to say I may have rubbed off on her a little. Everly is strong, stubborn, but with a heart of gold. She will break you down and peel back the layers before she rebuilds you, like she did me. I was never one for emotion. She knows that. But I've caught myself awed by her ability to adapt, morph, and change herself into the woman she is.

Valarian, too. I can see he will grow to be a great Alpha one day, and hopefully, you will be part of the reason he is. Don't let this knowledge of my existence tarnish what you have. Don't let this be the Blood Alpha's regret. Let it be the change that is so needed in this City. Love them, and you will not only gain a Luna and a son, but a family and home. She built her village; I just hope she lets you be a part of it.

So, with that, I'm sorry for not being a part of your life like I wish I were. Just know I love you, and I always will.

Love Mom x

P lacing the letter on the bedside table, I sit up and pull my clothes on before leaning down and kissing Everly's cheek. *I owe her this much*, I think as I get dressed and slip out of the apartment.

By the time I've organized buses and pulled all my men from border patrols, it's nearly midday. Poor Marcus has been run off his feet as I gave him orders and a never-ending list of tasks for the day.

I pull up at the school and walk in with Marcus to find Valarian. My son squeals loudly and rushes over to me when I walk into his classroom. Marcus scoops Casey up and holds her upside down by one foot, jiggling her like a teabag while she squeals loudly. The teacher stops her lesson and looks over at us, interrupting her class.

"Can I help you, Alpha?" she asks.

"Yes. Tell the kids to pack up; I've already spoken to the principal. The school is moving," I say, and she turns, picking up the small internal phone as students start flooding the halls, led by their teachers. Valarian's teacher jumps when the phone starts ringing in her hand. She answers, and I can hear the principal telling her what's going on.

"What's happening, Dad?" Valarian whispers as he watches the students gather what little belongings they have while the teacher directs them.

"I'm sorry you saw me like that, buddy," I tell him, and he drops his head. I pepper kisses all over his face, and he starts giggling, pushing my face away.

"Do you forgive me?" I ask him, and he wraps his arms around my neck.

"Always," he mumbles, and I suck in a shaky breath and rub his back.

"Are you shutting my school down?" Valarian asks curiously

while pulling away and looking at everyone leaving out the door. "What about my friends? Where will they go?" He looks uncertain.

"With you to your new school!" I tell him.

"But they're still rogue, Dad; they can't go to a pack school like Casey and me. What about Taylor?" Valarian pouts, his brows furrowed.

"Taylor is coming. Your village just got a hell of a lot bigger," I say, feeling the happy buzz inside of me.

"You're letting them come to the school in your pack?"

"I'm doing more than that. I'm letting them join our pack," I whisper to him before kissing his cheek and heading out the doors toward the buses.

CHAPTER
SEVENTY-THREE

Everly

Finally, everything is back in order, and I decide that I can't put it off any longer. Since Valarian is with his father for a few more hours, I decide I'll go out to the reserve and shift. After everything with the forsaken and the missing rogues, I've been putting it off because I promised I would take Valarian with me next time. Yet, as much as I want to keep that promise, it isn't a promise I can keep without putting him at risk. Plus, it's been ages since I last shifted, and I'm nervous about what I know will be an excruciating transformation.

Going through the gate, I pull my small backpack off my shoulder before glancing around uncertainly. This place is too quiet today, far too quiet. It sets my senses on edge. Yet, I'm already here, and I need to do this as much as I'm dreading it. I remove my clothes and quickly tuck them into my backpack, stuffing it inside a hollow log.

The shift takes a bit longer than usual, but surprisingly, it's not nearly as painful as I expected. I flex my claws in the moist soil and stretch out before running deeper into the forest. After a few minutes

425

of running, I realize my wolf form isn't tiring as fast, and after half an hour, where I would usually be dead on my feet and dragging my ass out of the forest, I feel eager to keep going. I suppose I had marking Valen to thank for that.

In spite of that, my wolf is still tiny and not what you would expect from an Alpha female. After another hour, I'm about to turn around when I hear the sounds of a whimper. My ears prick and twitch on top of my head while I try to find the source of the noise. I hear it again.

The breeze switches, and the soft scent of blood reaches my nose. My eyes scan the trees as I follow my nose. I swear I've smelled this scent before, but for the life of me I can't place it. All I know is that it's rogue. The next whimper tells me that someone is definitely in trouble or hurt. I pick up my pace, sniffing the ground and air while listening, looking for indication of where he, she, or they might be.

I find myself coming dangerously close to the boundary line that leads into forsaken territory, a place I hope I won't have to venture out to. Yet, the choking cough I hear next has me running toward the high fences without a second thought. My eyes blow wide when I see a pair of forsaken ripping into something on the ground. The scent of blood hits me even stronger now, and I quickly identify where I've smelled the scent before. Bile rises in my throat as I try to find a way through the fence. Racing along it, I try to find a gap big enough for me to squeeze through. Otherwise, I'll have to climb it and risk being torn to pieces by the razor wire that runs along the top.

My growl is surprisingly louder than I expected as I snarl at the two forsaken tearing into Emily, or maybe, what used to be Emily. Terrified but determined, I try to draw their attention away from her. If I leave and come back, she'll be dead long before I got help. I curse myself for not letting Valen mark me because we would have the mind-link, and my phone is still tucked in my bag closer to the hotel. One of the forsaken looks in my direction before growling just as my paws hit the fence. Suddenly, I feel the bottom of the fence pull away slightly from the ground, the mesh flimsy in this section. I start digging, my claws ripping into the soft earth as I try to dig under the fence and create a hole just big enough to squeeze through.

Yet, my wolf form is still too big for the gap, so I shift back. My bones snap painfully as adrenaline shoots through me, and I force the shift too quickly, making it increasingly painful. I'm about to shove my head and shoulders under but quickly turn, knowing my neck would be too exposed.

"Hang on, Emily!" I call, forcing my legs under the fence and grabbing the mesh with my fingers while on my back. The wire scratches and cuts into me, and I hear a snarl just as I lay flat on my back, attempting to shimmy under it. Teeth immediately sink into my legs before I'm suddenly ripped through the tiny space by one of the forsaken grabbing me; my face, torso, and arms are all cut by the wire. I scream as the wolf tears into my leg. I kick my other leg out, hitting its head before trying to force the shift back as I pivot, only for the beast to sink its teeth into the side of my torso.

Grabbing the mesh fence with one hand, my other reaches out, finding a rock. I grab it and swing, smashing into the top of its head as hard as I can; it lets go of my leg and shakes its head. Desperately, I swing again, not giving it a chance to get its bearings, smashing the rock repeatedly into its head. Blood coats my skin on the back-spray as I cave its skull in and nearly make myself sick at what I'm doing. Its dying whimper evidently gets the other one's attention, and my eyes widen when it snarls and rushes at me. My heart is pounding almost painfully as the forsaken hurls itself at me, all teeth and claws, going for the kill. My panic forces the shift quickly as I run at it full force.

Our bodies collide in a mess of fur, claws, and teeth.

Memories of pack training, things I thought I would have surely forgotten after all these years, kick in as we fight. The forsaken starts ripping into me, but being smaller, I'm able to move a little more efficiently, escaping some of its more lethal blows just in the nick of time. Aiming my teeth and claws at the softer tissue of his torso, I start tearing into him, piece by piece, slowly weakening him.

His teeth sink into my hip and I sink my teeth into his armpit and chest, which makes him let go. I pivot, sinking my teeth into his stomach above his thigh and shaking my head. He bounces back with a yelp before staggering, his intestines and organs protruding from the wound I gave him. I know I have no time to waste. I immediately clamp my jaws onto his neck and shake my head. His body falls limp on the ground.

I stand still for a moment, panting, trying to catch my breath, when I hear a groan that makes me spin. Shifting, I race to Emily, who is lying naked in the dirt in her human form. I skid along the ground mid-shift, grazing my hands and knees as I stop beside her, gripping her shoulders. Her hands are clutching the back of her neck as she lies twisted on her side.

The forsaken have torn into her severely and appear to have been eating her thigh and hip. It's almost as if she were too weak to go on and had collapsed, and they had stumbled upon her, thinking she was a leisurely meal in her weakened state. Rolling her onto her back, she whimpers, and her eyes fly open, scary and bloodshot, her hair matted. She blinks rapidly, and her eyes roll into her head for a moment before trying to focus on me again.

"Everly," she murmurs, and I look over her body, trying to figure out how I'll get her back through the fence.

"Right here, Emily. I'm right here," I try to tell her, looking around for something that will aid us.

"You need to get my son," she murmurs, and I look at her in shock.

"Where is Ben, Emily? Where is he?" I ask her, looking around for any sign of the boy.

"The facility," Emily gasps. "I have to get my son," she whispers, and her eyes roll into her head.

Tears brim in my eyes as I shake her, gripping her shoulders, trying to rouse her awake.

"What facility, Emily? Where is he?" I yell, and her cracked, bleeding lips move, but no sound comes out. Her face is burned and blistered from the sun, which tells me she's been out here for a while.

"Emily!" I cry, shaking her, before cursing when she falls unconscious. Grabbing her under the arms, I start dragging her toward the fence. If I can roll her under, at least to that side, I can go for help. But she'll be left open for predators on this side in my absence. I get her to the fence and start making the hole I was digging bigger. As soon as I think it's big enough, I use my feet to push her under while lifting the mesh as much as I can by pulling it toward me. Once she's mostly through, I use my hands and start pushing her so I can squeeze under next.

I hear growls behind me, and I freeze.

Emily is now safe on the other side of the fence while I'm still in the forsaken territory. I turn my head to see three forsaken stalking toward me, teeth bared. I frantically start pushing her, hoping to get under before they reach me.

Forcing my head and shoulders under the fence, I am just pulling myself through when I feel teeth sink into both my ankles. I scream, holding on to Emily's naked, unconscious body as they try ripping me back under the fence. My fingers slip and I desperately try to turn in an attempt to grab the fence, when another set of teeth sink into my thigh, and I'm yanked back under the fence at an alarming speed. My scream of agony makes my own ears ring as I stagger to my hands and knees, only for one of them to pounce on my back and start tearing into me.

CHAPTER
SEVENTY-FOUR

Valen

"Everly!" I call after walking up the steps to her apartment and pushing the door open. I get no answer. Valarian ducks off to his room, and I can hear Zoe coming up the steps behind me. Wandering through the place, I walk into her room to find her uniform on the bed. As I head back to the living room, Zoe enters, dumping Casey's stuff on the table.

"Have you seen Everly? She didn't answer when I called on my way here," I ask her.

"No, she was in the restaurant earlier; I thought she would be here." Zoe shrugs. "Maybe ask Tatum? Wasn't he on guard duty today?"

"No, he had to go to a border patrol meeting today," I tell her when Zoe picks up her phone.

"Ah, she's gone on a run at the reserve," Zoe says, and I walk over, snatching the phone from her fingertips. The text message was sent two hours ago. My heart skips a beat. That's far too long, and I'm worried, knowing the borderlines aren't secure.

"Watch Valarian," I tell her, taking off and jumping over the

430

guardrail on the balcony. Landing on the ground, I race toward the back end of the hotel property. I've been calling her for over two hours. She wouldn't have been gone that long. She told me herself, she can't last that long in her wolf form. I have a bad feeling about this.

As I run for the back of the property, I hear Zoe call out to me, but I don't stop. Instead, I hit the gate so hard it flies open and smashes into the fence, sniffing the air for any sign of her as I run. I find her scent coming to a log before reaching into it and pulling out her bag. I open the mind-link, ordering all my men to this side of the border to find her as I frantically look between the trees.

"Everly!" I scream out to her. My chest squeezes painfully—something feels like it's tugging. Goosebumps are rising on my arms, and I just know something terrible has happened. I don't even get three steps before the shift takes over, and I'm racing through the forest on huge paws, looking for any sign of her. I cursed myself that she wasn't marked because I would have found her in seconds.

Partway through the woods, I hear a scream, and my stomach drops.

Adrenaline courses through me as I tear toward the sound, her screams becoming louder and the sounds of snarls and fighting reaching my ears. I skid into the fence, my paws digging into the earth as I slam against it. My heart stops at what I see.

Three forsaken are tearing into her, and she's covered in blood as she tries desperately to shift. Racing along the fence line, I try to find a way out to her when she yelps. She just managed to shift when a brown, matted one rips into her neck, flinging her across the dirt.

I back up, looking at the fence and its coils of razor wire wrapping around the top. I shift back before backing up further and running at the fence, grabbing the mesh with my fingers and climbing it before jumping over the top. The wire tangles around my arms, torso, and legs, tearing at my flesh, and I feel it drag across my entire body before my weight carries me to the other side.

My entire body slices to pieces as I hit the ground mid-shift. My paws hit the dirt, and I growl viciously, the sound more of a roar. They freeze, all spinning toward the new intruder. My eyes immediately go to Everly, who is trying to crawl away, looking on the verge of death. One of her legs is broken, her shinbone jutting out past her skin, and I can't see a clear speck of flesh that isn't drenched in blood.

The forsaken turn their full attention on me, snapping and snarling as they try to circle me. Not giving them time to make the first move, I attack, tearing into one while the other two rip into me. I barely feel their bites as I pull them apart, utterly numb with my rage as I tear into the brown one's neck and shake my head.

Fur and blood—including mine—sprays around everywhere, coating the ground. I can feel my men getting closer as I instantly kill the first one before pivoting and sinking my teeth into the second one's face, tearing his ear off before biting his muzzle.

The crunch of his teeth breaking and his blood getting into my mouth makes me lock my jaw while the other tears into my side and back leg, trying to get me off him. His wails and screams echo as I feel his jaw snap and pop. I let go, turning on the third and ripping into his right, hind leg, the bone cracking between my teeth under the pressure, and I shake my head.

He yelps and howls as I rip his leg off just as the other one hits me from the side, but he has no control of his jaw as it hangs limply. I tear into his neck, slamming him down into the ground before tearing a chunk out.

Tatum is running toward us, and I gasp when I see Alpha John's giant, gray wolf lock its jaws around the forsaken's neck, snapping it in one bite before he repeatedly slams it on the ground.

My men emerge from everywhere. Blood drenches me and my wounds aren't healing very quickly, but I only have one aim, and that is Everly. Rushing toward her, I find her leg is indeed broken, her side is torn open severely, and a chunk from her thigh is gone. I start licking her wounds, and she pushes my face away.

"Stop, you're injured," she whispers, pushing my head with her hand again, and I snap at her fingers, ignoring her.

"Tatum, help Emily!" Everly cries, and I lift my head from her hip to see her point toward the fence line. Tatum rushes over, and I see my men help him tug at the panel to get to her better. Everly's hand drops, and so does the rest of her as she passes out, almost as if her body just gave up on her now she knows she's safe.

I keep licking her wounds, sealing them, so they stop bleeding before shifting back when I notice her father coming over. He sniffs her neck, and I snarl at him before scooping her up in my arms. He also shifts back, looking everywhere but at his daughter's naked body in my arms. I tuck her closer, shielding her nudity.

"What are you doing here?" I growl at him.

"Your men rushed out of the meeting; I figured something had happened and followed," he snaps back at me. His eyes go to Everly's face, her head falling back in my arms.

"She's going to be alright?" he asks before clenching his jaw and looking away.

"She will be," I tell him, turning my back on him and stalking off to the pulled-down fence.

"Get your men to fix that fucking fence, John; they were supposed to be on patrol today," I call over my shoulder. He growls but says nothing as I step through into the reserve. One of my men scoops up Emily and I stop. The girl doesn't look too good.

"She okay?"

"No idea," he says.

"Get her to the pack hospital," I tell him, and he takes off running with her.

"Already mind-linked for ambulances. They'll be waiting out front. I told Marcus to hang back for them. He's out there flagging them down," Tatum says, and I nod before looking at my other men.

"Guard the fence until John's men get here to fix it," I command.

"Yes, boss," I hear them say just before I take off running.

CHAPTER
SEVENTY-FIVE

Valen

I place Everly in the waiting ambulance, ordering Marcus to watch Valarian for me since he's still with Zoe. Once we get to the hospital, Emily is placed in a medically induced coma; they have no idea what's wrong with her. However, forsaken saliva can be poisonous; the number of bacteria they carry has baffled us for years. We aren't certain why, but something changes in their DNA once made forsaken, which is part of the reason our city rarely banishes people. Everly is slowly healing and has IVs of fluids and antibiotics coming out of her everywhere. The infection ravaging her body is mild, and the few wounds I received have already healed.

I've noticed that forsaken bites have never really affected me; something to do with the same genetic mutation in my bloodline that results in amber eyes, which is now shared with Valarian. Everly, however, doesn't share it, although her marking me seems to have some effect on her ability to heal a little quicker, whereas Emily is knocking at death's door.

I've been sitting here at Everly's side for three days now, waiting for her to wake up. At least now, she has a bit more color about her.

One of the pack doctors enters, carrying Everly's notes in his hands. He's an older man around my father's age, with gray hair tied at his nape accompanied by a short beard. He checks the charts on the end of her bed before hooking another bag of something to her IV.

"She's doing much better. I suppose she has you to thank for that. Although, she would heal a lot faster if you mark her," Doc says to me.

I scowl, furrowing my brows.

"I know you don't want to mark her against her will. But Alpha, I am sure, given the circumstance, she would understand," Doc says when I go to protest.

"You said she's doing better," I tell him, and he nods,

"She is, but she isn't out of the woods yet. You know how forsaken bites go; one minute they're fine, then the next..." he doesn't finish and instead shoots Everly a worried look. I scrub my hands down my face before rubbing my eyes that feel like sandpaper.

"What of Emily?" I ask. Scouts had scoured the area for her son but found no sign of him. We don't even know where she came from. Nothing makes sense, and we have zero leads.

"She isn't doing so well; I'm not sure if she'll make it. We had to amputate one of her legs already," Doc tells me, and I sigh.

"Also, Everly's mother keeps calling the hospital; Alpha John has also called to check on her."

My brows furrow. For years, they wanted nothing to do with her, and now, suddenly, they give a shit?

"What did you tell them?" I ask him.

"Nothing, of course. They aren't on her list of emergency contacts, but..."

"But what?"

"They are her parents, Alpha. Maybe you should let them know. You should probably go home, too. I will call if anything changes or if she wakes up."

I look over at Everly, still unconscious. The thought of leaving makes my stomach turn.

435

"And think about what I said about marking her. She isn't dying, but it would speed things up," Doc tells me. I bite the inside of my lip and nod. If she's on the brink of death, I would take her wrath, yet I wonder if she'll hate me if I mark her just to speed up the healing process.

Valarian keeps asking for her. I've managed to shield him away from what's really going on, but that will only last so long before he demands to see her. Getting up, my back cracks and I stretch, having been in that chair for days now. I walk over to her bedside, running my fingers up her arm. Sparks zap at my fingers from the bond, and goosebumps rise on her arms from my touch.

"Forgive me," I whisper, leaning down and cupping the back of her neck. I kiss her lips and tilt her head to the side. Feeling my canines elongate, I sink them into her neck. Sparks rush over my body everywhere, and I can taste the remnants of the poison in her blood, taste it on my tongue before I feel my heart thump erratically in my chest.

My chest feels like it's expanding, the bond forging, and I feel the moment our souls entwine, her sleepy state rolling over me; she moans in her sleep. She's always reacted to my touch, even comatose it seems, but this is something else. There's a deep longing, like she's fighting to come back to me, plus her worry for Valarian; so many things plague her even while in this state, and I can feel everything that makes her bleed into me. Everly completes me and fills a void I wasn't aware existed until I marked her.

Moving her over on the small hospital bed, I climb in beside her, not wanting to leave her side, hoping my warmth and our bond will be enough to rouse her awake, while also praying she doesn't want to kill me when she wakes up and realizes I marked her without consent. But Doc is right, it will speed up her ability to heal, and she has our little boy waiting at home with my father for his mother to come home.

I end up falling asleep beside her, only to wake up when my phone starts vibrating in my back pocket. I quickly look at Everly, but there's no change; she remains unconscious. Pulling my phone out, I yawn and glance at the screen. My father is calling. Answering it, I hold the phone to my ear.

"Yep," I say, shortness in my tone. We still aren't talking yet. but I trust no one more than my father with Valarian. He may be why my mother is dead, but he was a good father, and I know he would protect my son with his life.

"Valarian wants to see his mother. Now, don't be mad, but I've brought him to the hospital. We're downstairs."

I growl. I don't want Valarian to see her like this.

"Valen, don't make my mistakes. Don't keep him from her," my father says to my silence.

"I would never make your mistakes, Father," I tell him before giving him the room number. I hop off the bed, trying my best to cover her a little better and hide the tubes and needles in her veins. However, it's pointless. Nothing I do will shield our son from her helpless state. Hearing a knock on the door, what feels like moments later, I open it to see my father. Valarian stands there, peering around him with frightened eyes. I glare at my father. He shrugs.

"You shouldn't have brought him here; he looks terrified," I tell my father, reaching down to pick up my son.

"He misses his mother and you. What else was I supposed to do? He refused to go to school until he saw her," he answers. I growl, turning to look at my son. His eyes peer over my shoulder at his mother. I step into the room, and my father follows, standing off to the side.

"See, she's alright; she's just sleeping," I tell Valarian, squeezing him tight. It feels like ages since I saw him last.

"When will she wake up?" Valarian asks, kicking his legs to hop down. I place him on his feet and hesitantly walk over to her. His eyes wander over her, and he tries to climb on the bed. I sigh, grabbing him around the waist.

"Mommy has needles in her arms; you have to be careful," I say.

"I want to lay with her," Valarian whines, clutching her blankets, and I look to my father. He presses his lips in a line and nods toward the bed. I suck in a breath.

"Okay, just let me move her around. But you have to stay still," I tell Valarian, and he nods. I rearrange the cords and different devices attached to her, and my father helps me prop her up better, so she's kind of on her side. She doesn't show any kind of response as we move her around, which terrifies me. I get nothing through the bond unless my skin actually touches her.

Lifting Valarian up, he rolls on his side to face her, sharing her pillow while my father and I try to untangle the cords attached to her hands. I end up draping her arm over him so the IV doesn't kink. The trickiest part is moving her around and not ripping out the catheter. Thankfully, I manage it because that would be embarrassing—being scolded by the doctor for moving her when I probably shouldn't.

"If you want to hop off, tell me," I tell him, but he snuggles down under the blanket with her, his finger tracing over her face. I sigh and fall back into the chair.

"Go get a coffee and something to eat. I'll sit with them," my father says, and my eyes go to my son, who's whispering to his mother to wake up.

With a nod, I get up when Valarian speaks. "You marked her?" he asks, sitting up on his elbow and glancing down at the wound on her neck. He brushes her hair back to look at it better before sniffing her. "She smells like us now," Valarian beams. "Officially part of our big village, Momma," he says, sniffing her again. His eyes go to me. "So, that means we can come live with you now? Your house is bigger."

"Let's just see what happens when your mother wakes up."

Valarian nods before prodding her mark with his finger as if he could rub it off. "Why do we have to bite them to mark our mates? I don't want to bite Casey. She'll probably taste like a troll," Valarian says, pulling a face.

"Casey?" I ask him, and he shrugs before his little cheeks heat.

"I think the little man has a crush," my father announces with a chuckle.

"I do not, Papa," Valarian says, glaring and pursing his lips angrily.

"Then why would you say you didn't want to bite Casey because she would taste like a troll?" I laugh.

"Because she'll be my mate," Valarian announces, and I scratch the back of my neck awkwardly.

"But what if she isn't?" I ask him.

"But she's my best friend. But... so is Taylor. I don't want to bite them and get girl germs," he says, confused.

"Well, lucky for you, you don't have to bite anyone any time soon," I tell him, and my father chuckles.

"But aren't mates our best friends?"

"Yes, in a sense. But not all mates grow up together, Valarian. Casey and Taylor may have someone else for a mate," I try to explain.

"No, I'm their best friend. They can't have another boy as a best friend," Valarian growls, startling me.

"I thought you said Casey was annoying?" I laugh.

"She is, and she is messy, so is Taylor," Valarian states. "Can I have two mates?"

I laugh, turning to my father. "Have fun," I laugh, ditching him with the awkward questions.

"But–" my father complains, looking like he also wants to bail out with me. Sucker!

"I'll bring you back some coffee," I tell him, laughing as I duck out of the room.

Heading to the cafeteria, I order something to eat, grabbing something for Valarian and my father too. After waiting for my order, my name gets called and I go to the counter to retrieve the bag and cup tray. Turning around, I sigh when I see John and Ava looking out of place in my pack hospital.

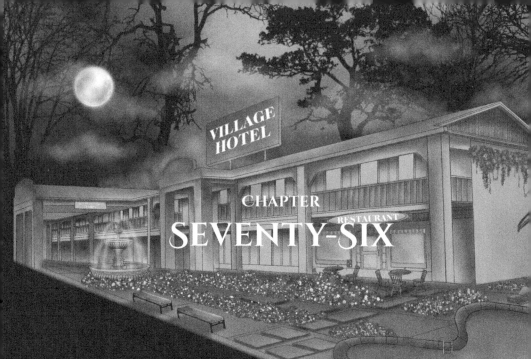

CHAPTER
SEVENTY-SIX

Valen

Pressing my lips into a line, I walk over to them where they stand harassing the receptionist.

"Why are you on my territory?" I snap at John, and he turns his attention away from the girl behind the counter, looking relieved.

"Your doctors won't answer my questions, and one hung up on my wife," John says, pointing an accusing finger at me.

"Your point being?"

"She is our fucking daughter," he snarls.

"What, now she's your daughter? Because you had no issues disowning her for five years," I snap at him, and he glares at me. Seeing him here when his daughter is on the verge of death pisses me off. He has no idea what she's been through. None of us do.

"Leave!" I tell him, unable to contain my anger.

Ava grips my arm and I pull mine away.

"Please," she says, and I look at her. I know Everly doesn't have issues with her sister—she's hurt, perhaps, by the fact she never continued their relationship, but she doesn't blame Ava. Her father, however, she has washed her hands of, after what he did.

"You can come to see her. *You* remain here," I tell her father, who growls before Ava looks up at him.

"Please, Dad."

He sighs. I raise an eyebrow at him to see if he'll challenge me on this, but he nods to her, and I tell her the room number before she starts to head for the stairs.

"Give this to my father and son," I tell her, giving her the paper bag and one coffee. She nods quickly, taking it and making her way up to see her sister.

I sip my coffee, and John stalks off to the cafeteria to order his own. A minute later, I receive a text from my father asking if it's alright that Ava just got there or if he should make her leave. I reply that it's fine and that I'll be back up soon before hanging up and placing my phone in my pocket.

"I'm not here looking for trouble, Valen," John says when I come up behind him.

"Good because if you are, you just found it," I tell him. He glares at the barista, who rushes around quickly, making his coffee.

"Why are you here?" I ask him.

"She is my daughter."

"Bullshit. You didn't care that she was your daughter when she got pregnant with my son," I tell him, pulling a chair out at a nearby table. The barista hands him his coffee, and he pulls out the other chair. The entire cafeteria falls silent, and I look around to find it empty except for the barista, who stood staring wide-eyed at us, sitting at a table together.

"Tell me the real reason, or leave. I will drop Ava back at your borders later; who let you cross?" I ask him.

"Nobody. I just drove in. You dropped your border patrols, remember? For the rogues," he says. I had forgotten entirely. I nod, sipping my coffee and sitting back in my chair. I can tell he's uncomfortable.

"I won't let you ruin her again," I tell him.

"I didn't ruin her. You did. She was a good kid; I had no issues with her growing up until you got your filthy hands on her," he snarls.

"Yet you have no issues trying to pawn your other daughter off to me, so what is it you want?"

"Nothing. I am just here to check on her."

"I don't believe you," I tell him, pinching the bridge of my nose.

"I need–" he begins sheepishly.

"There it is. You aren't here to check on Everly at all. You want something," I tell him.

"Your father and I had a deal; he broke it."

"A fucking deal for what? I marry Ava. Then what?"

"We have an alliance, that's what."

My brows furrow at his words. "I don't buy it; you're hiding something," I argue.

John sighs, scrubbing a hand down his face. "How is she?" he asks, taking a long sip from his cup.

"Alive, and now marked," I say.

"So she's awake?"

"No, not yet," I answer, shaking my head. I lean forward and brace my arms on the table. My beard has started to grow over the past few days of sitting in the hospital, and I scratch at it; I feel dirty. I actually don't mind how it looks, but as soon as I get my hands on a razor, it's going.

"The other girl, Emma? Emery?" he asks, and I can see he's trying to make small talk.

"Emily?" I ask.

"Yes, that one."

"She lost a leg, and they aren't sure she'll make it. Emily isn't strong enough to fight off the infection."

"She never found her mate?" John asks.

"She's rogue. What do you think?"

"I know she is rogue, Goddamn it. I'm just saying she might stand a chance if she had one," John snaps at me.

"As far as I know, she hasn't, and since when do you care about rogues?" I ask.

"I don't," he says, folding his arms across his chest and staring at me. His eyes run over me before they flick away.

"You look like shit," he says.

"And you look old. Time to retire, don't you think?" I retort, and John scoffs.

"This is the last time I am asking; if you don't answer, you can leave. Why are you really here, John?"

He scowls before looking at me. "It scared me seeing her like that; I thought they killed her," John says.

"And where's your wife, Claire?" I ask him, and he looks at the table.

"Staying with her friend; we had an argument," he says.

"Over Everly?" I ask, and he nods.

"So, what? You thought coming here would patch things up with your mate?" This guy is such an ass.

"No. Yes, but no. I just wanted to make sure Everly is alright."

"Because now you realize she isn't a rogue whore?" I ask him.

"How the fuck was I supposed to know?" he snarls at me, gripping the edge of the table.

"That's one thing I don't get," I tell him, watching the man that is supposed to be my father-in-law.

"What?" he asks.

"Since finding her and my son, as a father, what I don't get is how you could look at your own flesh and blood, the child you raised, and turn your back on her like she meant nothing. Throw her out and abandon her; I would kill for my kid. There is no way I would abandon him," I snap at him.

"You don't know what you're talking about; I was protecting her!" he snarls.

"Protecting her? Are you fucking serious? She was living in her car with a newborn fucking baby, choosing between food for herself and fucking diapers. Don't give me that crap, John!" I tell him before standing up. "You are a shitty excuse for a father and a man," I spit at him before turning to leave.

"Because you are such a great one yourself? You didn't even know Valarian existed for how long, Valen? And what of your father? Perfect fucking example there after what he did to your mother," John sneers, and I stop, turning back to face him.

"The mother that raised your daughter when you refused to?" I retort. "My father knows he fucked up. At least he admits it and is trying to make up for it. You? You just look elsewhere to blame. And me? I wish every goddamn day I was there, even if she wasn't my mate. I would have taken her as one had I known her or known she had my son."

John curses, shaking his head.

"You see her as your biggest shame, John, when you should have seen her as your daughter and for who she is."

"Because you are suddenly an expert on my daughter. She wasn't some sweet, innocent little girl. She got herself knocked up," he says.

"You're right; she got herself knocked up with my help. It takes two people to create a baby, John, so why are only the women punished for it? It's sickening, but as much as I hate you for what you did, I suppose I should thank you also," I tell him, and he scoffs.

"For what?"

"Because she turned out great in spite of you. You showed her what not to do, and I can't wait for her to bring this city to its Goddamn knees," I growl.

"Haha. You fool. You may own half this city, Valen, but Everly won't know the first thing about running a pack—a business, yes, but a pack? She was a fucking rogue. Ava would have known," John tries to argue.

"Ava is not my mate, and I would never choose her over Everly. And a pack? You fucking idiot. Her pack outnumbers all of ours."

"Great, now I've heard it all," John laughs. "Your numbers are only three or four hundred bigger than mine. You may have more people, but I have alliances you don't have, Valen.

"Think with your fucking head," John snaps, standing up.

"Try a thousand more than yours, John. You want to go to war over me refusing to marry Ava, so be it, but you won't win; I will gladly watch her destroy you—take everything from you."

"Pft, you idiot, you don't know what you've done. War? You have seen nothing of the war that will be headed our way. You need my pack," John tells him.

"What fucking war? I don't need an alliance with you because I have Everly's. They will fight alongside mine. You are forgetting something, John. Everly isn't just an Alpha—she was also a rogue. I've come to realize that they have more guts than any pack I've known, including my own. They band together, forced to survive and rely on each other," I tell him, stepping closer.

"The rogue population outnumbers any pack when banded together, and guess who just opened their borders up? Guess who has her army, and she didn't even realize it."

"Everly?" John laughs. "They're rogues, Valen, pull your head out of your ass. She can't control them."

"She doesn't need to control them, John. They're family. Everly has done more for the rogues than any Alpha in this city has, so when push comes to shove, who do you think they'll stand behind? An Alpha?" I laugh. "No, they will fight for the woman that gave them a fighting chance.

"Do you think she isn't Alpha material? She has her own land— that hotel is solely owned by her. Everly didn't just build a business; she built a pack. She has more members than any of us. Now, last I checked pack counts, my pack is the largest at 847; the rogue population is well over a thousand."

"Means nothing, Valen, and you know it. Unless she can get those laws changed, nothing in this city will change. Your merry band of rogue whores wants to stand behind you, who are more a fool than them? It's a quick way to become forsaken," he says, and I stop.

He laughs as I turn back to face him.

"You forget, any rogue that steps out of line receives instant banishment. They are already the dregs of society. Her being your Luna won't change that. You own half the city, but you don't own the council. It will never pass in the courts. Everly would be attempting the impossible. This city doesn't want things to change; she won't succeed. All she will do is start a war she can't win," John claims.

"She will win, John. I know Everly, she won't give up until she does," I tell him when Ava comes back down. I turn to look over my shoulder. She has tears in her eyes.

"Everly, is okay, she..." Ava shakes her head before glaring at her father. "This is your fault," she snaps at him. John growls at her words.

"Get in the car. You don't speak to me like that," John snaps at her, and she shakes her head at him before stalking off, leaving me with John.

"Tell Everly to call her mother when she wakes up," John says, and I nod. He turns to walk away, then pauses.

"And tell her I stopped by. And I meant what I said, Valen. War is coming. Make sure you aren't on the wrong side of it," he says before walking off. I stare after him, wondering what he's talking about.

CHAPTER
SEVENTY-SEVEN

Valen

Returning to the room, I find Valarian tucked in beside his mother, the blanket pulled high under his chin. My father is still seated beside the bed, and he holds a finger to his lips, pointing to the bed.

"What was that about?" my father asks as I drop into the chair beside him.

"John. And I have no idea. Something is going on with him, though. He kept talking about some impending war," I tell him, and his brows furrow.

"I'll ask around, see if I can find anything out," he sighs. "Do you want me to take Valarian?"

I glance at the bed where Valarian is lying and shake my head. "No, I'll take him home with me later; you head home," I tell him, despite not wanting to leave Everly. Our son needs me, and I know she would like one of us with him.

"Valen, I–"

"Not now," I growl. I don't want to talk about him betraying my

447

mother, and certainly not here in front of my son, even if he is asleep. My dad has terrible timing, that's for sure.

He closes his mouth and nods, getting up. "Call if you need anything or want me to take him, but it will probably be good if he stays with you; he hasn't been sleeping well," he says, making his way out the door, as I sit back in my chair.

After an hour or so, my eyes start growing heavy, and I find myself nodding off. Yawning, I get to my feet to find Valarian still asleep with his mother. Everly starts stirring, her nose crinkling, and I feel her consciousness slowly coming back as she sniffs our son. I was planning on taking him home, but as I watch her, maybe he's what she needs to wake up. So instead of taking him away, I move him closer to her before climbing in beside her and pulling Valarian onto my chest.

I place his tiny hand on the side of her face and her breathing evens out again. I kiss his little head, and he rubs his face against my chest when I hear her inhale deeply, making me look over at her to see her hand move. She rubs her eyes, though her hand doesn't do what she wanted and becomes tangled in the cords attached to her.

Rolling on my side, Valarian sliding between us, I reach over and untangle her hand, making her eyes snap open. She looks really out of it, but her eyes suddenly clear of their dreary state and widen after a few seconds, and she lurches upright, looking around the room. Gripping her shoulders, I push her back down.

"Emily?" she gasps.

"Alive! She's down the hall; stay still. You just ripped out your cannula," I whisper, and she blinks, her heart rate slowing as she exhales. I tug the cords away, hitting the button for the nurse when the machine starts going berserk. Then I lean over to shut the device to the IV off too—the nurse will fix it. Grabbing Everly's hand, I run my tongue over the little spot of blood where she ripped the needle and tape off, watching it heal before lying back down.

"Try not to move. You have cords everywhere and a catheter,

which I'm sure you don't want to be ripped out," I tell her. She nods, watching our son before brushing his hair with her fingers.

Valarian stirs under her touch, and she leans forward, sniffing his little head. My heart leaps at seeing her awake, and her eyes flick to me behind him.

"You're forgiven," she smiles softly, and my brows furrow. At first, I think she's talking about not getting to her fast enough, until she touches her neck. I let out a breath of relief.

"You forgive me?"

"There's nothing to forgive. I should have let you do it when I marked you. I heard you ask me to forgive you before you did it; I thought I dreamed it," she says, rubbing her eyes and yawning.

"How long has it been?" she asks, her foggy mind becoming clearer and clearer by the second.

"A few days."

"Did you find the facility?" Everly asks. I tilt my head to look at her better. That's the first time I heard about a facility.

"What facility?"

"The one where Emily's son is, where she escaped from. She didn't tell you?"

I wonder if Everly is confused; perhaps she dreamed something about a facility.

"Emily is in a coma, love; we haven't spoken with her. I'll notify the patrols and send some scouts out. Did she say anything else?" I ask when Valarian stirs and yawns widely. Everly smiles, watching him before burying her face in his neck and peppering his face with kisses. He pushes her face away and giggles before recognition hits him.

"Mom?" he whispers, and she smiles. He pounces on her, making her grunt.

"Careful, she's still sore," I tell him, gripping his waist, but Everly shakes her head, ignoring her discomfort as she hugs him tight.

"You're awake," Valarian murmurs, breathing in his mother's scent, and she nods.

He pulls his head from her neck and looks down at her critically. "You need to brush your hair."

"Do I, now?" she asks, and he nods. "Can I wake up properly first?"

He looks at her neck and smiles. "Daddy marked you, so now you belong to him," Valarian beams. I clear my throat and Valarian looks at me while Everly shakes her head with a laugh.

"Pretty sure it's the other way around," I tell him.

His brows pinch together. "But you're the Alpha?" he says.

"Yes, when your mother lets me be," I chuckle.

"So Mom owns you?"

"We belong to each other. No one owns anybody," Everly says with a shake of her head.

"But we can live with Dad now?" Valarian asks, and I raise an eyebrow at her, interested to hear her answer.

"*What's it going to be, Luna?*" I mind-link, and her eyes widen as my voice floats through her head. I can feel how giddy she is at being part of a pack again.

"Yes. Uncle Marcus is living with Auntie Zoe now, so it'll be a little squishy, don't you think?" Everly asks him. Valarian beams with excitement and nods his head just as the nurse opens the door.

CHAPTER
SEVENTY-EIGHT

Valen

I notice that the nurse who enters is older than the other one, who's usually on the afternoon and night shifts. She pops her head in and sees Everly awake before looking at me.

"I'll get the doctor," she says, smiling kindly before stepping back out when I nod to her.

It took a few hours for Everly to be checked over, but eventually, she was given the all-clear to head home. I had Marcus bring her some clothes to change into. The doctor wanted her to stay an extra night for observations, but she wouldn't have it, wanting to go home, and refused to take no for an answer. By the time we got home, it was a little after 7 p.m. We got Valarian McDonald's on the way home, but he fell asleep in the car, and I had to pry a chicken nugget from his fingers. Both Everly and I were shocked he even ate in the car, which proved how tired he was.

Carrying him upstairs and inside, I get him in bed, stripping him down to his underwear and shirt as I tuck him in before setting the night light's timer and closing the door.

Going back out to the living room, I panic for a moment when I

451

notice Everly is gone, but when I hear the shower turn on, I stop, heading back to our room to find her in the bathroom. I come up behind her, placing my hands on her hips as she tests the water with her hand.

"Can I join you?" I ask her, kissing her naked shoulder.

She looks at me over her shoulder, and I cup her cheek before pressing my lips to hers. She answers my kiss instantly, her lips parting, and my tongue invades her mouth, dominating it as I kiss her hungrily. Everly moans softly before turning in my arms and kissing me more fiercely, her hands undressing me as she tugs off the wrinkled suit jacket I had wanted to burn all day.

Her fingers run over my chest, fumbling as she undoes my shirt buttons, and I help her as her lips go to my neck, licking and nipping my skin, making me groan. Her hands move to my bare chest once I discard my shirt, then up to my shoulders and neck to the beard I despise because it's itchy.

"Hm," she hums, her lips going to mine. "I like this rougher look," she chuckles against my lips.

"It's not staying," I growl against hers while undoing my belt buckle.

"We'll see," she chuckles, and I growl, biting her bottom lip between my teeth, making her moan and press against me. My pants fall and I grip her waist as I step out of them before her claws slice through my boxer shorts. I raise an eyebrow at her when I feel the fabric drop at my feet. Then she curls her hand around me.

Her small fingers barely wrap around my cock as she strokes it. I kiss her harder, pushing her into the shower, my lips going to her neck, and she sighs. Her head tilts to the side, giving me better access, before I lean down and grip her thighs, lifting her and pressing her against the tiled wall.

Everly shrieks at the tiles' harsh coldness, making me chuckle as she wraps her legs around my waist. Her nails dig into my shoulders where she clings to me. I nip gently at her mark, and she moans, wiggling her hips against me.

My erection is painfully hard pressed against her warm, wet core. I want to bury myself in her, and she whines, gripping my hair.

"Ah, what are you waiting for?" she growls, and I can feel her arousal, fiery hot, burning through the bond.

"Permission," I chuckle.

"Valen!" she growls, rolling her hips against me. I kiss her slowly and can feel her building annoyance as she rocks her hips against me.

"Valen! Either fuck me, or I will pin you down and take what I want," she snarls, pulling her lips from mine and biting into my shoulder.

"Hm, that I would like to see," I tell her. A growl vibrates through her, her teeth breaking my skin as she bites my mark, making my cock twitch against her. I groan, gripping her ass before adjusting myself. In one last tease, I press the tip against her before slamming into her in one motion, burying my cock in her tight confines until our hips are flush. The sigh of pleasure that escapes opens her mouth, releasing my shoulder, and her fingers escape into my hair, gripping it and tugging my mouth back to hers.

I pull out, only to slam back into her; her slick walls grip my cock as her muscles spasm around it, coating me in her arousal. I groan at the texture and the ridges of her smooth channel, gliding along my length and squeezing it with each thrust.

Her hips move to meet my thrusts as I crash into her repeatedly, pinning her against the wall. I let go of one of her legs and let it slide down my side until her toes barely touch the ground. At the same time, I lift her other leg higher, slamming my cock into her and making her cry out as she grips my shoulders.

The back of my legs burn. I want to bend her over and fuck her, but that's not happening in the shower, so I pull out of her, earning a growl. Shutting the water off, I shove her out of the bathroom toward the bedroom.

"Valen! We need to dry ourselves!" she squeals when I bend her forward on the bed.

Without answering, I grab her thighs, dragging her to the edge. My hands grip her hips, pulling her ass into the air. Her protests about ruining the bed cut off when I squeeze her rounded cheeks, pulling them apart before adjusting my cock at her slick entrance once more.

I thrust into her, and she moans loudly, pushing back against me as I watch my cock slide in and out of her wet pussy. Her ass jiggling hits my pelvis with each thrust, driving me on. My hand slides up her back, forcing her further into the mattress as my fingers slide into her hair. I grip a handful, tugging her head back, and arch her back while I continuously slam into her. Her moans and the sound of slapping flesh resonate around the room. The bed is ruined, but that's inconsequential right now.

I feel the moment she comes as her walls grip my cock. The sensation of her pulsating squeezing and pushing against my dick makes me shiver, and her loud moans send me over the edge.

Finding my release with one last thrust, I fill her with my hot cum. My grip on her hair loosens, and she falls against the mattress as I pull out of her. I slap her ass, then gasp, realizing my mistake as I stare at her lying face down on the bed. I forgot...

She groans and rolls slowly onto her back. "I think you broke my back," she grumbles, but then laughs softly.

I bite my lip, noticing how her pussy—red from the ravishment she just received—is glistening a little too much. How angry will she be when she realizes what I've done? I figure I should get it over with, not wanting to hide my mistake from her.

"Uh, Everly?"

She cracks an eyelid open, a silly smile on her lips, and I look between her legs, the evidence of my release making her thighs slick.

"I wasn't wearing anything," I mumble, biting my lip, and she chuckles.

"I figured that," she murmurs and yawns. I expected a murderous rage, so I'm surprised when she doesn't seem that fazed.

"You could get pregnant," I press, wondering if she heard me.

"I know how babies are made—I had one—but it's doubtful with all the drugs in my system at the moment," she giggles before sitting up with a groan.

"Ugh, my back," she whines as she stumbles back to the bathroom to finish her shower, making me chuckle.

CHAPTER
SEVENTY-NINE

Everly

The next morning, I wake up to a knee in the kidney as Valarian climbs into the bed, causing me to grunt. He weasels his way in between us before yanking Valen's pillow out from under his head as he steals it. Valen lurches upright, and I chuckle and close my eyes as Valarian wiggles closer to me.

"Ah, good. You're up. Can I have pancakes, please?" Valarian whines at his father, as if he didn't just wake him by thieving his pillow.

"I am, thanks to you!" Valen says, rubbing his eyes.

I open my eyes to see my mate groan and scrub a hand down his face, trying to wake up.

"Please, Dad. Please, Dad," Valarian repeats, shaking his father's shoulder.

"What time is it?" Valen yawns.

"Breakfast time!"

"Isn't your mother up?" Valen yawns, and I quickly close my eyes, pretending to be asleep; I really don't want to get out of bed. Valarian rolls beside me, his fingers prying my eyes open, and I try not to smile as I fake sleep, though I notice his lips are covered in chocolate.

"Leave her, let her sleep," Valen says, hauling his ass out of bed while tapping Valarian's leg. Valarian stands on the bed before jumping off it onto his father's back, clinging to him like a spider monkey and causing him to groan.

"Geez, what's got into you?" Valen whines.

"I want pancakes, but we need more chocolate chips."

"There's a whole packet in the fridge."

I chuckle, knowing the evidence is on Valarian's face. Valen turns, hearing me, and I quickly close my eyes again and snuggle back under the blanket, trying to dive back into sleep.

I'm awoken from snuggling beneath the blankets a while later when Valen's voice whispers in my ear.

"Faker, I know you're awake; you just didn't want to get up," he says, jamming his fingers in my ribs, making me jump. "Make sure you take an umbrella to work, too. I heard on the radio a storm is headed our way," Valen tells me, and I groan.

"I'm not going," I tell him, adding some fake coughs for dramatics. He tickles me, gripping the tops of my thighs through the blanket.

"Stop, stop! Okay, I'm awake, I'll go to work!" I laugh when I hear feet rushing up the hall. Valarian calls out for his father, and I giggle as Valen yanks the blanket up, climbing under and hiding behind me.

"What are you doing?" I ask.

"Hiding from the hyperactive demon-spawn—he ate an entire bag of chocolate chips, and he made me iron his shirt twice. He's like OCD on steroids," Valen growls, trying to lie as flat as possible behind me and failing. Valarian wanders into the room and peers around.

"Have you seen Dad?"

I point to the mound under the blanket beside me with a smile.

Valarian walks around the edge of the bed to my side before throwing the blanket back and looking at his father.

"My shoelaces don't match," our son says, looking down at his shoes. Valen peers over the edge of the bed.

"They look fine to me," he says, but Valarian looks at him expectantly, and I chuckle.

"Your mother will fix them."

"But Mom ties them funny; can you fix them?" he says, pulling on his father's arm. Valen groans, but climbs back out of bed and bends down, fixing his shoelaces.

"There, better?"

"No. That string is long now."

Valen's frustration comes through the bond as he tries to fix the shoes. It's only on the third attempt that Valarian is finally happy enough about them. I glance at the alarm clock on the bedside table, knowing he'll have to run him to school soon. Valen lies back down and sighs.

"Uh, you gotta run him to school," I tell him.

"We still have half an hour; it's like a five-minute drive at most. And don't you have work?" he asks.

"I'm faking sick."

"Well, you better fake it better than your lame fake sleeping; you know it doesn't look good when the boss fakes sick, right?" he mocks.

"Don't you have work to do?" I ask him.

"Nope, Dad is handling it."

"You know it doesn't look good when the boss sends daddy in to do his work for him, right?" I ask, laughing to myself.

"I said I didn't have work to do; I never said I wouldn't work," Valen retorts before getting up and walking into the closet. I hear him moving around in the closet before he walks out dressed in his suit and throws my uniform on the bed.

"Up. If I'm working, so are you."

"I nearly died. Cut me some slack."

"*Nearly* died. Now up."

I roll my eyes but haul myself out of bed before hopping in the shower to wake myself up.

Halfway through washing my hair, Valen comes in, telling me he's running Valarian to school, and he'll see me tonight. I nod when he opens up the shower door, the cold draft making me shiver as I try to wash the shampoo from my eyes. He grips my wrist, yanking me to him and pecking my lips.

"Dad! We're going to be late!" Valarian calls out. Valen laughs, letting me go while I blink through the soap before stepping back under the shower spray.

"Hold your horses, I'm coming! And don't forget your raincoat, it's supposed to rain today!" I hear him yell back as he walks out of the bathroom. I chuckle to myself and finish my shower before hopping out and drying myself. I have things I need to do today, or at least look into. My first mission is stopping by the council chambers to see if I can petition to be heard in court, and then I need to check up on Emily at the hospital.

The day flies by quickly. It's overcast, and I figured the rain was coming. What I wasn't expecting was to step out of the city council to a storm brewing and coming in fast. We hardly get storms here, but when we do, they're always terrible.

Walking back to the car, the wind howls, whipping my hair across my face. Thick, dark clouds roll across the sky, the thunder rumbles loudly, and streaks of lightning light up the heavy clouds above. Reaching my truck, it takes nearly all my strength to close the door with the wind pushing against it.

This storm is going to be a doozy, and I have to get back to the hotel. I need to double-check the backup generators just in case and prepare to lock it down. Trees bend over with the wind as I drive toward work. The drive takes longer when rain and hail start belting down halfway there, the road barely visible, and the windshield wipers are struggling to clear the windshield through the downpour.

Pulling into the staff parking lot, I notice a pool umbrella flying across it. *"Shit!"* I mutter to myself while tugging the keys out of the ignition. I force my door shut before chasing after the damn thing, only to slip on the slick ground.

Macey, I see, comes running out after the umbrella, and I get back to my feet, soaking wet, my hair dripping.

"Go secure the pool area; I'll get this!" Macey calls over her shoulder. Her blouse has turned see-through from the rain, and her normally curly hair is straight and dripping. I chuckle as she curses the umbrella, chasing it down while I race to the pool. The wind is tossing the lightweight stuff and I shove it in the garden shed behind the fence where we keep the pool supplies. Rushing back out of the pool area, I turn to lock the fence. You never know when someone will be stupid enough to try to go for a swim during a storm, and I don't feel like scooping out a cooked werewolf in the morning. Once the chain and padlock are secured, I race toward the restaurant. Macey comes up behind me.

"Did you catch it?" I ask.

"Nope, gave up after it tried to whisk me away like Mary Poppins," she says, wringing her outfit out under the awning. I swing the door open and step inside, the warmth welcoming.

Macey shivers behind me. "Geez, it came out of nowhere," she says, shaking her head. One of the housekeepers comes over to us, handing us some towels, and I try to dry myself as best I can. Walking into the back to the kitchen, I look for Zoe, but she isn't anywhere to be found. I turn to the head chef, who's chopping potatoes.

"Amy, have you seen Zoe?" I ask her. She looks up from her station, her red hair in a hairnet and her chef hat sagging to one side.

"She said she wasn't feeling well and went to lay down before the afternoon rush."

I look at Macey behind me, and she shrugs. "She was in here before I went out on my futile mission."

"I'll go check on her. You alright to check the generators, or do you want me to do it on my way back?" I ask.

"I'll do the generators; you can check to make sure the event room door is locked," she laughs, and I glare at her; that's a 30-meter dash with no shelter. She laughs, sauntering out, and I shake my head, heading for the restaurant's rear exit. Forcing myself to brave the storm, I suck in a breath and run like mad for the ballroom, cutting through the gardens and making a beeline for the building at the end of the property.

All the doors are wide open, and I quickly race around and shut them before flicking the lights off. The wind has carried leaves and debris inside the place, and it will need to be cleaned tomorrow. After checking everything is secure, I race back to the main building before detouring for mine and Zoe's apartment.

I climb the stairs two at a time and burst through the door. *Well, that's my cardio for the day*, I think. My shoes squelch and squeak on the floors. I can hear a groaning sound coming from somewhere up the hall and I quickly kick my shoes off, searching for Zoe and the strange noise. Stepping into the hallway, I turn toward her room, but her door is open, and the room is empty. After sniffing the air, I pick up her scent, but gosh, it's strong. Approaching the bathroom door, I knock softly, hearing a whimper on the other side.

"Zoe?" I murmur, listening. She doesn't answer, but it sounds like wherever she is, she's in pain.

"Zoe, I'm coming in," I tell her, gripping the doorknob. I twist and push the door open to find Zoe lying on the cold tiles, a towel wrapped around her like she just climbed out of the shower. I rush to her side and kneel next to her.

"Zoe?" I ask, gripping her arms and rolling her on her back. Her skin is hot to the touch, her face flushed and cheeks rosy red like she has a fever, and her scent is sickly sweet.

"Everly, I don't feel too good. Get Marcus," she murmurs, her eyes fluttering before she jolts upright and scrambles for the toilet. She throws up before hugging the toilet bowl. "Ugh, I feel like shit; I think I may have that stomach bug," Zoe whines. I touch her head; her skin seems even more swelteringly hot.

"No, I don't think you have a bug, Zoe. I think you're in heat!" I tell her. Pulling my phone from my pocket, I dial Marcus's number just as the lights start to flicker, a moment before the power suddenly goes out. Great. Just fucking great.

CHAPTER
EIGHTY

Valen

It's pouring down as Marcus pulls up out front so I can pick Valarian up from school. I step out of the car straight into a puddle; the drains have gotten blocked, and the gutters are overflowing and spilling onto the sidewalk, rushing like a river and filling my shoe with water.

I growl, shaking my foot to get the water out before racing for the school's front door. Marcus waits in the car because he's still on the phone with the scouts, checking if they've found anything about Emily's missing son, and the audio is going through the car's Bluetooth. My toes squelch in my shoes as I walk on the slippery floors to the grade school office.

On the way here, I called ahead, so the moment the secretary sees me step into the small office, she calls up to Valarian's class to let the teacher know I'm here to collect him.

"He'll be right down, Alpha," the secretary tells me, and I nod to her, then begin wandering around the room, looking at the school awards hanging on the brown, brick walls. I shrug my coat off, which is drenched from the downpour, and drape it over one arm as I stroll.

"Scouts found nothing," Marcus says, walking into the small school office. He shakes his head, spraying water everywhere, and I growl, wiping my face with the back of my hand when he gets some on me. He laughs, running his fingers through his wet hair.

"You tell them to head back? This storm looks like it'll be a big one," I ask him, and he nods before dialing a number into his phone. I watch as he holds the phone to his ear, his face lined with worry.

"Zoe's not answering her phone; I've tried to call five times today," he whines when I look at him questioningly. He hangs up when she doesn't answer and sends her a text instead. His lips purse in frustration, and I raise an eyebrow at him as he glares at his phone screen.

"She's probably working," I tell him, and he sighs.

"I know, but she feels funny through the bond. Goddess, I feel so hot!" he says, tugging at the collar of his shirt. "They have the heaters up way too high here," he growls, looking around. He's been complaining all day about the heat and spent most of it in just his button-up shirt, while I spent most of the damn day shivering; I only took my coat off because it's drenched.

"Just go if you want. You don't have to come with me," I tell him just as his phone starts ringing.

"Hmm. Everly," he says, showing me the screen. I motion for him not to tell her we're together by pressing a finger to my lips.

"I know, I know," he whispers, walking off to take the call out in the hall. A few moments later, Valarian appears in the office with his teacher, his bag slung over his shoulder, and I reach down. After taking it from him and tossing the strap over one shoulder, I kneel before him.

"Here you go, Alpha, you just need to sign here," she says, handing me a printed slip and a pen with his student information and photo. I reach up onto the desk and quickly sign it before grabbing Valarian and pulling his raincoat from his bag. Once it's on him and buttoned up, I pick him up and get to my feet to leave.

"I forgot my umbrella, so we need to make a run for it," I laugh, and he pouts, unhappy about getting wet. Just as I'm about to head for the door leading out to the hall, Marcus comes rushing in, the door narrowly missing us as he bursts through it. He looks frantic and tosses me his keys—I only just catch them before they fall on the floor.

"I gotta go! Zoe's in heat!" he says,

"Uh, I can drive you home," I call out to him, but he's already shifting into his wolf, his shredded clothes trailing up the hall before he bursts through the doors leading out, hitting them in his wolf form so hard they smack against the walls.

"He'll get wet," Valarian says, watching him.

"It'll be quicker, though. He won't be restricted to the roads. He'll be fine," I tell him, walking down the corridor. Valarian sighs, and I hoist him higher before draping my jacket over his head and pushing the door open. We make a run for the car out front, and I become drenched even worse, my white shirt turning see-through. Valen squeals and whines that he got drenched too, despite having the jacket covering him. I place him in his booster seat before jumping into the driver's seat.

Valarian's teeth are chattering, so I turn the heater on high at full blast to warm him up and try to dry my shirt a little. Pulling away from the curb, we head further into the city on the way to our destination when my phone starts ringing through the Bluetooth.

"Who is Love Muffin?" Valarian asks, looking at the screen, and I snicker. Everly will probably demand I delete that name from my contacts.

"Your mother," I chuckle, and he scrunches up his face.

"Aren't you going to answer it?" Valarian asks, and I shake my head.

"Nope, I don't want your mother to know I kidnapped you from school early."

"She'll keep calling. And she probably already knows. My watch has a GPS tracker in it," Valarian says just as the phone cuts out, only for it to ring again.

"It has a what?" I ask him while looking in the rearview mirror at him. He holds up his wrist to show me his black watch.

"Yep, it's linked to her phone. She got it after I went looking for you when I ran away; said it's so she can keep an eye on me," he says with a shrug. "Where are we going anyway?" he asks, looking around.

"To the jewelry store," I tell him, and his tiny brows pinch together.

"Is that why you pulled me from school? To go shopping? I wanted to do the show and tell; I brought my dinosaur to school today," Valarian pouts.

"Well, I need you to help me. Since your mother never seems to wear jewelry, I don't know her tastes, so I want you to help pick it out," I tell him.

"Mom doesn't wear jewelry. Maybe you should get her flowers. Mom likes flowers, but make sure it's in a pot. She said cut flowers die and are a waste."

"You want me to ask your mother to marry me with a flower?" I ask him, glancing in the mirror, and he nods before I see his head whip up, a big grin on his face.

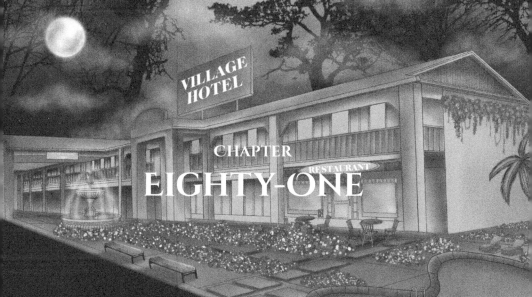

CHAPTER
EIGHTY-ONE

Valen

"You're going to marry Mom?" Valarian squeals, hurting my ears. His little eyes light up as he dances and wiggles in his seat.

"Well, I hope so. That's why we're going to the jewelers; we need to find her a ring."

Valarian claps his hands excitedly. "Oh, I know! What about grandma's rings? Grandma had bunches!" Valarian says.

"Her mother?" I ask him, a little confused. But he shakes his head.

"No, Grandma Valarie—*your* mom. They're in the storage shed mom has, where she keeps all Grandma's stuff," he says.

"I don't remember seeing a jewelry box in there," I tell him.

"No, mom packed it in a box after I dropped it. It has all my grandma's family jewels in it. Grandma gave them to her, she said. But she didn't feel right keeping them, since they're family jewels. Mom said they should go to a blood relative and that Grandma has already given her too much. Mom left them for me when I'm older, but I won't wear them—that's girl stuff."

I smirk at his words. However, I have no idea why Everly wouldn't wear them if mom gave them to her. Mom clearly thought she was more than worthy to keep them.

"Do you know where the jewelry box is?" I ask him.

"Yep, in the yellow box in the far cupboard. She kept them in the safe in the hotel for a while, but then we got robbed one night, so Mom put them in the cupboard in the shed and stacked boxes in front of it," he answers.

"The hotel got robbed?" I ask and Valarian nods.

"Yep, they didn't take anything though, just wrote *rogue whore* on the brick walls. Auntie Macey scared them off."

"Language! And you remember this?" I ask him, astounded.

"Uh huh, it was only last year, when Mom got her 5-star rating for the hotel, just before Christmas. Mom thinks it was another hotel owner. Auntie Macey smacked one in the head with her bat when they tried to get in the office area," Valarian laughs, making a swinging motion with his hands before he shrugs.

"And she didn't call the police?" I ask him.

"She did, but they laughed at her and said it was her problem, so Mom moved the jewelry from the safe—said it would be the first place they looked for valuables."

"And how do you know where she hid it?" I ask and Valarian drops his head.

"I accidentally knocked a box over and broke the jewelry box. Mom spent hours crying, trying to put it back together with glue. She wouldn't stop crying; she said it was Grandma's favorite possession," Valarian tells me, making my brows furrow.

"You made her cry?" I ask him, unable to imagine Everly crying.

"Yeah, but I don't think it was the jewelry box. I think it was 'cause I lost a stone out of one of the rings when it smashed. It was Grandma's mother's wedding ring. She said it was a priceless family heirloom. And the jewelry box was *given* to Grandma, so it must be the ring 'cause the box looked ugly," he says with a shrug while looking down at his hands in his lap.

"Do you think we can sneak in the back way?" I ask him.

"Back way of where?"

"The storage shed," I tell him.

"Like a secret agent?" he asks, and I chuckle when my phone starts ringing again.

"You should answer it. She's probably freaking out," Valarian states. I sigh and quickly answer it.

Everly's voice comes through the speaker. "Uh, where are you taking our son?" she asks. Valarian snickers.

"Father-son outing. Where are you?"

"I just got home. Zoe went into heat, so I had to call Marcus. Luckily, Macey is going to take Casey for the night because I feel exhausted today. Damn wet weather always makes me tired!"

"Well, we should be home before dinner," I tell her before turning the car around at the roundabout and heading for the storage locker.

"Where are you taking him? It's pouring, Valen; not suitable weather to be out and about! I heard on the radio it's going to get worse overnight, too!" Everly screeches through the phone.

"Father-son outing," I repeat, and she growls. I glance at Valarian in the mirror before pressing a finger to my lips. He giggles and nods.

"Fine, I'll start dinner, I guess. Oh, can you grab more milk and coffee on your way home? Oh, and Oreo ice cream?"

"Oreo ice cream?"

"Yeah, I feel like ice cream."

"But it's raining?" I ask her.

"Just get the ice cream, Valen!" she says.

"Fine, I'll go grocery shopping too, then. I love you," I tell her.

"I love you too. Don't forget my ice cream," Everly, hanging up.

The rain has eased off a little by the time we reached the hotel, but the parking lot is flooded, and the wind is horrendous. I drive around the back of the hotel, pulling up behind the event room where the storage locker is before grabbing the spare key from my glove box. The trees are bent over from the wind whistling past the car, and the storage locker door rattles loudly. Yeah, I can't take Valarian out in that. I sigh, not wanting to get out in this weather either.

"Yellow box?" I ask while turning to look at Valarian sitting in the back.

"Yes, it's in the brown cupboard, unless Mom moved it. It has boxes stacked in front of it. Maybe call and ask her."

"No, this is a surprise. You can't tell your mother," I remind him, and he nods.

I turn the car off and hold my pinkie out to him. "Pinkie, promise?"

"I can keep a secret," Valarian whines, but wraps his little pinkie around mine.

"And it isn't a secret; it's a surprise. You don't keep secrets from us."

"Isn't that the same thing?" Valarian asks.

"No because I'll be telling her—well, *asking* her—so it's a surprise."

"Sounds like a secret to me!" Valarian says, and I don't bother arguing with him. The kid would win.

"Wait here. I don't want you to get wet. The last thing I need is your mother going off at me for getting you sick," I tell him before shoving the door open and rushing out toward the storage locker.

It takes me a good thirty minutes of moving boxes before I get to the cupboard and find the yellow box he mentioned at the bottom of it. Taking the lid off, I nearly choke on my spit as I pull it out and wipe off the dust. Tears brim in my eyes as I chuckle. I always wondered what happened to this ugly thing. I made it in wood class the first year of high school and gave it to my father. Opening the lid, I see my name burned into the wood. Dad must have given it to her. I thought he threw it out.

It has a huge, gaudy-looking wooden flower on top. We were making Mother's Day boxes. Growing up, I always hated Mother's

Day because I didn't have mine around, so I always gave them to Dad. However, it's definitely broken, and I can see Everly had used superglue to put the splintered wood back together. Some bits are still broken and have gaps where she couldn't glue the pieces back together in it.

Biting my lip, I now know it wasn't the jewelry Everly was upset about. It was because she knew Mom treasured the box she kept the jewelry in. She had to have known, or she wouldn't have put it back together because it's the ugliest box I've ever seen and definitely not a work of art.

Suddenly, I feel glad I'm an Alpha because I'm not going anywhere with my carpentry skills, that's for sure. But she kept it. All these years, and she kept it. I chuckle and grab a towel, wrapping it around the box before tucking it under my arm and rushing back to the car. Opening the door quickly, I place it on the passenger seat before rushing back to lock the shed back up.

CHAPTER
EIGHTY-TWO

E verly
　　　Hours pass, and dinner is going cold while I wait for Valen and Valarian. Not that I made anything special; I was too tired and wanted to sleep, so I whipped up something simple, spaghetti with meat sauce.

However, Valen said he would be home before dinner and I finished cooking two hours ago. It's already 7:30 p.m. and the storm outside has only intensified. Lightning streaks across the gloomy sky, and there's not one star in sight; the clouds block out even the moon. Walking back into the living room, I snatch my phone off the coffee table and redial his number. The phone doesn't even ring, but instead goes straight to voicemail. Ok, now I'm starting to get worried.

Another 10 minutes, I pick up my phone again to call when it begins ringing in my hand. A private number shows up and I sigh. Finally, he thought to call back! Only, when I answer, I hear an unexpected feminine voice.

"Hello, is this Everly's phone?" comes my mother's voice.

Shocked, I pull the phone from my ear to look at the screen before placing it back.

"Mom?" I ask.

"Oh, thank the Goddess, I thought your receptionist gave me another wrong number," she says. I don't know what to say; it's one thing seeing her the day of the Alpha meeting, but I find myself suddenly lost for words on the phone. I no longer know how to speak to the woman who gave birth to me. So much has changed. I have changed. My family are suddenly strangers to me. I no longer identify myself with them anymore.

"Are you there?" she asks.

"Uh, yes, sorry. Why are you calling?" I blurt without thinking. She has never called before, not even when she promised to when I turned up on her doorstep that stormy night. So many broken promises—relationships now non-existent.

"I, um, I wanted to check on you after the incident with the rogues. Your father tried to see you, but your mate wouldn't let him in."

"Well, you could have visited; he let Ava in," I tell her, and she falls quiet. I find it hard to make chit-chat with her. The silence as we try to think of what to say is awkward.

"So, how have you been?" she asks, and I bite my lip, hesitant to answer. Does she genuinely care? Something bothers me with how she called out of the blue.

"Yeah, good—waiting for Valen and Valarian to get home," I tell her.

"He looks so much like his father," she says, and I nod, moving into the kitchen and covering their dinners.

"So, uh, how is Ava?" I ask, trying to divert the conversation.

"Ava is Ava. She's being difficult."

"And why is that?"

"Because she wants to go away for university; she doesn't want to take over the pack," my mother says.

"Well, find someone else to take over then," I tell her, looking at the clock as the minutes tick by. I'm starting to worry that something has happened because I've heard no word. Placing the phone on the loudspeaker, I search for Valarian's tracking device on his watch.

"It's not that simple, and you know that," she answers.

I watch it load before seeing he's at the mall, and sigh when I see it leading toward the parking lot and know they must be on the way home now.

"Are you listening?" my mother asks.

"Yes, still here," I tell her, turning the loudspeaker off. "Sorry, I was checking an email," I lie. I have no idea why I lied, but it isn't like it's any of her business.

"There's another thing I wanted to talk to you about."

"What's that?" I ask.

"Your father said you put a petition in to change the laws surrounding the rogues."

"Yes, interested in signing it?" I ask, knowing I need at least four Alpha signatures.

"No, but you should pull it. You're drawing unwelcome attention. Your father nearly had a heart attack when it hit his email. Withdraw the application, Everly," my mother says.

I laugh, shocked by her words.

"I'm being serious. You have no idea what's at stake!" she snaps.

"Did Dad put you up to this?"

"No. Yes... But he's correct. Are you hoping to start a war? It will change nothing. No Alpha will sign that petition. It will change nothing but cause issues within the city."

"I am not pulling the petition, Mom. I don't care who it upsets. It's time things change. This is a good thing," I tell her, unable to believe that the first time she calls in five years is only because she wants something—no, needs something—from me.

"It's reckless and will cause trouble for your father. You have no idea what you're getting yourself into. You've been Luna for all of five minutes and are making poor choices already!" she says, and I scoff.

"I know exactly the trouble it will cause in the city, and it's why

I'm doing it. Try living in the rogue's shoes for once, Mother. Without your credit cards or the pack's money, you wouldn't last one day. Nothing you say will get me to pull that petition, so jump on board and accept it. I don't care for your reputation or Dad's. You never cared for mine," I snap back at her.

"YOU ARE GOING TO START A WAR!" she screams.

"War?" I laugh. "I've been at war with the packs since I was seventeen. Packs don't scare me, Mother. I learned to live on my own without a pack. Instead, I built an empire. I sure as hell don't need a pack because I have something far more valuable than a pack of mindless idiots that follow orders from an Alpha that has no care for his people. I have a family, and families fight for each other. You may not have fought for me, but I will fight for mine!" I tell her before hanging up.

I curse, annoyed she would call me just to get me to pull a petition and berate me. Shaking my head, I'm about to try and call Valen when I hear the front door open and close.

"Finally!" I sigh with relief as I walked toward the hall. Valarian comes rushing toward me excitedly, soaking wet.

"It's raining," Valarian says, and I chuckle.

"I can tell. Where did you and your father go?" I ask him just as Valen steps past me, pecking my cheek as he heads for the kitchen with grocery bags.

"Uh, we went to get groceries," Valarian says, looking around me to look at his father, who's unpacking the grocery bags.

"Where else did you go?" I ask him when Valen calls out to him.

"Go get out of your wet clothes, quick. Mom made dinner," he says, and Valarian rushes off before I can question him more. I purse my lips, watching him run off.

"How was your day?" he asks before I can turn my interrogation on why they took so long to him.

"Good, yours?"

Valen shrugs and turns to the microwave to heat Valarian's dinner.

"Worked at the homeless shelter; you should come by tomorrow so I can show you around," he says, and I nod while he rummages through another bag, pulling out my ice cream and tossing it to me.

"Oh, you remembered," I tell him, placing it in the freezer. Yet Valen is being awfully quiet, making me wonder what he's up to. I start to ask when Valarian rushes out in dry clothes and sits at the table. Valen pulls his dinner from the microwave and takes it over to him while I watch them both.

"You two are up to something," I tell them, and Valarian looks up at his father. I narrow my eyes at them both.

"What?" Valen asks.

"Well, first of all, he usually tells me all about his day when I see him, and I got vague answers; you were both two hours late; and it doesn't take two hours to get two bags of groceries from a store that's two minutes from here," I tell him.

"Hm, well, care to explain why our son has a tracking device on his watch?" Valen retorts.

"You know why. Besides, it's for his safety, so don't change the subject. Where were you both?" I told him.

"Shopping," Valen says, and Valarian nods his head.

"Fine, don't tell me. I'll check his tracker data later," I smirk, folding my arms across my chest.

"No need, I made him leave it in the car, but you'll know soon enough anyway," Valen chuckles, and so does Valarian.

Valen returns to the kitchen and heats his own dinner up along with mine, and we sit down and eat. After dinner, Valen stays busy working on his laptop while Valarian does his homework. Bored with watching TV, I walk over to see what Valen's working on.

"What are you doing?" I asked, peering over his shoulder.

"The design company wants to know what I want on the sign."

I look at his design. It looks good but is kind of dull, as "Mountainview Homeless shelter" is rather predictable.

"You don't like it?" Valen sighs.

"How about you let me design it?"

476

"You want to help? What about your petition?"

"I can do both. Is this the designer you're going through? I do know a better designer who's local and has a cheaper signage manufacturer," I tell him.

"Who is your designer? The same one that did the murals along the restaurant walls?" he asks, and I nod.

"Yep, I know she would love to do it."

"She?"

"Me," I tell him.

"Wait, you did the murals in the restaurant?"

I nod. "Yes, and the one in the pool area along the fence. We couldn't find anyone to do them back then, and I used to paint. Your mother found one of my drawings and asked me to have a go at doing a mural. I did one, then she got me to paint all of them," I laugh.

"You don't paint anymore?"

"No time anymore, but I was going to ask if I could do a mural out in front of the homeless shelter anyway, so I can design your sign and send it off to get it made?" I tell him. He thinks for a second before nodding.

"Any other cool things you can do?"

I shrug. "No, but Macey did all the welded statues in the gardens," I tell him.

"Macey can weld?"

"Yep, she used to do odd jobs as a welder/metal fabricator around the city," I tell him.

"Huh, I didn't know that," he murmurs thoughtfully, and I shrug before messing Valarian's hair. I glance at his homework to see he's finished and now just doodling on the edges of the paper.

"Right, that's sorted then. When you can, if you give me a list of what you want, I'll order it in," Valen says, and I smile. I haven't painted in so long, so I'm excited about the challenge.

Hearing my phone ping with a message, I check it. I don't recognize the number, but I know undoubtedly where it came from by the statement it holds.

Think, Everly, you could destroy everything you worked so hard for, pull the petition, or the packs will come for you.

I growl, annoyed at the threat, and Valen looks over at me.

"What's wrong?"

"Nothing, I'll sort it out," I tell him before placing the phone back down and walking off to get Valarian ready for bed.

CHAPTER
EIGHTY-THREE

Valen

All night, I can tell something's wrong with Everly, feel her stress through the bond. I can also feel she doesn't want to worry me about whatever is bothering her. She's so used to dealing with her struggles herself, I think she forgets she can actually share them and that she's never a burden to me.

"Are you going to stop by the homeless shelter today?" I ask her as she gathers her handbag and keys.

"Yes. I'll stop by after I see Emily. Any news from the patrols about any more forsaken sightings, or anything about her son?" she asks me. I really wish I had an answer for her, but I don't. We have no leads, no scent trails, nothing. It's like they vanished altogether.

"No, but as soon as I hear anything, I promise you will be the first to know. There have been talks about a city meeting in the coming weeks to figure out something to do about the forsaken sightings and missing rogue situation. Pack members are becoming nervous, and it might also be a good time to bring up the rogue issues?" I tell her, and Everly nods.

"Yes, let's hope the petition goes well, and I get a date to be heard sometime today," Everly sighs and rubs her temples when her phone goes off in her handbag. She pulls it out, glances at the screen, and shakes her head.

"What's wrong?" I ask, watching her as I tie my shoelaces.

"Nothing. Mom has been pestering me to pull the petition and drop the rogue issue," she says, and I notice she sounds tired. She *looks* tired, actually. And I noticed she was tossing and turning all night in her sleep.

"What did she say?"

"That I would start a war," she says with a shrug.

"Funny, your father said something along those lines at the hospital," I tell her. Everly chews her lip nervously.

"What war, though?" we say simultaneously, and she giggles.

"Jinx," I tell her while getting to my feet.

"I have no idea. Mom called me last night," Everly explains.

"So that's why you've been in a weird mood, then," I tell her while wrapping my arms around her shoulders.

"Maybe I can try to get a hold of Ava. I'm not sure what's happening, but even your father thought something was going on behind the scenes with my dad," she tells me.

"Try your sister and come see me at the homeless shelter when you aren't busy. I'll be there all day; I have contractors coming to assess the damage," I tell her. I'm dreading the bill for that.

"Well, you're going in the opposite direction, so I'll run Valarian to school," she tells me before calling out to our son.

"Yeah, I am coming," Valarian growls, making me raise an eyebrow at his grumpy mood.

"What's wrong with you?" I ask him.

"I don't want to go to school. I want to come to the homeless shelter," he pouts.

"Not today, Maybe on the weekend. Besides, there's too much machinery and people working there at the moment. It isn't safe," I explain, and he sighs. Everly quickly fixes his school tie and blazer while I place his lunch in his bag.

Waiting for them to leave, I quickly clean the kitchen, packing up the school supplies Everly left out. I didn't want to say anything, but when she's rushing around, she tends to forget to put stuff away and leaves it out. It's a pet peeve, but damn, it makes me flustered. Finally leaving, I catch the elevator to the underground parking lot. But I don't go straight to the homeless shelter. Instead, I head to the jeweler.

Valarian said Everly doesn't like diamonds, which I had wanted to put in my mother's ring, but Valarian wanted to pick. And he chose Serendibite—he liked the color of it. The only issue is sourcing one to fit in the ring because Serendibite is a rare mineral and hard to source. The jeweler only had one, but it was tiny, and the ring I want it in would need to be altered to hold the stone.

Once I get to the mall, I walk up the side alley where the jeweler is, pushing the door open. The bell sounds to alert Dion of customers. He's around my age, and we went to school together.

"Hey, Dion, any luck?" I ask, closing the door behind me and walking toward the counter. Dion is looking at his laptop, chin propped on his hand; his glasses are perched on his nose as he stares at the screen. He sighs, pulling his glasses off and placing them on the glass display cabinet.

"Your son *had* to pick Serendibite," he chuckles while shaking his head and running his hand through his gelled hair. He leans back in his chair, folding his tattooed arms across his chest. Dion looks more like a biker than a jeweler.

"Can't source one?" I ask.

"Oh, I can get one, but are you sure you want to use that ring? Your mother's ring? I can melt it down and remake a nicer one using the gold?"

I shake my head, and he sighs.

"Well then, you best get your wallet out then, Alpha. Serendibite is $18,000 a carat, and the earliest I can get it is in six weeks. Then, I'll have to cut it to fit. I can only find raw material so far," he tells me. I did already research it last night while Everly was asleep and knew it would be costly before I walked in because they're rare and in scarce supply.

"Invoice me and I'll transfer it. Also, the band, you said it was thick enough to engrave?" I ask. Dion nods. I pull the piece of paper from my pocket and hand it to him, and he reads it.

"So much for big, bad Alpha, you big softy," he smiles.

"Send me the invoice and call when it's ready," I laugh, turning and heading for the door.

Driving to the homeless shelter, I feel prepared to get my hands dirty no matter how much that thought makes me shudder. What I'm not prepared for is to find the roof completely ripped off from the storm, as if it had been peeled away. My jaw drops when I step out of the car to see a huge cleanup. The structure still stands. However, the inside is flooded, and I groan with annoyance. Just what I need.

The storm is the worst we've had in years. The damage I can see on the main street is shocking enough, but this side of town seems to have taken a more brutal hit. It makes me wonder how Everly's hotel is. No doubt it will have been smashed by the wild weather too.

Walking over to one of the project managers, I find him ordering around his leading hand and a few supervisors, directioning them to designated, specific areas to start the cleanup. When he notices me, Bill turns around to face me.

"Alpha," he nods, stroking his beard before twirling the end through his fingers. "So, do you want the good news or the bad news first?" he asks.

"Is there any good news?"

"There is. The building didn't collapse," Bill states.

"Is that the good news?" I ask, and he laughs.

"Yep, now the bad news. This just added another month to the timeline and raised the cost."

"Anything else?"

"Yep, the sewer overflowed out the back, and it seems the entire city's shit washed into the far playground in the rear," he tells me.

And there's my queue to leave because... shit? Naah, I ain't touching, smelling, or going within the vicinity of the sewers out back.

"Got you some gumboots," Bill says brightly, and I shake my head.

"Nope, just remembered I have an emergency meeting," I tell him, and he laughs.

"I thought you were willing to get your hands dirty for once, Alpha?" Bill taunts.

"*Important* meeting," I tell him.

"Yeah, with who?"

He knows I'm full of shit, no pun intended, and is determined to call me out on it.

"With someone important."

"More important than the Blood Alpha?" he asks, scratching his chin and squinting at me. I swear he twirls that beard on purpose because he knows it irritates me. I want scissors to cut it off.

"Of course; far more important," I tell him.

"Name?" he challenges, and his eyes crinkle around the edges while he watches me try to get out of helping.

"Luna!" I tell him.

"Ah, nice save, Alpha. I see, hiding behind our Luna now," he laughs. "I'll be sure to tell her that next time I see her," he laughs before motioning for me to go.

Yep—blood, puke, I can kinda manage those. Shit? Nope! I draw the line at fecal matter.

"I'll be sure to send Marcus over. He would love to help," I tell Bill as I climb back into the driver's seat. Marcus had called me early this morning when he was on his way to get Casey from Macey's. Zoe's heat had finished, although she would be remaining home today to rest. Marcus said he was ready to come back to work, and I now have the perfect job as my replacement.

"Siri, call Marcus," I tell my car stereo as I pull away from the curb. Marcus answers as I pull into traffic and stop at a traffic light.

"Hey, what's up? I was actually about to call you," he says.

"Can you do me a favor?" I ask him.

"Depends," he says warily, and I try to suppress my laughter.

"I'm supposed to help at the homeless shelter, but something has come up. Bill needs extra men, so can you grab Tatum and a few others and go help him in the rear playground to help clean up?"

"Yeah, sure thing. Just give me an hour."

"I'll let Bill know," I tell him.

"Sweet. I don't suppose you're going anywhere near the council chambers?" Marcus asks.

"No, I was headed to the hotel. Why?"

"Everly got a rejection letter. I just dropped Casey off to Zoe, and she said Everly is on the warpath. I was about to head over there."

"I'll go; I'm turning around now," I tell him before screeching into a U-turn and earning some blaring horns from other cars. I curse. This is not good.

CHAPTER
EIGHTY-FOUR

Everly

I take a bite out of my muffin, looking at Zoe, who looks like absolute crap. I chuckle and shake my head at her slumped form draped across the table. I came here to check on her and bring her some breakfast. Marcus had gone to collect Casey, so Macey could take Zoe's shift today, and I now understand why she can't work.

"Stop laughing," she groans before getting up and walking to the fridge with her melted bag of frozen peas.

"Ew, throw them away," I tell her, taking another bite from my muffin. She snatches another bag of frozen vegetables, stuffs them down the front of her pajama shorts, and sighs. I snort as she awkwardly walks back to her chair and sits on it.

"My vagina feels chaffed. Is that possible?" Zoe groans, resting her head on the tabletop. "It's like he broke it," she whines, and I laugh at her.

"So unfair. Marcus has a great time while here I am stuffing frozen vegetables down my pants because I feel like I have carpet burn where I shouldn't have carpet burn," she growls.

485

"I'm eating," I tell her, shaking my muffin at her, not wanting that image in my head.

"Sorry, but let me whine; I have a literal fire-crotch situation going on here."

"Again, I am eating. You are the little sister that over shares; I don't need to know what's going on with your lady bits," I tell her when my phone pings, telling me I've received an email.

"Could be worse," Zoe rambles, but her words fall on deaf ears as I pull my phone out and see the email from the city council.

One step forward and two steps back—always the same shit on repeat. A growl slips out of me, startling Zoe, as I read over the rejection letter. When I see the signing Alphas, I wrap my muffin back up in its wrapper, and Zoe looks at me.

"What's wrong?" she asks, instantly alert.

"It was rejected."

"What was?"

"My petition for the rogues," I tell her, getting up from my seat.

"What are you doing?" she asks as I dump the rest of my coffee in the sink. Only, when I do, the mug shatters in my hand. I blink at the blood pooling in my palm.

"Shit!" I curse under my breath, picking up the broken pieces of glass and dumping them in the bin before snatching some hand towels out from under the sink. I rinse my hand, pulling a shard of thick glass from my palm before wrapping it in the towel. Zoe shrieks, seeing blood dripping from my hand, yet I feel nothing; I'm distracted from the pain—pissed off that my father would sabotage me like this. I quickly wrap a clean towel around my hand before snatching my handbag off the table.

"Everly?" Zoe says, reaching for my hand.

"I'm going to try to fix it," I tell her.

"Wait, you need to calm down. Just wait, I'll come with you," she says, hopping up and wincing. I shake my head.

"Marcus will be here soon with Casey. And you have to freeze your rug burn," I tell her, not realizing what I said as I storm out. I rush down the steps and around the side of the building before climbing into my truck.

Reversing out of my parking spot, I navigate through the full lot before jumping into the traffic and heading for the council chambers.

Finding a parking spot takes me twenty minutes when I arrive, only adding to my pent-up anger. After slamming the car into park, I grab my bag off the front passenger seat and storm into the brick building, nearly ripping my arm off as I yank the door open and shove my way through the security checkpoint. Guards rush toward me, and I'm not sure if it's the furious look on my face or the fact my hand is dripping blood everywhere. However, one growl from me makes them stop in their tracks as my aura flies out and batters them.

They stand struck, stunned, and blinking at me. It startles me momentarily before I shrug. *Thank you, mate bond!* I think as I move toward the front desk to the clerk behind it, who's on the phone chatting away. She hangs up and gives me a warm smile that slips off her face immediately when she sees mine. I try to relax my facial features, only realizing there's no hiding my tension when she speaks.

"Luna," she stutters, and I try to remember this woman isn't the cause of my anger. I glance at her name tag.

"Hi, Amanda, I need to speak to someone about my rejected petition," I tell her, leaning over the counter and showing the case number on my email. She quickly taps away at her keyboard.

"It says you needed four Alphas to sign off on it before it could be heard," she says.

"I have four Alpha signatures," I tell her, showing her mine and Valen's, along with the Alpha and Luna from the southeast borders. Amanda shakes her head.

"Yours and the Alpha Valen's don't count since you are the one filing the petition," she tells me.

"Since when?" I snap at her before sucking in a deep breath. Not Amanda's fault, I remind myself. "I'm sorry. Is there someone I can speak to about it?" I ask, trying desperately to put a smile on my face.

"I can see if my supervisor is in?" she offers, and I nod, my fingers drumming impatiently on the desk.

She makes a call and turns away from me. I watch her a moment before glancing at the clock behind her on the wall. I need to get back to sign off on a delivery in an hour.

"Sir? I have the Blood Luna here. She wants to speak with you."

I blink at what she called me. Hearing them call Valen that is one thing, but me?

"I understand, sir. I'll let her know," she says before hanging up the phone. She turns in her seat and smiles apologetically at me.

"He's in a meeting and said you'll have to book an appointment," she says, shrinking in her seat. I purse my lips. This is some bullshit! I can guarantee they wouldn't pull this shit with my mate.

"Your supervisor's name, please?" I ask.

"Scott Peters, Ma'am."

I click my tongue. Of course, he won't see me—he's a member of my father's pack.

"Thank you," I tell her, turning on my heel to leave and heading for the doors. The security staff quickly opens the little gate I barged through on my way in, and I see another guard waiting there with a bandage in his hand. Sniffing the air, I can tell he's one of Alpha Nixon's pack members. He nods to me when I take it from him.

"Thank you," I murmur, pushing the door open with my shoulder. Getting back to my car, I stare out the windshield, trying to think. My father and mother rejected the petition. That stings more than it should for some reason, but seeing my father's signature on the email really gets to me. It's one thing for them to kick me out, going without knowing if I was alive or dead for years. Now, they want to publicly join the crusade against rogues.

Even after all these years, he can't do one decent thing—not even for his disgraced daughter. This is bigger than me, it isn't for me, and still, he rejected it. It's like he's shunning me all over again. When will I be enough? I blink the tears away.

Valarie's words come to my ears. *"They don't deserve your tears!"* Knowing she's right, I sniffle and wipe them away. I don't need them; I proved that. But that doesn't mean I don't want them or miss what I once had. I want Valarian to know where I came from, to know the parents who raised me before they shunned me.

Starting my car, I head back to the hotel. Halfway home, my anger is still festering beneath the surface though, my emotions trying to strangle me. *My workers don't deserve my anger, I think to myself.*

Yanking the car off to the side of the road, I drum my fingers on the steering wheel, debating what my next move should be.

"Fuck it!" I growl, glancing in the side mirrors. When no cars are coming, I crank a U-turn heading in the opposite direction from the hotel and floor my beast. The engine growls just like me as I head back to the one place I haven't been to in years—I head to the place I once called home, to the very man who shunned me.

He doesn't deserve my tears, but he fucking deserves my anger, which is what he will be met with. When I get to the border patrols, they wave me down to pull over, but I flip them off, laughing my head off as my truck smashes through their boom gate, ripping it off before heading to the packhouse. If my father isn't already alerted to the border breach, he sure as hell will hear me coming with the way the engine roars as I put my foot down, heading straight for the center of his pack land—what should have been *my* pack land!

CHAPTER
EIGHTY-FIVE

V alen

While caught in traffic on the way to the council chambers, I try to call Everly repeatedly. Her anger is all-consuming, and I'm worried she might do something reckless. As her fury becomes too much through the bond, I find myself becoming angered by it. The traffic back-up only adds to my anxiety.

Honking my horn, I try to see around the cars ahead to see what's holding up traffic. Only then do I notice the police lights flashing and realize it's a damn accident. How? It's a straight stretch of road! How does someone take out the only damn traffic light pole in the center median strip? I shake my head, annoyed.

Drumming my fingers impatiently on the steering wheel, I try to call her again, but no answer. Yet, her anger slowly simmers down as I feel anger replaced with something else—she's overwhelmed. Her emotions scattering all over the place make me feel manic. That's one of the downsides of the bond. I feel close to her, but I also don't feel like I have complete control over my own emotions. I've been waiting for ten minutes, and we haven't moved an inch. However, when I feel through the bond she's moving further away, my heart races, wondering where she could be going. Her anger has returned full force—maybe even angrier than before—and my heart races and thumps wildly in my chest as panic sets in.

Sticking my head out the window, I see the tow truck start hauling the wrecked vehicle away. Surprisingly, the buffoon driver survived, but he's clearly intoxicated. He's out of the car, stumbling over his feet, when I notice Officer Derrick dragging him into his squad car's back seat. Yes! He's one of my guys!

Sticking my fingers in my mouth, I whistle to grab his attention. He looks up at the line of cars backed up, and I open the mind-link.

"Clear the other side of the road. I need to get my mate," I tell him.

He nods, jumping in his car before turning the sirens on and pushing into the oncoming traffic while workers try to remove the busted light pole. He leaves his sirens on as I pull into the oncoming traffic that has begun to move to the shoulder of the road before coming up behind him and following behind his car as he forces the traffic to move.

Once I'm on a clear stretch, he moves over so I can overtake him. I press my foot down on the gas, heading for the council chambers. Yet, the closer I get, the more I feel the need to keep going. Passing the council chambers, I didn't see her truck parked and curse, knowing where she went. There's only one pack in the direction I feel the tether forcing me towards, and that's Shadow Pack—her father's pack.

This woman will be the death of me. *She's going to give me a damn heart attack,* I think as I race to get to her. Coming to the gated community, I slow down, but the guards aren't posted like usual, and the boom gate has been smashed all over the ground; splintered wood in chunks litter the road. Fuck!

Shaking my head, I head toward the packhouse. After a few more minutes of me tearing up the blacktop, I arrive at Alpha John's street to find people lining it, all looking toward the packhouse. People jump out of the way of my car as I drive up the road. I soon find out why they're staring.

Everly, Ava, and John are having a confrontation.

Everly

The men from the border patrol shift instantly, chasing after my car. I don't stop. Instead, I navigate around the suburb I haven't been through in years. I end up driving right past my old street, which is a cul-de-sac.

"Shit!" I curse. Slamming my foot down on the brake, my truck comes to a screeching halt before I shove it in reverse, making the border patrols chasing me skid along the road and scatter out of my way as I speed backwards. Spinning the wheel, I floor it again.

Howls ring out loudly, alerting pack members to the intruder. I laugh maniacally. I'm not an intruder but, by birthright, their true Alpha. Driving up the street, I begin to slow as déjà vu hits me. The street looks the same, the houses precisely the same. I pull into the driveway and hit the brakes just in time to avoid smashing into the ass end of my father's black Mustang parked in the driveway; my old beasty would have destroyed it. Not that I would have minded seeing my bull bar imprinted on its backend.

My father's guards circle around the car, growling and snarling, but I pay them no mind as I toss the door open and hop out.

I am furious—murderous, even. Never in my life have I been so damn angry. No one, not even Valen, has pulled anger out of me like this. It briefly comes to mind that maybe it's years of pent-up anger, and my father is the tipping point that opened up the floodgates, inadvertently unleashing something else—my aura!

Slamming my door, I silently apologize to my beloved car for mistreating it. Wolves have circled it, but I can't be bothered to engage with them. Recognizing me, or maybe recognizing my mate's pack scent—scratch that, *my* pack scent; I am their Luna now, making them also mine—they back up. I stalk around my car toward the front door, though their eyes track my every move. Stepping onto the lawn, the front door bursts open and my mother steps out, her shock dominating her features as she cups her mouth with her hands.

"Everly?" she murmurs as I move toward her, the men following at my heels, ready to protect their Luna if need be. My father's stomping footsteps are heard from outside as he storms through the house. The screen door creaks as it opens, and it bangs hard against the wall on the porch.

"What is the meaning of this, Everly? My border patrol said you smashed through my barriers?"

"No 'hello', Father?" I ask, stopping at the bottom steps as he stomps down them to stop in front of me.

"You have no business being here, Everly," he booms, shaking a fist in anger at his side.

"I wouldn't be here except you signed my rejection letter for the fucking petition I handed in yesterday!" I yell back at him just as the door opens again, and I see Ava step out.

Oh, was she a defiant piece of work! Give him hell, sis! Ava waves her fingers at me, and I smirk as she strolls down the steps, slapping my mother's hands away as she tries to stop her. Ava smirks like she's been waiting for this showdown all her life and wants a front-row seat.

"Get inside, Ava!" my father snaps at her as she walks past him to lean on the hood of his car. He growls at her when she doesn't listen.

"Sign the petition, Dad," I tell him, diverting his attention away from her. He turns his head to glare at me and takes a step forward. The shock on his face when I don't move makes his eyebrows rise and almost disappear into his hairline.

Ava laughs, falling into fits of giggles holding her stomach, and my father snarls at her before nodding to one of his men. That's when I feel a strange tingling sensation rushing over me. I laugh at the realization that he tried to use his aura on me, and it had no effect whatsoever!

One of Dad's warriors, Lance, shifts back to grab Ava and drag her inside. Her shriek has me turning my head from my father to look at him.

"Do *not* touch my sister," I warn him. When I see his hand reach for her arm, he freezes, glancing at my father, who waves him off.

"We can discuss this inside," he says to me before turning his back on me and heading for the steps.

"No. Here will do, Alpha John," I tell him, and he stops.

He pauses on the step as he turns to face me; my mother looks terrified behind him. He glances around the cul-de-sac, and I turn to see what he's looking at. Pack members have flooded the sidewalk as they emerged from their houses to see the commotion. I shake my head.

Same shit all over again. All he cares about is his reputation and how he looks to others.

"This is a family matter, Everly. We will talk inside. No need to air our dirty laundry for the world to see," he growls, his eyes flickering black.

I laugh and shake my head. "What, now I'm family? Funny, last I checked, you shunned me and banished me from the pack along with your grandson—the Blood Alpha's son!" I tell him.

My father growls, his eyes darting around to his pack members who watch on.

"Inside!" he spits through gritted teeth.

"No, you won't save face this time. Now do the right thing and sign off on the petition," I tell him.

"This debate will not be settled in front of my pack!" he snarls, stomping back down the steps.

"You mean *my* pack? I am the rightful heir to this pack!" I tell him, and murmurs break out around us at the challenge.

"Sign the petition, John, or you leave me no choice," I tell him.

Despite my blistering hot rage at him, I am surprised at how cold and calm my voice comes out.

Ava laughs, and my mother's mouth opens and closes like a fish as she looks nervously between us. The sound of screeching tires and the roar of an engine tearing through the streets can be heard easily as the car drifts through the streets. I know it must be Valen; I can feel him getting closer to me through the bond. His panicked voice is flitting through my head, wanting to know what's going on and if I'm alright, yet I can't answer without becoming distracted.

My father laughs. "You dare come here and threaten me?" he growls.

"It's not a threat, Alpha. Threats mean you can back out, mere words, not actions. I intend to do what I say. Words are of no use to me. Actions are. So, final warning," I tell him.

He laughs and shakes his head, stepping down the last step. Now he's pissed off. But I won't back down—not this time. I'm not a little girl anymore. I'm not a child. And if there's one thing being on my own for so long showed me, it's that I don't need a pack to fight for me. I can stand on my own two feet and still succeed.

He scoffs, folding his arms across his chest. "Think, Everly, just because you have Alpha Valen behind you now doesn't mean I will submit. Your mate doesn't scare me."

"I don't need him to challenge you—and I would never ask him to—but as the rightful heir to this pack, I have every right to challenge you for *my* title. Now sign the damn petition. This isn't about me or you. It's the right thing to do!"

"They are rogues for a reason, Everly. You can't expect us to suddenly grant them back their rights for their misdoings," he states. Whispers break out from the crowd that has gathered. Turning, I see most of them are in agreement with my father, which just makes this even more disgusting. They're sheep, all of them.

"Misdoings? They are rogue for having a fucking child, the same as all of you here. The only difference is they were banished for who fathered them, their children then forced to live in poverty and with the weight of their parent's so-called misdeeds on their shoulders, labeling them for something that shouldn't be shameful," I tell them.

"How can you say that? They are home-wreckers, whores," comes a voice from the crowd. I look around and see Amber's surly face sticking out in the crowd. I turn to look at her as she steps out from behind my father's Beta, who is also her father and my family's neighbor.

"So, what does that make Micah?" I ask her. "You dare label my friend because your mate stuck his dick in someone that wasn't you? Sorry to tell you, Amber, but clearly you aren't aware how a child is made. You seem to have it stuck in your head that Micah tripped and fell into her vagina." My crude words earn some whispers and a couple of laughs, but I'm done being slut-shamed, done hearing the term rogue whore.

"She should know better!" Amber screams, her face turning red.

"And so should he. They had sex, and she got pregnant. Yet, she's punished for it. How is that fair? How is any of it fair?" I ask. Fools, the lot of them. It makes me laugh.

"I could call out," I look around at all the staring faces, "easily *ten* men here I know that fathered an illegitimate child!" I yell, glancing around to see some men stiffen.

"You call us whores for raising the children you turned your backs on, yet we are the deadbeats? The scum of the city? The ones labeled? So where are all your labels, huh? Punishing your own children for something they had no part in. They never asked to exist— that was the decision of two consenting adults that had sex—yet you shame them, too, for who their mother is."

"They made that mistake! They brought it on themselves! We are all taught the same thing: to save ourselves for our mates! I did the right thing, yet your friend has a child with my mate!" Amber screams at me.

"No, Amber, she had sex and got pregnant! Don't stand here and make yourself out to be better than her, just because no one here is willing to talk about the fact that the Beta's daughter was also the school bike. It doesn't make you any better just because you didn't get knocked up!"

"How dare you, I am the Beta's–"

"Whore? Half the football team ran through you from what I remember from school, but let's not mention that," I tell her.

"And let's not forget half the school! Daddy must be *so proud*," Ava chimes in behind me. Woah, clearly, these two aren't friends anymore.

"Ava, stay out of it!" my father snaps at her, looking lethal. Seconds later, Valen's car squeals as he drifts around the corner at the end of the street. Everyone on the road jumps out of his way as his car screeches to a stop in front of my father's house.

He jumps out of his car and growls, and everyone jumps back as my mate stalks toward us, only to stop when Ava keeps talking.

"Why? It's the truth. What Everly says is the truth! You all shunned my sister—your future Alpha—because she had a kid. Well, joke's on you, isn't it? Because it turns out she isn't a rogue whore, and is mated to the most notorious Alpha in the city, the very man who fathered her child," Ava says, pushing off the car to stand beside me as I confront my father and the pack that should have been mine. "But you knew that, didn't you, father? I knew it. We all knew it. Only one bloodline has those eyes," she continues.

I turn to face my father, who does his best to look away. I glance at my mother, who looks down, confirming her words.

"Can't have that, can we, *Dad*? Daddy's little girl sleeping with her father's rival? So instead, you shun her, sweep her disgrace under the rug," Ava says. I press my lips in a line. Her words sting. What I'm not expecting is for him to admit it, especially in front of Valen.

"Of course, I fucking knew! Do you think I didn't check hotel security cameras when neither of you returned home? I knew exactly where you were and whose room you were in. Who do you think had them wiped?" he bellows. "You ruined everything. You had one job, Everly, and you fucking disobeyed me." His face is red with fury. "You nearly cost me my pack!"

My brows furrow at his words, which make no sense to me whatsoever. Me having a child was the downfall of his pack? However, upon hearing my father's words, Valen growls before taking a mighty step forward and swinging at my father. My father, blinded by his rage, doesn't see it coming—or at least, by the time he does, he has no chance to block it—and Valen's fist connects with his face.

CHAPTER
EIGHTY-SIX

My father stumbles back, blood spurting from his broken nose, as Valen swings again. The impact knocks my father down before my mate pounces on him, raining blow after blow. My father curls up, trying to block the punches. My father's warriors, the ones that chased me here, race toward Valen as he pummels my father.

My father snarls, blocking the next hit and punching Valen in the ribs, then splitting Valen's eyebrow open with his next hit. My heart races as my father's wolves circle around us, trying to get to Valen without attacking my father.

Valen punches my father again before my father lifts his leg and kicks Valen in the chest. My mother screams as they continue the fight for supremacy. Valen is forced back and is now open, vulnerable. The wolves charge toward him, and I gasp, flinging myself in their way.

"STAND DOWN!" I scream, and my aura erupts outward. It washes over them, and they all freeze where they stand. The realization that my command worked on them shocks me. I suppose I *am* technically their true Alpha; however, I still didn't think my command would have an effect on my father's pack, since I'm no longer a member.

Valen snarls, and my father goes to tackle him when Ava shoves herself between them. Both are breathing heavily in their rage, and I can feel that Valen is on the verge of shifting. I grab his arm, pushing him away while Ava and my father stand off. She is tiny between the two Alphas, and if they attack each other again, she would get caught in the crossfire and so would I. Thankfully, my mother rushes down the steps, tears streaking her face as she grabs my father's arm, tugging him back.

"You knew I had a child?" Valen snarls behind me and stalks toward my father again. My hand hits his chest as he goes to attack him. Yes, he has every right to be pissed at my father, but this isn't his fight. We are also severely outnumbered. This wasn't supposed to happen, though the information that he knew all along is shocking. I don't want this to become a fight; not for Valen, anyway. *I* came here, and I will not look weak by hiding behind my mate.

My father shrugs my mother's hand off and wipes his nose with the back of his own hand, then spits blood on the ground. "Of course, I knew. I wasn't about to hand over my daughter to the likes of you to use against me," my father snarls.

"But it's alright that you try to pawn your other daughter off to him years later," I scoff.

"Yes, to clean up the mess you made! All you had to do was have the abortion, Everly. Instead, you've put my entire pack at risk of breaking the treaty. How was I supposed to know Valen would turn out to be your mate!" my father snarls.

"What fucking treaty? I had a baby! A son! A precious little boy— your grandson. You didn't just punish me, you punished him! You punished my son because of who his father is?"

"Yes, because you were promised to another! Your future was planned out, and you ruined it all!" my father screams at me.

"John!" my mother gasps behind him.

"To whom?" Valen demands with an angry growl. My father glares at him before turning his attention back to me.

"You have done enough damage, Everly. Now get off my pack lands," my father says, turning to walk inside.

"Sign the petition, Dad! You owe me this!" I tell him, and he stops. His entire back tenses as he turns to face me.

"Owe you? I fucking SAVED YOU!" he screams at me, and I laugh.

"*You* saved *me*? No, you *abandoned* me. You tossed me out in the fucking rain and threw your grandson and me into the streets to fend for ourselves. You didn't save me! But I should thank you because if you hadn't, I would be wearing the same rose-colored glasses as the rest of you here," I tell him before looking at the crowd gathered.

"You are all blinded by your own ignorance and ego. Blind to those that reside in the city, those you all once promised to protect. Packs, packs are supposed to be family. Not one of you here knows the meaning of the word! If you did, your children and grandchildren wouldn't be homeless; they wouldn't be living in deplorable conditions because of a label you bestowed upon their mothers—your own kids!" I scream at them.

"Your kids, the children you watched grow, the same children you taught how to use a spoon, how to talk. You claim you are the city's elite, better than them, but you're not. Because despite the labels you gave them, they stood up when the rest of you backed away. They stood up and raised the children that your mates pretend they don't have! And if you think you're good parents, then why aren't you fighting for them? Love, nurture, protect—that is what a parent is, and not one of you deserves that title," I tell them.

They whisper amongst themselves. I notice more of my father's warriors have appeared in the crowd, some in wolf form as they creep closer. I chuckle. He would have them attack his own daughter over the truth.

"I suggest you leave, Everly," my mother murmurs, glancing around nervously, then suddenly looking at my father in horror. He looks smug and folds his arms across his chest in a show of intimidation.

Yet, I don't scare easily. Not anymore. What should have frightened me no longer does. That was one thing being a rogue showed me; fear changes and morphs into something else.

You don't fear being forsaken. You fear the next day and how you will feed your child. You fear them growing up with the same label you hold. You fear the regret for the opportunities you know they will miss. You fear them being suppressed and silenced.

I refuse to be silent, yet I also know that Valen and I are severely outnumbered here if my father orders his warriors to attack. We can't risk that, not with Valarian.

Our pack wouldn't get here before they ripped us apart, and there is a reason my father has the status he does—why he's second only to Alpha Valen's pack. They're just as lethal. The only difference is they don't have his pack's numbers. But numbers mean nothing when they can't get here in time.

Although I have no doubt we could take down a vast majority of them. I know for sure Valen could and would for me.

"Get in the car, Valen," I tell him, not taking my eyes off my father. My father smirks as if he won, but he hasn't. And he won't.

Valen glances around, realizing my father has called in the troops. He growls, pushing me behind him, but I grab his arm, and he glances at me.

"*We need to leave,*" he tells me through the mind-link.

"Get in the car," I tell him, holding eye contact with him. He growls, pushing me toward my car.

"Get in your car!" I tell him again, and he stops, looking at me, then glancing around before his eyes meet mine once more.

"*Everly, what are you doing?*" he mind-links.

"*What I should have done years ago, now get in the car. I refuse to be seen as hiding behind you,*" I tell him using the link. Valen blinks at me before growling.

"I am not walking away until I know you are safely in that car," Valen growls loud enough for everyone to hear.

"Listen to your mate, Everly. It's time to leave," my father says softly. He actually sounds like he doesn't want it to come to this, which, I think, is odd considering he ordered them here. The retaliation all comes down to reputation. Well, looks like I'm about to earn mine.

Valen nudges me toward my car, but I don't budge. "Do not ask me to walk away," he murmurs. I know everyone is waiting for the Big Bad Blood Alpha to drag me away kicking and screaming, but if Valen truly meant what he said, that I'm his equal, he will do this for me.

"Please, just this once," I mind-link, and he looks around me before growling angrily, leaning down, and kissing my lips.

"He touches you, I will kill him," he says through the mind-link.

"No, you won't. But no one is dying here today. Just get in the car."

He pulls away, looking at me. "You're not..." he whispers.

"I am. Now, go," I tell him. Valen curses, not happy, but suddenly seems to understand. He shakes his head before he chuckles.

"Just this once," he says, walking off toward his car. The murmurs of him walking away from me and leaving me out in the open are loud, shocked he would let his Luna fend for herself. They don't realize I don't need to hide behind anyone. I was born an Alpha. It's my birthright, and now I am going to claim it.

"Run along, Everly," my father says, watching Valen climb into his car.

"No," I tell him, and he growls, taking a step toward me. His eyes dart over my shoulder to Valen's car before flicking to me.

"Everyone here will now bear witness!" I call out. My father growls. However, I keep going.

"I, Everly, Luna of Nightshade pack, challenge you, Alpha John, for my rightful title and birthright as Alpha to the Shadow Pack," I cry. The collective gasp is loud at the challenge. My father seems stunned that I dared speak those words.

He glances around at his pack, witnessing the reactions of his members to the challenge. He'll look weak if he backs down; I know he won't. He growls.

"So what will it be, Dad? Stand down and submit? Or accept the challenge?" I tell him.

"You foolish girl," he growls before looking around and pressing his lips in a line.

"Challenge accepted. Next full moon, council arena," he snaps before leaning toward me.

"You are going to get yourself killed. Rescind it. You don't stand a chance, and you know it."

"That is where you are wrong, Father. For seventeen years, you trained me. I didn't suddenly forget. I was taught by one of the best."

"Yes, taught by *me*. You think you can beat me? You spent years as a rogue. Think of your son."

"I am thinking of my son. I can and will win. You forget why a title is handed down to the eldest child, each generation stronger than a predecessor. Step down, Dad. You're looking at the next generation, someone that rivals you now, your mirror only stronger. You told me that. Promised growing up, I would be stronger than you one day. I saw no one bigger than you growing up. I held you up on a pedestal. You were my hero. Not anymore," I tell him before turning my back on him and walking toward my car. Ava presses her lips in a line, trying not to smile.

"You're making a mistake, Everly!" my father calls, but I keep walking to my car and open the driver's side door.

"You have until the next full moon to back out," my father says, earning some gasps from his pack. He doesn't want to fight me. What father would? No one wants to potentially kill their child, even one who he claims to hate. Which is precisely why Alphas handed the title down. Rarely are they challenged. It's also unheard of for an Alpha to offer the challenger a way out.

"Don't hold your breath waiting for me, Father; I would hate for the challenge to be over before it starts," I tell him, giving him a nod. He nods back before folding his arms across his chest, his face turning hard as he tries to hide whatever emotion he feels.

Climbing into my car, I start the engine, only for the passenger side door to open. I look at it to see my sister climbing in.

"What are you doing?" I ask.

"What I should have done the day he banished you! I'm coming with you," she says, clipping in her seatbelt.

I smile and start the car.

Watch Me

They might not see your vision, but they'll witness the success. Remember, you've got the power to turn CAN'T into CAN and IMPOSSIBLE into DONE. So, as you turn dreams into reality, let the world be your audience and make them watch.

Follow my Facebook Page Jessica Hall Author Page for the release date of Book 2

Alpha's Redemption-My Luna Has A Son.

Made in the USA
Coppell, TX
30 March 2024

30711137R00298